"I do

"Battling a giant is one thing, but taking on a _____
that's something completely different."

Nidhogg was asleep. He was snoring in his cave, and it wasn't a pleasant sound. Zeke shuffled up to the cave entrance, his hand gripped tightly to the Staff of Urd. The fear began to burn him. The darkness reached up to him as he drew nearer the place as dreadful as the worst of fears, the worst of dreams.

"Nidhogg!" he called. His voice faltered slightly as he spoke. "Nidhogg! Wake! Wake, wise serpent of Niflheim!"

There was a stirring from within the shadows of the cave. Movement. Plodding. The shuffling of great-clawed feet.

And then the beast, the dragon, the devourer of dead corpses and the destroyer of the great ash Yggdrasil, stepped into the small, flickering light of the torch. His yellow eyes reflected its weak light.

"Who calls me from my sleep and bids me speak?" the dragon hissed.

"I am Zeke Proper," he announced. "I am the slayer of the Korrigan, wielder of the stones, wanderer of the Mist, and holder

Praise for Brad Cameron's
The Serpent's Ship

I read the latest book in the Zeke Proper Chronicles: The Serpent's Ship, at one sitting - I couldn't put it down! As a high school librarian I read a lot of YA fiction and this fantasy has it all: Adventure, mystery, and murder! You won't believe what is happening this time in Alder Cove! 5 stars for The Serpent's Ship!

- Ann Sindelar-Trahin, MS EdML
Beaverton School District Libraries Coordinator

An unforgettable adventure! Brad Cameron has included spine-chilling action delivering bravery in the face of impossible odds, enchantment, and shear satisfaction. I can't wait for Book Three! I gotta see what happens next.

- Loni Thompson, MS. CCC-SLP
Speech Language Pathologist and Reading Coach

Praise for Brad Cameron's
Odin's Light

I finished it virtually overnight! Praise for Odin's Light, Book One of the Zeke Proper Chronicles. As the mystery unfolds, we are introduced to fabulous characters. My favorite: Taylre. She is spunky, enthusiastic, and totally geeky. I immediately wanted to reach my arms into the novel and give her a giant hug.

Moreover, the climax had me biting my lip in anticipation, almost yelling at the characters to, "Hurry up!" The book is addicting. I am excited for the sequel.

- Golda Lobello
High School English Teacher

Did you grow up on Nancy Drew and The Hardy Boys or (insert name of favorite kid detective here)? Then you gotta get a load of Zeke, Devon, and Taylre! The town of Alder Cove has some major supernatural secrets and these kids are out to solve the mystery! Little do they know how deep into the Norse pantheon those secrets delve. Look out Alder Cove! Here comes The Three Investigators for the next generation!

- *Tonya Macalino*
Author of Faces in the Water

More reviews for **Odin's Light** from Amazon readers:

I would have to say that Taylre is my favorite character in Brad Cameron's debut novel, Odin's Light. She's spunky with a lot of life and enthusiasm. Cameron's writing is very descriptive and easy to follow. He weaves a story that is both fun and exciting.

As a high school librarian, I read a lot of YA fiction and this fantasy has it all: adventure, mystery and murder! I can't wait for the sequel!

Cameron is a great storyteller and a master of description. He really brings all his characters to life and knows how to keep you wanting more. I can't wait for the next book.

Through a complex series of connections and realizations the reader is led on a grand, funny, and at times frightening adventure. As a teacher I am always looking for well-written, high interest stories that my students can make connections to.

Odin's Light is one of those great books that makes you feel as though you are taking part in the story, not just reading it. By the end of the first chapter, I was eagerly reading to see what

The Zeke Proper Chronicles

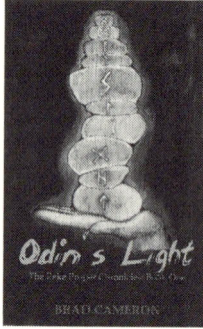

Book One: Odin's Light

Book Two: The Serpent's Ship

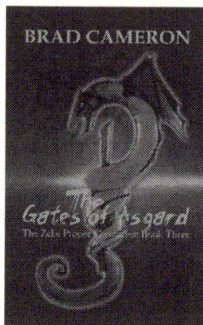

Book Three: The Gates of Asgard

The Gates of Asgard

The Zeke Proper Chronicles: Book Three

Brad Cameron

WORLD TREE
FANTASY

THE GATES ASGARD

For information, address World Tree Fantasy, PO Box 264 Hillsboro, OR 97123

ISBN: 978-0-9852417-5-9

Printed in the United States of America

To Laurie,
Who has a keen eye for detail and who is
absolutely smarter than a fifth grader.

To Corey,
whose vision brings dragons to life.

And to Tonya,
my personal builder of books.

Chapter One
Stone Walls

An odd diffusion of light and movement, reflected through the broken lenses of her glasses, caught Taylre's attention. She thought that the thing that crawled out of the small hole was a cat, one that had encountered a brutal life of near starvation and the mange. But then she saw the tail, the long, skinny appendage that dragged itself behind the animal like a dead snake. In horror, Taylre realized that the pitiable small cat was in fact a hideously large rat. As she reared back on her tiny cot next to the cold bare, stonewall; drawing her knees up to her chest and wrapping her arms around her legs, she wondered how the creature had managed to squirm its fat body through such a small opening.

The rodent - perching itself on its haunches near the barred wooden door - looked up at Taylre and appeared to be smiling, its jagged, sharp teeth reflected the dull light that managed to penetrate the minute cracks in the granite walls. Taylre felt her heart sprint as a shiver parted the middle of her back, both from fear and from the coldness that surrounded her in the tiny cell.

Taylre woke from a fitful sleep about an hour before and found herself curled up in a fetal position on a filthy cot. A thin mattress that covered rotted wooden slats displayed a myriad of stains that exuded an odor that she couldn't quite identify, but tried hard to ignore. When she rose she found her mind still raced with nightmarish visions of burning flesh, snarling wolves, and the vile, contemptible grin of Almar Loden, whose face seemed to peer down at her from some faraway place, a place shrouded in mist and memory. She struggled to shake the cobwebs from her thoughts and push away the mental pictures that haunted her. She hoped she could make some sense of her present surroundings.

As she stared through the broken lenses of her glasses, occasionally sobbing with an inescapable sense of loneliness and dread, she had a vague recollection of someone entering the stone enclosed cell at some point during her captivity, but the memory was shrouded in a hazy fog, like a hard, cold mist that settles amongst a forest of thick trees. The person who entered brought in a plate of food that still sat on the dirt floor beside Taylre's cot. The rat eyed the platter and appeared to weigh the possibility of making a run for it but couldn't seem to decide what kind of threat Taylre might be. Taylre looked again at the food and saw that a thin layer of green fuzz had begun to grow on its surface. Her appetite, meager though it was, instantly left. She reached down from her tucked position - careful not to startle the creature - and grabbed the plate of food. Then she threw it hard. The mangy rodent barely moved as the fuzz-covered meal hit the wall above its head. The metal plate clattered against the stonewall. Immediately the rat raced to the largest piece of moldy food, grabbed it in its jagged teeth, and dragged it into the narrow hole it crawled out of. Taylre shuddered with relief as she watched the creature disappear into the narrow fissure between the granite.

With the food now gone, Taylre discovered her hunger again. She thought of her grandmother; how she used to hum quietly to herself as she baked cookies in the kitchen, the thick aroma of molasses and ginger wafting through the air. She thought of her own bed with its cozy down comforter, the one she would sometimes grab and drag into the family room, wrapping it around her shoulders as she and her grandma sat on the couch watching old movies together. She reflected, with a brief smile, how they would share a big bowl of hot buttered popcorn and savor each crisp bite.

Her stomach began to growl.

Suddenly, the thick wooden door that kept her prisoner shook. Taylre assumed a fearsome wind had begun to blow, but then quickly realized that someone was trying to enter. She began to panic. Once again she brought her knees up to her chest and drew them in tightly with her long, skinny arms. Her breath came out in bursts of terror, and she imagined with horror that her worst fears had come true: her life would now come to a violent end in this godforsaken place, and she would never have the chance to ask her grandmother for forgiveness.

The door rattled again, but its warped edges refused to yield to the force that pushed against it. There was a brief moment of terrible silence, a kind of calm before the storm, when suddenly the solid bulwark burst open. The wooden edges splintered wildly as it swung wide.

Taylre screamed. She drew her arms up over her head and sheltered her face from the flying pieces of slivered wood that scattered about the tiny cell. Then slowly, as if she were testing the air for impurities, Taylre brought her arms down and looked toward the gaping doorway, its opening filled by the imposing frame of Teddy Walford.

"How ya doin' brat? Long time no see."

Taylre reached up and adjusted her glasses. She pulled on the frames, which allowed her to look cleanly through a small section that wasn't marred by the cracked lens. "Teddy?" she said, her voice revealing an overwhelming fear.

"I don't go by that name anymore," he snarled. "I'm Hrym. The giants have taken me in. They've given me a place among them. I'm no longer one of you."

Taylre tried to muster some courage, but her voice continued to betray her. "I...I thought we were friends, Teddy..." she managed to say. But then she saw the scowl on his face. "Sorry. I mean Hrym."

"You're not my friend, scum. You're my enemy. And if it weren't for the fact that Loden wanted to see you right now, I'd kill you myself. I'd strangle you with my bare hands for your treachery. You broke the law. You don't deserve to live. But I follow my master. *I* know where my loyalty lies," Teddy said, his thumb confidently pointing toward his broad chest. "Now get up. He doesn't like to be kept waiting."

Chapter Two
Cleaning Up

The winter storm - originating somewhere off the coast of Greenland - crept over the white capped waves of the Atlantic Ocean. Its icy grip wrapped itself around Alder Cove with an angry fist. A light snow fell, but weather forecasters were predicting a blizzard that would soon turn the gray, wet skies of autumn into a scrim of white confinement. Local city officials anticipated the possibility that their town may be forced to a near standstill under the weight of the oncoming tempest.

With Christmas quickly approaching, holiday decorations lined Main Street. The string of lights and garland that adorned the light posts wavered in the steadily increasing wind, and the red and green glow from the lights flickered each time a gust of air blew through the vacant corridor of streets.

Early on, the morning began with the promise of a mild day. The sun rose late and crested over the eastern horizon turning the clouds beyond it a deep blood red. Zeke and Devon - hoping for a lengthy break in the weather that had recently hung over the town - took the *Skipper Jack* out of the marina and headed her south, keeping their sights on the rocky shoreline to the west and safely away from the winter currents to the east, those treacherous tides that could inadvertently pull small ships out to the deep sea. The boys, solemn in their duties aboard the sailboat, took turns at the helm, their thoughts always turning to their late father, Percy Proper, the man who had purchased and named the boat.

Zeke found it hard to believe that his father's tragic death had only been three months ago. He reflected on the many events that had happened since. Life had certainly been difficult, and perhaps even a little despondent. Percy Proper's death had left a large hole in the hearts of the members of the remaining Proper family. And the kidnapping of Taylre by Loki had worsened that feeling. It became more and more difficult to find hope in life as both Zeke and Devon felt the loss press heavily on their meager shoulders.

Sailing the *Skipper Jack* into Gonzales Bay and then into the sheltered confines of the marina, Zeke felt the despondency deepen in his chest. He had hoped that a day on the ocean would be the balm he needed to rid himself of the cloud of depression that had hung over the family during the last few months, but the oncoming storm, like a harbinger of doom, seemed to inflame that feeling.

When the boat bumped softly against the pier, Devon leaped from the deck onto the wooden dock, a sturdy rope in hand. His deft hands secured the *Skipper Jack* to its berth. Zeke began tying down the sails when a small movement to his right caught his attention. He turned to look at a normally unused section of dock, and was surprised to see Bartholomew Gunner, the Captain, sitting on the edge of the wharf while his legs dangled over the side, his feet nearly touching the green water. In his hands he held a fishing rod, its line cast a few yards in front of him, a small red and white bobber rose and fell with the tide. The Captain's head was bowed, his chin rested on his chest, and his hands gripped the rod tightly, as if he feared someone might try to take it from him. A small plume of blue smoke rose from his pipe and drifted into the cold air above his head.

Zeke raised his hand as if to call out to the Captain, but he stopped himself. He had the feeling something was very wrong.

"Devon," he whispered. Devon paused in his attempt to tie a figure eight around a small metal cleat fastened to the dock and looked up at Zeke. "Check it out," Zeke continued, using his chin to point toward the Captain.

From his crouched position Devon glanced over his shoulder. He squinted for a moment, as if in deep thought. "I think we have a serious problem," Devon said, his eyes still focused on the Captain.

"Yeah," Zeke agreed. "Should we go over?"

Devon turned to Zeke. His look revealed disgust. "Well, duh. What do ya think; we should just let him suffer over there? We're his friends, monkey boy. Probably the only true friends he's ever had. So yeah, we definitely go over there."

"Why d'ya have to be such a dork about it? I was just askin'."

"I know," Devon said, "but you always ask the most obvious questions. Obvious and stupid."

"Look, goober, do we go now or do we finish up here first?"

Devon looked up to the darkening sky and shook his head. "We better tie things up first. Those clouds are starting to look really scary."

As the boys continued to secure the boat to its moorings and close up the hatches, they kept a wary eye on the Captain who remained fixed at the edge of the pier. His expression radiated defeat and discouragement. When the chores aboard the *Skipper Jack* were complete, the boys marched their way along the wooden maze of docks. Eventually they reached the place where Bartholomew Gunner sat and swayed, the fishing rod still gripped firmly in his hands.

Neither Zeke nor Devon made any attempt at stealth as they approached the Captain. In fact, they tried to make as much noise as they could, hoping their strident advance would rouse him from his apparent reverie. But the Captain remained still, almost like a wind and storm eroded statue. Finally, Zeke stepped forward and cleared his throat.

Bartholomew's shoulders arched, a slight movement that gave life to the sculpture. "Captain," Zeke said, bending at the knees and reaching a hand to rest on the Captain's shoulder. "Are you okay?"

Loosening his grip on the fishing rod, the Captain turned slowly, but he kept his head bowed and his shoulders slouched. When Zeke saw the Captain's eyes, he sighed as a deep sadness enveloped him. What he saw on the Captain's face reminded him of what he felt on the inside: despair, gloom, and hopelessness.

The Captain's face seemed to sag. His eyes were red and watery, accentuated by dark rings of flesh that hung down like withered flowers. His beard had been left to grow out, unkempt and peppered with shades of grey and black, and his hair was matted and tangled, so unlike his normal closely cropped cut. The pipe that hung from his mouth seemed to personify the Captain's mood as it drooped and smoldered. A weak remnant of pencil thin smoke rose from the tattered, ash-filled bowl.

"Zeke, is it," the Captain slurred, his breath stinking of cheap whiskey. "I...I've been fishin' today. Can ya see, lad. But no fish are to be had. Nope, nothing to be had today." The Captain swayed as he spoke, his mouth trying hard to form his words.

"Oh, Captain," Zeke said. "You're drunk again."

"No...nope, lad. Just a wee...wee bit on the tipsy side," the Captain exclaimed.

Both Zeke and Devon exchanged glances, shook their heads, and reached down. They grabbed the Captain under his arms and lifted him awkwardly to his unsteady feet. "C'mon," Zeke said, "We're takin' you home."

"Got...gotta' catch a fish," the Captain slurred, trying to clasp onto his fishing rod. "So as to feed the folks ya know. Got...got ta feed the folks."

The brothers continued to hold the Captain upright, both of them straining with his weight and unsteady stance. "There's no more fishing today, Captain," Devon said through clenched teeth. "We're taking you home. We've got a nice batch of hot coffee brewing, and I'm sure you could use it right now."

ᚴ

By taking the back roads, Zeke drove the Captain's rusted Ford F150 pickup truck back to their house, a task that was made even more difficult because the truck had a stick shift.

Zeke managed to stall it seventeen times, a number that Devon kept accurate track of during the arduous journey. He announced the number loudly each time the truck came to a lurching stop at the side of the road.

When they finally pulled up into the Proper's driveway, the truck shuddered while its engine continued to spit and cough like a sick old man, even after Zeke had turned off the key. Zeke and Devon then looked at their reluctant, sleeping passenger, aware that their task was not even close to an end.

The steps seemed steeper as Zeke and Devon heaved their burden up the incline. Devon held the Captain's left arm, Zeke his right. When they entered the house the aroma of freshly brewed coffee hung in the air.

"Sit him here," Vivian Proper urged. She removed a pillow from the couch and threw a blanket over the Captain as the boys plopped him in the comfort of the cushions. "I'll go get the coffee."

Marjorie Anders, who had been a frequent visitor at the Proper home, squeezed in between the boys and knelt down in front of the Captain. She removed his shoes and jacket and placed a comforting hand on his cheek, mouthing some silent words of reassurance.

The boys stood back and let the women tend to the Captain as Vivian returned from the kitchen. She held a steaming cup of black coffee. "Drink this, Bartholomew. It'll make you feel better."

The Captain stirred uneasily, as if he'd been awoken from a restless, nightmare-filled sleep. He took the proffered cup and drank greedily, slurping the hot, black liquid like a man dying of thirst. Vivian held the cup under his chin, tilting it as if the Captain were a mere child longing for the guided touch of his mother.

"There you go, Bartholomew," she whispered. "Drink it all down." Then, exchanging the coffee mug for a tall, clear glass of water, she forced the Captain to consume its contents along with a small handful of aspirin.

As Zeke, Devon, Marjorie, and Vivian positioned themselves in the small living room, the Captain nodded off. His snores reverberated off the walls like a cave bear hibernating the winter away.

Marjorie was the first to fill the spaces between the snorting. "It seems like it's getting worse," she said.

Vivian nodded her head. "I agree. I think it's time to get to the bottom of this. Bartholomew needs to know that his behavior isn't helping. In fact, it's setting us back. We're depending on him to help us get Taylre back. But this," she said, pointing at the Captain with a glare of frustration, "is getting us nowhere."

ᛣ

For a brief moment the Captain was confused. The last thing he remembered was sitting in a bar called Eddie's, located at the north end of town just beyond an old lumber road that heads up Mt. Sif. Beyond that everything else remained very fuzzy. He thought he had a brief recollection of going aboard his boat to get a fishing rod, but even that was lost in a tumble of scattered images and muddled dreams. His head ached, too. And when he tried to sit up, his back and limbs screamed with pain and stiffness. *I'm gettin' too old for this,* he thought.

As he looked about the room, recent events began taking shape. He remembered the jerky drive home with Zeke at the wheel of his truck, the slow march up the steps of the Proper home, and the eventual plunge into unconsciousness after being stuffed with black coffee and what felt like a gallon of water. He remembered the disappointed looks in the eyes of Marjorie Anders and Vivian Proper, too. That, more than anything, brought about the deep pang of regret he felt rise in his chest, a pain that seemed worse than his aching head and throbbing back and limbs.

Bringing his hands up to his face and rubbing briskly at his overgrown beard and scruffy, matted hair, the Captain considered what he could possibly do to make amends for his outrageous behavior. But before he could think much further than a badly rehearsed apology, he heard the loud pounding of feet as Devon descended the stairs. The Captain looked up to see Devon's grin and was forced to smile a bit himself, despite his current level of discomfort.

"He's awake!" Devon shouted. The Captain groaned while his fingers pressed against his temples to try and cancel out the shockwave of sound that echoed through his hung-over brain.

More footsteps were heard but this time they came from the kitchen. From around the corner came Vivian, Marjorie, and Zeke. They stopped and stood by the entrance to the living room and stared at the Captain. A momentary blush crossed over his face, as he suddenly felt trapped in his shame.

"Wow, Bartholomew. You look really awful." Vivian shook her head sadly.

"Yeah, dude," Devon added. "You look like you've been beaten repeatedly with an ugly stick."

Zeke turned toward Devon, his face crossed with anger. "Really? Don't you think the guys been through enough? Maybe *you* should take a look in the mirror and see who really took a hit with the ugly stick."

"Oh, yeah. Well maybe you should just shut up."

"Boys!" Vivian interjected. "That's enough." A sudden silence filled the room as Zeke and Devon glared at each other, but Vivian ignored their looks and focused on the Captain. "How are you feeling, Bartholomew?"

"Well," he answered slowly, his hands trying in vain to rub some of the redness and sting out of his eyes. "I feel like I've been hit with an ugly stick," he said, chuckling painfully at his own awkward joke.

Devon turned his attention away from Zeke and snorted as he tried to hold back his laughter. Vivian shot a warning glance at him, enough for him to know that he was about to cross the line.

"Bartholomew," Vivian said. "I'm not going to mince any words here. What I have to say comes from my heart, so please know that I still love you. You will always be a forever friend to this family, but I'm disappointed in you. Very disappointed. This type of behavior simply cannot be tolerated."

The Captain remained slouched over, his hands pressed to the sides of his face, his eyes closed, his head bowed. At first Vivian thought that the Captain had fallen back to sleep, but then he sighed heavily and his shoulders began to shudder. A muffled sob escaped his guarded face.

Vivian approached the Captain slowly and rested a gentle hand on his arched back. "Talk to us Bart," she whispered. "What's breaking you down like this?"

The Captain sniffed back some tears and gradually raised his head. He scanned the room, and then he looked at the assembled group that stared back at him, love and concern etching their expressions. "I...I...don't know what to do. I was never prepared for somethin' like this. Taylre's lost, and I have no idea how to get her back. I'm useless. Don't ya see? I'm completely useless."

Marjorie Anders stepped forward and placed her hands on both Vivian and the Captain's shoulders.

"Bartholomew." He turned his red eyes toward her. "This isn't your fault. Don't ever think that it is. It's Loki. You know that and I know that. We'll figure out a way. I know we will. But your drinking isn't going to help. We need clear minds right now, not foggy drunkenness. Please, Bart. Bring your strength back to us. We need it, and Taylre, especially Taylre. She needs it."

Though it hurt to do so, the Captain raised his head and looked at both Vivian and Marjorie. His bloodshot, tear-filled eyes reflected the light that shone through the living room window. He nodded slowly. "I can do that. For Taylre, I can most certainly do that."

§

The bathroom was filled with the fading residue of steam from the shower. The Captain sat on a stool; a frayed beach towel that depicted colorful seashells and sandcastles was wrapped tightly about his waist. Behind him, with a small black comb and a pair of scissors in hand, stood Vivian Proper. Her attempt at giving the Captain a haircut was mediocre at best, and Devon, who sat in the hallway adjacent to the bathroom door, peered in, unable to hold back occasional spurts of laughter.

"Judging from your incessant gigglin, boy, I'm assumin that the beauty treatment I'm gettin isn't goin to be havin me appear on the cover of any magazines real soon," the Captain said. He winced each time Vivian took another snip at his hair.

"No, no," Devon said innocently, his hands waving in the air as if he were trying to ward off an attack. "I think you look real good. In fact I'd say that the shower and the much needed shave, along with the rather lopsided hair cut, are really starting to clear up some of the effects of that ugly stick."

"Leave the man alone, Devon," Marjorie said playfully as she reached the top of the stairs. "I do believe the man's been through enough for one day." She stepped past Devon and looked in on the Captain, his glum expression meeting her look of amusement.

"Vivian," Marjorie continued. "You do know that both sides are supposed to be the same length, right?"

Vivian sighed heavily and dropped her arms to her sides in frustration. "Oh, Marjorie," she said. "I'm really not very good at this am I?"

"Well," Marjorie said, tilting her head to one side as if the change in perspective might somehow improve the look of the bad haircut, "to be perfectly honest, no, you're not very good. But still, you're doing better than I could do."

Soon both women were huddled within the confines of the small bathroom around an embarrassed Captain, his big belly and hairy chest bared for the entire world to see. Their combined efforts at grooming allowed the Captain's appearance to become at least passable.

Finally, Vivian stepped back and stared at the Captain. "If we stick a hat on him," she said, a note of exasperation in her tired voice, "I'm sure he'll look just fine."

Chapter Three
Volva

As the day continued the storm outside raged. Snow began to accumulate into towering drifts as strong winds battered the sides of the house. An icy cold seemed to penetrate the very core of the small group of observers who crowded around the living room window watching the oncoming blizzard, its chill fought against the large fire burning in the fireplace. The scene produced an eerie sense of déjà vu in the watcher's minds.

Zeke backed away from the window and looked around the room, his thoughts entangled with the nagging, inescapable vision of Taylre floating away on a flying ship called Naglfar; and Loki, his arms surrounding Taylre in a perverse, evil grip, his smile taunting Zeke as if to say *Come get her, if you can.*

"Tell me about the Valkyries, Zeke. What did the one that you saw say to you again?" It was Marjorie who spoke. Zeke was startled out of his thoughts. He jumped at the sound of her voice and instinctively reached for his leg as a phantom jolt of pain seized his thigh muscle. Marjorie placed a tender hand on his shoulder, suddenly aware that she had unintentionally triggered a searing memory.

"I'm so sorry, Zeke. I completely forgot. Are you alright?"

"I'm fine," Zeke said. He clenched his teeth as he massaged the muscle. "Sometimes I forget, too. I can never tell when it's going to act up."

"Is there a scar?" Marjorie asked.

"No, nothing. It's as if the spear were never thrown by Loki, but it hurts all the same, a low nagging kind of ache that's there all the time, but then, like now, it really flares up. Those are the worst."

"We even took him to the doctor," Vivian interjected. "They couldn't find anything. Strange isn't it?"

"Very strange," interrupted the Captain, "but the Mist is a curious place. Take Zeke's wound, for instance. Why is it that he can suffer a horrible injury in the Mist, but show no sign of it here in Midgard? Other than the pain o'course." The Captain reached into his pocket for his pipe and gave Vivian a sideways glance. She nodded and offered a reluctant, silent approval.

Devon moved away from the window and let the curtain fall in place. He circled a room that had fallen silent. "But that's our problem isn't it?" he said. "I mean, we've been in the Mist, at least Zeke and I have, but it seems like a place without rules. We've been able to pop in and out of it with no idea how we did it. Zeke, at least, has been able to identify a feeling that happens when he starts to go into it, but how do *we* choose to do it? If we were able to figure that out, I feel like we'd be halfway to getting Taylre back."

"And that's why I've failed all of ya's," the Captain snorted. "I've been taught a lot of things about the Norse myths, but the Mist...well, that's a puzzle. And it's downright frustratin!" he hollered. His hand slammed hard against the coffee table.

The shock of the Captain's unexpected outburst settled quickly while the nervous occupants of the room settled into a hushed reverie. Finally, after a few awkward moments of quiet contemplation Marjorie placed a comforting hand on Zeke's back.

"Zeke, take us back to the ship. You met a Valkyrie, which, if you think about it, is a miraculous experience. What did she say? I know you've described it before, but I think there's something there, a clue perhaps, that will lead us in the right direction."

Zeke, who continued massaging his leg absentmindedly, leaned back in the comfort of the couch while his thoughts spun in a whirlpool of memory.

"She was beautiful," he began, "more like a porcelain statue than a real person. I was afraid of her at first, but not in a bad way. It was more like fear in a respectful way. She looked at me as if she knew things. Things I could never know, things both terrible and wonderful at the same time. But the thing I remember most is when she asked me if I was a warrior. Funny, huh?" Zeke shook his head slightly; a pained smiled creased his face. "Me, a warrior. Could you imagine?"

Devon scoffed, "If a Viking screamed like a little girl, then yeah, I could imagine you being a warrior."

"Devon." His mother glowered at him. "Let him finish."

"It's okay," Zeke said. "For once Devon might be right. I'm sure if I were put into the position of having to fight hand to hand, I probably would scream."

"You fought Loki," Marjorie said matter-of-factly.

"Well," Zeke muttered, "that was different. Taylre was there. I was trying to help her. And, I didn't have a choice. It was either fight, or die. There was no sense of bravery. It was just pure adrenaline. Besides that, if the Valkyrie didn't show up, I would have suffered much more than a spear through the thigh. "

The Captain took a long draw on his pipe. He let the blue smoke escape from the corners of his mouth while it shrouded his wrinkled features in a sagely haze. "You've mistaken honor with bravery, lad. Sometimes doing the right thing requires something far beyond mere bravery. The greatest warrior conquers incredible odds not because he's brave, but because it's the noble, honorable thing ta do. Sometimes our greatest motivator is our integrity and our desire ta protect the things that are most precious."

"I suppose that's true," Zeke responded. "But a warrior also needs to know how to fight. Just because there's a good cause doesn't necessarily mean that he's going to win the battle. I absolutely felt a desire to protect Taylre, but all the desire in the world wouldn't have saved me from Loki's battle-axe. I suppose that's why Shaker's next words of advice have stayed with me. Stayed with me and haunted me at the same time."

"What did she say, Zeke?" Marjorie leaned in closer; a look of concern, tempered with curiosity filled her eager expression.

"That I need to prepare, and that I need to get stronger and learn how to act like a warrior. But the problem is that I don't know how. How does a person learn about the Mist? How does someone like me learn how to fight?"

Marjorie turned her gaze toward the frosted window where a hushed, gray light permeated the room and where a steady snowfall pattered against the glass. "You're an athlete, Zeke. You've pushed yourself before. You know what it's like to drive through pain to grow stronger. That part I know you can do. But the thing you really need is a coach. Someone who..." Marjorie paused; an odd, reflective look shadowed her glazed appearance. "Someone who really knows the Mist."

An impish grin spread across her lips as her voice trailed off like an elusive thought, making her look almost child-like.

"Of course," she said, turning to look at the others who stared back at her. Their confused expressions asked a thousand unvoiced questions. "We need a Volva. We need a Volva to lead us through a Seidh."

Chapter Four
The Cabin in the Woods

"What the hell are you talkin' about?"

"Devon!" Vivian shouted. Her angry stare sent dagger-like looks across the room.

Marjorie tried to hold back laughter, but was embarrassed when a snort burst from her mouth. "It's okay, Vivian. I don't blame him for his reaction. I don't blame any of you. Seidh and Volva are strange words, but they're part of Norse tradition. A Seidh simply means to speak or sing. Kind of like a séance, but really, so much more than that. And a Volva is the person who guides people through it."

"Wait," the Captain said, "you don't mean Sinmora do ya?"

"I do," Marjorie replied.

"Why, she was an old woman when I was a wee lad. She can't really still be alive can she?" The Captain puffed on his pipe, which sent a plume of blue smoke into the air.

"As far as I know she is," Marjorie answered. "But getting to her, well, that's going to be difficult."

"Wait...what...who...who are we talking about?" Vivian sat forward. Her mind was reeling with several unanswered questions.

"Sinmora," Marjorie repeated. "She's a Volva. A seeress. If there's anyone who can tell us about the Mist it's her. But she's...well... she's strange. And like I say, very difficult to get to. She lives on Mt. Sif. And as far as I know, there's no road to her house. If we want her advice - and I really think we do - then it'll be a tough journey."

"So let me guess," Vivian said, "this is going to be another one of those times when I'm going to have to suspend my beliefs, isn't it? You'll expect me to set aside all those hours spent in church on Sunday afternoons, all the sermons I've heard from a preacher behind a pulpit, and all of the lectures from my parents as I grew up. Is that what you want?"

"You don't have to set aside anything, Vivian." Marjorie rested a comforting hand on Vivian's arm and prodded her back into her seat. "What you need to do is combine what you already know and put it together with the things Bart has told you. You'll see that it's all connected."

Vivian stared about the room and saw the eyes of everyone looking at her. But they held no judgment. "I suppose you're right," she said. "But it's not going to be easy."

"No," the Captain said, tapping the end of his pipe against the bottom of his shoe. "None o' this is going to be easy. Not for any of us. But we've waded our way through some horrible things of late. We know what adversity is. We've gotten through it before; we can get through it again. So," he huffed, turning to look directly at Marjorie, "when do we leave?"

"As soon as possible," Marjorie said, rising quickly from her seat. "We've already wasted enough time. Taylre needs our help. We can't wait anymore."

"Wait," Vivian said, looking at the others who were all standing. "We can't leave now. Look at the weather. It's a blizzard out there."

Snow continued to pelt the frost-covered window. The sky remained white and cold. The small group edged toward the window and looked out on the threatening day feeling the ominous pressure of destiny squeeze and pull at their minds. Marjorie turned back to hesitant eyes.

"We have no choice," she declared. "We have to leave now."

ᛣ

A heavy accumulation of wet snow encased the Captain's truck in a vault of white, turning the chore of clearing its hood and windshield into a monumental task. Marjorie and Vivian sat inside with the engine running, defrost turned on high, and the two women enveloped in knee length coats, hoods, and thick gloves. Behind them, sitting in the small extension of the rusty cab, sat Devon. His knees were pressed tightly against his chest as a puff of frozen air escaped his open mouth.

"You should really be out there helping," Vivian said.

"There's no way I'm going out there," Devon responded. "It's like, arctic cold out there. I'd have to be mental to be standing out in the wind brushing snow off a truck."

"Well, your brother's out there."

"Like I said, I'd have to be mental."

The driver's side door opened quickly as the Captain slid his big body over the cold vinyl seat. "Cold as hell out there," he said, breathing a current of warm air into his cupped hands. "You sure about this, Marjorie?"

"As sure as anything I've done, Bartholomew. Taylre's in trouble, I can feel it. Sinmora's the only one who can help. And from what I've heard, there's not supposed to be much of a let up in this storm for the next little while. So, we have no time to waste."

"Whatever ya say. I'm just along for the ride," the Captain said. His foot pushed nervously on the gas pedal to rev warmth into the cab of the truck. "C'mon, Zeke. There's no need to wipe all the snow off," he muttered.

The passenger side door swung wide and let in a rush of cold air as Marjorie leaned forward allowing Zeke entrance to the small extension. He crawled in clumsily and tripped over his own feet. He uttered a silent curse under his breath and looked up nervously at his mother.

Finally, the Captain shifted the truck into reverse, released the clutch, and plowed the ancient four-wheel drive Ford out of the driveway and onto the abandoned street. With the road ahead clear, he pressed on the accelerator and unknowingly directed the group of adventurers into a journey far beyond anything their minds could have conceived.

ᛉ

The road ended.

Beyond was a gate that looked as if it had been there for over a century, its weathered split-wood frame gray and moldy with age.

"This is as far as we go, in the truck that is. The rest is all on foot." The Captain's hand instinctively reached for his pipe and tobacco. Its fragrance soon filled the cab of the truck with a sweet aroma.

"How much farther is it?" Vivian asked.

"Far," Marjorie said. "The most important thing is to keep warm. Take everything you can carry."

Fortunately, all members of the small troupe had come well equipped. Nevertheless, the cold was intense, and even the warmest garments couldn't keep out the iciness that penetrated even the tiniest niches in the clothing.

They walked single file up a narrow, snow-filled path; the weight of the heavy snow caused the branches of the trees that lined the trail to sag like depressed shapes leaning toward an ominous future. The Captain led the way. His pace was slow, but his big boots filled the trail with hollows that were easy to follow and imitate. Breathing became more difficult in the surrounding cold as the path continued to ascend Mt. Sif, and the air about the travelers fogged as the their breath escaped their mouths like exhaust from an un-tuned engine. An eerie silence pervaded the woods. The light was gray and sullen, and an impression enveloped the hikers giving them the sense they were not alone in this dark forest, that their movements were being closely watched.

Soon the weary travelers crested a small knoll that looked down on an open meadow. Here, the silence of the forest seemed almost tangible as the snow was piled in deep drifts, natural barriers that either kept something out, or prevented something from escaping.

"We're close," the Captain whispered. His voice quavered, but it carried easily over the frozen ground. "Look." He pointed with an unsteady hand toward another group of tall trees. There, a spectral amidst a background of shadows, rose a tendril of smoke.

"Sinmora's cabin," Marjorie said. "There's no need for stealth. In fact, I'm quite certain she's known for some time that we were coming. She has that gift, you know." Vivian looked up from under her fur-lined hood and hoped for some further explanation, but Marjorie pressed on. She marched past the Captain and pushed her own trail in the deep snow.

It took the group an additional hour to finally come in sight of the dwelling. As they walked, the snow deepened and the trail disappeared completely, almost as if no one ever ventured in or out. The cabin, a moss covered log cottage, stood waiting. Its shutter- covered windows appeared like the droopy eyes of an ancient sage. The roof sagged with the weight of the snow, and darkness continually enveloped the tattered abode, as the surrounding forest seemed to draw in closer by the minute, hoping to reclaim the trees from which it was originally built. A trail of white smoke drifted from the crooked stone chimney, the rising swirl added weight to the already over burdened limbs of the surrounding trees. Zeke, his toes and fingers numb from the cold, focused his attention on the front door, a narrow entrance that looked as if one would have to stoop in order to enter. There, standing in the threshold, was a girl. She was young, and, Zeke thought, quite pretty.

"Is that Sinmora?" he asked.

"No," Marjorie answered. "You'll know Sinmora when you see her. That girl, well, I'm not sure who she is. My guess is that she's an assistant or an apprentice. Someone who will offer aid during the Seidh."

"I wonder if she's real," Zeke muttered quietly under his breath, "the girl I mean."

"That," Devon said, "would be a scary thought." He shifted in the deep snow, his own feet throbbing from the cold, and stared at Zeke. For a moment the two brothers looked at each other, a flash of understanding passing between them. With it came the vivid recollection of their father struggling helplessly in the green waters of the Atlantic while Loki, in the guise of an innocent little girl, called for help.

The Captain, sensing the horrid images that must be playing out in the minds of the boys, turned to Marjorie. "What now?" he asked as his gaze drifted toward the cabin and the lone figure who stood at its entrance.

"We continue," she said. "But slowly and reverently. They're waiting for us."

Chapter Five

The Wooden Palace

The land that surrounded the broad inlet was barren. And the vegetation, the few patches that had the strength to grow, barely clung to life among the scattered rocks. The sky, a leaden gray with a scent reminiscent of an oncoming rainstorm, pressed down on the foreboding landscape like an intolerable affliction. The wind blew steadily and occasionally burst into gusts that tore at the skin with an icy chill. Taylre felt it the moment she stepped out of the stone hut where she had been held prisoner. She tried in vain to wrap her skinny arms around herself for warmth, but the cold was relentless. It penetrated her to the core. She stepped awkwardly over jagged stones that littered the frozen ground as she tried to keep up with Teddy's speed. Even Taylre, with her long legs and ardent stride struggled to keep pace.

"Walk faster, brat; I haven't got all day. Things to do, ya know." Teddy walked with purpose, his head down, and his shoulders slumped forward.

"Teddy, please. My legs are tired. I've been crunched up in that little room for so long. And I'm cold."

Teddy stopped abruptly. He turned quickly on his heals and grabbed Taylre by the front of her thin shirt, his face coming within inches of her own. "First of all, my name's not Teddy, not anymore, it's Hrym. Secondly, I don't want to hear your stupid complaining. Just keep up and do as your told." He shoved Taylre backward; the back of her heel scraped over a rock. She tripped and fell to the ground landing painfully on her backside. Teddy stood over her, his eyes narrowed to slits of malice. "Get up," he ordered, "or I will drag you by your hair."

Taylre groaned as she slowly pulled herself to her feet finding that her elbows were scraped and bleeding from the fall. She adjusted her glasses on her face and raised her head defiantly. Her chin jutted out resolutely. "Lead on, Hrym. Let's get this over with."

ᚱ

With the wind blowing steadily from the north, Taylre and Teddy climbed to the top of a steep hill. The view from the top was impressive as Taylre's kaleidoscopic vision revealed a narrow bay and the open expanse of ocean that extended far beyond. Her skin prickled with goose flesh as the cold continued to mock her, but her attention could not be swayed as the image of Naglfar came into view. Its hull rested in the water; the iridescent glint of artfully placed fingernails reflected the gray light. Taylre removed her glasses to rub her eyes and discovered that the view of the ship seemed to waver like the image of a fading dream. At times she could see it clearly: vibrant and real. At other times it appeared to move, edging to the corner of one's vision: it seemed to be there, but it always managed to elude one's direct stare. She pointed with an unsteady hand toward the vessel. "Is that our destination?" she asked, fearful that Teddy would once again lash out at her.

Teddy turned with the look of a master toward an annoying underling. "You talk too much, brat. But for your information, no, that's not our destination. The ship's under repair, but don't worry, Loden has asked us to prepare some temporary, but rather comfortable accommodations." He continued to stare at Taylre with hatred and loathing. "People who love and revere Loden take care of him. Remember that, traitor."

ᚱ

Taylre expected to see another stone edifice, something that had been hastily built under harsh conditions. What she saw, however, was completely unexpected. Before her, sitting on a gentle rise just above a sharp cliff that fell quickly to rocks and waves, was a palace, of sorts, one made completely out of thick, broad timbers. Taylre looked about her and noted the barren rocky landscape. She wondered where the trees had been felled to produce this massive structure. The question rose to her lips, but she repressed it quickly knowing that Teddy would not tolerate another query from her.

As they got closer, the building seemed to take on a sinister appearance. Tall, ornately carved pillars stood like sentinels on either side of a huge door. On its surface Taylre noted some of the most beautiful, yet disturbing artwork she had ever seen. The artist, Taylre thought, must have added magic to his work; the engraved figures seemed to take on a life of their own, mingling on deeply grained wood in a hideous dance of death and carnage. Battles of the past, the present, and future appeared to take place right in front of her eyes where blood flowed from dead or dying warriors in grotesque quantities. She shuddered as riders fell from their mounts only to be speared with long, sharply tipped lances, or to have their skulls crushed by heavy, spiked maces. Sound and smell combined themselves in a hurricane of vision as Taylre felt herself become faint. She reached for Teddy's shirttail and attempted to find a hold to steady herself, but Teddy shrugged her off. He pushed her hand away and let her fall once more to the frozen ground. She landed with a solid thud on her back while her mind continued to be lost in a whirl of images, each one more horrible than the next. She fought to pick herself up and tried in vain to turn her eyes away from the macabre mural. But its spell drew her in. It compelled her to become part of the wicked dance.

"Pick her up, boys. Let's get her inside," Teddy shouted, his voice seeming to come from some distant place as he continued to walk up the wooden steps, his back to Taylre.

She felt rough hands grab hold of her arms. They forced her to stand and walk as her mind slowly came back to reality. Then the great door swung open and her view of the carving ended. Suddenly the majesty of the open hall loomed before her.

A great fire burned in the center of the enormous citadel. Above the flames, rotating slowly on a thick spit was the carcass of a roasting pig. Its juices dripped into the fire's heat and sizzled, crackling as it cooked. Taylre's feet barely touched the ground as the short, bulky figures carried her into the hall. She inhaled the aroma of the cooking meat and realized once again just how hungry she was. Her stomach groaned, and her mouth began to water. She looked longingly at the food as an errant drop of drool escaped her open mouth. Taylre followed the rising smoke and noted how the ashes were carried to the pinnacle of a domed ceiling. Their remnants passed through a large round opening where the gray light of day penetrated the large enclosure.

"Set her there." A voice boomed from somewhere beyond the flames, its tone rich and confident. "And bring her meat and drink. The poor girl looks like a pathetic starving waif, you see."

Taylre was taken to a small wooden table where she was forced to sit. The heat from the fire breathed toward her. For a moment she allowed herself to relish in the warmth. She felt at once a longing for home and family. To her right stood a heavily bearded man. He was short, but very stout. He appeared, as far as Taylre could tell, to be a miniature warrior; his small body was clad in leather and metal armor; a sword hung at his side. He handed her a carved wooden plate heaped with slabs of meat, crisp seasoned turnips, and a chunk of thick-crusted bread. A wooden cup was also placed within reach, its contents filled with a golden liquid that begged her thirsty mouth to drink. She looked up tentatively from her meal and glanced about the room. When she did, she saw several faces lit up with the glow of the fire, staring at her. She shuddered with shame and embarrassment.

All of them appeared to be warriors: blond, bearded, weapons by their sides, and eyes that hungered for battle. Many of them were giants. Their immense statures offered an imposing image. Others were short and bulky, like the miniature warrior who gave Taylre her meal.

Taylre returned her attention to her food opting first for the goblet of golden drink. Her thirst outweighed her hunger and she drank greedily, tasting first the sickly sweetness of the honey brew and finally the burn of alcohol that scraped the roof of her mouth. It trickled down the back of her throat and made her cough as she felt the weight of the fluid reach the bottom of her empty stomach. Her head spun wildly. From around her came the derisive laughter of the watchers. Their mirth reddened Taylre's cheeks with shame. She looked up momentarily, but returned to the food. Her hunger easily overwhelmed her embarrassment. She took large bites of the meat and turnips, immediately feeling a renewal of strength, oblivious to the atrocious manners that she was sure her grandmother would find so deplorable.

Soon, Taylre longed for another drink, but shuddered at the thought of tapping into the honey sweet beverage before her.

"May I have some water?" she asked timidly. Her eyes searched the cavernous hall for the little man who had served her before. But her request was only met with silence as the yellow eyes of the hushed watchers continued to stare. Finally, the scraping legs of a chair, a sound coming from just beyond the tall flames, broke the silence. Taylre looked up to see Loden. His tall, slender form was striding toward her.

"There is no water for you, Taylre. Only this mead, you see. Drink it. It will warm you inside."

"I...I can't drink it," she protested. "It burns my throat and makes my head feel funny."

"Well, Hrym was right, you do complain a lot. But I can let that pass, you see. I can be much kinder, even to those who betray me." Taylre opened her mouth to object, but Loden held his hand up. "No," he said, "say nothing. It is not necessary. All will be forgiven when you help me. Then you can take your place beside me again, like Hrym, and be part of the great victory that will come."

"The victory? Help you? What do you mean?"

Loden looked at her, his mouth turned up into a malefic grin. "Have you eaten sufficiently? Is your stomach full?" he asked.

Taylre looked down at her nearly empty plate, surprised that she had eaten as much as she had. "Yes, I suppose."

"Good. Follow me and we can talk. There's so much you need to know and so much for you to do."

Taylre rose slowly from her seat, but her head still spun from the potent mead. She waited until Loden had moved beyond the fire before she began her slow advance behind him, determined to keep her distance. There was something about his voice that disturbed her. Something that sounded very dangerous, and she didn't want to be too close when that threat was finally revealed.

Chapter Six
Sinmore and Erna

The sky began to lighten as the weary travelers approached the cabin, and the dim gray of fading light turned to a softer white. Snow continued to fall, but it felt lighter, as if a solemn, meager change in the climate were about to take place.

Zeke felt his heart skip a beat when he reached the warped steps. His toes were still numb from the cold, but his breath came in warm, rapid wisps. Devon, who was standing next to him, glanced once at the girl who stood in the doorway and then turned to look at Zeke. He grabbed him gently by the arm.

"Easy there, tiger. Don't let those eager teenage hormones get the best of you," he said, his infamous grin finding a hesitant place on his frozen face.

Zeke jerked his arm away as a scowl replaced his look of pleasure. "I don't know what you're talking about," he whispered sharply.

Marjorie was the first to reach the porch. She pulled her hood back and revealed a nervous smile. "We've come to see Sinmora," she said quietly.

The girl, clothed in a knee length dress and draped with a thick, dark gray shawl, bent low in a graceful curtsy, her long auburn hair, wrapped tightly in a braid, fell over her shoulder. "We have been expecting you," she said, a slight accent marking her speech. "My name is Erna. I am pleased to welcome you into this humble home. Please come in." She stepped aside lithely while the visitors entered, their shoulders and knees forced to bend as they stooped through the low entry.

A few moments passed before everyone's eyes adjusted to the darkness, but soon the room was exposed. It revealed a rustic enclosure with thick beams overhead for support and solid wood floors beneath. A fire burned brightly in the corner while the room took on a smoky blur that shrouded the air in a misty haze. Sitting next to the fire in a chair that appeared to be made of polished driftwood, was the oldest woman Zeke had ever seen. Her eyes were bright, and she stared directly at him while she puffed on a long pipe.

"You are welcome, Chosen of the All Father. You are most welcome. Come, sit before me that I may study you further." Then her eyes shifted slightly toward Devon. "And you," she said, making a subtle motion with her pipe, "sit by me as well. I must look at you both."

As if on cue both Devon and Zeke looked at their mother. Confusion and fear filled their eyes. Vivian stared back; her expression was blank and empty. Finally, after a moment of awkward silence, Marjorie stepped forward. She bowed low but kept her eyes fixed on the old woman.

"Sinmora, we've traveled far to seek your help and advice," Marjorie said, her voice revealing a nervous stammer.

"I know why you've come, child. I hear the wind. It speaks to me. The earth shudders with the echo of evil, of horrible deeds of malice and revenge. Your journey will not be in vain." Sinmora leaned forward in her chair, looking past Marjorie and once again eyeing the two boys. "But these," she said, pointing a crooked finger, "these are the Chosen. I have heard the whispers of the Valkyries. They speak of warriors, of buds on the vine who must be nourished, for they will help defend the gates of Asgard."

"They are aware of the Mist, that is true," Marjorie said, "but a true understanding is only secondary to our purpose. My granddaughter has been taken. Loki has her. We must get her back. That's why we've come." Marjorie's voice rose as she began to lose her composure, her anxiety over Taylre edging the line of decorum.

"What you perceive and what is real are two different things," Sinmora scolded. "Do not suppose to tell me what must be done. I am wiser and I see beyond your temporal vision." She waved her hand dismissively toward Marjorie then struggled to rise from her seat. Erna hurried over and grabbed hold of the old woman's arm. She assisted her onto shaky legs. Slowly, shuffling her feet as she moved, Sinmora stood before the two boys, her head barely reaching the middle of Devon's chest. Then she reached out a twisted hand and touched Devon's smooth, unblemished cheek. He winced slightly at the old woman's touch as her fingers traced the soft lines of his chin and jaw. "This is ore from which hard steel will be forged," she said, dropping her hand to her side and staring at the boys with a wrinkled, satisfied smile.

Sinmora turned to Erna. "We must eat before the Seidh. Bring us bowls and place them on the table. Fill them from the cauldron and bring us milk and mead," she ordered, though her request was soft, gentle, and respectful.

Erna nodded her head as the green of her eyes glanced toward Zeke. When she moved obediently to her duties, the tips of her fingers brushed his arm as she turned. Zeke's back stiffened at the touch and a gentle flutter of warmth kneaded its way up his spine. For a brief moment his eyes met hers and they shared a smile, a wordless interaction that filled Zeke's heart with tenderness.

The small group sat on rickety chairs around a broad, solid table. Erna pulled a blackened cauldron away from the heat of the fire and filled large wooden bowls with a thick stew. In cups that resembled golden goblets from some lost treasure, she filled with buttermilk, and in another, honeyed mead. The Captain, ignoring the looks from the rest of the group, dove into the meal with the fervor of a man who had trudged many miles through the thick snow. He drank deeply from both of the cups, pausing long enough to wipe his mouth on his sleeve and tear another crust of bread from the loaf that sat on a plate in the middle of the table.

Devon watched with silent amusement as the Captain devoured his meal, but Vivian picked at her stew reluctantly. She carefully inspected unidentified lumps that lay in the thick gravy and tried in vain to determine what kind of meat had been added.

Marjorie ignored her food completely. A glum look spread across her face. Her thoughts still lingered on Taylre as a sense of frustration mounted with each bite the Captain took, his satisfied moans making his meal an audible delight.

"Really, Bartholomew. Must you make so much noise when you eat?" Marjorie asked.

The Captain looked up from his empty bowl, his spoon still gripped tightly in his hand. "Marjorie," he said quietly, "I'm quite certain you've noticed that a man of my size needs his nourishment. That's all I'm doin'. But if I happen to enjoy the taste of the sustenance while I get it, then why not just let it be. Let a man eats in peace will ya." He lifted his bowl and Erna refilled it along with his cup of mead. Devon laughed despite the scowl that Marjorie wore on her face, and then he too tore into his meal discovering his own voracious appetite.

Zeke, though a nagging hunger pulled at him, struggled to raise his spoon. Erna sat beside him. Her arm and shoulder touched his and the smell of her skin tugged at his senses.

"You must eat," Sinmora called from across the table. "The Seidh can be a tiring process. You will need all the strength you can muster."

Zeke looked up as an embarrassed tinge of red shaded his cheeks. "Yes, ma'am," he answered. Erna took his spoon and placed it in his hand. Her fingers lingered on his, and a gentle flutter once again rose up his spine.

Soon everyone was eating, relishing the satisfaction of a hot meal. Even Vivian found the stew to be delicious as the thick broth mixed with turnips, carrots, onions, and venison gave warmth to her hesitant soul. Both she and Marjorie sipped at the mead finding its honey sweetness to be a pleasant combination with the stew and the bread. Its touch of fermentation gave strength to their weary limbs and warmth to their cool, red cheeks.

Marjorie, finding her frustration slowly passing as the food and the mead filled her stomach, turned a questioning eye on Sinmora. "You live so far from civilization, Sinmora. Where does the meat come from? Who brings you the vegetables and keeps the fire going?"

Sinmora lifted droopy eyes toward Marjorie as teary sadness filled their depths. "Erna, my apprentice, sees to my needs," Sinmora said, lifting a gnarled hand toward the girl who sat beside Zeke, her hand now resting on top of his. "She hunts the beasts of the forest and grows the vegetables. She chops the wood that provides our heat, and she provides a strong shoulder to lean on when the winds speak of death and the coming of great evils."

"Is it true then?" the Captain exclaimed. "Are there terrible things on the horizon?"

"Aye," Sinmora answered, "but the Mist keeps secrets well. Long have I sought the answers to what the future holds, but now, now that the chosen have arrived, perhaps the answers will finally be revealed?" She pushed her chair back, its legs scraping against the wooden floor, and rose unsteadily to her feet. Erna, releasing the light grip she had on Zeke's hand, stood and held tightly to Sinmora's arm, directing her slowly to her seat by the fire.

The travelers watched quietly as Sinmora sat. Then her tired eyes looked up at the expectant visitors. "We will begin the Seidh," she announced softly. "I feel the Mist calling. It is time."

Chapter Seven
A Fettered Fenrir

The great hall, filled with feasting giants and dwarves, soon receded into the distance, as did the warmth of the fire. Taylre found herself shivering in the darkness of a narrow hallway as she continued to follow Loden. His pace was slow and even, as if he deliberately meant to prolong the journey and add to Taylre's discomfort in both body and mind.

A few dimly lit torches placed in iron sconces lined the corridor. Their flames flickered and danced as shadows appeared on the timbers, adding mystery to their final destination. Occasionally, Loden would look back at his reluctant follower and smile, a joyless smirk that pressed heavily on Taylre's weary, troubled mind.

"Not much farther," Loden said as the shadow of his tall figure leapt amid the other bleak shadows. "Soon you will be warm again. I have a special place of comfort that I reserve just for myself, you see. It is my sanctuary, if you will. It allows me the chance to get away from the warrior stench." He chuckled as he said this, glancing back toward the great hall from which they came.

"You should feel privileged, Taylre. There are very few that have ventured down *these* corridors. That should *prove* that I look highly upon you." Loden stopped and turned quickly to face her. "I have high expectations, you see. I think in time you will discover that I *am* your friend. Your only *true* friend. When you do, I'm certain you will help me." He spun around, once again leading Taylre down the darkened hallway.

The passage soon widened, giving way to another massive door. Taylre looked on with kaleidoscopic vision and watched the images carved in *its* surface sway and jig in their deathly ballet. A brush of nausea threatened to wash over her as the movement from the magic doors held her. It pulled her into its wicked embrace. However, the spell was quickly broken as Loden reached up and slid away a thick metal bolt that kept the entrance secure. The friction of steel on wood echoed down the length of the hall like the scream of an injured child. Loden leaned into the door. His strong shoulder pushed the barrier inward exposing a room that was both magnificent and horrible to look upon.

Taylre was awestruck.

The room glittered with gold. It was as if all of the treasure of Ali Baba had been opened to her and its secret exposed. Loden turned to Taylre and stepped lithely to one side allowing her entrance into the room, his exaggerated bow and royal gesture balancing precariously on the edge of mockery.

"Enter, my dear," he said. The wave of his hand beckoned her. "Your chamber awaits."

Taylre hesitated, her fear of Loden fed her reluctance but curiosity filled her desire.

She entered.

"Here you will find all of the comforts your mind can conceive," Loden boasted. "There is food, there is warmth, and there is bedding so plush that it would make even Freyja blush, the fairest of all the goddesses of the Aesir."

Taylre scanned the room, peering awkwardly through the shattered lenses of her glasses. High above she saw a familiar domed ceiling. Its broad timbers ran in a crisscross pattern, giving way to an opening that allowed both the smoke from the brilliant fire lighting the room to escape, and the gray light of day to enter. The light, though weak, shone upon a treasure that was piled in heaps on the floor. It sparkled with an outward and inward iridescence, almost as if the cache held a power of its own. But there was something else. Something that made

Taylre's senses curl. A smell. An odor. A stench, perhaps, that underlay the pleasant aroma of incense that drifted through the chamber. Taylre looked about the room trying to find the source of the smell when she suddenly stopped. A gasp of horror caught in her throat.

In the corner, just beyond the reach of the firelight, was a set of huge glowing eyes, eyes that stared at Taylre with hunger.

Taylre stepped back as an all-encompassing fear filled her soul. She turned in an attempt to find the door, a way to escape the beast that must surely belong to the eyes. She began running, but was immediately seized by the strong hands of Loden who pulled her in, embraced her and filled her with a chill of loathing.

"Relax, Taylre," Loden said soothingly. "He won't hurt you, unless I tell him to of course. He's my son, you see, the eldest of my devious union with Angrboda, a most lovely giantess. She had a way of soothing me during those lonely cold nights in Jotunheim, the land of the giants." Loden, still holding tightly to Taylre, swiveled around. He bent down and faced her.

"He is my favorite, you see. He is destined to make quite a display in the days to come. Quite a display indeed."

"Wha...what is it?" Taylre stuttered.

Loden released his gaze on Taylre and turned toward the eyes that continued to stare. "Not an 'it', Taylre. He. It's a he. Fenrir, the giant wolf... my son."

Loden placed a heavy hand on Taylre's shoulder, giving it a soft pinch before standing and walking toward a bejeweled throne. He sat lightly and reached toward an ornately carved table to his left and hefted an oversized jug of mead, filling an ivory cup. Loden took a long swig from the mug, letting the excess spill from the corners of his mouth. Slamming the cup on the table, Loden gazed once again on his child, the giant Fenrir whose stories of wrath had turned to legends and myth.

Taylre tried to back away when the beast stood, but Loden called to her, soothing her with a soft hush he forced her to look at the advancing figure of the largest animal she had ever seen, a caricature of an insane artist's interpretation of a living nightmare.

Fenrir seemed to slither from his darkened corner, an impression of thick liquid oozing its way toward the throne where Loden sat. Soon it perched next to Loden and sat lithely upon its haunches. Loden stroked his fur tenderly and the animal closed his eyes, moaning with pleasure at the touch of its master.

"Fenrir has had quite a traumatic past, you see. It's no wonder he appears so violent and destructive. But he's really quite gentle, once you get to know him."

Taylre located a small table that stood close by and lifted it, placing it securely between her and the beast. Its protection was scant, almost nonexistent, but its presence made her feel safe nonetheless.

"The gods have been cruel. They can't really appreciate power in others, they want to hoard it for themselves, you see. They want to punish those who exhibit strength beyond their own." He stroked the animal's fur again and Fenrir sat, groaning as he did, a quiet exhibition of satisfaction.

Taylre tilted her head to the side as her sense of fear toward the beast diminished while she listened to Loden's words.

"Gods can't be cruel," she stammered. "Gods are good. They're always good. That's why they're gods."

Loden looked up, astonished. "Why Taylre," he exclaimed, "you *can* speak. And quite forcefully too." He gave Fenrir one last pat and then stood, making his way toward Taylre and her makeshift barrier. He knelt in front of her and looked steadily at her, his eyes, though dark and malicious, locked her stare. "Let me tell you a thing or two about the gods, Taylre. There's nothing good about them. Nothing but lies and more lies." He turned to look at Fenrir. "My boy, the one you're so afraid of, he is a living testament to their cruelty."

"Then tell me," Taylre said. "What makes him so special?"

Loden smiled and reached his hand toward Taylre's cheek, caressing it lightly. She cringed, the touch cool and lacking tenderness. "There is hope for you yet, Taylre." He rose slowly and returned to his seat on the gilded throne. "Let me tell you a story," he said, once again drawing his hand across Fenrir's back and brushing the thick fur. "It is a tale of immense deception and jealousy, an attribute that can only be found in the disposition of the gods. You may not believe that it's true, but I assure you that it is." Loden reached toward the decanter of mead and poured himself another overflowing mug. "It all began when Odin, that one eyed ass, discovered that I'd fathered more children with Angrboda. He called the gods together and they decided that my children had no place within the nine worlds, that their existence was somehow a threat to mankind. How typical! They were *children*! Can one really make such a judgment on *children*? Especially without first seeing their worth?" Loden drained the contents of his mug and stared at Taylre, a look that called for an explanation.

Taylre remained mute. Her head shook, but her thoughts secretly sided with the gods.

Loden continued. "He put together a clandestine kidnapping, you see. While we slept the gods snuck into Angrboda's house and stole the children!" Loden's voice rose to a shout, and his eyes widened. "I tell you, it was a thing that only the gods could do. And *you* call them good. What is good about stealing children, I ask." His mug slammed against the table.

"From Jotunheim they dragged them to Asgard where they brought my beauties to Odin's throne, a long and perilous journey, especially for ones so young. The gods made them stand in their night clothes, feet bare on a cold floor, and look up in forced respect at the supposed All Father of us all." Loden dragged his hand through his hair, his jaw tightening. "I can only imagine the fear and anguish they must have been feeling at the time."

Fenrir's jaws gaped wide in a groaning yawn, much like a family dog lying beside its master. Taylre watched as the beast bared its teeth. She crouched lower behind her meager defenses, waiting for Loden to resume his tale.

"My children," Loden continued, "were not what one might consider...beautiful. They had their faults, to be sure. My daughter, Hel, for instance, she had some slight deformities, but I blame her mother for that. One can never fully trust the giants. They all come from a line of ancestors that never managed to look just right. They are not," Loden said, his hand waving in the air, a blush of embarrassment reddening his cheeks, "the most attractive people, you see.

"She was, my daughter that is, somewhat...difficult to look upon. The upper portion of her body came out to be an interesting shade of pink. All of this, even though it did attract some unwanted attention from onlookers, could have be waved off. However, the lower part of her body appeared to be decayed with a greenish-black hue. Also, there was an... odor, you see. That was difficult to ignore, even as a parent. She was not a happy child, to be sure. She shunned others quickly. Her expression was always gloomy and grim." Loden stood again and paced the wooden floor. His boots scuffed noisily across the solid surface. Finally, he stopped behind his throne and rested his hand on the high back, his head lowered with an expression of defeat. He looked up at Taylre once more. "But can you blame her? With all those people looking at her all the time, running away when they saw her approach. That's no life for a child, no matter what they look like or who their parents were!"

Loden stepped from behind the throne and placed his hand on Fenrir's back. "The gods shunned her too." Anger returned to his voice. "Odin took one look at my daughter and with disgust painted all over his face, hurled her out of Asgard. She sailed through the Mist and darkness and finally came to rest in Niflheim, the world beneath the worlds. It became Odin's decree that she should serve the dead, all those of the nine worlds who died of illness or old age. I have not seen my daughter in many ages. I'm told she still suffers. That her palace is in ruins and her realm is a kingdom of darkness and despair." Loden sighed heavily and stepped away from Fenrir, advancing once more toward Taylre's meager defense. "Do you not see my anguish, Taylre? Can you not feel at least a little pity for me?"

Taylre rose slightly from her crouched position. Her head nodded slightly. "It must have been terrible to see your child treated so harshly," Taylre admitted

"Oh but it was!" Loden exclaimed. "Terrible, terrible! But the worst occurred to my other son, Jormungand. He appeared even nastier than Hel. He was born in the form of a serpent. Odin, upon seeing him, cast him into the deep sea of Midgard where he remains to this day, suffering a horrible existence alone, friendless, and without hope." Loden, standing just in front of Taylre's table barrier, turned again to face Fenrir. He raised his arm and drew with it Taylre's gaze which now rested on the napping beast. "But my son has become my hope for the future. The hope for us all, you see." Loden's eyes moved to glance at Taylre but his head remained fixed.

"I don't understand," Taylre said. "How can *that* be the hope of the future?"

"*That*," Loden exclaimed, stiffening his arm toward Fenrir, "will destroy the gods. He is destined to do so."

"But you said the gods punished him."

"Aye," Loden answered, "but he's escaped their punishment, as I have. And the gods are shaking in their boots. They know the end is near."

"The end?" Taylre questioned. "The end of what?"

Loden chuckled, his head shaking as if he were talking to a small child. "You are so naïve, Taylre. You know so little. You are trapped in a world of ignorance and plenty. You think that it will always be thus. But make no mistake. It will end. It always does, you see."

ᛦ

Taylre began looking around the room and saw the treasure that was scattered about, the roaring fire that kept the immense room warm, and the rich food that adorned the long table. She sighed heavily. "I still don't see, Mr. Loden. We sit here in a land of cold and ice. We're barricaded in an incredible wooden palace, and yet you seem to think that *you're* going to win some great battle. That *you're* going to conquer the gods."

For a moment Taylre saw Loden's nostrils flare, as if he were about to explode with anger. But Loden took a deep breath, which seemed to calm his nerves. "Let me relate the rest of the story, Taylre. When I do, I think you will see things quite differently."

Taylre slunk slowly behind the table. "Go on, Mr. Loden," she said grimly. "Tell me the rest of the story."

Loden smiled, a calculated look gleaming in his eyes. "Odin saw Fenrir as just an ordinary wolf, you see. A puppy if you will. What he didn't realize is that he'd grow, his strength increasing with each passing year, the greatest deception of them all. Fenrir was set free, allowed to wander without restraint among the green and golden fields of Asgard. The great buffoon, Tyr, the supposed god of war, left him chunks of bone and gristle to gnaw upon, making him stronger and stronger, you see. Eventually, in the midst of their selfish control of the worlds, the gods suddenly stopped and took notice. Fenrir had become the immense beast you see before you, a power to be reckoned with. *Now*, the gods were afraid," Loden exclaimed. His hand rose, his finger pointing toward the domed, open ceiling.

"The cowards knew they couldn't kill Fenrir; he was too powerful. So they made up some excuse to appease their countless, idiotic followers: they didn't want to stain the sanctuary of Asgard with his evil blood. The gods also knew that Fenrir was smart." Loden turned and faced Fenrir. Fenrir raised his head, his eyes heavy from the short nap he'd been woken from. "Didn't they, my child."

"Yes, father," Fenrir answered sleepily. "They knew indeed."

ᛦ

Taylre almost screamed, but the lump of fear and surprise that filled her throat made it impossible. Her eyes grew wide;

the broken lenses of her glasses made them appear disjointed, as if there were several astonished looks coming from the same face.

"How...wha..."

"My, you *do* have a way with words, Taylre," Loden said sarcastically. He chuckled lightly under his breath. "I assume by your dumbfounded look that you didn't know Fenrir could talk. But why should you think he could? He is, after all, just a dumb, ugly beast. Right, Taylre?"

"I'm...I'm...I'm so...so sorry. I...had no idea. I just thought..."

"I know what you thought, Taylre. You, just like the ignorant gods, thought Fenrir was a ravenous animal, capable of nothing more than destruction. But you see you're wrong. And when the gods finally discovered that, they feared even more. They realized that the predictions of the Norns might actually come true; that the death of Odin might actually become a reality." Loden returned to his throne and sat. Once again he reached for the mead decanter and filled his mug.

Fenrir, still lounging beside Loden, stood and stretched, arching his back as the tips of his fur brushed against the high ceiling. Then his eyes turned on Taylre, their hue a pale yellow, and the centers burning bright red. He walked slowly. His claws clicked on the hard floor. Soon he stood before her, his shoulders hunched as he bent to stare at her.

Taylre could feel the beast's breath on her face and she tried to step back, but she had nowhere to go. A sturdy wooden pillar blocked her retreat, and the table she used as a barrier of protection now seemed like a helpless tree before a rushing avalanche.

Taylre shut her eyes and hoped death would come quickly.

Fenrir growled. "Open your eyes, you little fool." The voice was deep, like a thick river of sweet syrup. "I have no intention of harming you. Do you really think me such a brute?"

Taylre's eyes opened, slowly and reluctantly.

Fenrir continued to stare, but there was no kindness in the look. "Father," Fenrir's eyes shifted in the direction of the throne, "we could assist this child. Mayhap one of the dwarves could fix the spectacles she wears. The look she gives is deceiving."

"Aye," Loden answered. "I have thought the same. I will see to it while you finish here."

Finish here? Taylre thought. *Does that mean he's still going to eat me? But why would he? He wants my glasses fixed.*

Loden stepped down from his throne and took the glasses off Taylre's face. "I'll have them back to you in a jiffy," he said smiling. But before he could exit the room, Fenrir grunted.

"Father." Loden paused as he moved to open the large door. "Are you sure this cowering child is the right choice? She seems too frail."

Loden's smile faded and a sad look spread across his face. "She is all we have, my boy. She will have to do. Yet I'm confident she will suffice." Loden slipped through the small opening and disappeared into the darkened hallway.

Fenrir's yellow eyes turned back to Taylre. "My father has faith in you it seems. Though I wonder..." His voiced trailed off thoughtfully.

Taylre stared at the huge face that stood in front of her, though her view was unfocused by her myopic vision. "Please don't hurt me," she muttered.

Fenrir shook his head. "Perhaps if I were to finish the tale, the one my father started, you will begin to see me in a different light. Yes?" Fenrir's head tilted slightly to the side.

"I...I suppose," Taylre answered.

"Good. Now where did he end? Ah yes, the god's deception to their followers and their continued lies to me.

"Well, they feared me. There's no doubt about that. But the gods are cowards. Don't ever forget that. They knew they couldn't kill me, so they planned a way to imprison me. I remember it clearly; the sun shone distantly, almost as if it feared to be part of the day. I'd grown, as you can clearly see. I was no ordinary wolf, and I'd found a sanctuary among the vast trees of Barri, the great forest. I woke from a frightful dream to find myself surrounded by the gods.

"'Fenrir,' they said, 'we have been told that you are the strongest among the nine worlds. Even greater than the God of Thunder.' Then they showed me a chain, its links made from a material that sparkled with an inner brilliance. 'This is Laeding,' they said. 'Its strength is magnificent. Can you break it?' I studied the chain, but only with the eyes of one who was still caught in the throes of sleep. 'It looks strong,' I answered, 'but I am stronger.' And then, in my drowsiness, I allowed them to wrap the chain around my body, its strength making breathing difficult. But I planted my feet firmly on the ground, filled my lungs with air, and flexed every muscle in my body. When I did, the chain broke, the sound of its destruction caused the trees surrounding me to tumble. I looked up, feeling immense satisfaction, only to see the terror written across the faces of the gods. I knew then that this was no casual game. I knew that their intent was to destroy me.

"I look back on it now and know that I should have left and sought the comfort of my father, but my heart was prideful. I didn't want the gods to win.

"For a short time things returned to normal. I found pleasure once more in the forests of Barri and slept peacefully. But then the nightmares returned, and I again found myself staring into the eyes of the gods. Their arms were laden with the weight of another chain, this one called Dromi, its strength twice that of

Laeding. In my pride I let them wrap its weight around my back and neck, confident that I could also break its bonds, but it was strong, the effort to shake myself from its hold took all of my strength. Nevertheless, in the end I won. Dromi snapped, its links shattered and scattered in a hundred different directions. The sound it made when it broke not only set the forest aflame, but it also made the gods flee. They ran like frightened children, stumbling over roots and branches. I could not help but laugh. The image of their flailing arms and the sound of their terrified screams still makes me chuckle. Nevertheless, I knew they'd return. They were stupid to be sure, but they were also persistent.

"In their failure they sought the help of the All Father, perhaps the only intelligent being among them. But don't get me wrong," Fenrir implored, "I still think the man is a buffoon, it's just that below him there is little that can be considered worthy of affection. Nevertheless, the advice they sought was valuable, very valuable indeed. They sent a messenger to the world of the dark elves, Svartalfheim. Beneath Midgard he traveled to the dank, gloomy, twilit grottoes seeking the help of the dwarves, promising them gold and more gold if they could make a fetter that could bind me. I am told that even in the gloom the eyes of the dwarves glowed with greed, and they whispered and schemed and set off to work. In the end they did produce a fetter, but this was no ordinary restraint. No, child, this was no clumsy set of linked chains that rattled when it shook. This was Gleipnir, a fetter as smooth and supple as a silk ribbon."

Fenrir shook his head sadly; his eyes closed tightly, a reflection of pain and humiliation scarring his features. He looked again at Taylre, her eyes wide with expectation as the tale continued to unfold. "The dwarves brought together their dark magic to create a spectacle that could only be wrought in the land of the dark elves. Its construction and the materials they used are almost laughable, now that I think about it."

Taylre managed a weak smile as she held on tentatively to her fear. "Wh...what was it made of?" she asked quietly.

"Made of? Why only the best ingredients, of course," Fenrir answered. "First, they used the sound a cat makes when it moves. Next, they included a woman's beard." Fenrir chuckled lightly when he said this, though to Taylre it sounded more like a snarl. "You must keep in mind the makers of the fetter were dwarves. The thought of a woman's beard may not be so funny to them. You must also consider why a cat makes no noise when it moves and why most women you meet *have* no beards, but many things that seem not to exist are simply in the dwarfs' safekeeping. Nevertheless, they continued by adding the roots of a mountain, the sinews of a bear, the breath of a fish, and finally a bird's spittle."

Taylre laughed, in spite of her fear. "You're kidding, right?"

"I am not," Fenrir answered, his snarl-smile exposing white fanged teeth, "though I can understand your reluctance to believe such things. You come from a world of faithlessness. You believe only in what you see. But as the saying goes, 'there are more things in heaven and earth, Horatio...'"

Taylre nodded her head knowingly. She'd read most of Shakespeare's plays. *Hamlet* was her favorite. "So they bound you," she said matter-of-factly. "Did you break it too?"

"No, not this one," Fenrir answered sadly. "The dwarf magic was strong, stronger even than me. At first I was hesitant to allow them to fetter me as before, but again my pride took over. They took me to an island called Lyngvi, in the middle of Lake Amsvartnir. I knew they were trying to trick me. I even told them so. But they lied to me. They told me if I was unable to break Gleipnir that they would set me free again. They *promised* that they would do so. But something in their eyes made me skeptical. I demanded collateral, something to ensure they keep their word to me. I insisted that one of them put his hand in my mouth as a token of their good faith. If they didn't keep their word, the hand would be mine.

"Tyr, the son of Odin, the god of war, he who had fed me bone and gristle to keep me strong when all others shunned me, placed his hand in my mouth. Even in my anger I felt pity. I sensed this would not end well. I had come to feel compassion for Tyr. I thought he was my friend." Fenrir's voice seemed to soften at the memory of something lost, something heartrending. He padded away from Taylre and took his place beside the fire that burned big and bright in the middle of the chamber.

Taylre looked on, feeling a sense of sadness envelope her. She pushed away her meager defenses and followed Fenrir, finding a seat near the fire, her frightened, cold body soaking in the warmth. Fenrir looked at the dancing flames, mesmerized by their colorful glow. Taylre could see the colors reflected in his large eyes and was moved toward compassion; she felt his sadness; her benevolent character compelled her to comfort. She reached her hand toward his soft fur, thinking she would stroke it as Loden had done, but a faint impulse pulled her back. A warning, perhaps.

"Did they keep their promise? The gods I mean."

Fenrir stirred from his hypnotic gaze, surprised to see Taylre sitting there. "Their promise?" he said quietly. "No. There was no promise kept. Only lies. They wound Gleipnir round and round my neck, body, and legs until it was all used up. I struggled as I had before, kicking, shaking, shrugging and rolling. However, the more I strained, the tighter Gleipnir became. Soon the pain became unbearable and I lost my footing, falling hard on my side. Before me stood the gods, their laughter echoing in my aching brain, all except Tyr's; his was the cry of pain; he had lost his hand."

The door behind them swung open. Its immense iron hinges issued a faint rusty scream. Both Fenrir and Taylre turned to see Loden enter the hall. Delicately balanced in his hands were Taylre's glasses, their lenses smooth, the frames straightened and polished.

"Well," Loden said, eyeing the two sitting beside each other near the fire, "we've become fast friends I see. Taylre, your glasses." He stepped forward and placed the spectacles on Taylre's face.

When they were on, Taylre gazed about the room. Her eyes grew wide with amazement. "Oh, my gosh," she whispered. "I don't remember the last time I ever saw so well. Everything is so clear. So...so...clear."

"Dwarves have a way of making everything better. They make rather good allies. Would you not agree, Fenrir?"

"I would indeed, father."

Loden circled the large fire pit in the middle of the room and once again took his place on his gilded throne, pouring himself another mug of mead. "You've finished the tale I presume."

"Not quite, father. There is but one final detail to add. My subsequent imprisonment."

"Ah, yes. How could we forget that little bit of treachery," Loden said sarcastically. "Well then, please, let *me* continue the telling. For you see, Taylre, I could hear the howls of pain coming from my child. It broke my heart. But there was nothing I could do about it, because after the gods bound Fenrir with Gleipnir they proceeded to affix a large chain to the ribbon. Then they passed the chain through a hole in a huge boulder called Gjoll, looped it back, and secured it to itself.

"The gods then drove Gjoll a mile down into the earth. With this task done, my son realized he was helpless, you see. He opened his mouth to howl, but then one of the gods drew a sword and drove the point hard into the roof of Fenrir's mouth, ramming the hilt against his lower jaw. Now, not only was my son bound, but he was gagged as well. Cruel. So cruel are the gods."

For a long while there was silence. The only sound was that of the crackling wood on the fire that sent the occasional glowing ember floating through the smoky air. Finally, the silence was broken by Taylre's soft voice.

"I had no idea that people could be so cruel. How could they be? Why would they do such a thing?" She stood and faced the fire. Its heat enveloped her like a warm blanket. She watched the dancing flames with a kind of detached interest and then turned to look at Fenrir and Loden, her vision focused and clear. "Is there something I can do to help you?"

Loden breathed deeply and his nostrils flared. A weak smile wrinkled the corners of his eyes. "Perhaps there is, Taylre. Yes, perhaps there is."

Chapter Eight
Cat Skin Lining

As evening approached the temperature dropped, sending a cold draft through the tiny cabin in the woods. Far above, in the misty wintry sky, a timid crescent moon fought hard to peek its way through the rapidly shifting clouds, occasionally reflecting off the still falling snow.

Within the moss covered cabin a fire still burned, but its heat was subdued as it tried hard to press against the oncoming chill of night. Nevertheless, both Marjorie and Vivian huddled beside it, their gloves and scarves once again donned, their arms wrapped around each other for added warmth.

The table, once laden with food and mead, had been cleared, except for the candles that continued to sputter and flicker in its center. Their glow reflected eerily on the faces of Zeke, Devon, and the Captain as they watched Sinmora and Erna prepare for the Seidh.

In a darkened corner of the cabin, its edges just starting to take on the dim glow of the distant candles, Erna placed hen-feathered cushions upon a raised seat. When she was done she turned to Sinmora, sat her gently on the cushions, and began to dress her in the garments of the Volva.

Carefully, almost as if she were dressing a queen, Erna placed a blue cloak, ornamented with soft, round stones around Sinmora's shoulders. Next she placed a necklace of glass beads around her neck, coupled with a cap of black lambskin lined with white cat skin, a tribute, Erna explained, to the beautiful goddess Freyja who saw the cat as sacred. Upon Sinmora's hands Erna placed calfskin gloves and upon her feet calfskin shoes. Around her waist was a belt of boiled leather that supported a leather pouch.

"What's in there?" Devon asked, pointing at the pouch.

Erna stopped her work and turned, the soft smile never leaving her face. "This small purse contains potions of Volva magic," she explained. "It is also here that she will carry the Volva's knife. See how its hilt is adorned with walrus ivory. Its value is priceless." Erna tucked the knife into the tiny pouch and sealed it with a leather drawstring.

Erna, after placing a carven staff with a brass knob in the Volva's hands, stepped down from the small platform. Sinmora continued to sit quietly in her elevated seat. Her eyes reflected the yellow of the hearth fire. Her face was a mirror of trance-like reflection.

Erna turned to the small group assembled by the fire. "We are ready to begin," she announced, drawing their attention to the fur rugs that were placed upon the floor. "Please sit here. The furs are warm and there are blankets that you can use to wrap around your shoulders." But before they began to move, Sinmora stirred in her seat and lifted her arm toward Zeke and Devon.

"But let the Chosen sit here, by me," she said. "They must sit near me. I can hear the wind. It whispers this command."

While the others sat on the rugs, Zeke and Devon moved slowly up the small riser to the Volva's chair. "Here, by my feet," she said, pointing at the floor. "Now, touch the hem of my dress, I need your strength to carry me this night. There are portents of evil on the horizon and this journey will be long."

Devon turned to look at Zeke. His eyes reflected confusion, concern, and a myriad of questions.

"Erna," Sinmora proclaimed, "let us begin."

Erna stepped lithely over the fur-covered floor, carrying with her a small drum. Sitting on the riser at Sinmora's feet, she sidled up next to Zeke lightly touching his shoulder. The hair on the back of Zeke's neck fluttered with pleasure at the touch. He longed to reach out and touch her hand, hold it in his own, and caress her fingertips, feeling the warmth of her pearl skin. However, before he could lift his hand, Erna began hitting the drum with a broad, polished stick. The beat was slow and rhythmic; its timber filled the air of the tiny cabin with a reverberating shimmer, one that seemed to make the atmosphere shake, like tiny ripples on the surface of a calm lake.

It was Vivian who looked up first, sensing the change in the air, as if the room were somehow moving inward, getting smaller. Her first thought was that the fermentation of the mead had gone to her head, sending her mind reeling. But then she glanced at Marjorie and the Captain; both began looking about as well. Their faces reflected the same kind of bewilderment.

"Do you feel that?" Marjorie whispered.

The Captain nodded his head slowly. His eyes looked toward the decanter of mead that rested on a moldy wooden counter.

Marjorie shook her head. "No," she said. "It's something else. Something's happening."

The three turned their attention back to the riser where Sinmora sat and where the drum continued its cadence. Sinmora continued to stare past the small audience toward some distant vista while Erna, in time with the beat of the drum, whispered instructions. "Relax your limbs," she said, "and take deep breaths. Then, close your eyes. Visualize a forest at the peak of spring. The wild flowers are growing along a path that leads into the forest. The trees arch overhead. Imagine that you are now following the path. The trees form a tunnel. This will lead you to the Sacred Grove." Then, in a loud voice, one that startled its listeners, Erna shouted.

"Cease not, Volva, till said thou hast; answer the asker till all he knows!"

In a voice as loud but still more shrill, Sinmora spoke, rising quickly from her seat as she did. "I tell thee much, yet more lore have I; thou needs must know this...!"

The sound of the drum suddenly ceased.

Vivian, whose eyes were closed, looked up to see Erna, her arm raised as if to resume her beat on the drum. Beside Erna sat an empty chair. Beside the chair, where Zeke and Devon once sat, were vacant places, marked only by indentations in the soft fur.

Chapter Nine
Old Wounds

Someone was screaming.

Devon opened his eyes and discovered he was lying on the ground. Directly in front of him was a purple flower that bobbed up and down and side to side with a slight breath of warm wind. It issued a pleasant aroma that reminded him of spring in Nova Scotia when the battle with winter was finally won. He wanted to reach out and pick the flower and inhale its fragrance, but was distracted by the sound of the scream, coupled with the pattering of running feet.

He sat up quickly to see a much livelier and agile Sinmora pass by. Her calfskin shoes kicked up dust as she scampered toward Zeke who lay writhing in pain along the edge of a worn path, its graveled surface shaded from the sun by the trees that arched overhead in the form of a tunnel.

"Help me! Oh, god, please help me!" Zeke cried.

"Calm yerself, child," Sinmora said soothingly. "I'll take care of ye. Ol' Sinmora will take care of ye."

Devon scrambled over the path to find Sinmora leaning over his wailing brother. Blood was seeping from a cut in his thigh; a red stain was forming slowly in the blue of his denim jeans.

Sinmora reached behind her and felt for the pouch that hung from her belt. Devon rested his hand on her shoulder; she turned to look at him and pulled him toward her. "Take the pouch from my belt, lad. I'll be needin' the knife and some potions."

Devon's hands were shaking as he tried to release the leather tie. Gritting his teeth he fumbled with the thin line until he finally had it loose.

"Pull out the knife, lad. The one with the fancy handle."

Devon reached inside, pushing past tiny earthenware vials until his hand gripped around the thickness of the ivory. He extracted the blade and slid it out of its sheath. Sinmora grabbed it quickly. Then, holding it firmly in both hands lifted the knife, bringing it to eye level. Quietly and respectfully, as if she were uttering a silent prayer, she uttered murmured words that Devon could not understand. When she was finished she used the knife to tear away the clothing that covered the wound.

"The vial," she whispered sharply, drawing Devon's attention back to the pouch on the ground. "The one with the blue top. Take it gently. It is very potent."

Devon picked through the purse until he'd found the correct vial and removed it slowly, cradling it as if it were his grandmother's precious china. Sinmora reached for it, but this time slowly. Her movements reflected Devon's own caution. Releasing the cork stopper that sealed the vial, Sinmora tipped it and tapped the edge with her finger. A fine yellow powder sprinkled out, blending with the heat of Zeke's blood. The powder turned it from a deep red to a sickly pale orange.

Devon edged back as the yellow potion began to bubble and sizzle, sending out a rush of smoke that carried with it an odor so foul Devon had to turn and vomit onto the grass behind him. When he turned back to his brother, wiping his mouth with the sleeve of his jacket, he noted that Zeke's cries had diminished, turning from a painful shriek to an agonized moan. The rush of blood began to slow too, and the wound appeared to be magically closing in on itself.

Sinmora carefully replaced the blue-topped vial in the pouch, her movements careful and deliberate. Zeke struggled to sit up. Both Sinmora and Devon bent to assist him. "That's it, lad," Sinmora encouraged. "You'll be better now. Gotta' get the blood circulating again. That's it."

Zeke was shaking. His skin was pale, and a fine sheen of cool sweat glistened across his forehead. He began rubbing his leg vigorously. "What the hell was that all about?"

Devon stared at his brother while a crooked smile creased the corners of his mouth. "You know mom would slap you for saying that, right?"

Zeke paused as a shiver past over him, raising the tiny hairs on the back of his neck. He turned quickly, expecting to see his mother sitting right behind him, her mouth twisted in anger, her quick retort to his profanity slipping from her lips. What he saw, however, made him gasp.

The last thing he remembered was the beating of the drum and the cool draft that blew in from underneath the poorly fit door in the cabin. What he saw made him feel as if he were in a dream and everything that had happened in the last few hours had simply been a figment of his imagination. He considered pinching himself, and almost did, until Sinmora spoke, breaking his spell of confusion.

"'Tis the Mist, lads. We've come through to the Mist."

"The Mist?" Zeke questioned. "I don't understand. I've been in the Mist before, but getting here...well, it's been difficult. I get sick. Sometimes I feel like I want to throw up. This time it was...I don't know... seamless."

"Seamless. Aye, lad, Seamless is the right word," Sinmora chuckled. "It has been through countless hours of meditation and purification that I've been able to prepare myself to pass through the Seam into the Mist. The Seam is a fickle gatekeeper.

It allows only those who have the proper birthright. You," she said, her gaze resting on the brothers, "have both the strength and the heritage to do so. Consider yerselves blessed. For ye truly are."

With the blood and the screaming momentarily forgotten, Zeke and Devon finally began to take in their surroundings. Their first observation was the well traveled path they sat on, its edges marked with tufts of ungainly grass and fragrant wildflowers. The trail followed a slight incline toward a thick forest of tall trees, their bows sagging heavily over the pathway giving it the appearance of a darkened tunnel. Where they rested, however, a beam of sunlight shone brightly, casting a pleasant ray of warmth on their winter minds.

Both Zeke and Devon relished in the warmth. Their thoughts reflected on the arduous, cold journey to Sinmora's cabin in the woods. Then a shadow crossed their minds and Zeke found himself pointing toward the dark tree tunnel.

"Where does that lead?" he asked.

Sinmora was busy retying the pouch to her waist when she looked up from her task to glance along the trail. "I know not where it leads, Zeke. The Mist has many portals that continue to shift. Where it has allowed us to enter this time is not familiar to me."

Devon stood slowly and began moving toward the tunnel of trees. He stopped suddenly and turned to his companions. "So, what do we do? Sit here and wait for something to happen? Or start walking?"

Sinmora chuckled; the gravelly grating of her voice reminded Zeke of the Captain's pipe-smoking laughter. "Truly you are steel that has yet to be sharpened, Devon. Curiosity and courage, they are a most dangerous combination. But perhaps it can be polished. The wind whispers that it can. I believe it to be so.

"But to answer your question, I propose this query. Does the loss of Taylre genuinely afflict you? Are you willing to accept the challenge before you? For that road," she said, pointing a stern finger along the pathway, "is very long and so is the quest. There will be dangers far beyond your mind's eye that will destroy you if you're not careful. Are you willing to become the warriors you are destined to be? Will you ignore the pain and anguish that will surely come before you reach your desired end? Because if you're not, we must turn around now; I feel the Mist begin to shift. If we don't leave this moment, we may never find our way back."

"The choice, then," Zeke said, limping toward his brother and standing next to him, "is do we follow the path forward or the path backward?"

"Aye," Sinmora said, nodding her head.

"Then really," Zeke said, his arm resting on Devon's shoulder for balance, "there is no choice. We're talking about Taylre here. We'll do whatever it takes." He turned to Devon whose quick nod told Zeke all he needed to know. They turned back to Sinmora, their faces reflecting certainty.

"It is decided, then," Sinmora replied. "Well done. You may achieve your aim if the fates favor you."

Sinmora stepped off the path and rummaged among the grass and flowers. She retrieved her staff and her blue cloak, which she wrapped over her shoulders; however, the staff was handed to Zeke.

"You will need this," she said, placing the gnarled walking stick into his free hand. "The wound you received at the hands of Loki will never completely heal. Entering the Mist has made it real again. It will hinder you, but perhaps this staff will offer some assistance."

Zeke accepted the proffered staff. He felt its sturdiness and tested its stability as he leaned his weight into it. He released his light hold on Devon and turned toward the trees, a slight grimace tightening his face as a jolt of pain sent a flush of heat up from his thigh. "Let's get a move on." He said, pressing forward with a stalwart limping stride.

Devon reached for the once frail Sinmora, like a boy scout

helping an elderly woman cross a busy street. But Sinmora shook her head. "The Mist has strengthened me, lad. There's no need for your help, though I do appreciate the offer. You walk on. I'll follow to make sure nothing sneaks up on us."

Devon gave Sinmora a wary glance, but then smiled his impish grin. "You're kidding, right?"

Sinmora offered a weak smile. "I am, child. Now get a move on. Keep up with your brother. He's the one that will need your help."

Devon gave his usual curt nod and turned to catch up to Zeke. Sinmora watched him go, her smile gradually fading. Then she looked behind her, a quick glance into the woods before she turned and began walking the path that led the small troupe into the darkness of the wooded tunnel.

Chapter Ten

A Very Small Door

The Captain stoked the cooling embers of the hearth fire with a cast iron poker. He pushed the coals aside and added another log. But then cursed lightly under his breath as an errant spark flew into the light tufts of his beard, singeing the gray hair and sending a puff of acrid smoke into the cool cabin air.

"Leave it alone, Bartholomew," Marjorie said. "You're only making it worse."

"How can I make somethin' that's not there worse?" he snapped back.

"You're causing smoke to come out," she continued. "Is it really necessary to inflict us with cold as well as smoke?"

The Captain turned his head and gave Marjorie an icy stare. "I'm tryin' to make the flames bigger, Marjorie. Ya can't make it bigger if ya don't stir it up a bit. So if you'll keep yer mouth shut and let me go about my business, I'll have the fire goin' and the room warm. The smoke is somethin' you'll just have ta live with."

Vivian, who was sitting next to Marjorie, sighed as a gentle puff of breath escaped her mouth. "This isn't helping," she said.

"What isn't helping?" the Captain said as he struggled to push another log onto the flames.

"The arguing and bickering. We're all frustrated. I get that. But yelling at each other isn't solving the problem."

"It's not that we're yelling, Vivian. It's more like were discussin' things," the Captain said.

"What ever you say, Bart." Marjorie rolled her eyes and pushed herself closer to the now rising flames.

"What I mean," Vivian continued, "is that we're confused. I mean, what the heck just happened? One minute the boys are here, the next they're not. I can't wrap my brain around this."

"They've passed through the Seam."

The voice came quietly from the other side of the room. Nevertheless, its faintness made the Captain jump; the log he was placing on the flames rolled from his hands, striking Marjorie. She squealed in pain and reached for her foot, dancing around the room like a woman suddenly possessed.

Both the Captain and Vivian ignored Marjorie's moans, turning quickly to see Erna sitting quietly in a darkened corner of the cabin, their looks of surprise tempered by her gentle, disarming smile.

"Good heavens, lass. I completely forgot you were there," the Captain said. "You gave me a bit of a start, ya did."

"I am so sorry, Mr. Gunner. I didn't mean to scare you." Erna stood up from the low riser where the Volva once sat, her lithe, agile body almost floating toward the warmth of the building flames in the hearth. "So much has happened, and so quickly, that it's easy to understand why you'd forget about me."

"Oh, it's not like that, hon," Vivian said. "It's just that...well...we're sorry. I guess we did kind of forget about you. We're concerned about the boys, and Sinmora, of course."

The weak smile on Erna's face accentuated its softness, slightly wrinkling the freckles that ran across her nose. "There's no need to be overly concerned for the boys. They are in very good hands with Sinmora. She knows..." Erna paused, "the Mist."

Marjorie finally found a place to sit. She removed her boot to examine the swelling that was beginning to form on her big toe. As she rubbed the affected region, she looked up at Erna. "You seem like a very nice girl, Erna. But I get the feeling there's something you're not telling us. You hesitated when you referred to the Mist. *Is* there something more?"

Erna moved closer to the fire and extended her hands to feel its warmth. She looked up bashfully, a tinge of redness appearing on her cheeks. "I have more food...would you like more food? I have mead, too. Anything you like."

Marjorie squinted, her head tipped slightly to one side. Vivian and the Captain just stared. The air seemed to waver with an awkward silence.

"Erna," Marjorie said, her voice breaking the spell of the airy discomfort. "What's going on?"

Erna's eyes shifted uncomfortably. Her gaze moved from Marjorie, then to Vivian, and finally rested on the Captain. A tear edged its way to the corner of her eye. "They're lost."

Erna's words seemed to float in the air, waiting for someone to take hold and make sense of them. But there was only muted silence. Finally, Vivian cleared her throat, bringing everyone back to reality.

"What does that mean?" she said, her voice betraying the worried expression of a mother. "You said 'they're lost'. What exactly does that mean?"

"It means," Erna said, "that they're stuck. The Mist has shifted and there's no way to get back. Unless..." Erna paused again. Her gaze hovered toward the far end of the cabin where complete darkness shrouded the corners.

"Unless what?" the Captain said. His hand reached inside his coat pocket for his pipe as his own eyes followed Erna's wandering gaze.

"Unless," she said, motioning toward the darkness, "*he* decides to help us, but if he's not willing, I'm not sure what to do. Sinmora hasn't schooled me enough yet."

"*He*?" Marjorie questioned. "Who is he?"

Erna pointed toward the back of the cabin. Her hand was shaking slightly as she did. "Berling," she said, "the one who lives beneath the house."

A shiver rose up the spines of the three onlookers as they turned toward the darkness, a place where the light of the hearth had not reached.

"You mean there's someone else who lives here?" the Captain inquired.

"Aye," Erna said. "He's there, through the door. But Sinmora has told me time and time again, ever since I was very young, that I was *never* to bother him. He's been punished, you see. He wants nothing to do with folk like you and me. But he knows the Mist. Of that I'm certain."

The Captain stood, his pipe producing a sweet, aromatic plume of smoke, and edged himself closer to the corner, his body acting as a kind of shield for Marjorie and Vivian. "Here, ya say. A person lives here?"

"Aye," Erna answered. "Through the tiny door. He makes his home in the ground where he feels safe. Where he feels more at home. That's what Sinmora says."

Marjorie and Vivian stood, accepting the Captain as their shield. and moved closely behind him. "Are you telling us that there's someone who lives underneath this house, and the way to get to them is through *that* door? That tiny door in the corner?" Marjorie said.

"That's right, through the door. But he'll get angry if we disturb him. He's not kind. No, not kind at all."

"What did you say his name was?" the Captain asked.

"Berling," Erna repeated.

"And you've seen him, have ya?" the Captain inquired, his voice betraying skepticism.

"I've seen him once," Erna said. "He scares me something terrible though. Like I say, he's not nice and he likes to be left alone. That's what Sinmora says."

Both Marjorie and Vivian were standing on their tiptoes to look over the Captain's shoulder, afraid something might pop out at them from the darkness.

"But...what *is* he?" Vivian asked.

Erna looked from Vivian to the corner where the tiny door was lost in blackness. "Some sort of elf, I suppose. I hid for days when last I saw him. He was speaking with Sinmora, but it was late, and I'd been asleep. I woke to their whispers and was curious. I wanted to know who Sinmora was talking to. I crept down from my loft, and there they were." Erna pointed her trembling hand to the corner. "The tiny door was open, but I'd never noticed it before, not until that night.

"I shrieked when I saw him. I was startled, you see. I had never expected to see something like that. I must have startled them, too. They both turned quickly. Sinmora was angry, for sure, but nothing like him. He bared tiny sharpened teeth at me and made a little hissing noise. A sound I'll never forget. Then like a flash he was gone. Through the tiny door that slammed behind him."

The Captain produced a wooden match from his coat pocket and flicked the flame to life. It illuminated the darkened corner and revealed a miniature-arched doorway, its hinges blackened with age. It was missing a handle, but a small hole, one made especially for an ancient skeleton key, was prominent. The Captain reached toward the narrow cracks between the door and wall and attempted unsuccessfully to jam his thick fingers into the grooves along the side and pull the door open.

"It'll not open that way," Erna said, stepping into the small light cast by the match. "A key is what you'll be needin'. Sinmora kept it on a chain about her neck. But honestly, if Berling is truly the one that ya be wantin' to talk to - and I really don't suggest that ya do - you may just want to knock."

Vivian bent slowly into the light to examine the door. "Do you really think we should be doing this, Bart? Because - and

I'll be the first to admit this - in the beginning I was skeptical of all this myth stuff. But the things I've been seeing and hearing about are starting to make a believer out of me. So I'm wondering...do we really want to knock on that door? To be perfectly honest, I'm a little frightened as to what might answer."

The Captain moved the flame closer to the tiny door, his brow wrinkled in thought. "Yav' got a good point there, Vivian. Knockin' on that door is gonna take a lot more courage than I have. You all know that I've not been known for my bravery in life."

Marjorie rested her hand on the Captain's shoulder. "You underestimate yourself, Bart. The things you've done of late have taken more courage than I think most men can muster in a lifetime. And remember, we need to find Taylre and the boys. There's no more time to think this through. So I suggest you knock. Let's get this over with."

The Captain continued to look at the small door, but his thoughts were on Marjorie's words and the recollection of a tall, skinny girl in shorts and of two young boys whose strength he admired with the completeness of a grandfather figure.

"You're right, Marjorie," the Captain said. He took another short puff of his pipe. "Sometimes yav' got to stir up the ashes and make some smoke."

Marjorie smiled despite her earlier frustrations with the Captain. "That you do, Bart. That you do."

The Captain took a deep cleansing breath and then tapped out the ashes from his pipe on his boot heal. He bent and once again examined the blackened hinges and the rusty keyhole.

Then, he reached out his hand and knocked.

There was an air of confidence in the way Taylre strode through the hallway. It was nothing like the way she felt when she first ventured this corridor. Her head was held high as the mighty Fenrir strode along beside her with Loden leading the way. Taylre once again entered the great hall where giants and dwarves mingled, eating, drinking and practicing their swordplay.

The raucous voices quieted when Taylre entered. Some, like Teddy, watched with a kind of loathing that bordered on revulsion. Others, like the dwarves that brought her food and drink when she first came to the hall, smiled grotesquely. Taylre managed to ignore them all. She felt at ease with her two companions who promised their friendship and protection. And for all that, they asked so little.

"Prepare yourselves," Loden called as he stepped into the hall. "Soon we will sail again. Naglfar must be ready. The weapons must be stocked. There must be food aplenty, and of course lots of drink!" The sound of laughter filled the great room as several of the heads of the giants and dwarves nodded in agreement with Loden's mention of the strong honeyed drink.

The horde of creatures rose from their revelry and clasped on belts and swords. They fitted themselves with armor and helmets, and moved through the huge door to the outside, enthusiasm for battle filling the smoky air.

"Come," Loki's eyes gleamed, now brown, now green, and now indigo. His red lips parted and twisted into a wolfish smile. "We will talk some more while the preparations begin. Sit here beside me, Fenrir, my son. And Taylre, my daughter, sit here in this seat of comfort."

Loden's words took Taylre by surprise. She looked up quickly to see his gesture of friendship and warmth as he urged her to relax in a high chair, cushioned in crimson red, and plush with the comforting warmth of furs and blankets. His smile disarmed her and she smiled back, her acceptance of his address complete and welcoming.

Taylre took her place in the chair and at once relished in its comfort. She eased herself into its softness and even sighed a little. Warmth was creeping its way back into her body, and the aches and pains she once felt from her long imprisonment were soon forgotten.

"Taylre," Loden said, leaning casually over the arm of his great chair. "I insist that you try the mead again. Perhaps for you it is an acquired taste. Nevertheless, it will warm you and make you happy."

Taylre shrugged her shoulders; her contentment in her new environment neared completion. "I suppose I could give it another try," she answered sleepily. "As long as I can have something to eat. It seems I am constantly hungry. I'm not sure why."

"It's the fresh air, you see. It brings out the appetite in us all." Loden lifted his hand and made a slight gesture that was immediately answered by a tiny bearded man clad in a boiled leather tunic, a stained apron wrapped about his waist. "Bring us food and plenty of mead," Loden said. "And make it quick you hare-brained slave." The small man left quickly, his head bowed, his movements jagged and awkward.

Taylre watched the man go, feeling a twinge of sympathy. "That was a bit harsh," she said quietly.

Loden shifted his gaze to Taylre, but his head remained fixed. "He is a dwarf, Taylre. They are scum, all of them. Trust me on this. I know. I have had many dealings with them in the past and they are all the same. Treat them as the slaves they are, for that is all they're good for."

Taylre looked at both Loden and Fenrir, their expressions unreadable. "But he seems like such a nice man," she said.

"Scum," Loden responded. "But let us not linger on this. There is still much to be said, you see. Things are happening very quickly and there are some matters that must be taken care of." The tiny man returned with a rolling platter, its surface covered with a large assortment of food, a jug of mead, two gilded cups, and an immense bone that looked to Taylre as if it had come from the hind section of a horse. Bits of partially cooked meat still clung to its exterior as well as pieces of sinew and gristle. The dwarf hefted the bone off the tray and placed it in front of Fenrir who immediately began gnawing at its edges, moaning with pleasure as he ate. The remaining food was placed in front of Taylre and Loden.

"Here," Loden said, filling a cup with the golden liquid and handing it to Taylre. "Drink this, then we'll talk."

Taylre lifted the cup that had been filled precariously close to the brim and sipped at its contents. Its sweetness once again filled her mouth as a slight burn drifted its way down her throat. She cringed as the sweet honey-drink pulled at her jaw, but then relaxed, enjoying the sudden warmth that filled her. "It is actually quite good," she said, taking another sip.

Loden smiled. "You see. I won't lead you astray, Taylre. You can trust me." Loden poured his own overflowing cup of mead and took a long drink. He placed it back on the tray after he'd drained its contents. "But now to matters of business." He stroked Fenrir's fur absentmindedly.

"Your friends are looking for you, Taylre, as is only proper for good friends to do. However, they are being deceived. An evil witch is leading them. They are in great danger."

Taylre looked up from her mug, her eyes wide with surprise. "A witch? Does my grandmother know?" she said. "Is my grandmother looking for me, too?"

"No," Loden answered. "She has not the skill. But the two brothers, Zeke and Devon, they are devoted in their search. They have sought the help of one in whom they have given great trust. But they are being deceived. The one they follow is evil, and in the end she will destroy them. So, we must warn them. Or rather, you must warn them. I cannot, you see. They don't trust me as you do. But they trust you. *You*, Taylre, can save them from a horrible fate. The greedy gods that we've spoken of have led them to the witch. She is as wicked as the gods."

Taylre set aside her cup; the affects of the alcohol were making her thoughts spin. "Where are they?" she said frantically. "We must tell them now!"

"Patience, Taylre," Loden said, resting his hand lightly on her arm. "You see that we are making preparations. We will leave in the morning, after we've had time to rest. Then we will travel to Surtsey, an island of fire and ice. Your friends will appear in a few days. When they do you can warn them." A twisted smile stretched over Loden's face, but in Taylre's present state of mind she saw only acceptance and friendship.

Taylre sunk back into the plush comfort of the chair and reached for her cup. She took another large sip of the golden liquid. "I feel quite sleepy," she said, replacing the gilded cup on the tray.

Loden and Fenrir eyed each other, basking silently in their deception. "Then you should sleep, my precious daughter. Sleep and regain your strength. You will need it."

Chapter Twelve
Geirrod's Stronghold

The forest was a vast ocean of green, stretching in an endless array of shapes and sizes as varied as the terrain. Both Devon and Zeke marveled at the odd assortment of vegetation that surrounded them. Their heads moved quickly from side to side as they passed one vista to the next. The wildlife varied as well. Creatures both strange and familiar wandered by in search of food and shelter.

The boys had long since removed their coats and sweaters, tying them around their waists or dragging them behind as they walked. The heat, which seemed to rise with each step they took into this new world, caused sweat to accumulate on their foreheads. The air surrounding them felt thick and oppressive, weighing them down with an overwhelming exhaustion.

Zeke continued to limp painfully as Sinmora followed close behind. Her words of gentle encouragement sustained Zeke as he plodded along; nevertheless, his own words of self-motivation gave him that extra push. Devon, who kept a steady pace in front, would sometimes disappear amid the thick vegetation and then suddenly reappear when he crested a small knoll or when the path decided to take an odd turn.

At one of these turns, Zeke motioned toward Devon, calling him back to a small, level area of grass that sat next to a burbling stream.

"I need to rest," he said, and eased himself down slowly on the cool patch of green.

Sinmora reacted quickly, supporting Zeke as he bent to the ground, her strength in the Mist far beyond her normal fragile self in Midgard. "A good place to rest, lad. I'll scoop some water for ya to drink, and with it a measure of medicine to help take away a bit o' the pain." She reached for her pouch and brought out another vial, this one capped with a red stopper. She filled a small cup with water, and then added some powder. At once the liquid turned a thick, chalky white. Then she stirred the mixture lightly with the tip of her finger.

"Drink this," Sinmora said, lifting the cup to Zeke's lips.

At first, Zeke merely sipped the remedy, drinking slowly and hesitantly. His face crinkled with displeasure. "What is it?"

"Tis' the tea of the white willow," Sinmora answered.

"Sounds about right," Zeke said, raising the cup to take another drink. "It tastes like tree bark."

"Aye," answered Sinmora. "The bark is what it's made of. Though mostly I add a wee dash of cinnamon and honey to make it taste better. But there's none to be had now. A nice hot cup would be nice, too, but that can't be done either."

Zeke finished the cup and wiped away the white residue that clung to his lips with the back of his hand. "It does make me feel better," he said. "The pain is letting up a bit."

Sinmora nodded knowingly. "It'll keep the pain at bay for quite awhile, too. As long as we don't travel too far."

Leaning over the tiny creek, Devon knelt with his hand cupped to drink. "It's so cold," he said, "and sweet. Almost as if it were sugared."

"Aye," Sinmora answered. "Within the Mist you'll be finding both the finest and sweetest. But alas, you'll also find the harshest and the bitterest." She turned and looked along the path, a darkness fading over her features. "We have not far to go, I think, until we reach a place to rest for the night. Do ya think ya can walk a wee bit more?"

"I think so," Zeke answered, sitting up slowly from his place of rest. "As long as goober-face here slows down some."

Devon raised his eyebrow and wagged an accusing finger at Zeke. "Nasty remarks in the Mist, Zeke? Really?"

Zeke gave Devon a sour look. "You know you've been wanting to add your own comment. I can see it in your face. I just got in the first plug, that's all."

Devon shook his head sagely, and then started back up the path. "I'm a changed man, Zeke. Maybe you better start doing a bit of that yourself."

Zeke scoffed and then turned to look at Sinmora. She was staring at him, a look of confusion on her face. "Is this something brothers often do?" she asked.

"Well..." Zeke answered. "No...only if one of them is...well, a goober-face." He smiled at Sinmora, but she just shook her head.

"Perhaps you should change," she said, turning up the path to follow Devon into the tall growth. "The trail ahead may require it."

ᛟ

The shade of the forest opened onto a freshly plowed field. The path ended abruptly. Zeke and Devon, tired and sore from their journey, plopped themselves on the ground. Even old Sinmora found a place on the roughly tilled earth to rest, her Volva robes scattered about her as she sat.

The sun shone weakly. It fought hard to cast its light through the haze of smoke that hovered overhead. Sinmora watched it drift past. She sniffed the air and then nodded with understanding. "We're near a village," she proclaimed.

Devon, who was flat on his back, suddenly sat up. "Village?" he echoed. "Where...? I thought we were in the Mist. How can there be a village?"

"All sorts exist in the Mist," Sinmora said. "The Mist is a land o' connection, the limbs and roots of the tree, if you will. There are plenty o' worlds, to be sure, but 'tis the Mist that connects them. One must travel through it to obtain entrance to other realms."

"So...there are people here?" Zeke said, his hand vigorously massaging his aching leg.

"Aye...you both know that there are people here. You've seen them and spoken to them, have you not? And, well, there are other things in the Mist as well."

"So, if there's a village," Devon said hopefully, "then maybe there's a place to eat, too?"

"Perhaps," Sinmora answered. "But beware. Folks in the Mist are not like ones you might be used to in Midgard. They have strange ways. They don't trust others as you might. Don't take offense by it. It's just that their world is different. They have other concerns on their minds."

Sinmora rose to her feet, sniffing the air once again. "We should go this way," she said, pointing a steady hand toward the open field.

Devon picked up the remaining sweaters and coats while Zeke followed, the staff in hand and a grimace of throbbing agony reflected on his face.

Soon, after traversing the smooth plowed fields, the travelers came upon a group of men and women working. Their clothes were in tatters and their faces were covered with grime and filth. Zeke and Devon halted a step or two behind Sinmora who sauntered up to the workers confidently.

"Hail to all," she announced. "Who is it that lords over these fields?"

The women continued to work, ignoring Sinmora's salutation, as did most of the men. But one man did stop. His shovel sliced the ground with a kind of warning. "Who is it that be askin'?"

"I am Sinmora," she answered, "seeress of Midgard, keeper of the staff of Urd."

The man grunted, obviously unimpressed. He picked up his shovel and went back to work. Sinmora turned and looked at the boys and shrugged her shoulders. She turned back to the workers, but this time her voice expressed slight anger and a sense of authority.

"We are travelers from afar," she said. "The laws of hospitality, issued from the walls of Asgard, require you to help. So tell me, who is it that rules over these fields. Tell us so that we may find food and rest for the night to come."

Once again the man stopped his work, his shovel held in front of him like a weapon. "Our lord, seeress, is the giant Geirrod. He is the ruler of this land and a hard taskmaster who has little respect for the gods of Asgard or anyone else for that matter. So be gone. Take your weaklings with you and find another place to rest. If you remain here you will only find hardship. That is your warning. Now, I say again, be gone!"

Sinmora's eyes widened when the name Geirrod was mentioned. Zeke noticed that she even stepped back a pace or two before finally facing him and Devon. Her face was pale and she looked at the boys with a glazed, odd expression.

"This could be interesting," she said thoughtfully. "Are these the whispers of Valhalla?"

"What are you talking about?" Zeke asked.

The glazed look retreated from Sinmora's face, and she stared at the boys as if she'd forgotten they were there. "Nothing," she answered. "But we will not waste our time any longer with those who do not keep the laws of Asgard. Let's continue." She turned in the soft ground and began walking past the workers, bidding Zeke and Devon to follow.

The workers let them pass. All of them stopped their work to watch them go. Devon stared back, a shiver of dread running the length of his spine. *They look scared,* he thought. *But is it for them or for us?*

The smoky air thickened when they finally reached the outskirts of a small village. A rickety wooden fence marked the town's border. Within were people milling about with the laborious chores of peasants, most of them women dressed in ragged long dresses. Scattered about were children, dogs, and the occasional pig nosing its way amid the mud and muck of the streets.

In the distance, on a hill that towered over the rest of the village, sat an enormous building, its structure made of thick, sturdy logs. It appeared to gaze over the town with a malevolent stare.

"See, upon yonder hill," Sinmora said, "lays the stronghold of Geirrod."

"Who is this Geirrod?" Zeke asked. "And why are you afraid of him?"

Sinmora raised an eyebrow toward Zeke and gave him a questioning stare. "What makes ye think I am afraid?"

"I saw your face. When the man with the shovel said his name you stepped back. Your face got pale. I've seen fear before. I know what it looks like. You," Zeke emphasized, "were afraid."

Sinmora nodded slowly. A weak smile lifted her lips. "You observe well, Chosen One."

"Why do you keep saying that?" Devon questioned. "Chosen for what?"

"That I cannot say," Sinmora said. "But the halls of Valhalla whisper it. I hear it on the wind. Perhaps here we will find out. And soon." She pointed her crooked finger once more toward the great log palace. The boys turned to look, and saw, from its huge gates, riders, approaching fast and furious. They rode without order. The hooves of their mounts kicked up dirt and dust and their menacing shouts carried loudly, sending a shudder of terror that rippled up the spines of Zeke and Devon.

The boys watched in terror as they approached, paralyzed with fear at the oncoming rush. Finally, Zeke managed to move just enough to look for Sinmora, to call for help, to have her tell them what to do.

But she was gone. The boys were left alone.

ᚱ

Zeke and Devon lay on a hard wooden floor, their arms and legs bound with thick, rough twine. Mud and blood caked their torn clothing, courtesy of the treatment they received while being dragged from the ground, strapped over the back of a horse, and hauled to the timber palace. Nothing was said and no questions were asked. They were tired, sore, hungry and terrified. Their fear paralyzed them in place. Nevertheless, as uncomfortable as they were, neither moved.

Finally, the sound of footsteps could be heard. The boys looked up reluctantly to see standing before them one of the ugliest men they had ever set eyes on. He stood over them, large and menacing. A huge bulbous nose, red as a ripe apple and scarred with a crisscross of veins, accentuated his massive face. His eyes were set close together, but his cheeks were wide, pulling his features into a tight, painful smile. His hair was long and stringy, and appeared to drip with grease. His teeth, at least the ones he had, were crooked and yellow, marked by the stench of his breath which Zeke could smell from his curled, bound position on the floor.

"Well, looky what we have here. Fresh meat for the ovens, eh." The man chuckled, his laughter like tires on a gravelly road. "The master will be happy to see this, he will. Happy indeed. I'm sure he'll have a game or two to play with ya before he eats, though." He laughed again. Zeke had to turn from the odor. He exhaled as much air as he could and held what was left in his lungs so he wouldn't have to smell the odor of the man's breath.

"A wee bit o' rest first, though, eh," the ugly servant said. He reached down quickly to untie Zeke and Devon. "We may eats our guests, but we always treats 'em right." He lifted the boys from the floor with his two strong arms and planted them firmly on their feet. Zeke grimaced in pain as he reached for the staff that lay upon the floor.

The servant motioned with a wide gesture. "Come along, then. The master 'taint ready to see to ya yet. So, a morsel to eat and a place to rest is what we'll give ya."

He walked quickly, and the boys tried hard to keep up with the large man's pace. Zeke limped along behind with his staff in hand. The servant led the boys outside, past some smelly outhouses, and through a gloomy alley to a rank goat shed. When they stepped inside they discovered, to their dismay that it was furnished with heaps of rotting straw and a single chair.

"Here ya be," the servant said. "Rest. We'll come get ya when it's time. And," he said turning back quickly to the boys, "don't be thinking about going no place. We've got our eye on ya." He slammed the rickety door behind him and left the boys to themselves.

For the first time in several hours, Devon spoke. His eyes were wide with fear and his limbs shook from cold and fatigue. "We're going to die here," he said.

"That is definitely possible," Zeke responded sleepily. "Without Sinmora I think we're doomed."

Devon stared at the rotting straw and caught a whiff of its foul smell. His face took on a look of anger. "Yeah, what the hell was that all about? Where did she go? Is she helping us or trying to get us killed?"

Zeke shook his head. "I don't know," he answered solemnly. "I keep wondering if she's deceiving us or trying to teach us something."

"Oh, so this is a teaching moment?" Devon said sarcastically. "Well, I'm sure mom would be quite pleased. I can just imagine the smile of pride -"

Zeke ignored Devon's comment and moved painfully to the single chair in the middle of the room. He sat heavily, his fist clenched around Sinmora's staff, then he yawned. His fatigue was taking its toll, even surpassing his fear. Then, without another word, he fell asleep, his mouth hanging open while soft snores filled the putrid air.

Devon watched his brother with a duel sense of sympathy and frustration. They were in a tight spot; something needed to be done. But he also realized, because he felt his own overwhelming weariness, that Zeke needed the sleep. Zeke was hungry and tired just like he was. *Besides,* he thought, *there was no time for arguing, especially with death waiting just around the corner.*

Zeke soon slipped into complete unconsciousness. His breathing became regular and deep. But underneath the sound of Zeke's snores, Devon could hear the splash of water flowing nearby. He looked down at his filthy clothing and sniffed tentatively at his sleeve. "I think I actually have poo on me." He stood slowly and decided to find the water's source so he could clean up.

Devon opened the door and stepped quietly into the dim alleyway. He looked about to see if anyone was watching and was relieved to find that the street appeared empty. He stood silently for a moment and listened, once again hearing the flow of water. Stepping lightly into the narrow street, his feet slipped slightly on the muddy, moss covered ground as he strode back the way they had come.

On either side of the alleyway were dilapidated shanties and wood covered shacks that, he assumed, housed the town's meager inhabitants. At the moment, however, no one was around. He trudged forward, his insatiable thirst driving him.

After a few minutes of wandering the dim streets, Devon came to a wall, a dead end. But the sound of rushing water was strong; he knew he was near.

To his left was another much smaller shack, something, he thought, that might be home to a very small child. A door hung loosely from the side while its leather hinges appeared to be rotting with age. He pulled at its slimy handle but it opened easily, exposing a gray interior that sent a rush of cool air at Devon's face. The air was sweet and pure. Devon knew he'd found the water's source. He crouched low and stepped inside, and stared at a stonewall where a torrent of water flowed freely from a fissure in its side. He reached in eagerly, rubbing his hands in the cold water, feeling the grime of the day wash away and cascade into a narrow ditch that continued to flow underneath the shack and off to other parts of the village.

Drinking deeply, Devon tasted the water's sweetness. It reminded him of the tiny brook they'd come across earlier in the day. He drank again, this time throwing water on his face and head, reveling in its refreshing coolness.

"You are drawn to the sweet waters of the Mist, Devon," Sinmora said. "You are truly a sailor at heart. There is no doubt."

Devon whirled about and threw water across the tiny room as he fell backward. His butt landed squarely in the water-filled ditch. "What the...Sinmora. You scared the crap out of me!" Devon clutched his chest while his eyes grew wide with panic.

A soft chuckle came from a darkened corner of the shack before Sinmora stepped into the dim light. "I knew ya'd come here, lad. I just knew ya would. I've been waiting for ya."

"Waiting for me?" Devon said. "We've been looking for *you*. Where did you go? We were almost killed, ya know."

"Easy now, lad. Don't get yer anger up. Sinmora won't leave ya in a mess."

"But where did you go? We're going to get eaten ya know."

Sinmora chuckled again. "Don't go worrying about that. I *had* to get away. If I got snatched up with the two of ya then we'd all be in a pickle. Geirrod knows me well. Oh my, yes. He hates me more than ya could ever know. I once did him a great wrong. If he ever set eyes on me again he'd crush me without a thought, but you two, why he'll be curious. He'll want to know who you are, what ya know; who sent ya. *That*, ya see, will give us time."

"Time," Devon said. "Time for what?"

"Why, to kill him, o' course."

ᛉ

The goat shed door opened slowly and Devon entered. Zeke slept soundly in the chair, legs sprawled, arms hanging limply, but his hand still gripped Sinmora's staff. Devon approached and shook Zeke's shoulder lightly. "Zeke. Wake up," he whispered.

Zeke stirred uneasily, as if his dreams kept him captive in a dark place. "Wha.." he mumbled. A sling of errant drool escaped the corner of his mouth. "How long have I been asleep?"

"Not too long," Devon said. "Sorry to wake you. I know you're tired, but I've got to tell you something."

Zeke propped the staff against the arm of the chair and began rubbing his sleep-swollen eyes. "Tell me? What's there to tell me?"

"I saw Sinmora," Devon said.

Zeke looked up in surprise. "What? Where? What did she say?"

"That's what I'm going to tell you, dummy. Just give me a chance. I went to find water and she was there, waiting for me in this little shack."

"Why did she leave? Did she tell you?"

"It was to protect herself and us, too. But that's not the important part. You've got to know something, something about the staff..."

The door suddenly burst open and once again the big ugly servant stood at its threshold. "Geirrod is waiting," he announced. "He has in mind to challenge you to a game or two."

Zeke and Devon followed the servant and made their way back through the outhouses and shanties of Geirrod's hall. Soon they arrived in their original place of captivity, a place where the ceiling domed high, where the walls were covered with pine logs, and where the smoke of furnace fires, lined up and down the length of the hall, drifted heavy in the air. Their fires made the room too warm for comfort.

Staring at them from the far end of the hall was a giant of a man. His hair was long and hung well past his shoulders in blond and red waves. A bristly beard of the same color covered his face. He was tall, but more than that he was strong. Neck muscles flexed when he moved, blending with ripples of strength in his arms and chest.

"It has been a long time since our halls were greeted with guests, especially ones of such renown. We welcome you Light bearer, slayer of the Korrigan. My scouts tell me you must have traveled far. But surely you have not come on your own. Who, I ask, has been your guide?" he said. "Is it the witch Sinmora that brings you to these halls? Tell me, Light bearer. Tell me so I can tell you of her treachery, and of the great evil she has brought upon this kingdom." He smiled, but there was nothing happy about it.

Zeke's eyes opened wide and his mouth hung open, as if he was about to say something, but the words were stuck. All he could do was stare.

Geirrod laughed and stepped forward. "No?" he said. "You will not tell me? Has the witch got you under her spell? Well then, let us begin the games then. You, who so handily defeated Loki's daughter, will be quite the challenge I imagine."

Geirrod stretched forth his hand, but it was not to greet Zeke or Devon. It was to pick up a pair of tongs. With them, he reached toward one of the red-hot furnaces and retrieved a glowing piece of coal. "Welcome to my palace!" he shouted, and aimed the fiery lump straight at Zeke.

Zeke continued to stare, feeling as if time had suddenly stopped as he watched the sizzling missile advance toward his face. At the last moment, just before the red-hot coal struck him, he bent, his thigh muscle crying out in pain. The burning lump of coal jetted past him striking the log wall behind and sputtering to a dead, black ember.

"Ah! You're quick, boy. I'm quicker, though. In the end I'll see ya burn!"

Devon ran up from behind Zeke and grabbed him by the shoulder. "The staff, you idiot! Use the staff!"

Zeke dared not let his eyes leave the giant who was reaching toward another large piece of coal. The best he could do was to quickly scan his surroundings and look for a place to hide. "What do you mean? What am I supposed to do with the staff?"

"Sinmora gave it to you. It's to help you."

"I get that!" Zeke shouted back. "How do you think I've been able to walk, stupid?"

"That's not what I mean..."

Just then another ball of flame hissed toward Zeke and he fell to the floor. He struggled to rise as Geirrod chose another fat coal from the flames.

"Use the staff!" Devon shouted again.

Zeke turned this time and looked at Devon, his face pale with fright, his eyes wide with confusion. He looked across the floor at the staff that had fallen just beyond his reach and scrambled on his hands and knees to retrieve it.

Again, another ball of flame flew toward him, but this time it struck him. Its force spun Zeke around on the floor, and he felt the searing heat of its impact on the top of his foot. He kicked at the large lump of coal that clung to his shoe - melting the laces - pausing just long enough to be sure that it wasn't on fire. Then he continued to scramble forward, his hand gripping tightly around the shaft of the staff.

"He's throwing another one!" Devon shouted.

Zeke rose quickly and used the strength of his arms to push himself into a standing position. He gripped the staff with both hands and held it like a baseball bat. Geirrod sent another molten missile at Zeke's face, but this time Zeke stood his ground, his feet squared, and his eyes watching as the ball of fire approached.

Zeke swung the staff with every ounce of strength he possessed, connecting with the glowing coal like a major-leaguer, its trajectory bending toward Geirrod while everyone who stood as witness in the great hall, giants and dwarfs alike, scrambled under the tables. Geirrod himself tried to step behind one of the hall supports. However, the fiery ball punched through the support, passed through the giant's midriff, and continued through the wooden wall until it finally lodged itself in an earth slope outside the building.

Geirrod stood up straight - a strange, defeated look on his face - and looked down at the hole in his chest. He gasped and then hissed, as if all of the hate and venom inside him suddenly escaped. He gave one violent jerk, gurgled and was dead.

The fire in the hearth continued to flicker in the background making the cabin seem hotter than usual. Light danced on the ceiling and walls, accentuated by the tiny flame of the Captain's single match that gave radiance and substance to the small door.

The four onlookers stood waiting; their breath held and their muscles tightened in anticipation. Several minutes passed but nothing happened. Finally, the Captain stood, his back aching from bending over the tiny door. "I don't think anyone's..."

Suddenly, from behind the door came a solid thud, as if something were lifted and moved. Then there was a click, followed by the sound of metal scraping on metal. The Captain stepped back; the others moved with him. "Perhaps there is somebody home after all," he said.

The door swung open.

Within the dark entrance stood a little man, slightly misshapen with bowed legs, holding a flickering torch in his left hand and a sharpened dirk in his right.

"What great dunder-head has taken it upon himself to go a knockin' on me door," he said. "And at such a late hour as this?" The little man stepped into the light of the hearth fire and looked up at the four staring figures before him, his mouth twisted in anger, his eyes set with a look of fury.

"I...we..." the Captain stuttered.

Erna stepped in front of the Captain. "We have need of your help, Berling. Please don't be angry with us. We only knocked because we could think of nothing else to do."

Berling looked about the room, searching the corners as his narrow eyes squinted into the darkness. "Where is Sinmora?"

"Gone," Erna said. "Into the Mist."

Berling nodded slowly. "Has she now," he hissed. "Into the land of danger where she knows she is not welcome. Very brave," he said. "Very brave. So what is it that you want from me? Why have ya disturbed me from my sleep and my peace ya wretched child?"

"My friends," she said, pointing vaguely at the Captain, Marjorie, and Vivian, "they fear for the ones she has taken with them. And *they* fear for the one they've gone in search of."

"Fear?" Berling said with a grunt. "Why there's no need to fear with Sinmora. She can take care of herself and *usually* those who are with her."

"*Usually?*" Vivian blurted.

Retreating back into the tiny doorway, Berling hissed. His eyes widened with fear when he looked at Vivian. "Who is this, then? Have ya brought Freyja back to torment me more? Is that why you've lured me from my rest, ya great cow of a girl?"

"No. No, not at all," Erna said, her hands lifted in gentle supplication toward Berling while her eyes shifted back and forth between him and Vivian. "Freyja's not here. She'll not harm ya."

Berling squinted again, eyeing Vivian suspiciously. He turned his head to the side and examined her with a thoughtful gaze. "Why, she's the very image of the goddess herself, is she not?"

Every eye turned to look at Vivian. Her pale cheeks blushed a bright pink and her eyes clouded over with embarrassment. "Why are you all looking at me?" she said.

The Captain cleared his throat noisily, his hand automatically reaching for his pipe and pouch of tobacco. "It is said, Vivian, that the great goddess Freyja, wife of the All Father, is beautiful beyond compare. You, my dear, according to our little friend here, are the spittin' image of her. And if anyone should know that, it'd be him."

Vivian's cheeks turned an even darker shade of red. She found she had to cover her face with her hands in order to hide her embarrassment. "I've never heard of anything so silly in my life," she said as a brief smile escaped through the spaces between her fingers.

"No, woman. The big fat man here is right," Berling said. "I have set lustful eyes on the goddess. I know what she looks like. And you, well, you *do* have her beauty." Berling licked his lips and his narrow eyes flashed radiantly.

The Captain looked down on Berling, *his* eyes showing impatient anger. "Calm yerself, little man," the Captain said. "This woman is no harlot for your petty lusts. She is the mother of The Chosen. Don't you forget it!"

Berling raised the dirk he held defensively and glared at the Captain with a frightened expression. For a brief moment they both stared at each other, the Captain's courage rising in defense of Zeke and Devon's mother. Finally, Berling lowered the dirk, the darkness in his eyes softening as his mouth turned down into a weakened frown.

"I'm sorry," he said quietly, bowing his head and glancing quickly at Vivian. "I've let emotion take me again. It is my greatest fault." He looked at Vivian sadly. "I'm sorry, mother of The Chosen. Forgive me."

Vivian lowered her hands. Her innocent beauty filled the room with an unblemished light. "Who are you? And why do you live in the ground beneath this cabin?" Vivian said.

Berling lowered the torch to his side, his initial display of aggression slipping as his expression became like that of a frightened child. "I am Berling," he declared, "of the house Brising. I was once a great designer of metal, turning ore into treasure beyond belief. But my demise came the day that Freyja, wife of the All Father, ventured into my forge.

"Her journey, which took place hundreds of years ago," he said, "must have been long and tiresome. She would have had to travel from Asgard across the snow veils of Midgard beneath the dazzling, rising sun. She would have had to traverse her way across a twisting river, past the base of a great glacier, rounding a group of huge rounded boulders and then into a string-thin path that would lead her down and down to the land of Nidavellir. This is the land where I once dwelt, a sanctuary of underground tunnels and caves that are home to the dwarves. Much like the one I now possess here," he said, gesturing toward the small open door. "I have carved an abode beneath this house among the twisting roots of trees that make up the forest above."

"How long have you lived there?" Vivian asked.

"Long before Sinmora came to this place as a wee girl and an apprentice to the seeress, Var. She was a sharp tempered one, that one. No breaking of vows or promises around her, I can tell you. She would not tolerate such things. But Var let me burrow beneath this cabin after I fled the wrath of Odin. It has been my place of safety and my refuge from the anger that has filled the heart of the All Father because of my lust." Berling turned to the Captain. "You seem to know who I am, fat man. Why is that?"

Bartholomew puffed on his pipe. His eyes squinted against the sweet smoke that rose from the bowl. "I've been taught well in the old ways, little man," he answered. "My mother knew the gods. She understood their ways and tried to teach me to have an appreciation for their strengths as well as their flaws."

Berling nodded, eyeing the Captain's pipe. He reached into his coat pocket and produced his own long stemmed pipe. The Captain smiled and handed Berling his pouch of tobacco. Soon both men sidled up to the warped dining table and seated themselves, puffing thoughtfully, while Berling, whose feet barely touched the floor, swung his legs back and forth.

Vivian and Marjorie shook their heads and retired to stools beside the warmth of the fire. Erna sat beside Berling at the table; a kind of curious absorption filled her eyes as she stared at the little man.

"Why did the All Father hate you?" Erna asked.

"I'm embarrassed to say," Berling said. "It's been so many years, and yet my moment of lust still disgraces me. I find it hard to talk about." Berling turned to the Captain, his cheeks turning a deep red. "Will you tell the story? I can fill in any gaps, but to tell it in front of these pure-hearted women would be difficult. I fear I may turn back into my ugly, angry self."

The Captain nodded slowly and looked into the flames of the fire pensively. "It was the necklace of Brisings that brought Freyja to the forges in the first place," he said. "Her unquenchable desire for gold and jewels was her greatest weakness. When she made her way to the dwelling of the dwarfs and the smithy they worked beside, she was dazzled by the breathtaking brilliance of the work of Berling and his brothers. Before her was a necklace, a choker of gold cut with wondrous patterns, a marvel of fluid metal twisting and weaving and writhing. She had never seen anything so beautiful, and she desired it. She was willing to do anything to possess it." The Captain wiggled in his seat uncomfortably as Marjorie, Vivian, and Erna listened to the unfolding tale.

"Berling and his brothers...well," the Captain looked at Berling, a slight twinge of embarrassed red in his cheeks, "sorry, but I've got to tell it like I know it."

Berling nodded. "Go on, ya big oaf. Tell it like it happened. I won't be stopping ya."

"Well," the Captain continued, "they took one look at the goddess and desire took their hearts as well. This was not a desire for jewels and gold, but a longing for...well, you know." The Captain's cheeks turned an embarrassed red.

Erna giggled. "I know about the ways of men and women, Bartholomew. There's nothing to worry about. Continue with the story."

The Captain rubbed his hands together in thought and carefully calculated the words he should use to relate the remainder of the tale without offending anyone. "As I recall, Freyja thought the dwarfs to be too ugly and most unattractive. She offered instead silver and gold, but they refused. They were dwarfs of the house of Brising. They had all of the gold and silver that they wanted. When Freyja finally asked what their price for the necklace would be, they answered unashamedly and in unison: you.

"Freyja reluctantly agreed. Her distaste for the dwarfs - their ugly faces, their pale noses, their misshapen bodies and their small greedy eyes - was great, but her desire for the necklace was greater." The Captain again turned to Berling. "I'm sorry, old timer, but you said to tell it like I know it."

Berling grimaced and twirled his finger, urging the Captain to continue.

"A few nights passed. Freyja kept her word and the dwarfs kept theirs too. They presented her with the necklace, fastening it around her throat. She hurried out of the cavern and back across the bright plains of Midgard. Eventually she crossed the Bifrost Bridge safely into the realm of Asgard. Under her cloak she wore the necklace of the Brisings." The Captain bowed his head as if he were exhausted from the retelling.

Berling sat up and looked at the Captain. "Is that it, ya chubby boor? Surely you know there's more to the tale than that?"

The Captain shook his head. "I know. I know. But it is here that the story takes a turn that makes it hard to relate. This next character in the tale touches us all, and not in a kind way."

Berling eyed each member of the small group that huddled in the dim light of the cabin. His eyes squinted as understanding filled his senses. "Has the Sly One betrayed all of you as well?" he asked.

The Captain looked up and nodded. "Aye," he said. "He's taken one that we love. Where she is, we have no idea. That's why Sinmora's gone into the Mist."

"Ah," Berling said. "It all begins to make sense to me. I now understand your need. Loki is a rascal, to be sure. I had once been his friend, or so I thought. But in the end I realized that he does nothing unless it is for his own selfish needs. He thinks of no one but himself. Hence, my great trouble with the All Father and my need to hide all these years in an underground lair beneath this cabin."

"What did he do?" Marjorie asked. "How did he betray you?"

"He discovered the necklace and how Freyja had acquired it. When he did he immediately ran and told Odin, hoping to gain his favor, completely forgetting the many times I'd helped him in his ventures.

"Odin punished Freyja for her unfaithfulness, but it was nothing compared to the wrath that he let fall on Nidavellir. Our world became a battlefield of blood and carnage as he sent Huginn and Muninn, his faithful ravens, to peck out the eyes of my brothers and sisters. Then he sent Freki and Geri, his trusty wolves, to finish the job of destroying so many of my people. I, however, managed to escape. I crossed through many realms using the Mist as my guide, slipping through seam after seam until I reached this place here in Midgard. The seeress, Var, had pity on me and let me stay. I have been here ever since."

The crackle of the fire was the only sound in the smoky cabin as the exhausted inhabitants pondered Berling's words. Finally, Marjorie spoke, "I will not be the one to cast judgment on anyone, Berling. As everyone here knows, I have made some horrible mistakes in my life. Having said that, I hope you realize that you did make a huge mistake when it came to your dealings with Freyja. Odin's anger was justified. Wouldn't you agree?"

Berling nodded, but said nothing.

"Nevertheless," Marjorie continued, "the same entity that betrayed you has also caused us much grief. So, as far as that goes, we have a common enemy. It is our hope that you will help us."

Shaking his head and sighing, Berling answered cautiously. "I am reluctant to help. Please understand that I have put myself in danger just by sitting here by this table. The eyes of Odin's ravens are always watching, and the memory of the gods is long."

"But you must help us," Marjorie said. "Erna has told us that the Mist has shifted. If that is so, then Sinmora won't be able to get back. If she can't get back, neither can the two boys that went with her. And since their mission was to bring back my granddaughter, then I fear *that* may also be impossible. Without your help we are lost."

Berling sighed heavily while he rubbed his hands through his coarse hair. "Why, oh why did I answer the knock on that damned door?" He jumped down from the chair and waddled his way toward the small opening. He was about to slip back inside the door when he stopped and turned. "I'll help," he said, "but know that I do this reluctantly. For so long I have been safe from searching, vengeful eyes. But now my life may once again be in peril. However, I understand your need. If it is within me to help you gain back your loved ones, then so be it. Perhaps it will be the only way of making amends for my evil doings." He turned and disappeared into the darkness of his abode.

Marjorie looked imploringly at the Captain. "Is he coming back?"

"I hope so," the Captain said. "He took my pouch of tobacco with him."

᛭

The door stood open and Marjorie continued to stare at it impatiently as she, Vivian, the Captain, and Erna waited beside the warming fire.

"Steady, Marjorie," the Captain said. "The door stays open, so that must be a good sign."

Moments later they heard Berling's solid steps on the earth-packed stairs leading up from his home beneath the ground. The small group exhaled a sigh of relief and rose to meet Berling. In his arms he carried with him a large leather-bound book, one that appeared very old and fragile. He placed it gently on the table and then climbed awkwardly onto the chair.

"This is the *Ragnarsdrapa*," he said. "It is an ancient text written by Bragi the Old. Within are many secrets of the Mist.

Bragi describes places and times when portals into the Mist might open. By studying his calculations I've be able to slip in and out of some rather sticky situations. But know this: The Seam closes quickly. If you are not in the right place at the right time then your opportunity will be lost. The Mist waits for no one."

"So this book will tell us how to get into the Mist and find Zeke and Devon?" Vivian asked.

"Us?" Berling answered. "No. None of you has the gift to enter the Mist, with the exception of Erna. If anyone is going to go in the Mist to find your loved ones it will be me. Erna can come and assist if she chooses."

"But what are *we* to do?" Marjorie asked.

"Keep me hidden and take me to the place where the Seam will open."

"And whar might that place be?" the Captain asked.

Berling opened the book and began leafing through its pages, his finger drawing slowly down each column of script. Finally, his finger came to rest on a yellowed, stained section of the manuscript. "Here," he said, looking up at his attentive audience. "The place we must go is to Surtsey, an island of fire and ice."

Chapter Fourteen
The Road to Niflheim

Devon was running, but his feet seemed to be moving faster than the rest of his body. As a result, he stumbled a lot, cursing himself each time he did. Soon he came to a short rise in the wagon-rutted road that made his legs seem even shorter than they really were. He took a moment to look over his shoulder and saw that Zeke was lagging behind. His legs struggled to keep up with the staff that he held tightly in his hand; its occupation as a walking stick seemed to take on a life of its own. "You've got to run faster!" Devon shouted. "I can see the dust from their horses."

Zeke turned awkwardly to look in the direction Devon was pointing, and indeed, in the distance, passing through the gates of Geirrod's stronghold, a column of moving dust and dirt could be seen rushing toward them. Zeke turned back to Devon. "I'm trying, man, but this damn leg is killing me."

Devon hurried back to Zeke and took him by the arm. "I know you're hurting, Zeke. I know you are. But this time those guys aren't going to strap us on the back of their horses. This time they may just trample over us and be done with it." He began tugging Zeke up the hill, mindless of his own pain and exhaustion, fear of imminent death over riding all of that.

"Where is Sinmora?" Zeke said. "You saw her, right? So where is she?"

"I don't know, and I don't care," Devon answered. "Our only hope is to make it to those trees up ahead so we can find a place to hide. We'll worry about Sinmora later."

Devon pulled and Zeke continued to limp along as quickly as he could, cringing with the throbbing in his thigh. He persisted in using the staff as his crutch, placing it forcefully in the dirt with each step he took; his mind filled with hate as he recalled his enemy Loki and the injury he caused him, the one that continued to hamper his progress. He wondered if Loki had planned this all along, thinking that a tormented life of pain had a far more torturous effect than a quick death.

Within moments the brothers made it to the tree line and entered the darkened forest. The rutted road continued to weave its way into the darkness but was eventually lost among the thickness of the trees and undergrowth. Devon pulled Zeke off the path and they stumbled their way among brambles and weeds, eventually finding a tangle of blackberry vines, its branches thick with leaves and ripened fruit.

"Here," Devon said, "crawl under this. We'll hide here." The ground was littered with dry leaves that crackled and ground painfully into their palms as they shuffled inside. Thorns from the surrounding vines clung unmercifully to their shirt collars and sleeves, tearing small holes in the material and drawing tiny pinpricks of blood from any exposed skin.

"Bring your feet in," Devon ordered. "They'll see you."

The pounding of hooves shook the ground as a small army of Geirrod's followers entered the forest. A hurricane of dirt followed them into the thick confines of trees, burying the undergrowth in a layer of yellow dust. Devon and Zeke held their breath and tried desperately to calm the beating of their hearts, thinking the drumming in their own ears must surely be echoing through the forest as well.

The horses and men soon passed, following the meandering path that wound its way through the trees, unaware that the boys who destroyed their master were only a few yards away concealed under a thick blanket of thorns and briars.

Zeke released his breath slowly, still aware of the pounding in his chest and the searing ache from his leg. He tried to turn himself around within the tight confines of the hideaway, once again feeling the pull of thorns on his clothing. "Stop!" Devon whispered sharply. "I think there's someone still out there."

A thorn was sticking in his side, but the fear of jostling the brush made Zeke stop abruptly. He held his breath again and listened intently for any sound. "I don't hear anything," he whispered.

"Shhh..." Devon pointed urgently while he mouthed the words *there's a horse out there; I can see its legs.*

An abrupt snort, accompanied by a soft whinny resonated through the trees. Hooves padded softly on the dirt path as the horse shifted uncomfortably from side to side. "I know yer here, ya murderin' cads. Show yourselves before I decide to burn ya out." The voice sounded young, but his tone was strong and confident.

Zeke wrapped his fingers firmly around the shaft of the staff, drawing it tightly against his chest. "What do we do?" He whispered.

Devon held up his hand, his head tilted to one side. "Wait," he said. "Maybe he'll move on."

"Come out ya cowards. I can smell yer yellow fear! Come out so I can show ya what a real fight looks like!" Devon could see a man dismount the horse, though the shroud of brambles that concealed their own whereabouts hid his face. He poked at Zeke's foot, urging him to move.

"What?" Zeke said. "What do you want me to do?"

"Scoot out," Devon answered. "Maybe we can talk some sense into him."

"Are you mental!" Zeke's whisper was louder and sharper than he had intended.

"Just go out. You've got the staff."

"And just what the hell am I supposed to do with it? Swing it like a baseball bat?"

Suddenly, the mat of vines they hid under shook, as if a sudden, chaotic wind had just picked up. "You're here, aren't ya? Be warned, I have a lance. I'll start piercing it through until I poke ya both full of holes if ya don't come out!"

Zeke looked at Devon, his eyes wide with concern and fear. Devon shrugged. *Go*, he mouthed. Zeke shuffled his way from underneath the mat of thorns and Devon followed close behind. When they'd both escaped the confines of their hideaway they stared incredulously at their newest captor. Zeke's mouth dropped open with surprise and Devon gave a soft snort of laughter.

In front of them stood a boy, not much older than Devon, who held a small sword in one hand and a sharpened wooden stick in the other. His face was smooth and pale, with a soft patter of freckles smeared across his nose. His hair was a long reddish blond, slightly curled at the ends and in desperate need of a wash. He wore a padded boiled leather vest that appeared to be a hand-me-down from someone much larger and much older. Its presence made the boy seem younger than he actually was. His mouth was turned down into a fearsome frown, an attempt to look ferocious and threatening. But its true effect only made Devon laugh that much harder, despite the weapons the boy held.

"What're ya laughin at, cad? Don't ya know I could slice ya from here to Asgard and back?"

"I'm sorry," Devon said between bursts of laughter. "It's just that I expected something - I don't know - bigger?"

Zeke stared at Devon. "What are you doing? He's got a sword."

"I know," Devon said, "but look at it. I mean, it has rust all over the blade and it's probably duller than one of mom's kitchen knives. The only thing that it's good for is to spread butter on my toast."

The boy looked down at his sword. His frown lost some of its ferociousness. But then he quickly held up the stick and waved it in Devon's face. "But I've got this, haven't I? I could poke ya through with it!"

"Poke us through? Sure," Devon said sarcastically. "Or, we could build a nice little fire and cook up some hotdogs."

The boy stared at Devon and dropped the weapons by his side. A tear of frustration escaped the corner of his eye. "I'll never be a warrior," he muttered.

Zeke stepped forward cautiously, his hand raised with his palms facing up. "Sorry," he said. "Sometimes Devon can be a little insensitive. We didn't mean to hurt your feelings." Zeke looked at Devon when he said this.

"Right," Devon chimed in. "We were just, you know, a bit concerned is all. Nothing personal."

The boy looked at the brothers, a saddened expression on his face. Zeke placed a soft hand on his shoulder. "I'm Zeke," he said. "And this is Devon, my little brother."

"I am Vidar," the boy answered. "Named after the son of Odin. He who will avenge the death of Odin and live beyond the destruction of Ragnarok."

Devon nodded his head. "That's a cool name. Your mom and dad must be really proud of you to give you such an awesome name."

"Yes, I suppose they were. But they're gone now. Dead. Like so many others," he said matter-of-factly. "After they died Geirrod took me in and made me work in the kitchen. My parents owed many debts to Geirrod; because they could not pay before they died I have become his slave, and he is a terrible task master."

"Was," Devon corrected.

A brief smile flashed across Vidar's face. He looked at Zeke. "How did you do it? How did you kill Geirrod when so many others have tried and failed?"

"This, I guess..." Zeke held up the staff.

Vidar's eyes widened and he stepped back a pace. "That is no ordinary staff," he said.

Devon slapped Zeke lightly on the back. "See, that's what I've been trying to tell you, stupid."

Zeke stared irritably at Devon. "And when were we supposed to have this conversation?" he said sarcastically. "Because as I recall, I was in the middle of trying to defend myself from a barrage of flaming chucks of coal."

"True," Devon said. "But I did try. Sinmora said..."

"Sinmora!" Vidar said. "You know Sinmora?"

"She brought us here," Zeke said. "But where she is now is anybody's guess."

"Sinmora's a witch," Vidar proclaimed. "Geirrod feared and hated her more than any other enemy."

"What could an old woman like Sinmora do to make Geirrod hate and fear her?" Devon said.

"I'll tell you exactly what I did," Sinmora said, stepping out from behind a thick oak tree. "Then you will understand why the Staff of Urd can help you in your quest."

ᚷ

Vidar and Devon jumped when they heard Sinmora's voice, but if Zeke was startled, he showed no sign. His face was a mask of frustration. He simply stared. "So nice of you to show up," he said.

Sinmora smiled sadly. "You are angry, Zeke Proper. That I can understand."

"Angry? Oh, no," he said sarcastically. "I actually really like it when you disappear just when we need your help the most."

Devon nudged Zeke. "Careful, dude. I get a feeling you're treading in some rough water here."

"It's alright, Devon," Sinmora said. "Zeke has a right to be mad, you as well. But you must understand there is purpose behind my stealth."

"The only purpose I see is that you want us to die," Zeke said. "I'm starting to believe that you are a witch; that your motives in bringing us here are, let us just say, less than noble."

Sinmora shook her head slowly. "Zeke, listen to me. Do you remember the Valkyries' words to you? Do you remember what Shaker said?"

"Of course I do," Zeke said. A hint of irritation still echoed in his voice. "She asked me if I was a warrior. I told her I wasn't. I wasn't one then, and I'm not one now."

"You don't give yourself enough credit," Sinmora said. "Consider what you just did. You destroyed an evil, oppressive giant. One who was intent on killing you. That is not an easy task. Many might say it was a task that only a warrior could have performed."

"I got lucky," Zeke said. "Besides that I was scared as hell. Do you think a warrior would be as scared as I was? I think not."

"Ah, Zeke," Sinmora chided. "Do not underestimate the power of fear. Fear is not cowardice. Do not mistake the two. Fear is strength if it is reined in. Panic, however, is the problem. Panic *will* kill you. But you didn't panic did you? No, you pulled in your fear and with it you wielded the mighty staff of Urd and you slew the giant."

"But why didn't you stay?" Zeke asked. "We really could have used the help."

Sinmora took a deep breath. "You're an athlete - a runner - correct?"

Zeke's eyes narrowed. "Yes," he said suspiciously.

"If I were your coach," Sinmora continued, "and instead of allowing you to run the race on your own, I ran the race for you, then how would you get stronger?"

Zeke shrugged. "I guess I wouldn't."

"Shaker said you needed to work hard to become a warrior. No one just suddenly becomes a great warrior, just as no one suddenly becomes a great runner. You have to work at it. I left so that you could hone your skills. If I'd stayed you would've relied too much on me and in the end gained nothing."

Zeke nodded slowly, an uneasy understanding reflected in his expression. "I see what you mean," he said apologetically. "Sorry I called you a witch."

"There's no need to apologize. I understand your anger. If it helps, I was watching when you fought and I too was frightened. I care for you boys. Please know that." Sinmora looked at Vidar. "You too, Vidar. I knew your mother and father. They were good people. I'm sorry for your loss."

Vidar nodded and joined in on the awkward silence as the small group looked toward the crooked road before them, their minds eager to be on the move.

ᛤ

The narrow road was difficult to negotiate; deep ruts from centuries of passing carts had left their indelible impression. The travelers found that they had to walk carefully on the rounded middle section of road where brown grass stood in drying, ragged tufts. Vidar led his horse, Alsvid, with a frayed length of hemp, while Zeke, Devon, and Sinmora followed close behind, their feet occasionally slipping into pot holes and tripping over scattered rocks.

"Shouldn't we be keeping to the forest?" Zeke asked. "What if the riders come back?"

"They won't come back," Sinmora said. "If they'd found you they would have killed you, certainly. But it wouldn't have been because of any loyalty to Geirrod. They hated him as much as anyone did. He was an evil man who governed his realm with fear. No," Sinmora continued, "their real purpose in riding was to finally get away from Geirrod's stronghold, to be rid of that place once and for all."

"There's a lot of hate and fear being talked about here," Devon said as he stepped carefully over a fresh pile of horse droppings. "But you're not telling us why. What happened to cause so many bad feelings?"

"I killed Hrungnir with *that*." She pointed a calm finger at the staff that Zeke held, its strength steadying him as he walked. "It is the Staff of Urd. Urd is one of the three Norns, the goddess of destiny, and keeper of the Well of Urd. She gave it to Var, my mentor, and Var gave it to me."

"Who's Hrungnir?" Zeke asked, struggling with the odd pronunciation.

"Geirrod's brother, strongest of all the giants. He was a brute, especially when he'd had too much to drink. I was there the day that Odin brought him to Valhalla. I was permitted to walk the celebrated halls because Var had recently died. A place of honor had been set for her at the great table where the warriors feasted. And because I had honed my skills in entering and exiting the Mist so well, she invited me to sit beside her, a privilege few mortals have been given. I was her favorite, you see. I learned my role as Volva quickly from her and she wanted to show me off, I suppose.

"While we sat at feast, a great chase had been taking place. Odin had stumbled into Hrungnir's hall, boasting that his horse, Sleipnir, the eight-legged steed, could out run any other horse. Hrungnir challenged him with his own horse, Gold Mane, and a great race began. Odin and the giant raced across the flatlands near Jotunheim, but neither gained ground on the other. They raced into the uplands and crossed the nineteen rivers, finding themselves outside the gates of Asgard. Odin led him farther overland and waited for him at the outer gate of Valhalla. Odin was always a great competitor, but he respected the laws of courtesy, so he invited Hrungnir in, promising him drink to quench his thirst.

"When Hrungnir walked in, the halls of Valhalla erupted with angry shouts from the warriors who filled the benches feasting and drinking after a day of slaughter. But the All Father raised one hand and the clamor began to subside. 'Hrungnir comes unarmed! He comes in peace! Let him drink and leave in peace!' Odin shouted.

"Then the Valkyries, Shaker and Raging, brought out two massive horns, both brimming with ale. All of the company in Valhalla watched as Hrungnir drank down one horn without taking a breath, and then did the same with the other. It was not long before the giant began to feel the effects. His words were slurred and he began tossing boastful taunts at the other warriors who sat at the benches. 'I'll pick up this worthless hall and carry it home to Jotunheim,' he shouted. The warriors at the benches roared with laughter, and I must admit, I giggled a bit myself. Then he swung around to face the source of laughter, but his balance was wrong and he reeled sideways. Then he said, 'I'm going to shink Ashgard in the shea!" So the more he drank, the louder and more threatening he became.

"His threats scared me, I was becoming a bit frightful of this great beast of a man. He was dangerous and getting more dangerous by the minute. The rest of the warriors, I could tell, were becoming tired of the giant's taunts, but no one seemed to be stepping forward to challenge him. He continued to assault us all with a stream of boasts and curses that I was finding hard to listen to. I looked to Var for some help, but she seemed to be completely indifferent to what was happening, and Odin was just laughing it off, as if it were all a big joke. But I felt myself becoming angry. *How*, I thought, *could this pig of a man continue to treat the greatest of the universe's warriors in this way?*

"Finally, without even thinking about what I was doing, I stood up. 'What is this!' I shouted. 'What gives you the right to speak to us in such a way?'

"The giant waved an arm in the direction of Odin and slurred his words. 'His shafe conjuct,' he burbled. 'Ojin, he invited me in.'

"'Well, perhaps you have out-stayed your welcome,' I said. 'Maybe it's time you left so we can have some peace. We're sick of your ranting!'

"'Are you shreatening me, little girl? I could crush you between my finger and shumb if I wanted to!'

"When he said that, I felt a sudden, overpowering anger grab hold of me. It coursed through me like a bolt of lightening, a power that threatened to consume me. I stood with my staff in hand and waved it in the air. 'Bring on your worst ya pig. I'll not have ya bringin shame to this company!'

"Hrungnir reeled again, spun on his heels, and grabbed a massive whetstone that the warriors used to sharpen their swords. He picked it up and hurled it toward me with his incredible strength. But while the stone was launched at my head, flying through the air, I hurled my staff and the two met in midair.

"Now, one might think that a simple staff would simply shatter when it collided with the stone, but this was no ordinary staff. Carved alongside the waters of Urd and dipped nine times in the well, the staff received its magic. If the right person wields it, its power is strong indeed."

"My father used to tell me this story," Vidar interrupted. "I used to cheer when he came to this part. But I always did it quietly, lest one of Geirrod's true followers was close by and listening."

"Aye," Sinmora answered. "I've been told that the story has become legend. But I was there. I was the one who wielded the staff. I discovered its true strength!"

"What happened?" Devon asked anxiously. "When the staff and the stone hit each other, I mean."

"The staff and the whetstone met in mid-air with a dazzling light," Sinmora exclaimed, her arms open wide as she told her tale exuberantly. "The light was followed by a crack that some say was heard throughout the nine worlds as the whetstone was smashed into hundreds of fragments.

"The shrapnel flew in every direction, scattering amongst the hall while warriors, Valkyries and servants alike hid under tables and behind pillars."

"What about the staff?" Zeke prodded.

"The staff," Sinmora continued, "flew on and found its mark, striking Hrungnir in his forehead and crushing his skull. He spun around twice and finally fell on one of the great banquet tables, turning it to dust with his massive weight."

Vidar continued the tale. "The rest o' the story had to be spoken quietly. My father and I would hide underneath the covers of my bed as the end of the legend was revealed." Vidar had a sad look on his face as the fleeting memory of his parents drew across his mind. His horse plodded obediently behind him but he continued to speak. "News of Hrungnir's death traveled quickly, so it wasn't long before the hosts of Jotunheim heard what had happened.

"Geirrod was working in his forge, pounding out the great swords that he was so famous for when he heard the news. He flew into a rage, swinging his hammer and upending the furnaces. His servants tried to run from his anger, but he struck them dead: his wrath was unquenchable. It was a frightful sight to be sure."

"So that's when he heard about you?" Devon asked.

"Aye," Sinmora answered. "News did indeed travel fast. And though the warriors in the great hall of Valhalla cheered me on for what I'd done, they offered me no protection. Even Var was hesitant to help. But I don't blame her. She'd suffered a long and perilous life. She deserved her rest.

"Nevertheless I was forced to flee, wending my way through the Mist, clinging to the branches of Yggdrasil precariously, finally finding peace in Midgard in a cabin tucked in the forests of Mt. Sif. And that, my two budding warriors, is where you found me. Me and Erna."

ᛣ

The road had become straighter and less rutted as the travelers moved on. And the forest became an open valley with gentle rolling hills that spread out with a melodious rhythm of soothing highs and lows. Fields that were once plow scarred were now covered with green grass that shivered in the soft warm breeze.

"The road seems to go on forever," Zeke said as he gazed out across the distant landscape. "How far do we need to go?"

Sinmora, her gait appearing stronger by the moment, walked beside Alsvid and placed a gentle hand on its withers, caressing its mane absentmindedly. "We walk to the shadows," she said, pointing toward the horizon. "There, in the distance, are the mountains of Thrymheim. It is there that we will find a pass. It is very high and dangerous. But it is the road we must take before we can come to Niflheim."

Vidar gasped and stopped his horse. "We can't go there," he said. "Niflheim is a place of gloom and swirling mists. My father warned me of that place. No," he said, shaking his head, "I'll not be goin'"

"It is true," Sinmora replied, "Niflheim is not a place for the faint of heart. But it is the only place that we will receive the answers we need. You, Vidar, have no place to call your own anymore. You can choose to go your own way or follow us. It is your choice."

Vidar's young cheeks turned red. He bowed his head and mumbled some silent words under his breath, but made no move to leave. The matter was soon dropped.

Zeke stumbled up to the rest of the group who were now stopped in the middle of the road with Alsvid grazing lazily in the tall grass at the side. "What is Niflheim?" he asked, looking into the frightened eyes of Vidar.

"The place of the dead," Sinmora proclaimed. "It is where we will find Groa. She will tell us how to find your friend Taylre. And right now, Groa is our only hope."

Chapter Fifteen
A Prayer to Njord

The soft light of morning began to rise in the east just beyond Mt. Balder where its jagged peak sat black and silhouetted in its gentle glow. The snow had stopped falling and the air seemed warmer as melting drops fell from the heavy branches, marking the deep snow with only a memory of their existence.

Vivian marveled that a new day was upon them. The time that had been spent in the cabin seemed to pass like a dream making each member of the tiny troupe feel tired, but at the same time anxious to be off on the quest. The Captain led the way, finding his forgotten impressions in the snow from the day before. Behind him, his short legs struggling to keep up, was Berling. His breath clouded in front of him as tiny icicles formed in his beard. He complained often, issuing curse words that Marjorie and Erna, who followed close behind, found rather amusing.

"Great turds of Ymir," he mumbled. "Is this what I'm to expect for the rest of the day?"

The Captain glanced back as a bemused smile brushed his lips. "I said I'd carry ya on my back."

"I'll not be havin ya carry me, ya great oaf! Do I look like a wee child to ya?"

"Berling, please," Vivian said imploringly. "We haven't got much farther to go. Soon we'll be at the Captain's truck where we can get warm and we won't have to walk anymore."

Berling looked back at Vivian, still amazed by her beauty and her likeness to Freyja. "Truck? What in the name of Odin is a truck?"

Vivian's head jerked up. "It's a..." she began. "Never mind. You'll find out soon enough. Just trust me. We'll be out of this soon. And please, keep your mouth shut for a few moments. I think we could all relish in a little peace and quiet."

"Amen," the Captain said, glancing back at a frowning Berling.

ᚱ

The old split wood fence soon came into view; behind it sat the Captain's rusted Ford. The Captain wedged his way awkwardly between the rotting slats and offered a helping hand to Berling. But the dwarf quickly waved him off. "I can do it myself, ya odorous dropping of Skoll."

Berling's bowed legs struggled to find a foothold on the fence, and more than once Erna bent forward to lend a hand, but the look that Berling gave her as he squeezed his way between the fence forced her back.

Soon all five members of the group found themselves huddled within the confines of the truck, its engine rumbling as the flow of warm air from the defrost melted away the chill.

"Where're yer horses?" Berling asked

"Horses?" the Captain questioned. "What do ya mean?"

"I mean how're we to get down the mountain, ya big stupid mule. We can't just sit here in this *truck* o' yers. Something's got to pull it."

"Ah," the Captain said, suddenly understanding Berling's meaning. "Well ya see," he said, pointing at the hood of the truck. "The horses are under there. Miniature ones. Tiny, but very strong."

Berling's eyes grew wide. "This is dark magic if I ever saw it," he muttered.

The Captain chuckled under his breath, but Vivian quickly interjected. "It's not magic, Berling. It's an engine, a modern invention. We don't travel by horse and cart anymore."

"Don't travel..." Berling sputtered as his mind tried to wrap itself around a cart that moved without a horse. "Oh, this isn't good."

"Isn't good?" Marjorie said. "What isn't good?"

"We must travel in the old way," Berling said. "If we don't, the magic will be lost. We will never reach Surtsey in the appointed time. The Seam will close, and we will lose our chance to enter the Mist."

"The old way!" the Captain said. "Whadya mean, ya fussy little man. It'd take us hours to get down the mountain if we did it any other way."

"I mean," Berling emphasized, "the old ways must be followed. That much I do know."

"Berling is right," Erna said. "Sinmora has always taught the old ways. We've watched as flying machines have soared overhead and have heard the rumble of machines in the forest, but she said they hide the magic. Their existence has buried it in unbelief."

"So what're we supposed to do?" Marjorie asked. "Walk down the mountain?"

"Unless we have a proper horse to pull this truck of yours, then yes, we walk," Berling said.

There was a brief moment of silence in the tiny interior of the truck's cab as the group looked out at the frosty, chilly morning.

"Well," Marjorie finally said as she released the latch on her seatbelt, "let's get out and start walking. Taylre needs our help and we're not doing her any good sitting here."

"But, Marjorie," the Captain complained, "it's a good seven mile walk back to Vivian's place."

"Then we'd better get moving," Marjorie said. "I'll lead the way."

ᛉ

It took a long time to get the house warm, even with the thermostat switched to high and a roaring fire blazing in the fireplace. The blankets were the only things that kept the travelers warm. Vivian served mugs of hot chocolate while the Captain added logs to the fire. Berling, though his teeth continued to chatter, looked about the room in astonishment, the TV and the computer receiving his full attention. His eyes were full of amazement as he watched the dancing figures on their screens.

"I'll check the internet for flights," Marjorie said as she tapped away at the keyboard. "This Surtsey place is in Iceland. It might cost us a pretty penny to get ourselves there."

"No," Erna said quietly. All eyes turned toward her. "We must follow the old ways."

"And we have," Marjorie said, turning slightly in her swivel office chair next to the computer. "We made the walk all the way down the mountain."

Erna nodded. "But it must continue, else the magic will leave."

"What do you suggest?" the Captain said. "The ocean is wide and the waters are treacherous. Our only hope is to fly over them."

"We must sail, as they did in the days of old," Berling said.

"Are you crazy, you little dumpling of a man! A trip like that would be suicide!"

"Nevertheless, any other way would close the Seam."

The Captain threw up his hands, exasperated. "Have ya not seen the snow out there? Have ya not felt the chill of the wind? If you think that was bad, wait until you take a boat out on the sea! The wind will toss chillin' waves over the side, ice will cling to the masts, and navigation will be next to impossible. And let's not forget about the floating ice. If it's been a bad year up north of here - and I believe it has - then we'll be battling icebergs, at least until we get past the Labrador current."

The big chair Berling sat in seemed to engulf him, making him look like a small child huddled beneath a blanket. Nevertheless, all sense of the child-like impression soon left once he began to speak. "Listen to me, ya great heap of dragon droppings. The warriors who made their way here a thousand years ago brought their families and all of their belongings aboard ships that I'm sure aren't built half as good as the ones ya have today. Ya think they didn't see some treacherous seas? Ya think they didn't fear for their lives at one time or another? O' course they did! But they made the voyage because it was the right thing to do. It was the only way they could preserve their way of life.

"Ya keep telling me that ya've got a wee lassie that needs to be rescued," he continued. "That her life is in danger. Well, is that not a worthy voyage? Is that not reason enough to risk your life?"

The Captain opened his mouth to speak, but then quickly closed it, realizing that Taylre was indeed a worthy cause. He sat down heavily on the couch as his breath came out in a great sigh. He looked at Berling. "You have a point, little man. But I'll say this: I'll not be takin' Vivian or Marjorie. The fewer lives that are at risk, the better. I'll only be takin' those that absolutely need to be there."

"Now just a moment..." Marjorie began, but the Captain quickly raised his hand.

"My word is law, Marjorie. I know ya want to help Taylre as much as ya can, but it'd make me feel a whole lot better knowing you and Vivian were somewhere safe."

Erna quickly interjected. "It seems to me there'd be nothing wrong with you and Vivian taking a flying machine," she said quietly. "Those of us who enter the Mist must be the ones to keep to the old ways. The magic needs to stay with us, not you."

"Aye," Berling said, nodding in agreement. "The power lies with us so we must be the ones who remain pure."

"So what're you saying?" Vivian asked. "Are we to fly to Iceland and meet you there? Won't a voyage like that take weeks to accomplish?"

"It will," the Captain said. "My guess is that we've got over two thousand miles of open water to cover."

"But your boat has an engine in it, Bartholomew. Isn't that breaking the rules?" Marjorie asked.

"Aye, but who said anything about takin the 'Maggie'? We'll be takin' the *Skipper Jack*. It's a solid boat. It rides o'bit heavy, but it'll get us there in one piece. Besides that, the boys have kept it in tip-top shape. It won't take much to get it outfitted and ready to go."

A reflective silence took hold of the small group as they listened to the crackling fire. They continued to shiver with cold as they huddled under blankets and considered the enormous challenge that lay before them.

ᚱ

It took the Captain an entire week to outfit the *Skipper Jack*, much longer than he would have wanted. But he was determined to make sure that every detail of the voyage was covered so that nothing of importance was left to chance. Nevertheless, the Captain's meticulous scrutiny over every detail frustrated Berling who was constantly harping and complaining. He wanted to help, but found that he had to take cover either in the boat itself, or remain at the Proper home, keeping himself hidden from inquisitive eyes. However, the week of preparation proved to be invaluable as the weather began to change, melting the snow that covered the town and opening the waterways for easier departure.

"We've got to be moving, Bart. Today is the day. No more time for delay," Berling said as he wound a length of rope around a cleat.

"I know, little man. I've been hearin' ya everyday for the last week. I'm goin' as fast as I can, so stop pestering me."

Berling threw down the rope and picked up a bag of potatoes, intent on storing them in the galley cupboard. "And everyday ya say the same thing, ya big oaf. But ya don't seem to realize that the Seam won't stay open forever. We've got to get a move on!"

The Captain lifted the final bag of supplies on board and stared at Berling. "That's the last of them. When that's put away we're ready to set sail. There'll be nothing holding us back except a sudden change in the weather."

Erna popped her head out from the hold, her face smudged with the work of scrubbing and cleaning. "A prayer to Njord may do us some good," she said as she brushed away a length of hair that hung across her face.

"And we will," the Captain said. "When the ladies get here we'll say our farewells, but before we do we'll call upon Njord to help us on our way."

ᛦ

The deck of the *Skipper Jack* glistened in the sunshine. Its smooth wooden slats, polished to a shiny finish, reflected the waning light of day. Beside it were Vivian and Marjorie standing arm and arm on the gently swaying dock while Bartholomew Gunner offered a prayer to the god of seafarers,

Njord. His arms were extended while his voice rose above the sound of wind and waves.

Hail to Njord, Master of Ships.
Hail to Njord, Lord of Vanaheim.
Hail to Njord, loving husband.
Hail to Njord, devoted father.
Nourish our hearts, and minds and spirits
As the ocean nourishes the sand
And the sand hungers for the tide.

Save us, oh Njord, from the crushing waves,
On our voyage to outlands, glory beyond the waves
Leaving homeward shores behind,
To horizons abound, our sails filled with Northern breeze.
On this ship we will cut across the sea,
Never fearing death or the power of storms.
Grant us, oh lord Njord, safe passage amidst the tides,
Say, "No harm shall find you on your voyage across my seas."

Vivian looked up when Bartholomew finished, uttering a silent amen.

Naglfar glistened in the light of the muted morning sun. Cold waters in the natural harbor lapped lightly against its hull and a cool breeze, carrying the scent of oncoming snow, brushed itself against the rocky hillside. Overlooking the bay, Taylre's attention was caught by the frantic movements on the ship's deck. She smiled and looked back at the tiny entourage that followed, thankful for her eyesight so she could once again see the magnificent ship, but also glad to know that Loden had done as he promised: provided quick, feverish preparations, so she could warn her friends.

"Do you see my wonderful ship, Taylre? It takes on the light of the moon so nicely, does it not?" Loden strolled up next to Taylre with Fenrir and Teddy standing protectively by his side. He rested his hand gently on her shoulder. She shuddered, moving slightly as an uncomfortable smile appeared on her face.

Loden frowned. "You still don't trust me, Taylre?"

"No, I do," she stammered. "It's just that I have this thing about being touched." Which was a lie. Taylre cherished her grandmother's gentle touch more than anything. And if you asked her friends, they would be the first to say her hugs were the most enthusiastic. But Loden's touch, even the subtlest ones, produced a discomfort that Taylre found difficult to describe.

Loden slid his hand slowly from Taylre's shoulder and patted her tenderly on the top of her head as if she were a small child. "Trust me when I tell you this, Taylre. I am, and always will be, your friend. You can have faith in that. What you must fear is the witch that has taken over your friends, not me. She is a powerful sorceress. Why, even now Zeke and Devon believe that she is only there to help them in their quest to find you. But that is a lie. She knows how to weave a spell. And believe me when I tell you, your friends are being deceived. Their lives are in mortal danger. So, unless you put your utmost trust in me, without any reservation, then I cannot guarantee their safety or yours."

Taylre bowed her head in shame. Her cheeks turned an embarrassed red. "I'm...I'm sorry, Mr. Loden. I truly am. Your kindness and your friendship are something that I cherish more than anything. Will you forgive me?"

Loden placed his hand back on Taylre's shoulder, a hideous smile creasing his lips. "All is forgiven, my child. All is forgiven." He exchanged a knowing glance with Fenrir and then looked at Teddy. Loden tipped his head subtly and Teddy nodded back, his face covered in its usual sneer. Teddy turned quickly from the group and left, taking a worn zigzag path down the steep slope toward the waiting ship. "Come," Loden announced. "Preparations are almost complete, you see. It is a long voyage from these rugged shores to the island of Surtsey. We must be on our way."

ᛯ

The ship was immense. Taylre stared in awe as she boarded the vessel and walked the length of the glistening deck. Her mind frantically searched her memory for the time when she had first ridden these decks. But she could find no solid recollection. It was as if her initial voyage upon Naglfar had been a dream, some vision that took place in a faraway mist.

"It is a beautiful ship is it not, Taylre?" Loden stood close to Taylre, his mouth close to her ear, the sound startling Taylre out of her reverie.

"It...it is," she said. "It is so much bigger than I imagined. Bigger, even, then how it looks from the shore." Taylre looked at Loden as if she were a small child. "It's almost like magic."

"Not magic, Taylre," Loden said, his eyes squinting against the sudden breeze. "Just a trick of the light, you see. The only one who employs magic is the witch who leads your two young friends. For that reason we must rush to save them." Loden raised his hand, a signal to unfurl the sails. "Let us begin, shall we."

The ship heaved as the sails filled with wind. Muscular giants who sat on either side of the ship, their huge arms grasping the wooden oars, pulled against the tide. Soon it began to move forward, gliding its way into the open sea.

Chapter Seventeen
Decree of Asgard

The flags and banners, standing like sentinels before the gates of Asgard, fluttered in the warm southern breeze, their light material snapping with the tiny gusts of air that coursed their way across green fields and rolling hills.

Suddenly, the wind changed, and the light warm breeze became a cold rush from the north that caused the flags to shudder and turn back on themselves, clinging awkwardly to the sturdy poles that kept them aloft.

Within the gates, where fallen heroes and warriors sat feasting in the Halls of Valhalla, the boisterous talk of past deeds and glorious battles fell silent. The lifting of overflowing mugs stopped, and the clinking of metal on metal ceased as mock battles ended abruptly.

Shaker, the stalwart, beautiful Valkyrie who once appeared to Zeke Proper in his desperate time of need, froze, the mug she was attempting to refill with mead all but forgotten as she sniffed the air and whispered - *Naglfar. It sets sail once more. Our enemies are on the move.* The warriors who sat nearby could hear her hushed words. Soon they began to echo her whispers until the sound filled the great room. All of the warriors repeated the phrase, their confusion at the shift in the wind turning to pleasure as they anticipated the oncoming battle; it's what they lived and longed for.

Odin, the one-eyed, hooded ruler, the All Father, who sat in his shrouded corner of the hall with Huginn and Muninn perched on his shoulders, also heard the whispers. His closed look of indifference changed to an expression of anger. Slowly, he stood; his Staff of Light pounded heavily on the wooden floor drawing all eyes toward him.

"The wolf's father has escaped his bonds, and he moves toward battle as we have long expected he would." The warriors in the hall stirred in their seats as Odin's voice reverberated off the ceiling. "Soon, my heroes, we will see the battle to end all battles, the one we have anticipated for so long."

Shouts and murmurs followed the All Father's words. He raised his hands to bring quiet back to the hall. "Know this, my warriors. Our chance to fight is forthcoming, but it has not yet arrived. Before we stir from our hall of comfort I will send the

Frost Giants and their spineless leader a message! A message they will not soon forget!"

Odin stepped down from his corner of the hall - his place of shadows - and moved to the head of the great table where the feasting had ceased. He set his staff firmly on the floor and lifted himself up on a chair and then stepped lithely onto the tabletop, once again lifting his arms high above his head. "I call upon the Hafgufa the mother of all sea monsters, she who consumes whales, ships, and men - all that stands in her way. Ride with the tide, Hafgufa! Turn the voyage of these traitors into a plague of misery!"

The great hall erupted in cheers. Warriors who sat at the feasting tables stood and lifted their cups of mead and drank deeply. But Odin, he who saw all things and knew the past, the present, and the future, smiled sadly, taking a measured sip from his overflowing cup.

Chapter Eighteen
Hafgufa

To Taylre the sea seemed like a vast rolling landscape of mountains that rose and fell in chaotic rhythm. Their peaks appeared to be touched with snowcaps, while the faces of the mountain-waves looked black and angry, almost as if they concealed a secret that lurked just beneath their frigid surface. She watched hypnotically at the constant movement while she stood clinging to what appeared to be a bejeweled railing, its surface cold and rough to the touch.

Behind Taylre, his hands gripped tightly to the frayed ends of a length of halyard rope, was Teddy Walford. He pulled on the rope as he'd been instructed to do, tightening the sails to catch the best of the wind, but his eyes never left Taylre nor did the scowl that was constantly smeared across his face.

"Ya thinking about jumpin', brat? Cause if ya are, I won't stop ya."

Taylre was roused from her hypnotic state by Teddy's booming voice, but she was not startled. Teddy had been a constant annoyance. Every time she turned around Teddy was there, watching; mouthing some silent words of reproach or threat. Taylre was getting used to his presence and the fact that he loathed her beyond words.

She continued to stare at the roiling sea. "Would that make you happy, Hrym? If I were to heave myself out of the ship and kill myself? Would that really make you happy?"

"You're damn right it would. It would make a lot of us happy to see you do that."

Taylre turned slowly, her stare bearing a touch of sadness. "I know you hate me, Hrym. But there's nothing I can do about that. Perhaps there was a time when I lost my faith in Loden, but not anymore. I trust him. I just ask that you try to trust me too. I want to be your friend. We can help each other; that's what friends do."

"Help each other?" Teddy said sarcastically. "What kind of help could you possibly give me?"

"I don't know," Taylre answered. "Sometimes, like my grandma used to say, time reveals the things we need. Maybe that's all we need. You know, some time. Time to get to know each other."

"Yeah. I don't think so, brat. Besides, what kind of help would you need?" he asked suspiciously. "Are ya needin some advice on how to escape? Or maybe how to betray Loden again?"

"No," she said. "But maybe you could help me understand what I'm looking at. Over there, see? It looks like two moving rocks."

Teddy edged closer to Taylre. "Rocks?" he said. A trace of curiosity filled his voice. "I don't see any..." Teddy paused. His eyes grew wide and his face turned pale. "Those aren't rocks," he said. He turned quickly and ran across the deck toward the large enclosure in the mid-section of the vessel.

Taylre watched Teddy race off, a startled look marking her own expression. When he reached the edifice she saw him pound frantically on the ornately carved door that kept the structure sealed.

"Loden!" he shouted. "Mr. Loden! I think you need to come out and see this!"

The giants and dwarfs who pulled on the oars ceased their rowing to watch Teddy, their expressions a mixture of confusion and amusement. Black Surt, the forger of metal; he who brandishes a flaming sword, the strongest of the giants, also turned to watch Teddy, his concern more evident as he had come to respect Teddy's strength and courage, choosing to bestow on him the new name, Hrym.

"What is it, lad? Why are ye troubled so?"

"The rocks!" Teddy shouted. He pointed a steady finger toward the south.

Surt followed Teddy's gaze, noting the small islands that seemed to appear and disappear at random intervals. "I see, lad. And those definitely aren't rocks." Surt yielded the helm to another giant and walked confidently to the edge of the quarterdeck. "Listen to me, ye men of battle!" he shouted. The multitude of giants and dwarfs turned to listen to his plea. "The enemy is at hand. We must prepare ourselves for battle."

Suddenly the door to the enclosure swung open and Loki emerged from its confines, Fenrir the wolf quick on his heels. Loki's expression was eager, almost cocky.

"The call for battle, is that what I hear? And so right that it should be. I have expected this, but not quite so soon," Loki said. "I knew it would come, you see. The gods continue in their cowardly way by sending another to fight their battles." He stepped quickly atop the quarterdeck and pulled Teddy by the arm to stand with him. "This will be our fight together, Hrym. I will teach you to guide this ship, your ship, past the menace the gods have sent. We will prevail, you and I."

Surt turned his watchful eye toward Loki. "It is Hafgufa, my lord. She will try to capsize the ship and swallow us whole!"

"She will try, Surt. But I have other plans in mind," Loki said. "Ours will be a decisive victory. One that will show the gods that they are no match for me and my giant warriors."

The sky began to darken with the promise of heavy rain. The waves below Naglfar seemed to cast a shadow. A stiff wind blew steadily, sending a bone chilling cold through Taylre. She watched in horror as the objects she once thought were small islands drew closer, the rock shapes taking on large yellow eyes, a spine covered tail, and a massive jaw filled with snapping, razor-sharp teeth. She turned and began looking for a place to hide, sensing the oncoming conflict that would soon develop. But she was too late.

An icy wave suddenly crashed over the side, soaking Taylre and sending her sprawling across the deck. She reached out quickly, grabbed hold of the frayed halyard rope that Teddy had once pulled on, and saved her self from slipping through the railings and falling into the sea. The cold seemed to penetrate her soul and she felt her heart flutter with an uneven rhythm. She tried to stand but the ship tossed heavily to the port side sending another wave of cold water splashing over her.

"Help!" she managed to utter, though the briny water threatened to gag her.

A patter of heavy footfalls came from behind and she was suddenly lifted into the air, her body swinging over the open water and then back onto the deck where a sodden Fenrir stood over her, panting like an exhausted dog.

"You must follow me!" he shouted, his voice barely reaching over the turmoil of swinging swords, shouting giants, and a roaring sea monster.

"I can't see!" she shouted, as wave after wave hurled over the sides of the ship.

"Grab hold of my tail if you must. Just keep up with me and I will take you to safety!"

Taylre reached up and groped the air until she found Fenrir's tail. She gripped it tightly, feeling herself being dragged toward the middle of the boat. "You're going too fast!" she hollered.

"Stop complaining, child. We will be safe soon. Look," Fenrir said, nudging his snout toward the starboard side of the ship where the sea seemed to boil with the crash of battle. "Even now Hafgufa nears her doom. Her blood mixes with the salt waves while Surt and his giant warriors slice at her throat!"

Taylre, her hands covering her face to ward off the heavy surges of sea water, turned from the engraved doorway that Fenrir led her through, but not before she saw and heard the loud clash of battle. The sea serpent fought ravenously, tearing at the giants and dwarfs with her teeth. The men scrambled around her like tiny gnats, swinging their swords as she seized them one by one in her razor sharp jaws, their cries of pain and anguish sending a shudder of fear coursing down Taylre's spine.

Soon, however, Hafgufa's movements began to slow. Its great tail continued to lash the air and knock down sails and snap the masts like toothpicks. Nevertheless, the number of warriors who fought against her was too many. She couldn't stop the constant onslaught of sharpened blades and piercing arrows that continued to strike her hide, cutting away flesh and sending great drops of blood in every direction. Hafgufa whose roars at the beginning of the siege were deep and terrible turned to shrieks of pain. It frantically whipped its spiny head back and forth, fighting now for its own survival.

Taylre, her hands still covering her face, tried to block the ghastly vision of slaughter that she witnessed before her. But she found it hard to stop watching. She discovered the scene to be both horrible and exciting at the same time. She spread her fingers many times so she could observe a spectacle that she once thought only existed on the movie screen.

Then came a scream. At once Taylre was reminded of the Korrigan and its last moments of life when Zeke raised the stones touched by Odin, their light penetrating its eyes and turning its flesh to ash. The death throes of the dying serpent that tried unsuccessfully to topple Naglfar and send her crew of miscreants to the bottom of the sea was very similar. Taylre shuddered when she realized this dreadful image would also remain in her memory.

Suddenly she felt the strong grip of Fenrir as he pulled on her shoulder with his teeth, his sharp incisors nearly breaking her skin. He yanked her abruptly inside the enclosure and slammed the door shut. Taylre found herself shrouded in darkness so thick she could feel it oozing across her skin, while outside the sounds of battle subsided.

"Here there is safety," Fenrir said panting, his voice penetrating the viscous gloom. "We will take these steps down to the bowels of Naglfar. There we will find warmth, food, and drink."

Taylre listened as Fenrir descended the spiral steps that wound their way within the tight confines of the enclosure. She hesitated, a feeling of guilt and betrayal passing over her mind.

"Are you coming?" Fenrir asked from somewhere in the dark.

"Yes," Taylre answered, though secretly, she wondered what Fenrir would do if she said no.

Chapter Nineteen
Flight of the Eagle

More smoke than fire billowed from the small campfire as the weary travelers gathered around its edges seeking its warmth. Sinmora tucked her knife and flint back in her pouch after the tiny spark it produced lit the kindling. But most of the scraps of wood that surrounded them were wet, soaked from a mix of rain and snow that fell relentlessly. Devon and Vidar returned from scavenging the forest, their arms laden with dead branches and moss. They dropped their find next to the tiny circle of stones that surrounded the fire. Zeke looked at the scavenged wood and then looked up at Devon as a bitter expression spread across his face.

Zeke was in a foul mood. His clothes were soaked, his hair was wet and matted to his forehead, and his leg ached with a throb that echoed up the length of his spine and ended in a painful reverberation in the back of his head. He was hungry too, eager to devour the fish Sinmora caught in a shallow stream several miles back. But when he looked at the armload of wet wood Devon and Vidar had just dropped in front of him, his bitterness toward their current situation rose to a crescendo.

"Are you serious?" he said, staring at Devon with a loathsome look.

"Waddya mean?" Devon answered, glancing at the pile of wood then back to Zeke.

"This stuff is all wet. How're we supposed to keep a fire going with this?"

"What am I supposed to do? Everything's wet, goober."

"If you throw that on the fire it'll make more smoke. There's no warmth in smoke and no way that we'll be able to cook any food."

"So, you push the wood close to the flames we already have and it'll dry it out," Devon answered, kneeling down to tuck sticks and moss just inside the fire ring.

"That'll take forever and you know it," Zeke complained.

"Look, Zeke," Devon said, taking a deep breath to calm his own rising temper, "I know you're tired. I know you're hungry and I know you're sore. We all are. Maybe not as sore as you are, but still, we're uncomfortable. We're doing the best we can, so have a little patience."

"Devon is right, Zeke," Sinmora scolded. In her hand she cradled a tobacco pipe that she clenched tightly between her teeth. "There are still many miles to travel and much adversity to overcome. The road ahead is dangerous, to be sure. We must learn to work together. Our survival depends upon it."

At the mention of danger, Vidar clutched the handle of the sword he wore at his side, his eyes staring at the smoke and the tiny dancing flames within the meager ring of fire.

ᛦ

The four travelers slept underneath a makeshift shelter of pine boughs and willow branches. Zeke woke fitfully to the combined snores of Sinmora and Devon, while Vidar slumbered quietly under a pile of leaves in the corner of the primitive hut. The mix of rain and snow had stopped at some point during the night and the sky was filled with the growing light of a new morning. Zeke rubbed the sleep from his eyes and tried unsuccessfully to smooth down a patch of hair that refused to settle. He sat up slowly, finding that the ache in his thigh had subsided substantially allowing him freedom to stretch out his leg with very little discomfort. He looked at the fire ring and saw that the flames from the night before had died completely. The ashes in the small ring had become as sodden as the ground surrounding it.

His recollection from the night before remained foggy, with only brief images of sharp retributions, sharp pains, and sharp words. But in contrast to it all, Zeke also remembered the soothing taste of cooked fish followed by a sip of white willow tea. It was the tea, he remembered, that made him feel sleepy. The last thing he recalled was dozing by the rising flames of the campfire, its heat finally enveloping him in a blanket of warmth.

He yawned and stretched his arms out, at last feeling a measure of strength, when he looked out of the hut toward a small meadow and saw a deer grazing among the green grass and rolling landscape. At once Zeke began to feel the nagging pangs of hunger that had assaulted him the night before. He turned to Sinmora who continued to snore beneath the dripping sap of the pine boughs.

"Sinmora!" he whispered sharply. "Wake up! There's food!"

Sinmora stirred restlessly and turned quickly on her side, producing a loud snort. Her eyes flew open and she sat up straight, the hair on each side of her head sticking up like the horns of a bull. "What is it, lad? Are we being attacked?"

"No," Zeke said. "Look." He pointed a stern finger toward the meadow and the deer that still grazed among the tall grass.

"Ah," she said, licking her lips. "Breakfast."

Sinmora stood slowly and reached into her pouch. From it she brought out a small swathe of leather that had two long bands of hemp rope tied tightly to either end. She exited the tight confines of the tiny enclosure and reached down to pick up a thumb-sized stone from the ground. Then, she began swinging the sling around her head, the whizzing hum of the string bending and whirring against the cold morning air. Finally, she let go of the string and let the rock fly. The tiny projectile sailed quickly and silently. The deer, unaware that Sinmora was even there, dropped to the ground dead, the rough stone striking its forehead quickly and painlessly.

With Devon and Vidar roused from their sleep, a large fire was built and the deer was butchered. The venison was soon hung over the roaring flames and the meat began to roast. A sweet, crisp aroma hovered in the air.

The scent of cooking meat ravished the travelers who had barely eaten during the last several days. They were impatient and could barely wait to eat. As soon as they thought the meat was roasted to perfection, Sinmora cut off a large section, hoping to share it with the weary group. But she found the inside to be completely raw.

"This is strange," she said, watching the cold blood drip on the hot flames. "It seemed like it was on there long enough to cook it completely through. Maybe it's because we're so hungry," she said, placing the meat back on the fire.

There suddenly came a chill wind that channeled down the old road and struck the travelers as they sat before the fire. Each of them, without thinking much of the sudden change, wrapped themselves tightly in their meager clothing and scooted closer to the flames where the aroma of freshly cooked meat still hung in the air.

After a short time, Devon, who shivered underneath his sweatshirt and ski jacket, said, "Do you think it's ready? I'm starving."

This time Zeke stood with the help of the Staff of Urd and used Sinmora's knife to cut off a large hunk of meat.

"It must be cooked by now." Zeke handed the piece to Sinmora who looked at it with a perplexed stare.

"I don't understand. It's still not cooked," she said. Her eyes squinted in disbelief. "It's as raw now as it was to begin with."

Vidar shuffled up close to Sinmora and examined the meat. "The fire seems hot enough," he said. "Perhaps there's something working against us."

Suddenly, there came a voice from above. "Perhaps there is," it said, its voice scratchy and shrill like the blades of a sharpened knife.

The four travelers looked up into the tall trees above and saw an eagle, black and immense, its wings spread well over twenty feet. All four of them reared back in fright, even Sinmora, as the sight was hard to believe.

"If you let me eat my fill," the eagle said, "I'll allow the fire to cook your meat."

Zeke and Devon, along with Sinmora and Vidar, retreated into the makeshift shelter, a feeble attempt at hiding from the giant eagle that perched itself above them.

Devon looked up. "There's a giant talking eagle up there. What do we do?"

All eyes turned to Sinmora. "This is a new one," she said. "I've been in the Mist many times, but I've never come across a talking eagle. I think we should do whatever it asks of us. Something that big that also holds the power to keep our fire from cooking the venison must be very dangerous."

Zeke began shaking the staff, as if its gnarled, wooden frame would help him make his point. "We can't give up our food," he said imploringly. "Let the damn bird get his own food. We're starving here."

Vidar grabbed Zeke by the arm. "Wait," he said. "I've heard of this bird before. My father once spoke of her. This eagle sits upon the highest branches of Yggdrasil, the world tree. It is a beast to be respected. We cannot ignore its request. To do so would mean death."

All four members of the tiny troupe looked at each other, hoping some words of wisdom would prevail. Finally, Sinmora spoke, her voice even, without emotion.

"We let the eagle take what it needs. We are not warriors yet. A battle with this kind of beast would be futile."

Zeke raised the Staff of Urd and began to speak, but the others ignored his complaints, leaving him behind as they exited the shelter.

"Since we have traveled far," Sinmora said, raising her voice and arms to the tops of the trees, "we too are very hungry. But we see that you are a beast of great strength and are to be revered. Therefore, we agree to your terms. There is nothing else we can do."

The eagle, its wings still spread, swooped down from the tree and settled over the fire. It picked at the carcass ravenously, pulling at the rump and then at the shoulder. Then the bird turned its eye toward the travelers, watching them with a kind of taunt in its stare as it continued to pull at the meat.

Zeke, however, had had enough. His anger rose again as it had the night before. He was hungry, stiff, and sore, and he wasn't about to let some bloody bird take all his food. He yanked himself out of the shelter and ran toward the eagle, his pain all but forgotten. Then, with all of the strength he could muster he swung the Staff of Urd, smashing it against the giant bird's body. Zeke could feel the unusual power that the staff provided him, as if it took on a force of its own when it struck the animal. The eagle was thrown off balance and dropped the meat. It screeched loudly forcing Zeke's awestruck audience to cover their ears. The bird then took to the air, but not before it clutched the staff in its giant talons. Zeke discovered that he was unable to let go as he felt his feet lift off the ground. He pulled and twisted and yelled, Devon and Vidar even tried to reach for him as he flew over their heads, but already the bird was lifting high above the tree line.

Zeke's hands were stuck to the staff.

Sinmora, Devon, and Vidar watched in horror as the great eagle's wings flapped harder and faster, lifting Zeke higher and higher until finally he disappeared into the misty morning air.

ᛉ

The eagle flew at great speed climbing higher and higher with each powerful downward stroke of its giant wings. Zeke tried to scream, but his voice was caught in a gulp of fear. His terror seemed to be caught somewhere in his throat, and the best he could do was to swallow the chilly air that seemed to be getting thinner the higher they went.

Suddenly the eagle dipped its wings, careening hard to the left and swooping fast toward the ground. Zeke's legs kicked at the air in complete helplessness as he watched the tops of the trees draw closer and closer. Branches and tall limbs struck his feet as they circled. Then the eagle dipped again, this time soaring just above the rocky ground. Zeke was dragged across it. His knees and ankles banged into loose rocks and boulders, as well as dry branches and thorns until they were bleeding. The pain in his thigh was becoming a secondary affliction.

"Please, stop!" Zeke's voice managed to escape his lips, but the sound was hoarse and dry.

The eagle took no notice. It continued to drag Zeke across the rough ground as one of his shoes went spinning off his foot and his shirt and jeans began to tear.

"Please! I beg of you! Stop and let me go!"

The eagle looked down on its helpless victim, her yellow eyes with their black piercing centers glared angrily at Zeke. She rose slightly, giving Zeke some respite. "I will have mercy on you," the eagle said. "But only if you swear."

Zeke, who was still shaken by the fact that an eagle could talk, tried to calm his frayed nerves and push aside the pain that raked his body. "Anything," he cried. "Anything you want. Just set me down."

The eagle's giant wings spread wide, catching the wind like a great canvas sail. Zeke felt a sudden rush and then just as quickly found himself settled to the ground, his legs still shaking with fear. Nevertheless, his hands still clutched firmly to the Staff of Urd. Drops of blood spattered his one bare foot, while deep scrapes covered both of his knees where the pant material had been torn away. He stood unsteadily, but fought hard to stay on his feet; he feared the eagle might try to attack him if he were to fall. He kept the staff outstretched, ready to ward off the eagle's aggressive advances.

The eagle landed softly on the ground just in front of Zeke. She turned and hopped back, her wings tucked firmly at her sides.

"I am Hraesvelg," the eagle said. "My home sits at the pinnacle of Yggdrasil. From there I can see all that happens in the nine worlds and throughout the Mist. Why, I believe that I can see even more than the All Father himself. But I care nothing for what I see. Why should I concern myself with the affairs of gods, giants, and men? They are of no interest. However, what does concern me is the dragon Nidhogg, he who sits at the base of Yggdrasil constantly tearing at its roots with no thought for those whose homes and existence depend upon the tree. If he continues to gnaw away at the roots, Yggdrasil will topple over and I will lose my perch."

Zeke continued to take a defensive stance, the staff extended between him and the great bird. "So...what do you want me to do?" he stammered.

"I have up until recently employed a messenger to carry my messages of threats and anger down to Nidhogg. But I fear that Ratatosk, the giant squirrel who races between the worlds on the limbs of the tree, has turned on me. I believe he has taken sides with Nidhogg. I believe they sit together in the depths of Niflheim and laugh at me. I can no longer trust him. Therefore, you must swear to be my messenger.

"From my perch I have watched your progression through the Mist. I see that you are headed to Niflheim. For what purpose, I know not. Nor do I care. All I want is that you deliver a message for me to the filthy serpent."

Zeke began shaking his head as a sad smile creased his face. He lowered the staff slowly. "Why didn't you just ask? Why did you have to drag me to near death to get what you wanted?"

The eagle hesitated, eyeing Zeke cautiously. "You are a slayer, a killer of beast and giant. I feared you and your staff. But know this: if the dragon does not comply with my wishes, I will take my wrath out on you, staff or not. I will find you. I can see all," the eagle said quietly.

Zeke's face took on a curious expression. "You...you feared me?"

The eagle nodded, her eyes never leaving Zeke or the staff.

Zeke took a measured breath and nodded his head slowly. "Sure," he said. "I'll deliver your message. Since we're going there anyway. How hard can that be?"

ᚱ

Far below, on the rugged trail leading through the mountain pass, Sinmora, Devon, and Vidar rode on the back of Alsvid. She plodded along easily with its light load of passengers, never breaking into more than a slow trot.

"Won't this beast go any faster?" Sinmora exclaimed.

Vidar shook the reins and clicked his tongue, but it was all done gently, like one friend urging on another. "She's not a runner, that's for sure, ma'am. She's apt to go only as fast as she wants or deems necessary."

"But we have to find Zeke," she insisted. "This time I really do fear for his life."

Devon, who was sandwiched between Vidar and Sinmora, turned to Sinmora, his face turning pale as she expressed her concern.

"Don't worry, lad. 'Ol Sinmora shouldn't have said that. Have faith in the staff. It'll keep him safe."

As if Alsvid knew where to go, she plodded off the path, between some low hanging trees, eventually halting at the top of a rocky plateau. Devon was confused as to why the animal had stopped until he looked across the barren field below and saw Zeke stumble his way back toward them, the staff in hand and his limp much more prominent.

"There he is!" Devon shouted, sliding quickly off the bare back of Alsvid. "But where's the eagle?"

"That's a good question, Devon." Sinmora said. Then she smiled hopefully. "Maybe he has defeated it as well."

Both Devon and Vidar ran down the rocky slope to meet Zeke and assist him the rest of the way. Sinmora continued to sit atop Alsvid watching with curious wonder as Zeke wrestled himself up the hill. When he reached the top, Devon and Vidar on either side, their arms wrapped around his back for support, Sinmora spoke. "Well, Zeke Proper. You are a marvel, to be sure. Have you slain another beast? Do you continue to mark your wondrous journey to becoming a great warrior?"

Zeke was out of breath, but he managed to steady himself with the help of the staff and look abashedly at Sinmora. "No," he said shaking his head slowly. "I did nothing brave or wondrous at all. All I did was scream for help and cry out in pain. That does not make me a warrior or draw me any closer to being one."

"But where is the eagle?" Vidar asked.

Zeke looked back at the field of rocks that rested under the heights of a great mountain. "She's gone," he answered. "Back to her perch on the pinnacle of Yggdrasil."

Sinmora cocked her head slightly to the left. "She let you go? Why?"

"We made a bargain," he answered. "I am to deliver a message to some dragon guy named Nidhogg when we get to Niflheim. No big deal."

Shaking her head with a wry smile across her lips, Sinmora said, "This may be a bigger deal than you think, Zeke. Just what, may I ask, was the message she wanted you to relate?"

"I'm to tell him that he's nothing but a dog in cheap armor and to stop ruining her tree. She said she'd be watching from her nest to make sure I did it. But it seems simple enough, uh?"

"Aye, simple enough perhaps. But we shall wait and see. In the meantime let us get your wounds bandaged and mended. We still have a long way to go."

Chapter Twenty

Not a single wave or ripple could be seen on the surface of the water. Small icebergs dotted the frigid landscape and yet high above, overlooking the calm sea, the sky was a bright blue with a cold, merciless sun edging its way toward the west. The *Skipper Jack* sat on the water as still as a painting, its sails hanging limp in the late afternoon air.

"Doldrums," the Captain muttered. "I hate em'. I really do. No air movin' and the water as still as night."

"I know what the doldrums be, ya great stump. Do ya think I'm stupid?" Berling said.

"No one was talkin' to you. I was just mutterin' to myself, if ya please."

"Well I hear ya all the same. A little quiet for me own thoughts would be appreciated." Berling puffed angrily on his pipe, his face partially covered by a woolen scarf to ward off the chill.

"Yer own thoughts?" the Captain mocked. "Ya mean ya actually have those?"

"Oh, a clever retort from such a dumb wit. Will miracles never cease?" Berling stood carefully, grasping the low railing that enclosed the bow of the *Skipper Jack* and edged his way to the cabin door. "I'll be in my quarters doing my thinking there. The company here stinks." He disappeared through the tiny door leaving the Captain and Erna alone on the deck.

Erna looked up sadly from where she sat cross-legged near the stern. Her hands continued to work deftly with her knitting needles. A partially completed sweater was draped across her lap and a green ball of yarn sat by her side.

"Usually I'm not one to interfere in such things, Bartholomew. But the two of you have been bickering a great deal. I realize the close quarters and the length of our voyage so far has strained things, but don't you think you could try to be a bit kinder? Berling is a bitter dwarf, to be sure, but you. I think you can do better."

The Captain puffed gently on his pipe and shifted his eyes toward Erna, but his head remained still. "The little imp is a pain in me arse," the Captain said. "I've tried my best to be civil but he keeps kneading at me. I'm about ready to toss him overboard."

"It is hard, I know. I too am frustrated. But it is in his nature to be unpleasant. All dwarfs, from the beginning of time, have been this way. But it is not in our nature and we must practice understanding. If we don't, then I fear that you may indeed throw him into the sea. That would not be good. Our entire purpose for the voyage would be nullified."

This time the Captain turned to look at Erna. A guilty chuckle escaped his lips. "You're right, as usual. I just wish we could crank up that diesel engine in the back and get a move on. This sitting around is making me anxious."

Erna shook her head. "No, Bartholomew. To do so would erase the spell. The magic would die. We must keep to the old ways."

"But just a quick burst. That couldn't hurt, could it? Just until we find the wind. Our time is running out, I fear. "

"No," Erna repeated, her hands still working vigorously with the needles. "We know not what might cause the magic to cease. We best not test it."

ᛟ

Three more days passed. The air remained as still as Bifrost, glimmering just as brightly under the wintry sun. The sails of the

Skipper Jack continued to rest, the white canvas drooping lifeless and drained under a blue sky. The Captain continued to brood as well. His face shared the appearance of the limp sails: saggy and tired. He sat as still as a sculpture, like the wind that refused to blow. Occasionally, though, he would lift a flask of whiskey to his lips and drink, the woody liquid causing his mind to bend and swirl.

Below deck, resting in his bunk, Berling drank deeply from a mug of mead and munched on handfuls of raw potatoes and turnips.

It was clearly evident that a nasty storm was brewing.

"Enough is enough!" the Captain hollered. "I can't stand it anymore!" He rose unsteadily, clinging to the boom for balance. "The engine will be started and we'll get this blasted ship underway if it's the last thing I do!"

Erna stirred uneasily from her nap, a nearly completed woolen sweater resting beside her head. She sat up quickly, startled by the Captain's shouts.

Berling swayed as he tried to sit up, his head swirling with the affects of the potent mead.

"What in the name of Skoll is that fat scum hollerin' about now," Berling slurred. He placed unsteady feet on the floor and stumbled to the cabin door swinging it open with a flurry of strength.

Erna watched Berling trip his way out into the cold day, feeling the tense air shudder around her. She dropped her knitting and followed him out onto the deck. Immediately she felt the chill of the air race through her. She contemplated going back inside to retrieve the sweater, but changed her mind quickly when she saw the Captain trudging his cumbersome, unbalanced body toward the back of the boat. In his hand he held a dangle of silver keys. His determined gaze was intent upon the helm and the ignition that would start the small diesel engine. Erna skipped past Berling, gently pushing his sturdy little body to the side and tried to intercept the Captain.

"No, Bart," she whispered sharply, her hands lifted imploringly. "Go back to yer place at the bow. Yer not in yer right mind and I can smell the strong drink on yer breath. Go back now. The wind will come, I promise."

"Out of my way, lass," the Captain bellowed, his big body reeling unsteadily. He reached out a quick hand and grabbed hold of a length of halyard rope, saving himself from a cold plunge in the icy North Atlantic waters. "I'll not be spending another moment of my life drifting among icebergs when there's a perfectly good engine that can get us movin'."

"But the magic, Bart. Don't forget the magic." Erna tried unsuccessfully to push the Captain back, but her tiny frame could do nothing against the Captain's massive girth.

"Magic be damned!" the Captain yelled. "If it's magic ya want then watch what happens when I turn the key in the ignition. Then you'll see magic, that I'll warrant."

"Stop right there, ya great hunk o' dragon turd!" Berling slipped his way past Erna, his shoulders squared; his face a mask of anger as he stared up at the Captain. "You know the rules. We all agreed to them. If we're goin' to save yer friends then this is the way it must be." Berling pushed the Captain backwards, his tiny strength a surprise to both the Captain and Erna.

"Don't ya dare lay a hand on me, ya smelly little man!" The Captain steadied himself and took a swing, his fist catching Berling solidly on his right ear.

Berling lost his balance and fell hard on the deck. His mind began spinning as tiny sparkles of light glittered in front of his eyes. Erna let out a scream and covered her mouth in horror as she watched Berling tumble across the floor.

The Captain ignored Erna's entreaties and continued to advance toward the helm with the silver key extended in front of him. But Berling stood quickly, regaining his balance despite the potent effects of the mead, and rushed toward the Captain, his teeth bared while his eyes glowed a fiery red.

"You'll start that engine over my dead body!" Berling hollered. His head was down as he charged the Captain like an angry Billy goat. His body appeared to move faster than his tiny legs would allow.

"If that's what it takes," the Captain said. He turned rapidly to meet Berling's clumsy attack, "then so be it!" This time he let his arm fly with a solid backhand and caught Berling on the top of his head. Berling twisted hard to the left, his balance once again lost, his body sliding under the ship's meager rope railing and finally over the edge of the *Skipper Jack*, splashing heavily into the icy water.

Berling tried hard to grab hold of the passing lifeline, but his head was still whirling from the Captain's ferocious blow; his eyes began to blacken into unconsciousness.

Despite the icy chill of the water, Berling remained unconscious, his tiny, bulky body sunk quickly. The Captain, his mind and focus still intent on the *Skipper Jack's* ignition, heard Erna's shrill cries. At first he tried to ignore them, but this time there was something different, something much more urgent in their resonating call. Reluctantly he turned from the helm, the key just inches from slipping into the starter. He took one glance at Erna and noted the horror stricken expression on her face. He followed her shocked gaze and saw the brief outline of a small hand just as it began to sink beneath the still waters.

Immediately the Captain felt the sobering affects of the desperate situation. The influence of the whiskey no longer bound him and his mind began to clear. He dropped the keys on the deck and raced to the ship's starboard side. Pushing aside the ropes that barred his way, the Captain dove into the cold green water.

The chill struck him like a sledgehammer. He could feel his heart stammer as a shudder of pain drove its way through his chest. For a brief moment Bartholomew Gunner almost lost consciousness as he began to sense a light pass before his mind, a reminder of all the good and bad that had occurred in his life. The light was warm and the temptation to fall into its comforting embrace was almost too much for him to resist. But resist he did, knowing that to succumb to this temptation would surely mean death.

He fought hard, gritting his teeth and clenching his fists into tight balls of fury. His legs began to kick too, pushing him back to the surface where he gulped greedily from the chilly air. He filled his lungs before he plunged himself again, deeper and deeper, his arms extended, groping the dark for a hand, an arm, a leg, anything that he could cling to in this most desperate moment.

Finally there came a touch, a sleeve perhaps? Or a bit of hair? The Captain wasn't sure, but he grabbed at it, praying to Odin and to Njord for a miracle. The Captain's lungs were burning and the desire to gasp, to draw something into them became almost overwhelming. Soon he began to see the light again.

It called to him.

So warm.

So peaceful.

He kicked hard. Again and again he fought against the pull of warmth, the siren's call that would surely mark the end of both him and Berling. Finally, with one last desperate kick, one last stroke of his strong arm, the Captain broke the surface. He gasped and then began drinking the cool air, willing it to fill his flaming lungs with refreshment as if he were a man dying of thirst in the middle of a burning desert.

Erna, clinging precariously to the side of the *Skipper Jack*, reached a trembling hand over the side and grabbed hold of Berling's collar as the Captain literally yanked him from the clutches of death itself.

"Hold 'im there, lass. Don't let go. I'll climb the ladder and help pull 'im in." The Captain swam as quickly as he could to the back of the boat, but finding that his hands and arms were as numb as icicles, he struggled to climb aboard, exerting as much strength as he could muster.

"Bart, please hurry. I'm losing grip." Erna was now on her stomach, her arm still stretched awkwardly over the side of the ship.

"I'm comin', lass, just a moment more. Hold on till I get there." The Captain pulled himself up the tiny ladder and stumbled across the deck, his legs paralyzed with cold. He stepped clumsily over Erna and then knelt beside her, once again reaching into the icy water. He grabbed a tight hold of Berling's collar and lifted his dead weight safely onto the deck.

Berling's long hair was matted to his very pale face; his lips were blue. "I'll get these wet clothes off 'im, lass. You run inside and get a blanket or two." The Captain removed Berling's tiny jacket and shirt and then bent his head, listening for a heartbeat.

Erna returned, her arms laden with a pile of woolen blankets. "Is he breathing?" she asked desperately.

The Captain was trembling, and his voice stuttered when he spoke. "Th...there's a faint heartbeat," he said, "b...but he's not breathin'."

The Captain laid Berling's cold, lifeless body on the deck and tilted his head back, gently placing his hand firmly underneath Berling's neck. The Captain then took the thumb and forefinger of his other hand and squeezed Berling's nose. At the same time he covered Berling's mouth with his own and began to blow. Berling's chest rose dramatically with each breath.

After several attempts and some very tense moments, Berling's eyes fluttered open. He coughed and his chest heaved as a deluge of thick green fluid escaped his lungs, spilling from his mouth with a moan of agony.

Berling sat up slowly, his eyes opening wide, a look of terror painted across his face as he gazed about him. "I was there," he whispered, "walkin' toward the realm of Hel. It were an awful place, I can tell ya that." He looked up at the Captain, a tiny tear escaping the corner of his eye. He reached up and hugged the Captain tightly around the neck. "Thank you, Bartholomew Gunner. Thank you from the bottom of me heart. Ya brought me back from a terrible fate and for that I am ever indebted to ya."

The Captain's back stiffened as the dwarf enthusiastically embraced him.

"It weren't nothing," he said awkwardly, trying hard to release Berling's tight hold on his neck. "I'm to blame for what happened. I've got a bad temper and I let it get the best of me."

"No," Berling whispered, his mouth pressed up against the Captain's ear. "I was to blame as well. My temper is like the fires of Surtsey, always has been, and for that I'm sorry." He hugged the Captain once more and then leaned back, his hands still resting on the Captain's shoulders.

The Captain stared back at Berling. A slight scowl creased his face. "You're not goin' ta kiss me now are ya?"

Berling let out a laugh that filled the chilly air with mirth, a sensation that made Erna smile brighter than she had in weeks.

But then, just as abruptly, Berling's laughter ceased and he once again looked at the Captain, his smile fading, his eyes taking on a serious look. "I was walkin' toward the gates of Hel. I saw them, I tell ya. It's like they were callin' me in and beggin' me to enter. But I felt ya reachin' for me, I did. As if you were pullin' me back from that terrible place of darkness. But I'm so glad ya did, Bart. It's the dwellin' of the malformed daughter of Loki. 'Tis a place of shadows, I tell ya. It's full of hunger, sickness, and disease. You, my friend, have saved me."

And then, before the Captain had a chance to turn his head, Berling did kiss Bartholomew Gunner, a solid smack on the cheek.

ᛟ

Bartholomew and Berling sat comfortably on tiny folding chairs that were perched unsteadily on the top of the ship's deck. The Captain's legs stretched out in front of him while Berling's dangled uncomfortably, barely touching the dark wooden slats. Both of them had woolen blankets wrapped tightly around their shoulders while Erna carried steaming cups of freshly brewed tea from the galley and placed them gently in their still shivering hands.

"Can I get you two anything else?" Erna asked, her smile still beaming as she watched two former enemies sitting beside one another as friends.

"Perhaps something a bit stronger than tea, if ya've got it, lass," Berling said, holding his cup up to Erna as if he expected her to add a shot of whiskey.

The Captain snorted with laughter and nudged Berling on the shoulder. "Here, here, lass. Fill 'er up with somthin' that's got a wee bit 'o fire in it."

"They'll be no more o' that," she said sternly. She folded her arms defiantly across her chest. "We've all been witness to what happens when you two get too much of the strong drink in ya." Erna's voice was firm, but her eyes still showed a sparkle of laughter.

"All right, lass," Berling said, placing his hand tenderly on the Captain's shoulder. "But ya need not worry. Bart and I are the best 'o friends. There's nothing that can tear us apart. Not after all we've been through." Berling looked sadly at the Captain. His eyes spilled over once again as the vision of the ominous gates of Hel shaded his vision.

"Right ya are, my wee friend," the Captain said, clicking his teacup against Berling's. "To us," he continued. "And to a long and fruitful friendship."

"To friendship," Berling echoed.

Erna laughed and clapped her hands together with joy. But then her smile broadened even more as her long auburn hair blew away from her face. She turned from the two companions and gazed with wonder at the sails. They began to flutter, at first just a gentle flap that was barely noticeable, but then the thick canvas filled with wind and the *Skipper Jack* started moving forward.

Both the Captain and Berling tossed aside their blankets, jumped from their chairs, and grabbed hold of the ropes that kept the sails taut.

"Hold on!" the Captain shouted. "Njord has heard our prayers and I've got the feelin' there won't be much holdin' us back."

Berling scampered his way to the helm and grabbed hold of the wheel, his grip tight as his knuckles turned white. "Onward to Surtsey," he proclaimed.

The *Skipper Jack's* sails continued to fill with wind as the ship tilted heavily to the port side, cutting through the chilly water with ease and leaving a forgotten memory of their presence in its wake.

Chapter Twenty-One
Draugar

As usual, Vivian had packed too much and she and Marjorie had trouble boarding the small airplane that would take them to Surtsey. Besides that, the language was strange and the pilot's accent was strong and difficult to understand.

"But I need all of these things," Vivian protested, her pleading hands extended in front of her.

"It is not for me to decide," the pilot said. His English accent was thick with too many highs and lows. "The airplane is small. It has weight restrictions. If it's too heavy we may not get off the ground. We might crash. You don't want that to happen do you?"

"But it's very cold where we're going. I will need all of these items if I'm to keep from freezing to death."

The pilot smiled, but he was not about to give in. "Two luggage. Besides, it is Icelandic law." he said. "Make your choice what you will leave and what you will keep."

"I want to keep it all," Vivian pleaded.

Finally, Marjorie stepped in and placed herself gently between Vivian and the pilot. "We will decide. Please just give us a moment." She pulled Vivian aside and hauled with her the four overly packed suitcases.

The two women walked a few yards away from the tiny airplane, their boots crunching on the ice and snow that covered the tarmac of the Reykjavik airport, the capital city of Iceland. Marjorie looked at Vivian with pleading eyes. "You're not going to be able to take all four bags, Vivian. They just won't let you. So let's take a few moments to repack. We'll gather the most important items in two bags and leave the rest."

"But..." Vivian began. Marjorie placed her finger softly on Vivian's lips.

"We have no choice," Marjorie said. "If we want to get to Surtsey and meet Bartholomew then we'll just have to go along with the Icelandic law."

Vivian bowed her head, her hands wringing with frustration. "Fine," she muttered. "But let's be sure to get all the warm stuff out. I'm already freezing and we haven't even left the airport."

ᚱ

Sighing heavily, Marjorie shifted from one foot to the other, her lips pursed together as she tried to hold back her desire to scream. Vivian was still rummaging through her suitcases holding up one item and then the other as she tried to decide which item of clothing she should leave and which one she should keep.

Finally Marjorie's patience had come to an end. "For crying out loud, Vivian. It's clothing. Make a decision and let's get it over with. The pilot is waiting."

Vivian looked up from the clothing that lay strewn about her, some of it beginning to stiffen in the chilly Icelandic breeze. She glanced momentarily at Marjorie and then turned toward the pilot and the airplane.

Suddenly her eyes grew wide with astonishment and surprise. From her crouched position on the icy tarmac she stood straight up. Her face turned a sickly pale.

Marjorie stepped back, assuming that she'd finally pushed the wrong button, causing Vivian to turn from her usual carefree self to an angry, frustrated woman.

"I'm sorry," Marjorie said. She pressed a soothing hand onto Vivian's shoulder. "I didn't mean to make you angry. It's just that we have to get moving. We have people waiting for us."

Vivian ignored Marjorie's apologies and raised her finger, pointing toward the airplane, her hands visibly shaking. "Did you see that?" she stammered.

Marjorie turned and followed the direction of Vivian's pointing finger. "See what?" she asked.

"The man. He was working on the airplane. I saw him. I swear I did. He was standing there, just behind the tail section."

Marjorie squinted her eyes against the cold and the fierce wind that had begun to pick up. "I don't see anybody except the pilot," Marjorie said.

Vivian, lowering her shaking hand to her side, began walking slowly toward the plane. She continued to stare, the astonishment never leaving her face. Marjorie quickly stepped up beside her and took her by the arm. "What is it, Vivian? What did you see?"

The voice of Marjorie that was practical told her that Vivian was just seeing things in the wind. That her mind, exhausted from the time change and the distance they'd had to travel to get to Reykjavik, was causing her to only imagine she'd seen a man. But Marjorie's other voice, the one who knew about monsters that lived in a river, the one that also knew about flying ships and evil, vengeful gods, told her that Vivian wasn't imagining things at all. That in fact she did see someone standing behind the airplane, and that the sighting, whether imagined or not, deserved a complete investigation.

Vivian turned her pale face to look at Marjorie. "It was Percy. Percy was standing right there, looking directly at me."

ᛦ

Both Vivian and Marjorie were finally buckled in to the narrow seats of the tiny four-passenger airplane. The pilot sat just in front of Marjorie and adjusted controls above his head while the propeller whirred unsteadily in the front of the plane, its two exhaust pipes pouring out plumes of black smoke.

Vivian shuffled about in her seat, first staring out one window and then, shifting across Marjorie's lap, peered out the other. She was nervous about the flight, but more importantly, she was hoping to see the man again.

"You do believe me, don't you, Marjorie?"

Marjorie, knowing full well that this question was coming, bit her bottom lip, a gesture she often used when she was thinking. "Of course I believe you, Vivian," she said, her response brought to a severe whisper since she didn't want the pilot to overhear their conversation. "Considering everything that has happened lately, how could I not believe you? The problem I'm having is trying to decide what exactly it is that you saw." Vivian leaned in closer, their shoulders now rubbing up against each other.

"You see," Marjorie continued, "I have a great deal of experience with events that, well, might be considered dark," she said, her head bowed slightly with embarrassment.

"So you think this might be something bad?" Vivian asked. " Something that has to do with our being here?"

"Perhaps," Marjorie responded. "But it could be something simple too. Something very harmless and in fact, helpful."

"I'm not sure I follow," Vivian said.

"Well, let's consider the fact that we know that Loki can change forms. Bartholomew saw him once as a little girl standing in the grotto. Zeke and Devon saw him as Alicia Edda floating just outside of La Cueva del Diablo, and let's not forget that Zeke and Bart also saw him change into a wolf. He has that shape changer ability."

"So you think that maybe what I saw wasn't Percy, but was in fact Loki trying to lead me, or rather us, away from Surtsey?" Vivian asked.

"Maybe," Marjorie said, once again biting her lower lip. "But for some reason I don't think so. I think that Loki has too much to worry about right now than two useless females who just happen to be traveling to Iceland. No," she continued, "I think it's something else. I think it's a Draugar."

"A what?" Vivian asked. Her body suddenly pushed back in the seat as the plane accelerated and lifted off the ground.

Marjorie turned to look out the window of the ascending aircraft as the landscape of snow, rock, and city began to slowly fade away, turning to cloud and eventually, as they flew higher, to blue sky.

"A Draugar," Marjorie repeated. "It's a representation of the living, but only if that person has died and has never been buried, like Percy, for instance. He drowned. No one ever found his body and so he was never buried. It may be that Percy has become a Draugar: a non-living soul who still has uncompleted business to take care of. Maybe that's why you saw him. Maybe Percy has something important to tell you."

Vivian turned to gaze out her own window, staring at the white clouds below and the blue sky above. "But there was a smell," she said, turning once again to look at Marjorie. "It was an awful odor. Did you smell it?"

"I thought I caught a whiff of something," Marjorie offered. "That's mainly why I didn't just toss your vision off as just a crazy symptom of exhaustion. A Draugar also carries with it an unmistakable stench of decay. They are undead corpses from Norse/Icelandic mythology that appear to retain some semblance of intelligence. However, I'm not saying that what you saw was in fact Percy. It may have been a being that simply looks like Percy, so you'll trust him. That way he can pass on some important piece of information. Something we've missed along the way that will help us get Taylre back."

Vivian turned back to her window and stared at the passing clouds that were intermixed with patches of open water. "That's too bad," she said sadly. "I would give anything to see my husband again."

ℛ

The small island of Surtsey, with its plume of white smoke rising from its still active volcano, came into view on the left side of the aircraft. The pilot glanced back at his two passengers and removed the headphones that covered his ears. "We'll be landing very soon. Please make sure that your seatbelts are buckled. And by the way, the crew on the ground is asking what scientific institute you both come from. They want to make sure before we land."

Vivian glanced quickly at Marjorie as a pale expression returned to her face.

In order to officially set foot on the island of Surtsey, one must be a reputable geologist belonging to an established scientific institute that studies volcanoes. Surtsey is not a tourist destination. Therefore, all visitors must show credentials, proof that they have official business on the island.

"We're from the Nova Scotia Institute of Science," Marjorie lied, spouting her words quite matter-of-factly.

Vivian bowed her head, red shame and embarrassment shaded her usually pale skin. The pilot glanced back once more and surveyed the women a bit closer as if he had some measure of doubt. "Okay, fine. I'll let them know."

In a few moments the aircraft touched down on the rough, rocky runway. Both Marjorie and Vivian gripped the armrests tightly, a combination of uneasiness for the landing and apprehension that they may not be able to convince the other scientists on Surtsey that they really belonged there. Their hope, as Marjorie put it, was completely in the hands of the All Father, Odin.

The airplane taxied up to a small singlewide trailer. When the propeller finally came to an abrupt halt, two men emerged with bodies clad is hooded parkas and thick, knee high boots.

"Well, here goes nothing," Marjorie sighed. She unbuckled the seatbelt and gathered small items that had fallen around her during the short flight.

The pilot opened the door. Onrushes of cold wind whipped into the tiny cabin, prompting the two women to envelope themselves in their down-filled jackets and to tighten fur-lined hoods around their faces.

As they exited the aircraft one of the men approached, his hand extended. "Welcome to Surtsey," he said over the gust of wind and cold. "I'm Tony," he said, "and this is Mike." Pointing to his companion. Both men were stocky, heavily bearded scientists who'd obviously spent a great deal of time on Surtsey. "We'll grab your bags and carry them into the hut. You two just watch your heads and get in there as quick as you can. You don't want to be out in this weather too long."

Vivian and Marjorie scrambled to the trailer, their boots thumping hard on the ice-encrusted stairs that led to the metal door. Marjorie pushed it open, but the wind swung it the rest of the way, slamming it hard against the back wall. Vivian grabbed the door quickly and forced it closed with her shoulder, sealing the room in a quiet calm while the wind outside continued to batter the building with its fierce gusts. Both women turned to look at their new surroundings, noting with immediate displeasure the odd odor that hovered in the stale air and the rather disheveled appearance of the room: books and papers were strewn chaotically on the floor and the sleeping cots. Pushed up on the other side of the room were empty potato chip bags and old discarded tin cans.

Vivian curled her nose in disgust. "I can't believe I'm actually going to say this, but this place looks and smells even worse than Zeke and Devon's rooms."

The door suddenly swung open again, bringing with it blowing flakes of snow, tiny splinters of ice, and Mike and Tony, their arms laden with suitcases.

"We'll just dump these here for now, ladies." Tony dropped Vivian's two suitcases on the floor next to a pile of crumpled up underwear, while Mike propped his burden on one of the cots. "You'll be heading to the other side of the island as soon as the transport gets here. In the meantime, make yourselves comfortable."

Marjorie looked around the trailer, but didn't dare sit down. "I think we're fine standing," she said. "We've been doing a lot of sitting. It feels good to do some standing for a change." She looked at Vivian and winked.

"Can I get you ladies anything to eat?" Tony asked. "There's nothing too fancy here, but you're welcome to whatever we have."

Both Marjorie and Vivian sniffed the air again, wondering what the men's definition of "nothing too fancy" was.

"I think we'll pass on that too," Marjorie said, "although, we're wondering just how long the transport will take to get here and is there going to be any problem getting on?"

"Problem?" Tony asked. "No, there's no problem. In fact, you've both been given some very high praise from your colleague. What was his name?" Tony turned to Mike, leaving his question hanging in the air.

Mike shrugged. "Can't remember," he mumbled. "Doctor somebody. All I know is that he was one of the weirdest guys I've ever met. Never looked you in the eye when he spoke. Almost acted like he was looking right through you. You know, kinda' zombie-like. And," Mike said, bringing his thumb and forefinger up to his nose and pinching it, "he was in desperate need of a bath. The guy stunk real bad. And that's really sayin' something, considering Tony and I can be a little on the messy side, too."

Tony gave Mike a glaring sideways glance. "You'll have to excuse my buddy, ladies. He can be a little harsh at times. We didn't mean to put down your colleague. I'm sure he's a really nice guy."

Marjorie and Vivian eyed each other, confusion evident on both of their faces. "So this colleague of ours, what did he look like?" Marjorie asked.

Tony looked puzzled. "He said he was the team leader at the Nova Scotia Science Institute." Tony said this as if they should absolutely know who he was talking about. "Tall guy with dark hair, kinda' pale skin. He sounded funny when he spoke, too, you know, no inflection in his voice. Like he was talking in monotone. You know the guy I mean?"

"Oh him," Marjorie lied, trying to sound confident. "He's new to the institute...um...you know, it's funny, but I've gone blank on his name too."

Vivian shifted her gaze away from the conversation, her head slightly bowed, her hands wringing together nervously. She knew that if she looked up she would cause the two men to become even more suspicious than they already were. She was never a very good liar. Her hope was that Marjorie could pull off the deception so they could be on their way without any delays. For some reason she couldn't shake the nagging feeling that time was running out. If they didn't leave quickly they would miss the Captain and the chance to save Taylre.

Mike stepped forward holding a bag of stale potato chips. His hands glistened with a clear residue of grease as he dug into the bag to bring out another handful and stuff it in his mouth. "Oh, I remember his name now," he mumbled, as small bits of potato chip fell from his mouth and lodged themselves in his thick beard. "Said his name was Proper. He said he's been over on the north end for quite a while doing seismic research."

Both Marjorie and Vivian stifled a gasp at the mention of the name. Vivian turned away completely, her head swirled; a wave of dizziness settled over her mind.

Marjorie recovered quickly, however, turning and staring at the two men boldly. "Oh, Proper," she said. "Of course, how could I forget? It's just that he has been away so long - you know, doing his research."

Tony stared back, suspicion still evident in his narrowed eyes. "Right. Well, like I say, he seemed to remember you two well enough and he said you were both top-notch researchers. Apparently he's got a hut all set up on the north end. Said he'd wait for you there."

The cold wind continued to pelt the sides of the tiny trailer, but its thrashing noise was soon accompanied by another low grumble.

"That'll be your snowtrack," Tony said, moving to the door and bracing himself for the flourish of wind that would pour in when he opened it. "You ladies ready?" he asked, turning back to Marjorie and Vivian.

The two women nodded, donning their fur-lined hoods while Tony opened the door. Sure enough, the wind rushed in with enough strength that the trailer's occupants were forced to cover their faces as scant protection. When they stepped out into the freezing air the two women looked up to see a large boxy vehicle with a yellow cab and tractor treads.

"This is a snowtrack," Tony called over the howl of wind. "Mike and I will toss your bags in the back. You two climb up the ladder into the cab. Aron is your driver. He'll take you to the north side." Tony motioned toward a steel ladder that was welded to the side of the vehicle. Then he waved a final goodbye. "Best of luck to you, ladies. Something tells me you're going to need it."

ᛦ

It was a bouncing, bone-jolting ride. Aron, the young Icelandic native driving the snowtrack, handled the vehicle confidently, steering it over the rugged terrain with the ease of a seasoned veteran. Marjorie and Vivian both felt like they were riding in the roller coaster from hell as they found themselves clutching the dashboard to keep their balance.

"This place we're going to," Aron shouted over the rumble of the snowtrack engine, "it's not a place I'm familiar with, so you'll have to be patient with me."

Vivian raised her eyebrows with concern. "You mean you don't know where you're going?"

"Well," Aron said, smiling uneasily, "it's not that I don't know where I'm going. I'm just not familiar with this specific location. It's not a place where researchers like you normally go. There are a lot of open vents where steam and sometimes lava comes through. I'm actually surprised to hear that someone's got a station set up there. It can get pretty dangerous if you don't know what you're doing."

Vivian glared wide-eyed at Marjorie, her worried expression turning to outright fear. Marjorie patted Vivian gently on the hand, giving her as confident a smile as she could muster. "Well, no worries there," Marjorie said to Aron. "We're about as experienced as you can get."

The snowtrack continued to plod along the snow and ice covered ground for over an hour. As they traveled, they passed several solidified lava flows, deep crevasses, and shear cliffs that towered above them stretching to the tops of the high mountains that dotted the lonely island. Vivian struggled to relax as her tight grip on the snowtrack's door handles stiffened her already overtaxed muscles. She worried about her boys and where they might be. And she worried about what they would find when they eventually reached the north end of the island. Who, she thought, would be waiting for them? She thought back to the man she saw standing by the airplane. Was it really Percy? Or was her mind just playing tricks on her? And what about the man that Tony and Mike mentioned? How did they know about the name Proper? Was someone playing an elaborately cruel joke on them?

As they continued on the bumpy trek, the vehicle soon rounded a small hillock and they could see from their elevated position the sea crashing on a rocky beach below. About a hundred yards up from the beach, tucked into a protective alcove of rock and ice, stood an ancient box-shaped building constructed entirely of stone and blocks of turf. The earthen roof sloped steeply, mixed with walls made of woven sticks, rocks and mud. A low door, made of what appeared to be old driftwood, barred the entrance. The rest of the building looked as if it were dug just below ground level, perhaps to help it keep out the wind and the cold.

"What in the name of Thor," Aron whistled under his breath. "That building looks like something right out of the time of Eric the Red."

Both Marjorie and Vivian stared in disbelief. "Is this it?" Marjorie asked.

"As far as I know," Aron answered. He pulled the snowtrack around and parked it near the front entrance.

Vivian stared at the oddly constructed door and her mind filled with dread as she tried to imagine who or what might exit the building to greet them. The snowtrack's engine slowed but continued to rumble at a low idle.

"Out ya go, ladies" Aron said. "Best of luck on your research. I hope you keep warm." He looked again at the ancient edifice, trying to imagine why anyone would want to set up scientific research in such a dilapidated building. Marjorie looked at the hovel, too. And like Vivian, wondered who had built it and would they be coming out to greet them. But the door remained closed. It was left up to the two women to climb out of the snowtrack, retrieve their belongings, and watch as Aron drove away, leaving them standing alone in the chilly wind.

Because the building was situated in a sheltered alcove, the women enjoyed a momentary reprieve from the wind, though they continued to feel the intense cold that pierced them both to the core. But the women, although reluctant to do so, inched themselves closer to the hut's door finding that the wind was even more muffled. They stared at the closed entry; an uneasy trepidation filled both of their minds.

"Does this seem familiar to you?" Vivian asked.

Marjorie pulled her eyes away from the driftwood slab and gave Vivian a knowing glance. "You mean standing in front of a door waiting to find out what was going to come through it?" Vivian nodded. "Yes," Marjorie said. "This is far too familiar. Except the door in Sinmora's cabin where Berling came through was much smaller. This one," Marjorie said, returning her frightened gaze back to the door, "is a lot bigger."

Marjorie raised her arm, her hand tightened into a tiny fist. "Well, like I said before, here goes nothing." And then she knocked.

Three times.

✗

Marjorie looked at Vivian and shrugged, her hand raised once more to knock, but there was no need; the door was opening, its worn leather hinges remained mute, as it swung inward.

The hut's interior was dark and smoky. A small fire smoldered in the middle. The women squinted, trying to peer through the darkness, but the room appeared empty. They both stared fearfully at the door, their minds drifting toward the same thought: whoever or whatever opened the door was still standing behind it.

"Hello," Marjorie called. "Is anybody home?"

In answer, the door opened a bit wider. Marjorie took a deep breath and started to enter, but Vivian grabbed her by the arm. "What are you doing?" she whispered sharply.

"I'm going in," she answered boldly, but Vivian could tell there was a healthy amount of fear underneath Marjorie's confident words.

"No," Vivian said. "We don't know what's in there."

Marjorie gazed into the interior once more, her resolve becoming stronger. "That's true," she said. "But if we don't go in then we'll *never* know. We might as well get it over with." She pulled away from Vivian's grasp and entered.

Vivian followed closely with her hand gripped tightly to the back of Marjorie's jacket. They walked slowly through the darkened haze until they reached the center of the hut where a tiny peat fire burned warm and bright.

The door closed behind them.

The room was suddenly cloaked in blackness, except for the yellow flicker from the fire. And, there was a smell.

The odor of decay.

The stench of rotting flesh combined with the scent of stagnant seawater and seaweed that had been left to dry and putrefy in the hot sun filled the smoky hut.

"I knew you would come," a voice said from behind them. "Ganglati, the slow caretaker of Hel, said you wouldn't. But I just knew you would."

Both women spun around quickly as gasps of surprise caught in their throats. Finally, Vivian found her voice and took a step forward, her eyes wide with recognition. "Percy!" she said, extending her arms in a hopeful embrace.

"No!" the voice shouted, suddenly backing away, his body melding into the darkened corner. "You cannot touch me. It is not permitted."

"But I..." Vivian stopped while her arms dropped limply to her sides and her head recoiled from the powerful odor.

"Please," the voice begged. "I have so very little time and what I have to say is of great importance."

Marjorie reached out, grabbed Vivian by the shoulder, and pulled her back, away from the terrible odor, and away from the voice whose appearance and expression seemed to be that of Percy Proper.

"It's a Draugar," Marjorie whispered. "This is not Percy."

"But he's..." Vivian began, but Marjorie squeezed her arm.

"Do not be fooled by this apparition," Marjorie said. Her eyes never left the dark figure that continued to crouch in the corner. "He seeks to gain your confidence by his familiar appearance. But know this: he is not your husband."

Vivian squinted into the darkness, catching only brief glimpses of the pale, stinking shape. "Can we trust him?" Vivian asked. Her head turned slightly toward Marjorie, but her eyes never left the specter.

Marjorie hesitated as she tried to remember what she had once read and heard about Draugars. "I don't know," she finally said. "Let's see what he has to say."

The wraith stepped farther into the light, a small flicker of flame projecting a sickly yellow hue on his cheek and forehead.

"You must tell him this," the specter announced. "Shaker has made herself very clear, and yet he wastes his time on his own selfish needs. He must prepare!" The apparition began shouting, yet his arms and hands remained stiff by his side. "A great battle is at hand. If he does not prepare, all may be lost. Tell him! Tell him!"

Frightened by the shouting, the two women backed away fearing that the apparition's tone of voice would become physical. Marjorie pushed Vivian behind her, as if her physical presence could somehow protect her from the Draugar. "Who is *he*?" she shouted. "Is it Zeke you're referring too?"

The Draugar slowly retreated into the darkness, his stiff arm slowly rising as he slunk into the black corner, his finger pointing accusingly. "Tell him," he repeated.

And then he was gone, as if a mantle of anonymity had been released and the air suddenly filled with the residue of forgetfulness.

The two women held each other in a fearful embrace, looking on with astonished gazes at the place where the apparition once stood, their mouths agape.

"What do we do?" Vivian finally managed to ask.

"We find a way to warn Zeke," Marjorie answered.

Chapter Twenty-Two
Roots and Corpses

"We must step through the Seam here!" Sinmora said. Her stern finger pointed at the ground below her feet. "Since the time we left Midgard until now we have been wandering the Mist. But now we enter a new world, the world of Niflheim. The land of limbs and branches are over," she proclaimed. "Prepare yourself for the realm of the dead." She turned to look back over her shoulder and expected to see an enraptured audience of eager young minds glued to her every word. Disappointed, she saw instead the still waking faces of her fellow travelers.

Zeke sat behind Devon who was sandwiched between him and Vidar on the firm back of Alsvid. The mare walked slowly behind Sinmora who led her along the uneven path. Its halter swung with each step and her hooves clomped nosily on the stones.

The boys stirred unsteadily on the back of the mare, but their minds still swirled with unfinished dreams and their bodies still shook from the cold of the mountain pass. Zeke's head leaned hard against Devon's back as a fine line of drool coursed down the middle of his ski jacket. Zeke grunted and snorted a final time, his thoughts mixed with macabre visions of rivers overflowing with demons and dinner plates of elaborately dressed meals infested with squiggling maggots, when Devon shuffled quickly to one side. Zeke's snort seemed to soak in to his left ear with the dampness of a wet-willy.

"Get off me, ya freak," Devon hollered. He jerked his shoulder violently while Zeke, still struggling to wake up, found himself slipping off the back of Alsvid and landing with a solid thump on the stone-pocked path.

Zeke struck the ground hard. His right shoulder took the brunt of the impact. His eyes flew open wide as he looked about him trying to figure where exactly he had landed and why he was there. Sinmora rushed to his side. Her hands reached gently under his arms as she lifted him to his feet.

"What just happened?" he said, wincing with pain.

"Just a tiny accident," Sinmora said. She glanced up angrily at Devon.

Zeke followed Sinmora's gaze and saw Devon's cheesy grin appear on his face. Zeke scowled in response, but could say nothing; he still wasn't sure how he'd gotten to the ground.

Sinmora waved at the boys still sitting on the horse. "Come down, lads. This is something you must see."

As Vidar and Devon slowly dismounted, Zeke followed closely behind Sinmora to the border of a turbulent stream. "See here," Sinmora said, her hand sweeping the water's edge like a model on the Price is Right. "Where does the water go? Can you tell?"

The boys all reached the river's bank and their eyes scanned the water's movement as it meandered roughly over rocks and boulders, around tight corners, and through tight fissures to finally flow into...nothing.

Zeke looked up at Sinmora, his face a mixture of confusion and bewilderment. "Where did it go?" he asked. "It's as if the air just sucked it up and took it away."

"Aye," answered Sinmora. "But if ya'd been listening instead of sleepin' ya might have heard what I said before. Tis' the Seam, lads." She smiled knowingly as each boy looked at her in confusion. "We've reached the end. Don't ya see? When we step through here we'll be in Niflheim. No longer will we wander the limbs and roots of Yggdrasil."

"But Niflheim," Vidar said. His voice shook with fear. "It's the land of the dead. The land ruled over by Hel. My father has spoken of this place. It is not a place we want to voluntarily walk into."

"No. Tis' quite true, lad," Sinmora answered. "But it's a place where we'll find answers. And besides," she said, glancing sideways at Zeke, "there are messages that must be delivered if we're to continue safely on our journey."

ᛉ

The travelers continued to walk a narrow path of dirt and gravel after crossing the Seam into Niflheim, but to Zeke the crossing seemed too easy. He kept looking back at the tiny stream that seemed to flow out of nowhere into the now barren wasteland. He sidled up to Sinmora and left Devon and Vidar to continue their ridiculous conversation on who would win a battle of strength: Superman or Thor.

"That was too simple," Zeke said, his feet now matching stride for stride with the robust and healthy figure of Sinmora. His right arm continued to grasp the Staff of Urd.

"What was, lad?" she said, her hand still holding Alsvid's reins.

"Slipping through the Seam. Usually I feel like throwing up when I've passed through. And normally, I really have to think about it. But this time getting through was so easy. Why is that?"

Sinmora shrugged. "You're growing stronger, perhaps. Your body is becoming used to the transformation."

Zeke sighed heavily. "But why don't I feel stronger? I mean, look at me. I can't walk without this staff and sometimes the pain is so bad I want to pass out. But you, you seem to be getting stronger by the minute. When we first saw you in that cabin you could barely get yourself up the steps. But now we can barely keep up with you."

Sinmora nodded slowly, her expression sad with understanding. "Aye. But know this: my weaknesses are the afflictions of Midgard. A life lived in the shadow of forests and mountains that surrounded Alder Cove. Your afflictions, Zeke Proper, were the wounds inflicted by the shadow of darkness in the realm of the Mist. There's a big difference."

Zeke considered Sinmora's words as the soft sound of their footsteps on the dry ground marred the silence. Devon and Vidar's conversation still muttered behind them, but the new subject of their discussion was lost in the musing of thought and careful observation.

Above them the sky seemed to radiate a perpetual evening that was gently turning into a dark night. Gray clouds hovered in the lofty distance, their edges making up what appeared to be the ceiling of a vast cavern. Scattered among the well-trodden path were pale weeds that struggled to grow amid the faint stench of death and decay. Nevertheless, the new world the travelers had entered appeared empty of any inhabitants. There was no one to stop them from progressing along the path, no one to question why they had chosen to enter this new, bleak existence.

"Can you detect the odor of death, Zeke Proper?" Sinmora asked, her eyes remaining fixed on the path in front of her.

Zeke sniffed the air and once again the acrid odor of decay met his nostrils. "Yes. It reminds me of a lingering autumn. One that never seems to meet the winter snow, but is always plagued by rain and rotting fallen leaves."

"Well said, lad. Perhaps we'll make a seer out of you yet." Sinmora smiled, but she walked on, confident in her steps. "What you sense is the decaying roots of Yggdrasil, the tree of the universe."

"The Mist?" Zeke asked.

"Aye," Sinmora answered. "'Tis' one and the same." She took her eyes off the road for a brief moment and eyed Zeke. "You see, the eagle that procured your promise to deliver her message was not completely truthful. She did not really explain to you who Nidhogg really was. Or, perhaps, she just assumed you knew. Nevertheless, you must know that the recipient of your message is a powerful force to be reckoned with. I fear your task will be much harder than you think." Sinmora glanced once again at Zeke. "What did you think Nidhogg was, Zeke?"

"Just some guy," he said, shrugging his shoulders. "I was thinking he was probably like Geirrod. Some big ugly giant who needed a lesson taught to him." Zeke gripped the Staff of Urd in both hands and swung it around his head once for effect.

Sinmora snorted with laughter. "Then you truly have been deceived, Zeke Proper. Soon we will pass by the axis of the nine worlds where the roots of Yggdrasil originates. The great ash soars from here, fanning over gods, men, and dwarves. Here there is one great root dug deep into Niflheim and under that root the spring Hvergelmir. The waters of this spring seethe and growl like water in a boiling cauldron. It is there that you will find the dragon Nidhogg." She stopped her walking for one brief moment and looked directly at Zeke.

Halting abruptly in his limping steps, Zeke looked at Sinmora, his expression dazed with thought as he considered the word "dragon". Suddenly, his eyes filled with understanding, like a man waking from a pleasant dream to a real nightmare.

"Wait a minute," he said, his mind swirling with thoughts. "Are you saying that Nidhogg the dragon is really a *dragon?* Not just a nickname given to some big dude?"

Sinmora nodded slowly as sadness filled her eyes. "That's right, Zeke. Hraesvelg the Eagle has sent you to deliver her scathing message to a real dragon."

Zeke's jaw dropped open. He was suddenly at a loss for words.

Sinmora watched Zeke's expression change from confidence to hopeless uncertainty. "Fear not, Zeke. I will stand by your side. But know this: your quest to become a true warrior must continue with this task. The more I think about it, the more I believe the gods have guided fate in this undertaking."

The path they were on began to descend, its course taking on a rougher, rockier landscape, the air about them becoming thicker with dread. Zeke leaned on the staff, as if the weight of the oncoming task had grown too burdensome, the staff being the only thing that helped him remain upright. After crossing over several switchbacks the travelers found that the ground was becoming steeper and steeper with each step. Zeke, who was struggling to walk, finally gave expression to his dark thoughts. "I don't think I can do this. Battling a giant is one thing, but taking on a dragon...well, that's something completely different."

Sinmora nodded knowingly. "I understand. I really do. I've had to pass through many tests as well. But there's strength in you, Zeke. Something that is beyond my comprehension that leads me to believe you will prevail. It will not be easy, that is true. But the gods need you. For what, I don't know. But you must prepare."

Zeke shook his head. "What have I been thinking?" he said quietly. "I should be home sleeping in my nice soft bed. I should be in school, thinking about college, and running on the cross-country team. What am I doing here?" He looked at Sinmora imploringly as his leg began to take on a throbbing ache.

"Perhaps a quick lesson on 'knowing thine enemy' might help," she said, resuming her plodding steps down the trail. "Down there," she said, pointing into the darkness of the dissolving path, "the dragon Nidhogg is tossed the corpses of the most evil inhabitants of the nine worlds. He rips them apart with his jagged teeth and sharpens his scales on their decaying bones. But Nidhogg is not content with the meager supply of corpses to chew upon. To satisfy his never ending hunger he gnaws at the root of Yggdrasil itself, trying to loosen what is firm and put an end to the eternal."

Zeke stumbled on a loose rock, righting himself quickly but painfully with the help of the staff. "It almost sounds like the dragon has some kind of purpose in his hunger," Zeke said, resuming his awkward gait down the slope.

"Aye, Zeke, a clever observation. Nidhogg is without a doubt a servant of Loki. His allegiance is to the darkness and the eventual overthrow of the gods of Asgard. This is why I believe the gods are guiding your fate. Perhaps they see no other way to stop the dragon except by you."

Zeke shook his head. "You are giving me way too much credit, Sinmora. And I'm afraid you're expecting too much of me. Passing on a nasty message from an eagle is one thing, but stopping a dragon from destroying Yggdrasil...well, let's just say that might be a task for someone who's a real warrior. Not a pretender like myself."

Sinmora said nothing as she continued to navigate her way down the steep path. Beside her Zeke tried to keep pace. His breathing came in bursts of exhaustion. Alsvid followed closely. Her hooves stepped carefully over the uneven path, avoiding the sharp stones that would otherwise cause her to stumble. Behind Alsvid, Vidar and Devon plodded along, but their conversation became hushed as darkness settled over the travelers.

The uneven descent soon flattened to a smooth trail, much like the path they had first trodden on when they entered the Mist from Sinmora's cabin and the realm of Midgard. Zeke was feeling an immense pain return to his leg. He had been given very little time to rest but had also refused to complain; he didn't want Sinmora, or anyone else to think any less of him. Confessing weakness and the inability to handle the task of delivering the eagle's message had placed a bleak mood over the company. When Zeke openly declared his lack of faith in himself Vidar and Devon had quickly stopped their conversation. The look of disappointment he received from the two boys made Zeke feel like an angry parent had just scolded him. The look that Devon gave him was especially unsettling.

Devon's eyes seemed to exude a kind of regret, one that reminded him that the task they were on was not really about them at all, but about Taylre.

Leaning hard on the staff, Zeke finally stopped. "I've got to rest," he said, his breath coming in short spurts of suppressed pain. He dropped the staff along the side of the path and sat down heavily. His head dropped slowly between his legs.

"Is it the pain, lad? Shall I make up more tea?" Sinmora knelt beside Zeke, her hand already reaching for the pouch she carried on her hip.

"No," Zeke said, waving her off as if she were an annoying gnat. "I've made a decision." He raised his head slowly as the tiny group huddled around him, their looks of disappointment were still evident, but they were shaded with concern.

"I've decided to do it," he said breathlessly, staring up at the three sets of eyes gazing back at him, expecting some kind of reaction. A clap on the back perhaps, a small cheer of excitement, or maybe even a light pat on the head. Anything.

Devon leaned in close, his mouth almost touching Zeke's ear, and whispered, although everyone could easily hear. "You're really selfish, you know that?"

Zeke reared back, heedless now of the pain throbbing in his thigh. "Wha..." he began to say, but Devon quickly cut him off. His small hand grabbed him around the collar.

"We've all suffered, Zeke, everyone of us. We're hungry. We're tired. We're sore..." Zeke gaped up at Devon with a confused, ironic stare. Devon gripped his collar harder, shaking it. "That's right. We're sore. Maybe not as much as you, but none of us is particularly comfortable. Why, I've got a blister the size of a grapefruit on the back of my ankle, and don't even get me started on the chafing. I can't even begin to tell you how much my butt itches. So yeah, we're all feeling it! But do ya hear us complaining? Do ya hear us going on and on about how terrible everything is? How hard the ground is or how thirsty we are? No! We don't because it is what it is. We don't because we're here for Taylre, not because this is some sort of vacation gone wrong. So get over yourself! Start putting other's needs first instead of your own selfish problems! We're here for a reason, Zeke. Haven't you figured that out yet? This isn't about you. It's about getting Taylre and whatever else the fates or the gods or whoever they are have planned for us." Devon held Zeke's collar a moment longer, his eyes boring imaginary holes into Zeke's head. Finally, Devon let go, but not before he added a slight shove that pushed Zeke off balance, forcing him to lean on his elbow.

The tiny group continued to stare down at Zeke with a kind of loathing, as if they were all in agreement with Devon's sudden reproach.

Silence stretched into a long, awkward period of reflection. Devon, Sinmora, and Vidar retreated to the opposite side of the path, leaving Zeke alone with his thoughts as tears of frustration and regret etched small paths down his dirty face. Finally, after a heavy darkness settled over the barren land, Zeke wiped his face with the coarse sleeve of his jacket and smeared the drying tears across his cheeks.

"Have I..." he stuttered. "Have I really been that bad? Do I really complain that much? Am I really that selfish?"

Devon rose slowly from his failed attempt to nap in the chilly night air. He squinted at Zeke, his one eye shut while the other peered at him angrily, but then softened. His gaze reflected the kindness and maturity that Devon had managed to develop at such a young age. "You're no worse than the rest of us, Zeke. And I'm sorry that I was so mean awhile back. I didn't mean it."

"No," Zeke said. He pulled the staff in close and used its strength to stand. "You were right. I've had time to think. And you were right. I was being selfish, but not anymore. It's time to get things moving. I've been spending so much time thinking about my own woes that I completely forgot the real reason behind this journey: Taylre." Zeke bent and picked up some bits of discarded clothing and then looked up at his fellow travelers, his gaze directed specifically at Sinmora.

"We have work to do," he said, his voice taking on a power that to Zeke felt both strange and exhilarating. "Tell me what needs to happen, and then let's get a move on."

ᛧ

A gloomy night was descending and the once uninhabited land began to take on life. Shadows began dancing amid shadow, while howls of pain and anguish echoed like the death throes of the terribly departed. Sinmora reached into her pouch and retrieved a tiny torch, its miniature flickering flame casting light only a few feet ahead of the small troupe. They scampered among the rocks, tripping and stubbing their toes while yanking their clothing away from small scrub brush that almost seemed to reach out and clasp on, dragging at their shirts and pants with desperate claws. The travelers held to one another like frightened children. Zeke was surprised to find that even Sinmora, her hands shaking with fear or cold, held to the back of his jacket with a vice-like grip.

"Zeke," she whispered, her mouth so close her lips brushed the edges of his earlobe. "The place we seek is near, I can feel it in my bones. Remember the things I've told you. Repeat them word for word or Nidhogg will remain in his cave. He has lived much longer than any of us, to be sure. He knows the ways of the sly One, for he himself practices the dark arts. Nidhogg cannot be deceived. But he will answer your call. He must, for he is compelled by ancient magic to do so. But you must repeat the words exactly as I have explained."

Zeke nodded his head quickly, the movement abrupt, almost curt; his resolve had grown strong.

The group soon rounded a scattering of large boulders, the tiny light from the torch exposing a path littered with dried, withered bones. As they pressed forward the glow illuminated an immense cliff face, its surface marred by the jaw-like opening of a huge cavern. The tiny group stopped but Sinmora pushed Zeke ahead. "Go on, now," she urged.

Zeke stumbled, but not before he turned and caught Devon's cautious, fearful gaze. For a brief moment their eyes met. In Devon's eyes Zeke could see the face of his mother. And like Devon, she was crying, and there was, in just that brief glance, the feeling of unconditional love. The real meaning of family and hope radiated from Devon like the bright noonday sun, its warmth gripping and comforting. Zeke held on to it. His mind wrapped around it for strength and courage. For though he tried hard to show his strength in action, the truth was, he was weak and his fear was colossal.

Nidhogg was asleep. He was snoring in his cave, and it wasn't a pleasant sound. Zeke shuffled up to the cave entrance, his hand gripped tightly to the Staff of Urd. The fear began to burn him. The darkness reached up to him as he drew nearer the place as dreadful as the worst of fears, the worst of dreams.

"Nidhogg!" he called. His voice faltered slightly as he spoke. "Nidhogg! Wake! Wake, wise serpent of Niflheim!"

There was a stirring from within the shadows of the cave. Movement. Plodding. The shuffling of great-clawed feet.

Zeke looked back at Sinmora, but she twirled her hand rapidly in front of her, urging him to continue.

"Listen," he continued, his quivering frame turning back to the black opening. "Who can hear the sound of the grass growing? The sound of wool on a sheep's back growing? Who needs less sleep than a bird? Who is so eagle-eyed that, by day and by night, he can see the least movement a hundred leagues away?

"Nidhogg! Nidhogg! Nidhogg!"

And then the beast, the dragon, the devourer of dead corpses and the destroyer of the great ash Yggdrasil, stepped into the small, flickering light of the torch. His yellow eyes reflected its weak light.

"Who calls me from my sleep and bids me speak?" the dragon hissed.

Zeke stepped back. He couldn't help it. His knees began to buckle, but he held firm, his mind reflecting on Devon, his mom, his dad, but most especially, Taylre.

"I am Zeke Proper," he announced. "I am the slayer of the Korrigan, wielder of the stones, wanderer of the Mist, and bearer of the Staff of Urd."

This last part seemed to impress the dragon the most. His eyebrow rose, and the scales on his forehead glistened in the flickering firelight of the torch. Nidhogg tilted his head slightly to one side. "Slayer of the Korrigan are you," the dragon nodded his head slowly, his voice bending the air like thunder. "I have heard whispers of this on the wind," he breathed. "But the bearer of the Staff of Urd as well? Now that is a matter to be considered."

Nidhogg shuffled his huge body to one side. His tail brushed the rocks at the cave's entrance knocking down small boulders that littered the ground amid the dispersion of bones and partially consumed body parts. The dragon appeared to be thinking, his mind trying to work out the reason for this unusual visit. Finally, he turned back to Zeke, his rows of sharpened teeth protruding from his uneven jaw. "Why have you disturbed me, Zeke Proper, Slayer of the Korrigan? Why have you come here?"

"To deliver a message," Zeke stuttered. "A message from the great eagle Hraesvelg, she who sits upon the great ash and surveys the whole world."

Nidhogg laughed, a great snort that sent a cascade of green snot and saliva sputtering through the air. "That great feather-brained fool has sent you?" Nidhogg said. "And what, pray tell, has the winged idiot sent you to say?"

Zeke leaned heavily on the staff and pushed himself to stand a little taller. "You," he stammered, "are nothing but a dog in cheap armor and you must stop tearing away the roots of Yggdrasil." Zeke let go of his breath, something he felt he'd been holding the entire time he'd been standing in front of the cave. He glanced back at Sinmora and smiled; the task was complete.

"What did you just say to me? You tiny, insignificant son of Midgard." Zeke could feel Nidhogg's hot breath scraping his face.

He looked up reluctantly into the dragon's eyes. "I...I," is all Zeke could manage. His fear crested over and turned into complete terror.

"That's what I thought," Nidhogg muttered. "You're just a trivial messenger. You're no slayer. You're no warrior. Why should I listen to you? Perhaps I should just eat you and get it over with. I have a nap to attend to."

Again, Zeke tried to speak, but the sound caught in his throat. All that escaped was a kind of gurgle.

Sinmora quickly stepped forward, her hands held out defensively in front of her. "Nidhogg, hear me. I am Sinmora, apprentice to the great mother. He who stands before you holds the staff of Urd. No harm must come to him. The ancient magic dictates it."

The dragon shifted and slanted his head to one side, his yellow eyes glaring. "Sinmora," Nidhogg muttered. "Why does that name sound so familiar?" And then it came to him. He smiled, though to Zeke, who was standing beneath the great beast, the smile looked more like a hateful sneer with a growl to accompany it. "You are the slayer of the giant Hrungnir." Then the dragon laughed, his huge scaled head and neck bending with each chuckle. "Oh, how I despised that giant boor. Why, you did us all a favor when you rid the world of that ogre. Well done, Sinmora. Well done!" The dragon sat back on its haunches, his manner more relaxed, his gravelly laugh still echoing off the walls of the cliff face.

"You're brave," the dragon finally said. "Both of you. And I give you credit, Zeke Proper. You had the courage to call me from my cave. Not many have lived to tell a tale like that. Nevertheless, your message from the eagle is that I stop chewing upon the tree, a bold request indeed. But know this: I will not stop until my coffers have been filled. I want gold, Zeke Proper! If you can't fulfill that request then I will not listen to your message. Tell that to Hraesvelg, if you dare. My guess is that she won't be as gentle as I have been."

Zeke and Sinmora exchanged glances. Sinmora's expression was filled with hope, but Zeke had doubt strewn across his features.

After gaining Nidhogg's permission to talk in private, Sinmora led Zeke toward a tiny alcove beneath a tall rock overhang. Devon and Vidar huddled in close too, their minds befuddled with the thought of how one might outwit a dragon.

"Listen to me," Sinmora held Zeke stiffly by the collar, her eyes boring small holes of will and determination into his own. "We must comply with the will of this beast, else we won't be permitted to pass into the next leg of our journey."

"Comply?" Zeke said. "You mean do what Nidhogg wants? How can we do that? We have no gold."

"'Tis true," Sinmora answered. "But I know who has. If you are strong and if you are determined with will and strength, then you can get it. But it will require harshness, a quality that I have not witnessed in you yet. You are soft and too gentle at times, a trait that can often destroy a warrior. Can you be harsh, Zeke Proper?"

"Harsh?" Zeke questioned. "I guess. I mean if it will help Taylre, then, yeah, I can be harsh." He looked at Devon who gave Zeke a knowing and confident nod.

"Good," Sinmora said. "Because nothing else will do. In order to get the gold Nidhogg requires, you must be demanding. Andvari will not give it up willingly. You *must* demand it."

"Andvari?" Zeke said. "Please don't tell me this is another dragon. I don't think I could handle that."

"No dragon, Zeke. He's a dwarf, but a tricky one. Very tricky." Sinmora made ready to stand, but then turned suddenly, once more taking Zeke by the collar. "And one more thing," she said, her hand releasing its tight grip to rest gently on his shoulder. "Can you fish?"

Chapter Twenty-Three
Down the Rabbit Hole

Naglfar appeared to be limping. Its broken rear mast, jagged and snapped in the middle, dragged behind in the open sea while giants and dwarfs with makeshift oars tried to manipulate the floundering vessel through the cold green water. Most of the crew, those who could still walk, were battered and bruised, many of them covered in blood-soaked bandages. They were sullen and downcast; their visages mirrored the tattered remains of *Naglfar* after the long battle with the serpent Hafgufa. Nevertheless, the Isle of Surtsey was finally in sight, and the vision of land on the horizon at least gave the crew hope as they dragged their weary, battle-worn bodies to their posts, heaving the ropes and raising the sails on what was left of the main masts.

Loki stood at the helm, his back straight, his eyes fixed on the horizon watching the procession of men moving to and fro. To his left was Teddy, and to his right stood Fenrir. Just below, standing near the starboard rail, was the giant, Surt, his voice ringing out with orders to the crew, his right hand pointed his smith's hammer while his left swung a broadsword.

Taylre was hiding. She crouched low beneath a set of nail-covered steps, holding her knees in close and shivering. She'd seen enough of death and violence. All she wanted to do now was to go home, crawl into a nice hot bath, and then later, with a mug of hot chocolate gripped firmly against her palms, slip underneath a thick down blanket and sleep forever. But that wish was left unfulfilled as the call of "land!" tore open her silent reverie and brought her suddenly back to the present.

She stretched her aching legs out slowly and reached toward the lowest step, lifting herself to her unsteady feet with a heavy sigh. She began making her way to the port side when she felt the presence of Teddy; his loathsome, ever-present stare melting looks of hate and malice into her thoughts. Taylre turned around and sure enough, there he was, his arms crossed, his heavy, muscled frame standing firmly on the quarterdeck beside Mr. Loden. And he *was* staring at her, just as she suspected he would be. She tried her best to ignore his gaze as her head turned slowly toward the open sea.

The green-blue ocean stretched out in front of Taylre like a great empty desert, while a pale light fought hard to penetrate the cloud covered sky, its reflection spilling across the dune-like waves with a promise of hope. Taylre smiled in spite of the glaring look she'd just received from Teddy. In her heart she felt that beyond that horizon, not very far from where they were right now, her friends were waiting for her. Waiting for her with a tender kiss and a warm embrace. But as she looked across the sea, all she saw was water, water, and more water.

"Look there, Taylre." The voice was right next to her ear. She jumped with fright while her hands gripped the railing and her knuckles and face turned a pale white.

Taylre whirled around quickly, her face coming within inches of Mr. Loden's. She let out a grunt of surprise, her feet searching for a place to step back, but she was trapped between Loden and the railing.

Looking at Taylre's ashen features and sudden expression of fear, Loden laughed: raspy, deep-throated, and raucous. "I've done it again, haven't I?" Loden proclaimed. "How I will ever manage to walk up without scaring the wits out of you, I'll never know." And then he laughed some more.

"What I mean," Loden continued, his hand wiping tears of mirth from his cheeks, "is that if you look in that direction you'll see land."

Taylre followed Loden's pointing finger. Her eyes squinted as her gaze centered on the distant horizon. At first she saw nothing, just more water. And then suddenly, like a photograph suddenly coming into focus, it was there, like an oasis of green in a vast land of sand and dunes. A shadow, rising up beyond the waves, a billow of smoke rising from a crooked peak like the gentle curve of a finger.

"I see it," she whispered. She took a deep breath as the smell of wind and sea filled her senses and cleared her mind. "Are my friends there?" she asked, her face turning to look at Loden hopefully.

"Indeed they are, Taylre," Loden said. He patted her gently on the shoulder. "They are there and when you see them you'll be sure to warn them, won't you?"

Taylre turned back to the open sea, the wind lifting her limp hair and tossing its red curls into her face. "I will," she proclaimed. "I will warn them. I would never want them to get hurt."

ჯ

The *Skipper Jack* did indeed sail heavy. Its broad hull dragged itself through the water like an old woman walking up hill. But the Captain managed to keep the sails taut as the thick canvas caught every inch of wind and turned it into motion and power.

"Well done, ya big sluggard." Berling pulled hard on the limp halyard, tightening the sails and allowing the ship to tilt swiftly to the port side, its thick hull lifting off the starboard drag, giving the *Skipper Jack* a chance to ride the steady current and cut easily through the cold water. "We're makin' good time and keeping ahead of the storms. We'll be in sight of Surtsey before ya know it. Well ahead of time."

"Aye," the Captain mumbled. "The gods have been good to us, that's for sure." His thick hand gripped the tiller tightly, easing the vibrations of the boat with practiced expertise.

Erna stumbled her way up the short steps to the deck. She handed the Captain a fresh cup of hot black coffee and then steadied herself on the boom, reaching a second cup over to Berling. His tiny hands grasped the warm mug eagerly. He drew the cup in closely and took a brisk sniff of the golden aroma.

"Ah," he moaned. "Ya know how ta treat a man, that's for sure, lassie."

Erna chuckled to herself, proud of her accomplishments on board the ship and proud to know that the once fierce rivals were now great friends. It was a miracle that could only have happened through adversity.

Calmly she turned her face to the wind and let the breeze brush through her hair while it pushed away the auburn curls that framed her pretty face. With her eyes closed and a brief smile crossing her thin lips, Erna thought about Zeke and the warm, nervous touch of his hand. She thought about his soft blue eyes; the way they looked at her with innocence and longing. And then she wondered, her heart anxious with worry, if he was safe and if he had managed to find Taylre.

Suddenly, her eyes sprang open. She looked up, her attention drawn by a flash of white.

"Land!" she shouted. "Surtsey. On the horizon!" Her arm was extended and her finger pointed steadily toward the north.

In the distance, beyond a bank of white clouds that skirted the ocean's green horizon, stood a stalwart peak, its summit venting puffs of gray smoke that curled gently into the blue sky, its tail fading into the dark purple of the ozone. The Captain, who kept flicking his finger on the glass covering the speed indicator, looked up with surprise.

"It can't be," he remarked. "Have we really traveled that far already?"

Berling, who had just completed tying a figure eight of nylon rope around the tip of a metal cleat, looked up at the sound of Erna's shout.

"Great tales of Snorri!" he shouted. His hands grasped the boom tightly to keep himself from falling once again into the sea. "Can it be that we've really reached the end so quickly?"

The Captain locked the wheel in place and lumbered up on deck, his gait unsteady as he joined Berling and Erna. Their hands were pressed to their foreheads to shade the blinding glare of the sun that reflected off the sea into their upturned faces.

"That's really it, isn't it?" Erna said. Her awestruck stare glared into the distance.

"Aye," Berling said. "'Tis, indeed."

ᛣ

With the *Skipper Jack* safely anchored off the rugged coastline, the three sailors endured an arduous journey through mountainous waves and gale-like winds to finally reach the icy, pebble-streaked beach of Surtsey Island. *Ol' Nellie,* the Captain's trusty row boat, plodded through the cold water like a stubborn mule while the Captain's muscles strained with each pull on the oars, his eyes fixed on the outboard motor that hung uselessly from the stern.

When they finally reached the sand, the Captain stepped hesitantly into the waist deep water to pull the boat securely onto shore, his feet and legs numbing quickly as the icy water filled his boots and penetrated the thin layer of material that covered his skin.

Waiting on shore, their bodies covered in heavy furs and blankets, stood Marjorie and Vivian. With frozen faces, they smiled weakly, but inside they both felt an abundance of joy at seeing the fulfillment of a grueling voyage that had finally come to an end.

"Ahoy!" the Captain hollered. His left arm waved wildly while his right continued to tug on the rope connected to *Ol' Nellie.*

"We're here!" he continued. "Njord has seen us through!" The Captain's grin was wide. It showed his tobacco-stained teeth but reflected joy in his bright blue eyes. He trudged up the wet sand giving *Ol' Nellie* one last pull as the gravel and sand crunched around the hull.

Berling and Erna leapt off the side, their feet barely touching the cold water as they both ran up the beach. Erna reached the two women first. She wrapped her arms around them in a tight embrace. Berling stood back near the misty surf, a tight grin bending his features.

"Top o' the morning to ya, ladies," Berling said. His fingers brushed his forehead with a curt salute.

Vivian held out her arms, beckoning Berling forward. "C'mer, little man. You're going to have to endure at least one hug."

Berling stepped up reluctantly, his head bowed, but the smile never left his face. He let Vivian hug him, feigning disgust, but feeling the warmth of true love, nevertheless.

The Captain secured the soggy line between two hefty rocks and then strolled amiably toward his waiting friends. He gathered them all in a giant group hug while his beefy arms wrapped each of them in a welcome embrace.

"We're safe, ladies. Safe and glad ta see ya." His embrace tightened until Marjorie grunted, her lungs squeezing out the last of their air.

"Enough, Bart," Marjorie said. "A warm welcome is fine, but death by hugs is not the way I wanted my life to end."

The Captain grudgingly backed away, abashed that he'd been so enthusiastic in his greeting, but nevertheless warmed by the sight of his old friends.

Suddenly, Vivian grabbed him by the shoulder, spinning him around; her eyes cast beyond the *Skipper Jack,* as a look of terror filled her expression. "Look!" she said.

Bartholomew turned slowly, almost as if he feared what he might see. His eyes followed the length of Vivian's outstretched arm. He gazed over the rough seas and saw the broken masts of *Naglfar*, its dragonhead bowsprit limping between cloud and mist.

The Captain turned back quickly. "Hide!" he yelled. "Quickly, there must be some place we can hide."

Marjorie, who was now looking past the Captain and seeing the dreadful sight of the oncoming ship, hesitated. One part of her shook with alarm at the sight of the ship, but another part of her wanted to race to it, to find Taylre and rescue her. Thankfully the logical side of Marjorie took over.

She grabbed the Captain by the arm. "This way," she beckoned. "There's a small, well concealed hut we can hide in. But we have to hurry."

In spite of Marjorie's cry the tiny group continued to stand on the wet sand, their minds filled with the compelling urge to stay and watch the approaching ship; their thoughts were mesmerized by it legend, its myth, and the dreadful threat of its existence. All except Berling who understood the Mist, who had seen the beauty of other worlds amid the branches of Yggdrasil, and who understood the consequences of magic both black and white.

"Move!" he hollered. "There's no sense gawkin'. Get a move on!"

Pulled from their spell, the small assembly reluctantly turned and followed Marjorie and Vivian up the short ascent of sand and gravel into the hidden alcove where the ancient hut stood. Its interior still carried the odor of the Draugar, but the smoke of the peat fire seemed to overwhelm it all. Marjorie pushed the leather-hinged door open with a flourish while everyone filed past her into the darkened cabin.

The last to enter was Berling. His tiny legs fought to keep up with the others. He stopped in front of Marjorie. "I should keep a look out," he admonished. "Perhaps find a place to hide in the rocks and see where they land."

Marjorie considered the idea then looked imploringly at the Captain.

"Do it," the Captain said. Then added, "But be careful, my friend."

Berling glanced back at the Captain and quickly nodded his head. "You know I will. Hundreds of years hiding among the branches have taught me this, at least." He ran out into the gray light. His small feet crunched lightly beneath him as he disappeared amid the rocks and fog.

Marjorie closed the door and leaned against it. Her back pressed up heavily to its wooden frame.

"What do we do now?" Vivian asked, looking through the smoky air.

"We wait," Marjorie said. "We wait and try to be patient just like we've always been."

ᛪ

Berling watched as *Naglfar* battled between Midgard and Mist. At times the ship would flounder in the turbulent waves, at other times it would rise above them, gently gliding over the thrash of water and wind. When it did labor among the waves, Berling could see, from his hiding place amid the rocks, that the crew aboard was struggling. Something had happened to *Naglfar*. Some kind of battle had left both the vessel and the crew crippled. Berling watched as the crew struggled to guide *Naglfar* past an outcropping of rocks and sail beyond Berling's sight, well away from the tiny hut where his friends hid. He sighed and knew that they were safe, at least for now.

Leaving his place of concealment, Berling plodded his way amid the rocks and sand to once again gain sight of *Naglfar*. An anchor, heavy with the bones of man and beast, was tossed over the side of the ship. Berling watched as battered crewmembers lowered smaller versions of *Naglfar* into the waves and then, raising their squared sails, directed them toward the black sandy beaches of Surtsey.

An unnamed group of giants dragged the first of the boats onto shore, disembarking and setting up what appeared to Berling as a perimeter, a cordon of military-type protection for the next boats to arrive.

In the third boat, the one that seemed to shine more brightly in the gray light of day, sat a girl whom Berling did not recognize, but guessed must be Taylre; her hair was red, the glasses she wore were too big for her face, and she was the only girl aboard a ship full of dwarfs and giants. Besides that, she sat next to Loki, a figure that Berling *did* recognize. When Berling saw the Sly One he shuddered, despite his attempt to remain brave; Loki was a creature to be feared and avoided.

When Loki's boat landed, Berling watched him step off lithely, almost athletically, into the shallow water, his boots, reaching past his knees, protected him. Berling was surprised to see Loki assist crewmembers as they hauled the vessel onto shore; he expected to see a tyrant who considered himself too privileged to participate in such a mundane activity.

When the boat was finally dragged far enough onto the beach, Berling watched as Loki extended his hand and assisted Taylre over the gunwale, her feet touching softly on the wet sand and sinking while a fresh influx of water filled her empty footsteps. He watched her, too, with surprise, wondering why she was being treated so kindly and why she was reacting in such an amiable way.

As Berling continued to contemplate this mystery, his attention was suddenly drawn to another large figure that was quickly approaching on a fourth boat. He drew in a quick breath and was barely able to contain himself. The horror and dread he felt almost overpowered him. Sitting on his haunches in the back of the boat, his head lifted to the wind that crested and blew back his massive ears and mangy fur, was Fenrir, the giant wolf, substance of legend and myth.

How, thought Berling, *did the great beast escape the strength of Gleipnir?* Berling knew the tale well. The dwarfs that lived in the world of the dark elves and fashioned the silken chain used to bind Fenrir, were distant relatives. Their creation was supposed to be unbreakable. The fact that Fenrir was somehow able to escape its hold meant that time was unraveling quickly. Berling shuddered inwardly. He had hoped that recent events surrounding Loki were just a coincidence. But now that he'd seen Fenrir and the dreaded ship *Naglfar* both in the same day, he realized that time was not on their side. He and his companions would have to act quickly to save Taylre and the two boys who were traveling with Sinmora.

As more boats landed on the shore Berling could see a large army start to develop. When he glanced out to sea he shook his head with the knowledge that *Naglfar* still held more giants and dwarfs upon its decks and within its underbelly. This was indeed going to be a formidable array of soldiers. Eventually, Berling thought, their numbers would fill the beaches and the rocky hills that surrounded the area. His companions would soon be located; there was no way they could hide from such a huge army.

Suddenly there was movement and a large group of giants and dwarfs began marching down the beach, the great throng protectively surrounding Loki, Taylre, and Fenrir. Berling watched as they trudged along the black sand and then turned sharply, heading toward high ground and the rocky, icy fields beyond.

Berling reached into the pouch he had slung over his shoulder and retrieved the map he'd drawn based on his calculations from *Ragnarsdrapa.* He and the Captain had been following the map carefully, a skill that led them to this beach. He unfolded its creased edges on the ground before him and gazed urgently at the bold lines. His bearded face suddenly turned pale and he looked up at the retreating army.

"They know where the portal is," he said. "Somehow we've got to get there first."

ᛦ

Though the hut was dark, the Captain felt a measure of comfort in its closeness. Even the smoky air seemed pleasant as he breathed in the peat smoke, filling his lungs and somehow clearing them. It allowed him to breath better than he had in years.

Erna also appeared to be enjoying the thick atmosphere. Its dim light and smoky surroundings reminded her of Sinmora's cabin.

Marjorie and Vivian sat beside each other under the warmth of a fur blanket. Vivian struggled to stifle her constant urge to cough while Marjorie kept her head beneath the blanket to keep her eyes from watering.

The silence of the moment, however, was suddenly broken as Berling burst through the door, his face red in an effort to catch his breath. "They're on the move," he panted. "They... they know ware the portal be. I've no doubt of that."

The Captain stood quickly and raced his bulky body across the hut toward Berling. "What do ya mean, little man?"

"We need ta be on the move. Don't ya see? They know the way in. The portal is close by, just across the valley by my calculations." Berling again reached into his pouch and pulled out the map. He placed it next to the tiny fire letting its glow reflect off the parchment that showed the details of the island. Berling pointed a sturdy finger at one section of the map.

"We be here," he said. "And the portal is here," he continued. His finger slid over the folds to another boldly drawn location. Berling's companions, their eyes taking in every detail, crowded around the map.

"That looks like a long way," Vivian said, bending in closer to see the map more clearly. "How do we get there?"

Berling looked up as all eyes were suddenly upon him. "We run," he exclaimed. "We run as if the devil himself were chasing us. And we do it now before it's too late."

ᛦ

There was no way that Berling was going to keep up. His tiny legs just couldn't match the pace of the others. Even the Captain who labored hard to breath in the icy, windy air was able to out pace the dwarf.

"Oh, by Odin's one clear eye!" Berling called, his tiny fist raised in the air while his face and beard were pelted with minute crystals of ice that blew in the wind. "I can't go on."

The travelers stopped in their tracks at Berling's beckoning call. Even Marjorie came to an abrupt halt, her rapid stride leading the way.

"What is it now?" she said impatiently. She turned to see Berling in the distance fall to his knees, his arm still raised above his head.

Vivian turned to look at Berling too, but then gazed back at Marjorie. She understood Marjorie's anxiety. She knew how badly she wanted to be on the move so she could locate Taylre.

But Vivian also knew that without Berling they had no hope at all. He was their key to the Mist.

Erna was the first to reach Berling. She lifted him to his feet while his legs shook beneath him. "Steady now," she urged. "We can stop and rest here for a moment."

"No," Berling said breathlessly. "No, you must keep on. There's no time ta lose. Just leave me and be on your way, lass."

Gathering around the dwarf, protecting him from the worst of the storm, the small group assembled. Emotions within the gathering were mixed; nevertheless, each member felt the urgency of the moment and knew something had to be done.

Vivian was the first to act. She reached down and grabbed Berling by his arms and twisted his body around, placing him squarely on her back, his arms and hands wrapped forcefully around her neck.

"What're ya doin' woman?" Berling shouted. His face blushed a bright red despite the cold. "I'm not a wee child for ya ta be haulin' around, ya know!"

Vivian continued to cling tightly to Berling's wrists as he struggled unsuccessfully to release himself from her grip. Quick anger flashed across her face as she turned her head to look him in the eye. Berling stopped his thrashing immediately; something in Vivian's angered look frightened him.

"I'm only going to say this once, you disgusting, putrid, vile tempered little man! You are going to come with us if it's the last thing I do. I will drag you by your smelly little feet or pull you along with the end of your gristly gray beard if I have to. Either way you're coming! Have I made myself clear?"

Berling, his tiny legs hanging limply down Vivian's back, swallowed hard while the angry, forceful words reverberated around him finding their way slowly into his stubborn dwarf brain.

"I... I do," he stammered nervously.

"Good," Vivian said. Anger still boiled in her voice. "Now, hold on tight; I'm going to be moving quickly."

And she did. In fact there were times when even Marjorie had a difficult time keeping up with her. But exhaustion and fatigue soon set in, and Vivian was forced to rest. Her back and arms screamed with pain.

"Somebody else has to take him," Vivian panted. "I'm done."

Berling opened his mouth to say something, but Vivian quickly cut him off with one angry glare. Marjorie stepped forward and took Berling from Vivian, placing him on her back.

"Sorry, old boy," she whispered. Berling wrapped his tiny arms around her neck. "I've never seen Vivian like that. Never. She's scaring me a wee bit too."

"Aye," Berling said. "Scary is one way of puttin' it." And then as an afterthought said, "Are ya sure she isn't the goddess Freyja? She does have a similar sharp tongue."

Marjorie chuckled softly as she started forward. "Not that I know of. But then again, we have seen some strange things of late."

"Aye," Berling responded. "That we have. That we have."

ᛣ

By following Berling's map, the tiny group was able to locate a trail that skirted the edge of the cliffs overlooking the crashing sea and the long line of Loki's soldiers who plodded along another trail far below.

From her vantage point Marjorie could just barely make out the bouncing red hair of Taylre. Tears of regret and pain flooded her eyes. Anxious drops spilled down her cheeks and then froze. For a brief moment she considered the ache in her back and arms as Berling's weight began to slow her strides. But then she looked down at Taylre again. Determination filled her mind, giving her strength that might otherwise have faltered. Soon she was jogging along the narrow path, the other travelers in tow.

After crossing two or three miles of ice covered meadows and brimstone littered fields, the meager troupe came to an abrupt halt.

"We're here," Berling announced. "We've reached the place known as Gladsheim where the portal to the Mist will soon open. Be ready, those who will venture with me. But beware. Many sentinels, those who would seek to turn us back to Midgard, will guard this entrance. Because the Seam here is very weak, access to the Mist is much easier, so many of the unwelcome will find there selves turned away. But we must hurry. Loki's armies quickly approach."

Marjorie dropped Berling gently to the ground while they ran to the edge of a narrow gap in the earth.

"This is it?" Erna asked. "This is where we're to enter?" She looked down a dark opening that seemed to fall into nothingness, its narrow passage reminding Erna of a rabbit's hole. "But there's barely enough room for one to enter."

"Aye," Berling answered. "'Tis the only place marked on the map and it's only meant for one at a time."

The Captain stepped forward, his broad face red with exertion, his brow dappled with beads of sweat. "It'll take Loki's army days to get through that."

"Aye," Berling grinned. "That it will. And thank Odin for that. Otherwise we'd have no time at all."

Suddenly, the echo of marching feet and the cry of impending battle drifted through the chilly air.

"They're coming," Erna cried. "What'll we do?"

Berling smoothed the edges of the map on the ground and then retrieved another yellowed parchment from his pouch. He lined them up against each other as he closely examined each document. Then he looked up into the heavens as gray clouds drifted across the firmament like a time elapsed film, their fluffy tails leaving streaks across the bright sky. He stuck his finger in his mouth and then lifted it, testing the wind.

The Captain rolled his eyes. "You've got ta be kidding,"

Berling gave the Captain an angry glare. "This isn't science, ya dull witted troll. It's magic. Show a little respect." Berling brought his arm down and then consulted his papers once more before he announced: "Now! We go now!"

He stood quickly and refolded the documents, shoving them back in his pouch. He turned toward Erna. "If you're comin', lass, now's the time." He took Erna by the hand, the grip firm and steady. They both looked back as a measure of fear crossed over Erna's pale features.

Then, they jumped.

They fell quickly as they disappeared into the abyss, their bodies completely
 enveloped by the darkness.

The three remaining travelers stood in utter shock at the pair's sudden departure. All three of them were thinking the same thing: neither Berling nor Erna said goodbye.

The Captain broke the silence as he stepped closer to the edge and looked in. He turned back to Marjorie and Vivian, giving them first a soft grunt, and then a weak smile.

"We couldn't have gotten here without you two," he said solemnly. "Why, that little dwarf would've still been lyin' way back on the ice if you two hadn't carried him all this way." He turned around and looked in the hole one more time as the pounding of giant boots and the clanging of metal weapons sounded throughout the narrow valley, their footsteps drawing closer and closer.

Bartholomew Gunner turned back one more time toward the two women. A sense of urgency filled his deep voice. "You're going to be captured," he said, his earnest expression intensely focused. "I wish there were a way for ya both ta get away, but it's too late, Loki's coming. I can hear his army approaching. Please don't think of me as a coward. I'm not. Not anymore. I'm doing this because Zeke, Devon, and Taylre need ta get back safely. Something is compelling me ta go. So be strong and fight ta the end. And may the gifts of Odin be with ya."

Then, just like Berling and Erna before him, the Captain jumped, his large frame fading into darkness like the sudden stroke of a moonless night.

Chapter Twenty-Four
Andvari's Gold

Zeke walked alone. In his hand he clutched the Staff of Urd, almost as if it held some sort of strength, a power that enabled him to push on despite his fearful solitude. He looked around and noted the fading light of an October-like day and the oncoming dark of January night. Through the branches of the thick woods Zeke could see distant lights: candles and oil lamps sitting in rough hewn cabins and farm houses, or perhaps lazy hearth fires burning brightly in the midst of the tiny abodes. These were the homes of the myriad occupants of the nine worlds, a few of the billions and billions of inhabitants who lived among the branches of Yggdrasil seeking refuge from the cold or rest from a hard day's labor.

Zeke thought about trudging through the tangled undergrowth and knocking on one of the doors, just to have a chance to rest his leg and maybe even beg for a tiny morsel of food, but time was not on his side. His brother and his friends were still back in Niflheim under the constant and careful watch of Nidhogg the dragon.

The deal was quite simple, and even Zeke had to admit that it made perfect sense, although he couldn't understand why the accumulation of more gold was so important to Nidhogg. Didn't he already have enough? Wasn't his cave already filled to overflowing with treasure, piled high to the ceiling while it collected dust? Surely the dragon could be happy with what he had. Nevertheless, he wanted more. And so, Zeke was forced to set out toward the world of the dark elves while Sinmora, Vidar, and Devon waited, their lives held in ransom under the hungry eye of Nidhogg.

As the path twisted and bent before him, Zeke continued on, Sinmora's bulky pouch perched awkwardly on his hip. It shifted from side to side each time he stepped. Nevertheless, he patted it often, finding warmth and comfort in its touch.

After what seemed like many days and many miles, Zeke finally came to the edge of a particularly dark forest. The boughs of its trees hung low while the tips soared high into the ever-present gray sky. Here the path stopped, almost as if no one wanted to enter its bleak interior.

Zeke slowly parted the branches that barred his way and thrust the Staff of Urd in front of him as if it were a talisman to

ward off evil. He stepped carefully into the darkness as the soft
crunch of leaves and pine needles eased his way and softened
the pressure on his aching leg. He plodded through the thick
foliage and trudged forward with a kind of intensity akin only to
an Olympic athlete. And though he felt intensely the nagging
pangs of thirst and hunger, his mind was constantly thinking of
Devon and his friends, the ones he'd left behind. He knew that
their lives depended on him. If he didn't fulfill this task they
would be eaten. The possibility of that consequence drove him
on, notwithstanding his nagging discomfort.

Eventually, after dragging himself through miles of thick
forest and some close calls with unusual animals, Zeke reached
the entrance to the world of the dark elves. Its broad cavern was
a black opening, like the foreboding maw of an enraged eel. He
entered slowly, his senses enhanced and searched for danger in
every nook and cranny. However, the dim light that shone
through the large cave opening soon dissipated and left Zeke on
the virtual brink of night and day. He reached into Sinmora's
pouch and retrieved some flint and steel. Then from the pack
slung over his shoulder he produced a tattered t-shirt that he
ripped into strips, wrapping each one around the tip of his staff.
Once again delving into Sinmora's pouch, he produced a tiny
purple-topped bottle, the words "oil" printed boldly on its front
with black marker and a piece of masking tape. Sinmora had

prepared well, Zeke thought. The pouch always seemed to contain the necessary items. Though Zeke couldn't help but think there was some kind of magic involved here as well.

Emptying the entire contents of the tiny bottle, Zeke poured the oil over the tattered t-shirt and soaked it completely until the viscous liquid began to run down the smoothed edges of the staff. Then, as a chilly wind began to whistle from the tunnel ahead, Zeke took the flint and steel with trembling hands and struck it several times over the oil drenched material. Finally, as sparks continued to fly, a meager flame erupted, eventually spreading and engulfing the top of the staff in fire. Zeke held it high over his head. The light his torch now produced extended deep into the darkness.

Zeke began to trudge ahead, though without the staff as a crutch, his limp was more pronounced. Nevertheless, he picked his way down a chain of dripping tunnels and through a maze of twilit chambers, finally coming to another massive cavern, its high roof supported by columns of rock thicker than tree trunks. The corners, however, remained dark and foreboding. The little light that did manage to filter into the middle of the cavern from Zeke's torch and from a vertical shaft in the roof, illuminated what Zeke had ventured so far to find: the abode of the dwarf Andvari. In the center of the cavern was a large silent pool filled with water that seemed to spring from nowhere and flow nowhere. Standing at its edge, Zeke reached, once again, into Sinmora's pouch, retrieving a folded scrap of leather. Inside was a rotted piece of meat Sinmora had collected from the ground near Nidhogg's cave. What kind of meat, and where it had come from, Zeke did not want to know. This was the bait that would catch the flesh-loving pike that swam the cold waters in Andvari's clever disguise.

Zeke stamped out the flame that continued to burn brightly from the end of the staff and replaced it with a thin line of fishing wire. On the end he placed a barbed hook, its sharpened end catching the light from the vertical shaft. Then, remembering a brief moment in time - almost a year ago - when Taylre tied a fishing lure to the end of one of the Captain's fishing rods, Zeke tried to mimic her subtle movements: spinning the line several times and then pushing the end through the tiny loop. Then, using his teeth, pulling it taut until the knot tightened, a well blended marriage of hook and line.

Taking a deep breath, Zeke spun the line around several times, like a cattle rancher trying to rope a calf. He cast it swiftly into the depths of the pool. Then he pulled on the line slowly, dragging it through the water with a steady, even motion.

Suddenly the line pulled tight. The thin wire cut into Zeke's grip as he struggled to keep it from pulling him and the Staff of Urd into the frigid water.

Near its center, the smooth pool suddenly exploded as a huge fish leapt into the air, furiously lashing and writhing, its nasty yellow eyes taking one angered glance at Zeke before plunging back into the water. Zeke, his feet wedged between the narrow cleft of two rocks, wrapped the line around his hands while he heaved and pulled, fighting with the great fish until finally landing it on the rugged shore. Its massive tail beat against the rock while its mouth opened and closed in a vain attempt to gulp at the dry air.

Zeke stared at the dying fish, and for a brief moment felt pity for the suffering animal, but then he remembered what Sinmora had told him: *Andvari is a sniveling, spineless little imp who will stop at nothing to get what he wants. He's cruel and hoards his gold like the angry miser that he is. Don't be fooled by his supposed helplessness. He isn't helpless at all,* Sinmora had said. *He'd just as soon cut your throat and watch you bleed to death then give you a morsel of food if you're starving.*

Zeke freed his mind of his normally giving nature and grabbed the flopping fish by the tail, hanging him upside down, careful not to get too close to the pike's sharp teeth. He shook the fish fiercely.

"Change shape!" Zeke yelled. His voice echoed off the cavern's walls.

The pike stopped its thrashing about and looked up at Zeke with its yellow eyes. A look of confusion seemed to creep into its pupils, expanding them, pushing aside the yellow that filled the outsides.

Then suddenly, like a scene from some vivid nightmare, the fish morphed into a tiny man. Zeke fought hard to keep himself from turning and running. Instead, he found himself holding the dwarf by the back of his pants. The little man's arms waved around widely while his head bumped against the rocks.

"What do you want?" whined Andvari.

Hearing the poor little man's pathetic cries, Zeke almost let go. But he remained firm to his promise to Sinmora.

"What I want," Zeke said, trying to sound confident and mean, "is all your gold. Give it to me or I'll give you the beating of your life with this staff." Zeke held the staff close to the dwarf's face. He shook it threateningly, though the act itself seemed awkwardly comical.

Andvari's eyes widened when he looked closely at the staff; a fearful recognition stretched itself across his features. Zeke expected this kind of reaction. Sinmora had related her own grim experience with the dwarf and how she'd nearly fallen prey to his treachery. Yet it was the Staff of Urd that had finally saved her, though she wouldn't say exactly what she'd done with the staff to escape the deceitfulness of this lying little creature.

"I'll do whatever it is that ya want," Andvari said. His voice wavered with fear.

Zeke hesitated for a moment, his grip still strong on the back of the dwarf's pants. "Lead me to your smithy," Zeke ordered, his voice sounding much bolder. "But no tricks. Remember, I have the staff."

Andvari glanced once more at the staff, but then from his upside down position looked up at Zeke giving him a curious gaze. Zeke caught it, but just briefly. It was quick and subtle. And though it caused Zeke a moment of pause, he waved it aside.

He dropped Andvari to the ground, the sharp stones and jagged rocks bit into the little man's knees and hands. "Careful, lad," Andvari complained. "I'm not a sack of potatoes ya know."

Once again, Zeke felt a pang of guilt. His actions were cruel, so different from how he normally acted. And yet, didn't Sinmora urge him to remain firm? He had to follow through; Andvari was not to be trusted.

"Just get up and take me to the gold," Zeke said. "You're wasting my time."

"Alright, alright. No need to get pushy." Andvari stood quickly and brushed away the mud and sand that clung to his tattered clothing.

He led Zeke out of the echoing chamber and down a long twisting passage. Andvari walked quickly. Zeke had a difficult time keeping up; his leg pounded with pain and he winced each time he set his foot down. Andvari kept glancing back, his yellow eyes catching glimpses of Zeke's intermittent grimace.

Soon they exited the long dark tunnel and entered the smithy. It was hot and sticky. Zeke felt the heat suddenly envelope him like a heavy wet blanket. He found it hard to breath and even harder to walk. The warmth seemed to weigh upon him, pressing downward as if the ceiling were about to fall. He gripped the staff firmly and leaned on it for strength. Suddenly a feeling of power filled him, almost as if the staff recognized his need. He stood taller as the weight of the heat recoiled, pushing back against the solid walls of rock that surrounded him. Zeke looked at Andvari and saw him staring at him again, his yellow eyes widening as another curious look filled his expression. The dwarf then spread out his arms toward the well-stocked room that showed gold upon gold gleaming in the forge's firelight.

"Take whatever it is that ya like," Andvari said. "All that ya can carry is yours."

Zeke stared in wonder at the immense treasure that was laid out before him. Never in his life had he seen anything so wonderful. For a moment he was hypnotized by the sight, recognizing that this was probably what Nidhogg felt when he stared at his own miserly pile of gold. But it was this thought that brought Zeke back to the present as he once again remembered Devon and the others who were being held captive by the dragon. He turned to Andvari and put on his best angry face.

"Gather it up, dwarf. Put as much as you can in the wagon there. And be quick about it."

Andvari pinched his eyebrows together and was about to open his mouth to say something when he glanced once more at the staff. "Alright," he said reluctantly, and began scrambling around, cursing and moaning, his sharp words hidden under his breath.

Soon Andvari filled the small wagon with a pile of discs and chips and splinters of yellow gold as well as bars of red gold, of objects already made and of objects half made. Zeke looked at the pile and was very pleased, knowing that Nidhogg would have to be impressed with the contents of the wagon. He was about to congratulate Andvari for a job well done, but he stopped himself; praising the little man would show weakness. Zeke wanted to remain firm, though the effort to do so was difficult.

"Is that all you can get in there?" Zeke said, pounding the staff into the dirt.

"It's full. Can ya not see?" Andvari complained.

Though Zeke could see that it was well stocked, he didn't want the dwarf to think him at all satisfied. "I suppose it will do," Zeke said, catching the quick movement of the dwarf's hand as he tried to hide something behind his back.

Zeke held the staff firmly with both hands and stared angrily at Andvari. "What are you hiding?" he demanded, once again stamping the staff into the ground. "I saw you put something behind your back. What is it?"

Andvari's face seemed to wilt and the corners of his mouth began to quiver as if he were about to cry. "Please," he begged. He began shaking his head from side to side.

"Whatever it is," Zeke said, his voice reverberating off the smithy walls, "put it in the wagon with the rest of the treasure."

"Let me keep it," Andvari pleaded. "Just this one little trinket." Then from behind his back he produced a ring.

Zeke saw that it was tiny, something he would barely be able to fit on his own little finger. Yet it shone with a golden brilliance. As if its marvelous light came from within. It was beautifully wrought too. Zeke could make out intricate carvings on its smooth exterior, as well as a flash of color, one shade changing quickly to another. Zeke swallowed hard. He knew this would be the kind of prize the dragon would readily accept, all but assuring the release of his friends.

"Give it to me," Zeke ordered, his hand extended, palm side up.

"You must let me keep this," Andvari said. Giant tears flowed freely down his cheeks. "Without it I cannot make anymore gold. It's the starter, you see. I must have it or my smithy will be worthless."

Zeke saw the dwarf's tears, his hand nearly withdrawing as deep sympathy filled his mind. But he would not be dissuaded as Sinmora's voice echoed in his thoughts

He will deceive you, Zeke. Make no mistake of that. I would have surely died had I not relied on the strength of the staff. Use it. It won't let you down.

Zeke gripped the staff harder, the knuckles on his right hand turning white as a charge of power filled him, releasing him from the pain in his leg and clearing his mind. He pushed his hand out further and glared at Andvari. "I said give it to me."

The tears in Andvari's eyes quickly dried up, as did the sudden quiver that overtook the corners of his mouth. They were replaced with a red anger that filled his cheeks and set his yellow eyes blazing.

"If ya take this, ya blasted brute, then a curse I place upon it! It will destroy whoever owns it! Do ya hear me? It will destroy ya!"

Zeke grabbed the ring from the dwarf's hand and stuffed it in his pocket. He looked up at Andvari and smiled. "So much the better," he said. "I will never be the owner of this ring. It is a gift for someone else. Now, grab hold of the end of that wagon and start pulling. We have a long way to go."

Taylre observed Mr. Loden with a curious expression as he and Fenrir stared down into the dark cleft in the rock. With the bulk of the weakened, tired army milling about on the flat precipice overlooking the sea and even more trudging up the hill to join them, Taylre couldn't help but feel a bit frightened. She couldn't remember a time when she'd seen Loden get so angry. He was usually so together, so in control of everything and everybody around him. Now though, Taylre thought Loden was acting like a small child having a temper tantrum. She backed away slowly. She feared the ravings and curses that spilled from his mouth. Under her feet she felt the uneven mixture of moss and rock, the sharp contrast in textures causing her to become unbalanced. Thankfully her grandmother was there, holding her tightly by the shoulders in a loving embrace. One so tight and warm that Taylre didn't ever want her to let go. She turned to once again look at Marjorie and smiled, despite the unsettling scene that Loden was continuing to make.

"I'm sorry," Taylre whispered. She hoped her voice wouldn't carry in Loden's direction. "He's not usually like this."

Marjorie tried to hold back a snort of laughter in spite of their recent capture by the horde of giants and dwarfs. "Taylre," she began, her eyes and mouth softening as her voice betrayed a kind of warning. "You really don't know who he is, do you?"

Taylre's smile faded and her brow creased with confusion. "Mr. Loden, you mean?" She turned to watch as Loden continued to pace back and forth in front of the hole. His arms waved around madly as he struck one unsuspecting soldier after another. And his curses became more bold and offensive by the minute. "Of course I know who he is," she said. She stared back at her grandmother. "He's my friend. I know you think that he's a bad man, but he really isn't. He's shown me time and time again that he's good. That he wants to help."

Vivian, who was standing next to Marjorie, leaned across and took Taylre gently by the arm. "He's not, Taylre. You have to believe us when we say this: Mr. Loden is not your friend."

"But he's suffered. The gods have been so cruel to him," Taylre said. "Him and his son, Fenrir. They've both been through so much hardship. All they want to do is be happy, just like us. He even brought me here to warn Zeke and Devon."

Vivian's ears perked up at the mention of her sons' names. She stepped in front of Marjorie and ignored the huge, smelly men that stood around her. She grabbed Taylre by the shoulders, this time her grasp much harder. Her fingers dug into Taylre's skin.

"What has that beast said about my boys?" Vivian demanded. An unusual anger poured from her voice.

Taylre was taken aback; hardly able to comprehend that her normally calm, reserved aunt could be treating her so cruelly. Marjorie reached in and pulled Vivian away. Her own fingers dug at Vivian's; fighting to release the grip she had on Taylre's arm.

"Relax, Vivian," Marjorie said. "We don't want to frighten her." She turned to look at Taylre with a hopeful gaze. "I'm sure she's been through a lot. I'm also sure that the boys are just fine."

"Well, not really," Taylre said as she desperately tried to rub out some of the soreness in her arms. "Mr. Loden has brought me here to warn the boys. They're in trouble, you see. An evil witch is deceiving them."

This time both Vivian and Marjorie stepped back, their faces filled with shock.

"Loden told you this?" Marjorie asked.

"Yep," Taylre said, eyeing Vivian with a scornful expression while she continued to rub her arms. "In fact we're here to find a tree of some sort. Apparently Zeke and Devon are sitting on it, or walking on it, I'm not sure which. Anyway, that's what Loden said."

Vivian and Marjorie looked at each other; a mixture of puzzlement and alarm marked their features.

Marjorie was about to speak when a heavy hand dropped upon her shoulder. Its touch produced an extremely unpleasant sensation. She turned quickly to see Loki standing before her. A wicked smile creased his lips, and anger oozed from his eyes.

"Ladies," he said smoothly. "I really have to admit, I did not expect to see you two here. No, I did not." He looked at Taylre and draped his arm around her shoulders. "But you have to admit, it's good to finally be together again, isn't it?"

Marjorie tried to move, she even tried to speak. But she couldn't. Loki's touch had somehow paralyzed her. All she could do was stare at Loki. And though she tried to pull away, the effort was useless. Whatever Loki had done, or was doing, Marjorie Anders was helpless.

"Tell me, *grandma*," Loki said, his grip still firm on Marjorie's shoulder. "Who has ventured down that hole?" His eyes gazed back at the deep cleft in the rock. Its opening appeared to mock the horde of gathered, exhausted soldiers with a silent scream.

Pursing her lips and trying to remain mute, Marjorie swallowed a breath, but before it could enter her lungs it burst forth. "Berling!" she hollered, almost as if the words were pulled from her chest. "And...and...Bar...Bartholomew!" she said, spitting out the final words as if they were poison to her soul.

Loki began to laugh, raspy, deep-throated, and raucous. "You've got to be kidding," he said between bursts of laughter. "Berling? That stupid, banished dwarf, and the biggest coward of them all, Bartholomew Gunner? Oh, this is rich. This is really rich." Then he turned to Fenrir. "Did you hear that?" Loki continued to laugh.

"I did, father," Fenrir answered, though his words were more tempered and serious.

Loki turned back quickly to the two women who stood in absolute fear before him, his arm still wrapped around Taylre's shoulder. "We will find them," he said. Then he turned to Taylre. "To warn them, of course." He smiled and walked away. His hand released the grip it held on Marjorie's shoulder.

Marjorie fell to the ground. Her knees completely gave way while Taylre and Vivian surrounded her as they tried to raise her to her feet.

Meanwhile, Loki began pacing across the edge of jagged stone. He circled the hole where Berling, Erna, and Bartholomew Gunner entered the Mist. He pointed a stern finger at the ground at specific locations and barked commands to his men. "Dig here, you curs. And here. We will tie into the Mist from these places. Hurry, you spineless bits of dragon droppings. There is no time to waste. Holes must be dug, and quickly!"

Chapter Twenty-Six
Boiled Veal and a Warm Fire

The Captain fell through a rapidly shifting Mist, one that tossed and tumbled in a chaotic wind of time and space. He felt his mind swirl with visions of death and hope amid a million stars and billions upon billions of souls. A vision of their faces passed before his own, some happy, some sad. Some were full of regret, but others reflected on a lifetime of joy and love. The Captain felt a measure of both, mostly regret. Not for leaping into the Mist, though. This was his moment and somehow he knew that jumping into that dark cleft in the rock on Surtsey was the most important and noble thing he'd ever done. Nevertheless, the time he spent saying his goodbyes to Marjorie and Vivian would cost him; time and place would bend setting him miles away from the place where Erna and Berling had landed.

Soon the Captain began to feel himself slow, almost as if the Mist were pulling and surrounding him in a net of safety, preparing him for his final descent to a land hidden somewhere on the sturdy branches of Yggdrasil. For a brief moment there was clarity, like a bright light revealing a wonderful treasure. The Captain reached out his hand and tried to grasp at the empty air like a drowning man. But then the light went black and Bartholomew Gunner discovered for the first time in his entire life what it was like to really sleep.

He was on his back staring up into a blue sky. At first he was confused. He assumed he was still drifting amid the world of dreams and deep sleep, but then a gentle wind blew, fingers of wind coursing through his thick black beard that caused the mottled skin on his face to quiver. He breathed deeply, sensing the aroma of spring: a time for sowing and a time for harvesting fish from the clear shallow waters. He sat up slowly and peered ahead, noting the freshly plowed fields that surrounded him and the dense thicket of trees that edged the black dirt resting in neatly cut rows. He gazed to his left and then to his right, but saw no sign of Berling or Erna. He assumed they had moved on, not knowing that he would be joining them on their quest.

The sky, though filled with light, was tinted with the softness of late afternoon. Reveling in the beauty that the day held, the

Captain nevertheless felt a nagging sense that he should get a move on. Timing meant everything.

He stood quickly, surprised to find that the arthritic pains that would normally press upon him didn't fill his joints with pain. Instead, he rose to his feet and felt refreshed, as if he'd just experienced the best, most restful sleep of his life.

"I am definitely in the Mist," he muttered to himself. "No doubt about it."

The Captain began walking whichever way his heart told him to. He had no idea where Berling and Erna might have gone, but felt sure they would take the path of least resistance, something he would have done. So, with the wind at this back, he trudged on.

After many hours the sun dipped to the edge of the horizon and seemed to sputter, its life for this day soon coming to an end. The Captain walked steadily, skirting along the ruts of an old wagon road when he came upon a decrepit turfed hut. The evening air was still, but the shack looked so rickety that the Captain thought it might collapse if the eagle-giant Hraesvelg gave one flap of its mighty wings. The Captain timidly knocked on the roughly hewn door and waited. When no one opened it or answered, he slowly pushed it open, his limbs spent and exhausted from the day's journey. He entered hesitantly, stooping under the low doorframe. When he walked in, it took the Captain a moment to adjust to the rank, smoky gloom. But soon the air cleared and he was able to make out a trestle table, a bench, and a pile of seed wrapped in burlap bags sitting in the middle of the room. Beside that was a crumbling cupboard leaning against a battered wall where a straw-filled mattress lay next to it. On it were the snoring, sleeping forms of Erna and Berling, their faces smudged with dirt while their mouths hung open in complete and utter relaxation.

The Captain chuckled lightly to himself, secretly wishing that he were stretched out on the same mattress with his eyes closed shut and his mind drifting amid the world of dreams. But that nagging feeling tugged at him again and he knew that time was running out.

"Am I welcome here?" he said, remembering the greeting his mother had taught him if ever he were to venture into the Mist.

Both Berling and Erna stirred uneasily. Their snores turned to snorts while their eyes fluttered open like the wings of a humming bird.

Berling was the first to sit up, his beard wet with his slobber, while the corners of his eyes held onto the sandy remnants of sleep.

"Great Thor's hammer," Berling bellowed in shock and utter amazement. "What in the name of Odin are ya doin here?"

"And a fine good day to you too," the Captain responded. A brief smile lit up his dark eyes. Then he turned to the tiny pot that hung over a scant fire. "Is there vittles to be had?" he said, smacking his lips. "I'm starving."

Erna rose gingerly from the flattened mattress and smoothed the hem of her dress delicately as she approached the Captain. She spread her arms wide and gave him a warm hug and a soft smile. "I knew you'd be coming; Zeke is going to need you. I feel it here," she said, her hand resting over her heart. " *You* will obtain the gift that only a warrior can receive."

The Captain stared at her curiously, watching her pad her way over to a steaming pot of boiled veal. He wondered why she had just uttered those simple yet profound words, words that resonated in the air like an approaching storm.

Erna began filling two large bowls. Then she reached toward a stout oak chest. From it she removed a loaf of rye bread, a gob of butter, and some knives and spoons, arranging them neatly on a small table. Pulling the rickety chairs away she invited the two men to sit.

Both Berling and the Captain felt awkward as they approached the meager, yet well-dressed table and took their seats. They watched as Erna stepped to the front door and dipped a large jug into a vat of beer. She filled two cups to overflowing and then set them down lightly on the table without spilling a drop.

"Will ya not be eatin'?" the Captain asked.

"I will when you've had your fill," Erna answered kindly. "It is the way Sinmora has taught me. And it is the way I will follow."

The dwarf and the man looked at each other as a thin line of guilt crossed their faces. But then they looked down at the food. The mixed aroma of boiled veal with thinly sliced vegetables steamed into the air and filled their nostrils. Both of them took their spoons in hand and began to eat.

⚔

The night was growing darker and colder. Erna sat beside the fire holding her bowl of thick stew. Its warmth seeped into the palms of her hands while she delicately spooned meager portions into her mouth, filling her hungry stomach. Berling and the Captain stretched out on the floor, their heads propped up with blankets as puffs of sweet smoke rose from their pipes.

"Whose house is this?" the Captain asked sleepily.

Berling grunted softly, his eyes heavy with exhaustion. "'Tis the home of Afi and Amma," he answered. "Grandfather and Grandmother. They were kind and let us in when we knocked, but then fled when Erna told them that she was Sinmora's apprentice. They both went on about a witch, or some such nonsense. Then they grabbed their things and hopped on their cart. 'Course that was after Erna shooed them off with a big stick. The last I saw they were heading down the road with a donkey pullin' 'em."

This time the Captain grunted. "A witch, ya say. Do ya think they meant Sinmora?"

"Aye," Berling nodded quietly, his head heavy with beer. "'Tis' ta be expected though. She is a Volva and most folks think of them as witches."

Erna stirred uneasily by the fire and pulled the blanket tighter around her shoulders. "Sinmora is not a witch," she protested. "She is a kind woman who has taught me well. I'll not have folks talking about her in such an evil manner." She kicked at a tiny piece of peat that rolled from the fire and pushed it back into the flames.

The Captain looked curiously at Erna over the pencil thin line of smoke that drifted from the end of his pipe and wondered at the unique dichotomy of this child. How she could be so warm and humble, yet at the same time display a righteous anger that would cause even the greatest warrior to shrink in respectful submission.

Erna glanced at the Captain, almost as if she knew what he was thinking. "We should all sleep now," She curled up on the dirt floor beside the fire while the blanket enveloped her body, but her eyes never left the Captain's. "Tomorrow we must travel far to meet Zeke. Something tells me the burden he carries is very heavy."

Heavy snores were already spilling from Berling's mouth when the Captain pulled his eyes away from Erna's stare. He rolled over and kept his back to the warm flames and closed his eyes. But sleep was a difficult beast to wrangle, despite his complete feeling of exhaustion; Erna's words kept echoing in his mind, words that seemed to foretell a burden that both he and Zeke must bear.

Chapter Twenty-Seven
The Fork in the Road

The morning was frosty and cold with a thin layer of snow clinging to the frozen ground. The Captain was surprised to see his breath cloud in front of him; the day before had showed the promise of spring. But today, the threat of winter still clung to the frigid sky, painting the overcast heavens with a scrim of depression.

The Captain stood slowly. His joints felt sore and his head ached like a pounding drum. "Too much beer," he said, looking at the tiny stone ring where the fire had once burned, but it had turned to ashes. Even the smoke refused to rise in the cool air. He turned to his companions and saw that Erna was already awake, staring at him as if she'd never slept.

"Wake Berling," she said softly. "I'll prepare a quick breakfast. But then we must be on our way."

The Captain, so used to barking his own orders, obeyed quickly and swung his feet over and kicked Berling into a grumpy wakefulness. "Wake up, ya hairy bag of trash. There's things ta do and not another moment ta waste."

Berling pushed a woolen hat down over his eyes, grunted, and then rolled over, pulling his knees up into a tight fetal position. "Leave me be, ya mangy sea dog. Can't ya see I need my sleep?"

"Not today, dwarf. We need ta be up and movin'."

Just then, the sizzling sound of meat, placed gently on a hot pan, caused both Berling and the Captain to lift their heads. Berling pulled his hat off and sniffed the cool air. "Ah," he exclaimed. "Nothin' like the smell of cookin' breakfast ta get a man's blood flowin'."

The Captain nodded eagerly as an errant string of saliva escaped the corners of his mouth. "Aye, lad. Thar's nothing better."

Erna smiled tenderly as she watched Berling and the Captain devour the food she'd prepared. Their hums of enjoyment as they stuffed each morsel of food into their mouths made her want to serve them more. She nodded with satisfaction and mused to herself, wondering if Zeke would be someone who would value her cooking. She blushed at the thought and then recognized that time was running short. They had to get moving.

"All right boys," she said, lifting plates away from the barrage of forks and knives. "Time to get a move on. Zeke is out there somewhere and I have a feeling that finding him is going to involve a long walk."

ᛣ

As the tiny group plodded their way northward along a narrow rocky road the snow became deeper. At times they had to climb over tall drifts and fallen tree limbs to keep on the path. Berling became especially frustrated as his short legs hindered his progress, forcing him to rely on the Captain to lift him over obstacles that marred the way.

They stopped now and then and rested on rotting tree stumps or tiny boulders that edged the roadway, gathering their strength before setting out again. At one point the Captain even stopped to build a tiny fire. The exhausted travelers bent close and warmed their freezing hands over the tiny flames and cooked a small lunch of potatoes and salted meat.

After a few moments of quiet, while the travelers ate their meager meal, the Captain, his sighs heavy with fatigue, finally spoke, his voice hushed and calm. "I know this may sound like I'm giving up, but I don't think I can go on," he said, his head bowed while his hands rested in his lap.

"I thought there was a reason for me to be here," he continued. "That's why I jumped into the hole. But I'm old and weak and fat. I really don't know what I was thinking. I'm no good to anyone."

Berling looked up quickly from his meal and frowned. He opened his mouth to say something, but then thought better of it and went back to his meal. Erna, on the other hand, pushed her plate aside and rose to sit by the Captain, her arms wrapped tightly around his thick shoulders.

"Bart," she said, her gentle voice sending a shiver up the Captain's back. "You're old, you're weak, and you are fat, that I will not deny. But, there is a definite reason for you to be here. Your intuition was correct when you jumped into the cleft. You felt it then as you feel it now. You have a warrior's heart. There's no question about it. You've doubted yourself in the past, but that doubt has only made you stronger. You can sense it, can't you?" Erna turned to look at the Captain as his eyes stared blankly into the heat of the fire. She pushed the Captain lightly, a nudge with a touch of love. "Can't you?" she repeated.

A small smile curved the Captain's lips as he nodded. "Aye," he said quietly. "I can feel it. A wee bit anyway."

Erna pressed on. "That feeling is the warrior within. You've always had it you just didn't know it. But soon," she said, her grip on the Captain's shoulder becoming tighter, "you're going to need it. I said it before and I'll say it again. You will obtain the gift that only a warrior can receive. I will be honest, I don't know exactly what that means, but I feel it here," Again, she brought her hand to her heart. "Zeke needs you, Bart. Don't say that you're no good to anyone, because you are to Zeke, and that's all that matters."

Bartholomew Gunner raised his red, watery eyes from the tiny flames and looked at Erna, his forehead raised in question. "The gift of a warrior, ya say? I'm not sure why, Erna, but that expression has me feelin' a bit worried, almost as if thar's a nasty fate awaiting me. Almost as if I might never see Alder Cove again."

This time Berling set his own plate aside as he watched Erna try to console his aged and exhausted companion.

"No, Bart," she said soothingly. "I can't believe the Norns have fated an end here in the Mist. I'm sure we'll find Zeke and Devon and soon be on our way home. You'll die an old man in your home at Alder Cove. I'm sure of it." But even as she said it, Erna *wasn't* sure. Something pressed upon her, and though she tried to push it away, the feeling clung, like a memory of something willingly forgotten.

As the flames of the tiny fire flickered and then died, the trekkers continued on through the snow, lifting sagging branches that barred their way. Their feet left faint prints that were quickly brushed away by the blowing wind.

Soon they came upon a fork in the road and stopped. One path ascended into the higher reaches of Yggdrasil, while the other descended, a twisting trail that led to darkness and forest. In its path were overhanging trees that curved inward like an oppressive tunnel.

Erna turned to Berling. "Which way?" she asked.

Berling thought for a moment and considered the options before him. "If we go this way," he said, pointing toward the descending path, "we will reach the entrance to Niflheim. That is the realm of the dead and the home of Hel. We don't want to go that way." Then he looked upward. His eyes contemplated the trail ascending into the light of day, its canopy free of overhanging trees while the snow seemed to thin, leaving bare patches of ground and tender tufts of young green fern growing between the rocks. "But that way," he smiled, "is much better. There, at least, we'll find some warmth."

Berling started along the path, his tiny feet testing the upward slope when he suddenly stopped. "Did ya hear that?" he asked, his ear cocked to one side.

Erna and the Captain, who almost stumbled into the back of Berling when he came to an abrupt halt, looked at each other. "We didn't hear anything, ya paranoid goof," the Captain said.

"No." Berling raised his hand for quiet. "There's something comin', a horse and wagon by the sound of it."

The travelers stared up the pathway, a mixture of fear and curiosity filling their expressions. Finally, the Captain let out the breath he'd been holding, a small puff of mist floating in the air before him.

"Well, I'll be," he said. He raised his hand to rub the back of his neck. "If I'm not mistakin', that's Zeke makin' his way toward us."

And indeed, heading down the path, his staff firmly held in his right hand while his left arm swung in awkward time to his pronounced limp, came Zeke. Behind him, pulling a teetering, dilapidated wooden cart was the saddest looking dwarf the three travelers had ever set eyes on. Zeke, glancing up from his concentrated effort of walking, stopped dead in his tracks. He looked up in complete surprise at the mangy group that stood before him. At first his face showed uncertainty, a tint of defensiveness as he gripped the staff with both hands and spread his feet. But then, as if a light switch were suddenly flicked on, Zeke's mouth split into a wide smile. His eyes grew wide as recognition struck him.

"Wha...how...?" And then he ran, mindless of the throbbing pain in his thigh and completely oblivious to the dwarf who stood behind him with a wagon full of treasure.

Zeke reached the Captain first and threw the staff aside on the muddied ground while he wrapped his arms around Bartholomew's thick neck, hugging him in a tight embrace. He giggled like a small child as he pulled back from the Captain and looked him in the eye.

"You're here!" he exclaimed. "You're really here!" He laughed again and his voice sounded almost giddy. He gave Berling a quick glance, but then he turned and saw Erna.

Zeke's child-like expression faltered as the red in his cheeks deepened. Erna's cheeks reddened as well, but her eyes at once lit up with pure joy. She raced toward Zeke and wrapped her arms around him. She kissed him gently on both cheeks while Zeke stood in quiet, but delighted bewilderment, his arms, as if unsure of what to do, rose slowly and took Erna into a gentle embrace.

The Captain and Berling stood to the side, their heads bowed in embarrassment as they tried to look at something other than Zeke and Erna. Finally, the Captain cleared his throat and reached for Zeke's discarded staff.

"Here, boy. You'll be needin' this." Erna released her tight grip on Zeke and took the staff from the Captain and handed it to Zeke, her eyes suddenly shaded with concern.

"This is Sinmora's staff. Is she alright?"

Zeke nodded slowly and gripped the staff like an old friend. He put his weight on it once again. "She's fine," he said. Then he added, "I think."

Erna gave a slight gasp. "You think?" she said. "What does that mean?"

Taking a deep breath, Zeke looked at the tired travelers. Then with his free hand he pointed at Andvari and the wagonload of treasure. "That," he said, his voice filled with exhaustion, "is ransom. Nidhogg the Dragon has Sinmora and Devon held captive in his cave. The only way he'll release them is if I bring him this gold."

Andvari, who stood listening to Zeke's explanation, began fuming with anger. "I knew it!" he yelled. He dropped the small harness he'd been using to pull the wagon on the ground with disdain. "Treasure for a dragon, is it? Well not in my lifetime it won't be! I'll be turnin' this contraption around right here and now. No dragon is going to be getting any of my gold!"

Zeke, as if he'd completely forgotten that his friends stood near, bounded toward Andvari, the staff raised high above his head. "You will stay right where you are!" Zeke shouted. "I employ you now, dwarf. That gold will go where I say! Don't forget, I hold the Staff of Urd." Zeke shook the staff threateningly in Andvari's face.

Andvari tried to hold his ground as his face twisted and contorted with anger. But eventually he wilted, his fear of the staff forced him to bind himself once again to the harness at the front of the wagon.

Suddenly aware that his friends stood behind him, Zeke turned, his face red with shame. "I'm... I'm sorry." He looked directly at Erna's soft features. "I'm not usually like that. But Sinmora told me..."

"It's okay," Erna interrupted as she stepped toward Zeke and took him again in a soft embrace. "I understand."

Berling, who had been quiet up until now, pushed his way past Zeke and Erna. He stood before Andvari and glared at him. "Why if it isn't the ol' fish monger himself." He chuckled lightly under his breath. "Sinmora taught ya a lesson once before and now it's his turn, is it?" He laughed again, but this time there was no joy in his mirth, only a measure of scorn and disdain.

Berling turned quickly to Zeke. "You've done well ta keep this one under a tight leash," he said. "Why he'd most likely cut yer throat and walk away before ya got a chance ta bleed." Berling walked back to the fork in the path, his hands sunk deep into the warmth of his pockets.

Zeke looked at the Captain. "Who is that?"

Bartholomew looked once at Berling and then turned back to Zeke. "Sorry, lad. I'd forgotten that you and the scruffy dwarf over there had never been introduced." He reached over and pulled at Berling's tattered jacket, drawing him close so that Zeke could get a good look.

"This is Berling," the Captain said. He ruffled Berling's hair lightly but lovingly. "He's the one who got us here." The Captain then looked affectionately at the tiny man, crouched down beside him, and wrapped his arm around his shoulder. "And, he's my good friend. You can trust him."

Zeke nodded once and looked at the Captain with a knowing glance. "That's good enough for me," he said, urging Andvari on with a wave of the staff. "I trust you Captain. You can always depend on that."

As the ancient wheels began to turn and creak with the weight of the treasure, Zeke stepped forward and grabbed Erna by the hand while his other clung to the Staff of Urd. The Captain and Berling fell into obedient cadence behind the rolling wagon as the travelers descended the path. They turned right at the fork in the road and marched their way downward toward the darkness of Niflheim and the cave that housed the dragon Nidhogg.

Chapter Twenty-Eight
At a Loss for Words

The battered and exhausted soldiers dropped two by two and shoulder-to-shoulder through the holes burrowed into the solid rock that overlooked the roiling ocean and the cold, barren beach of Surtsey. Loki continued to bark orders, sometimes going so far as to force some of the warriors through the holes, especially the bigger giants whose immense stature and width made entrance into the gaps difficult.

Behind the chaos, shivering in the cold, stood Marjorie, Vivian, and Taylre. They watched as a procession of soldiers approached the newly dug holes, leapt into the air, and then disappeared into the blackness of the gaps and the enveloping shrouds of the Mist.

"They'll be in search of the boys," Marjorie said sadly. Her arms clung tightly to both Vivian and Taylre.

"I hope so," Taylre responded. "They need to be warned. The witch is going to kill them. Mr. Loden said so."

Marjorie pulled her granddaughter in even tighter and grabbed her lightly by the chin, raising her face so they could both peer into one another's eyes. "*Something* is going to try to kill them," Marjorie said. "But it isn't going to be a witch."

Taylre's eyes squinted. Her new glasses allowed her to see her grandmother's face much more clearly. "What does that mean?" she asked. Her voice echoed a tenor of betrayal. "Mr. Loden told me they were in danger. He brought me here to warn them about the witch and that's what I'm going to do."

"Taylre," Marjorie began. "Mr. Loden isn't who you think he is. He's lying to you. Whatever he's done, and I'm not sure what that is, he's convinced you that he's your friend. But he isn't. You've got to believe me. He is going to hurt the boys, not save them."

For a moment, perhaps just a millisecond, Taylre believed her grandmother. But then her brow furrowed and intense anger began to contort her normally pleasing, soft expression.

"You're the one who's lying!" she spat. "You're just jealous. You think I love Mr. Loden more than you. And maybe you're right. Maybe I do!" Taylre tore away from her grandmother's grasp and began to run until she fell against the soft fur of Fenrir where she began to cry. Her tears soaked Fenrir's soft coat.

Loki, who continued to yell and scream at his soldiers, stopped and watched as Taylre stumbled across the frozen ground, tripping and falling into the supple fur of his son. He smiled wickedly. "Wormwood," he said, his depraved smile bending and twisting his lips. "It never disappoints."

He strode toward Taylre; a sly, calculated smirk pressed his features. He glared at Marjorie as he crossed over the jagged rocks. When he reached Taylre, he gently draped his arm across her shoulders.

"Be not afraid, my sweet child. Your grandmother doesn't understand, you see. For she, too, has been led astray by the witch. Do you not remember me telling you that?"

He drew Taylre in and hugged her to his breast. Then he wiped the tears from her eyes. Marjorie looked on from a short distance, speechless, her horror-struck emotions tightening like a hot ball of flame that crouched inside her chest. She tried to blurt out a warning, a scream even, anything to distract the monster that held her granddaughter. But somehow, just by glancing at her, Loki had managed to once again stifle Marjorie's speech. Instead she was forced to listen as the Pied Piper whispered his lies and weaved his tales of deceit.

"Look at your grandmother, Taylre. Look at the way she longs to speak to you and confess her wrong. But she can't. Do you know why?" Loden said, resting his hand lightly under her chin and raising her head to look him in the eye.

"No, I don't," Taylre answered quietly.

"It's because the witch has bound her tongue. Sinmora, the evil one, can feel us near. She knows that if your grandmother were to continue to speak, she would reveal the truth of who she really is. The witch knows that we are coming for her, and she's frightened, you see."

"What should we do?" Taylre asked.

"Why we must go now and stop her. We haven't a moment to lose."

"But what about grandma? Will she be coming too?"

"No, child. That would be too dangerous for her. If Sinmora knew that she was with us, who do you think she would try to kill first?"

Taylre wiped a final tear from her cheek and looked over at her grandmother. She felt a sense of shame at having yelled at her, for now she understood that her grandmother really didn't understand, that it wasn't her fault that she said those awful things about Mr. Loden; the witch *was* controlling her and trying to stop them from rescuing Zeke and Devon.

"I understand," Taylre finally said. She turned back and gave a solemn look at Loden. "It will be safer if grandma stays here. I would hate it if she were to get hurt. I would blame myself."

Loden nodded. "That is right, my child. Besides, you'll see her again very soon. Then we can join together and be one happy family: you, your grandmother, Zeke, and Devon. Won't that be nice?"

Marjorie tried to reach forward, tried to step across the rough earth, but her legs wouldn't let her and her arms felt like leaden weights at her sides. She was helpless. All she could do was stare as tears began to fill her eyes and spill over onto her face.

Loden and Taylre were both looking at Marjorie. Taylre's face lit up with a warm smile while Loden's remained much colder.

"You see," Loden said. "She's trying so hard to break the witch's spell so she can tell you how much she loves you and how proud she is. How very brave. How very brave."

Taylre blew her grandmother a kiss. "I'll be back soon, grandma. And don't worry, Mr. Loden will take good care of me."

Marjorie, who felt the frozen, clinging grip of Vivian at her side, watched as Taylre let Loki lead her toward the same gap that the Captain, Berling, and Erna had jumped through. Then soon, just like her missing companions, Taylre disappeared into the darkness of the hole while a mist gathered about her, taking her away forever.

Chapter Twenty-Nine
The Strength of the Staff

Amid the branches of Yggdrasil, a traveler could, at any given time, look up into the night sky and see as many as twelve moons perched in the darkness. However, tonight the sky was shrouded in heavy overcast. The gray melded into the black of night like watercolors running in the rain. A light drizzle fell from the thick clouds and scattered a fine mist upon the warming ground, melting the remaining snow and urging the heads of the wildflowers to rise, turning winter into spring.

The weary travelers, spent and worn from their day's journey, finally stopped for the night and found shelter from the light rain beneath a tall evergreen, its branches spread wide, while its broad truck seemed to beckon the travelers to lean into its sturdy frame for support and rest. A tiny flame flickered from a campfire. Beside it, huddled beneath thin blankets, sat the Captain, Berling, Zeke, and Erna. They shivered, despite the warming flames that battled hard to produce enough heat to warm its companions while they munched on a meager meal of cold potatoes and strips of salted meat. A few yards away, huddled beneath the cart that contained the golden treasure, slept Andvari. His legs were pulled up tight into his chest while his arms wrapped tightly around his knees. He snored heavily, oblivious to the cold as exhaustion from pulling the burdensome wagon prevailed.

The Captain, his arms curled beneath the tentative warmth of the blanket, used his chin as a pointer, nudging it toward Andvari. "A friend of yours, is he?" he asked. He gave Zeke a prod with his elbow.

Zeke poked his head out from beneath his thin woolen blanket, his eyes puffy from exhaustion, but his mind somehow focused and awake. "No," he said quietly. "That is certainly no friend of mine. The only reason he's here is because I needed someone to haul the gold. I couldn't do it on my own." Zeke pointed at his leg, indicating with a wince that the pain from Loki's stab still throbbed and ached.

The Captain nodded slowly as he took another short puff on his pipe and pushed aside the cold remains of his meal. "And the dragon ya spoke of. You're not seriously sayin' it's real, are ya?"

Zeke pulled the blanket tighter around his neck and

shoulders. "I've never been more serious in my life," he answered. "Nidhogg is real. He's big. He's ugly. And he's mean. But worst of all, he's smart."

The Captain watched Zeke as he spoke and marveled at his maturity. He found that he almost didn't recognize him; he had changed that much over the course of his harrowing journey. And the Captain was sure, very sure, that Zeke had certainly witnessed many things that had forced him to grow up very quickly.

"You're telling me that you've actually seen a dragon? Up close?"

Zeke nodded. "Much too close for my liking," he said. "But because he loves gold and treasure, he's keeping Devon and Sinmora captive. The only way I could set them free and move past his cave into Niflheim was to search for Andvari. Sinmora told me where to find him. She said he was sneaky and that I was to be extra careful, because he'd kill me if he got the chance. This staff," Zeke said, holding the Staff of Urd up so that the Captain could get a closer look, "would bring him into submission. Apparently it has some kind of power. Sinmora said that I need to learn to use it before something really bad happens."

The Captain reached out and touched the wooden base of the staff. He recoiled, as if he'd   suddenly been shocked by a powerful surge of electricity. He pulled his arms in beneath his blanket and stared at Zeke. "There's magic there. No doubt about it. No wonder Andvari follows you. He obviously knows something about the staff that we don't."

With the staff held in front of him Zeke said, "There have been times when I've felt its power. It's lifted me and strengthened me at times when I really needed it. I only wish I could get that kind of strength from it whenever I wanted." Zeke's eyes began to close as exhaustion finally took its toll. His head nodded awkwardly to the side, and he slumped forward.

The Captain, straightening Zeke's slumping form, gently pushed him back against the tree while he draped a blanket around his shoulders. Then the Captain watched as Zeke's breathing slowed and his muscles relaxed, a slight twitch here and there that let the Captain know Zeke was now fast asleep.

Bartholomew looked toward his other companions and noted that they too were drifting amid the world of dreams as snores and heavy breathing emanated from their open mouths.

With only the peaceful crackle of the tiny fire to keep the Captain company and the light sprinkle of rain to remind him that his current situation was not in fact a dream, he considered Zeke's words and the path they were headed down. Bartholomew's mother had related many stories about Nidhogg;

he reflected on them uneasily in the quiet of the night. Then he looked at Andvari - a treacherous little imp indeed. But Nidhogg was worse. This the Captain knew. Andvari was not one you turned your back on, but he could be controlled. Nidhogg, on the other hand...

The Captain pulled up on his blanket and tried to sleep. But he knew, even as he closed his eyes that sleep would not come; there was a battle ahead, and Erna's words kept ringing in his head - *you will obtain the gift of a warrior.*

Bartholomew was more frightened than he could have ever thought possible.

Chapter Thirty
The Warrior Within

A dirty gray light managed to seep through the top of the cave's entrance, but the entire bottom half was blocked by Nidhogg's enormous body. Devon stared at the light, meager though it was and longed for it; it had been so long since he'd had the chance to really see it. Darkness was pressing a pall of depression on his mind. He needed sunlight.

Twelve days. That's how long they'd been stuck in the back of the cave with its putrid, rank odors of dragon dung, rotting corpses, and dank, black pools of water that festered with scum and floating entrails. Devon was tired of it. In fact, he'd gone well beyond tired. He was becoming downright angry.

Beside him, stuffed amid the musty gloom, sat Vidar and Sinmora. Missing was Alsvid. Nidhogg had eaten him days ago and the echoes of his screams still reverberated throughout the immense cavern. Devon tried to push the memory aside; he couldn't remember ever seeing anything so horrible. Even the death of Officer Teddy Walford in La Cueva del Diablo paled in comparison to the slow, agonizing death that Alsvid had to endure. To make matters worse, Vidar had to watch it too. Devon was suffering from the memory, but he was sure that Vidar's anguish was much worse

Alsvid was Vidar's horse, a friend who provided not only transportation, but also companionship. Now, not only had Vidar lost his mother and father, but he had lost his favorite pet as well. His tears seemed to be endless. Devon could hear him sniffling in the darkness of the cave's shadows despite his heroic efforts to remain brave. But after all, Vidar was still a boy. Devon understood this all too well.

As Devon continued to consider their hopeless predicament, he suddenly felt the warmth of Sinmora's hand grab his own. She reached over a tiny outcropping of rock and touched Vidar as well, her gentleness so very grandmotherly.

"Be at peace," she said, almost as if she could discern Devon's bleak thoughts. "Zeke is coming. I can sense it. And, he brings help."

As soon as Sinmora uttered these glad tidings, Nidhogg began to stir. His head rose slowly from his solid pillow of gold, emeralds, and diamonds. He sniffed the air as a sense of agitation grew within his scaled features.

Normally, Nidhogg slept most of the night and day, his long naps broken only by the occasional bloodied corpse that would wander dejectedly into the dragon's lair from the realm of Hel. Mostly, the dead looked the same: their eyes were gouged out while their tongues, what was left of them, hung from their mouths either from exhaustion or because their screams had been suddenly interrupted. They shuffled aimlessly into the cave and walked straight toward Nidhogg, almost as if it were their destiny, the force of it prodding them on to their final, torturous end. When they got close enough, Nidhogg would reach out with his narrow, sharpened jaw and grab hold of the mindless creatures, ripping them apart limb by limb until there was nothing left but some tough ligaments and tiny fragments of bone. Nidhogg would then gnaw on the last of these pieces until he once again fell asleep. Then he would snore loudly, satisfied once again with his meal, his gift from the caretakers of Niflheim, the land of the dead.

Today, however, was different. Nidhogg was rising too quickly; something other than a corpse was approaching. Vidar once again began to cry as his shattered emotions poured out in fear for Zeke.

Sinmora took Vidar by the hand and shook him gently. "Hush, now. There is nothing to fear. Zeke has the staff. Its magic ripples in the air before him. He has discovered more of its power. Of that I am certain. So, fear not. Zeke will take care of himself."

Suddenly, from somewhere beyond the entrance to Nidhogg's dwelling, came a distant shout. Its declaration pierced the gray light with familiarity and hope.

"Nidhogg!" the voice shouted. "Nidhogg! Wake! Wake, wise serpent of Niflheim! Listen, as the slayer of the Korrigan speaks to you. Listen as the wielder of the white stones beckons you from your cave. Who can hear the sound of the grass growing? Or, the sound of wool on a sheep's back growing? Who needs less sleep than a bird? Who is so eagle-eyed that, by day and by night, he can see the least movement a hundred leagues away?

"Nidhogg! Nidhogg! Nidhogg!"

Devon stood quickly and grazed the jagged rock of the cave with his back, but he remained oblivious to the pain; his brother was outside; he had come to save them from their captivity.

Nidhogg began to growl as his clawed limbs pushed aside piles of treasure. He then shuffled his immense body out of the cave where the tired remains of man and animal lay strewn upon the ground and where the stench of rotting flesh bubbled over like oozing black tar.

Once more, there came a shout, but this time closer. Though the words were difficult to decipher, the voice was definitely that of Zeke's.

The three captives followed Nidhogg from the cave, but kept their distance. Their fear of this beast overwhelmed any attempt at bravado. Devon tried to jump so that he could peer over the dragon's large behind, anything to get a glimpse of Zeke. But Sinmora gave him a sharp look and placed her hand forcefully upon his shoulder.

"Soon enough," she said. "Soon enough."

Devon shied and reddened at Sinmora's gentle reproach. He allowed her to take the lead, as they finally broke free from the darkness and the stink of the grotto, entering the gray light of day.

Heavy clouds hung in the air above, their weighty, dark linings threatening rain. Instead, they just hovered, as if this, too, were their permanent home. Devon glanced upward feeling the oppression of the clouds like a sentence of death. But his attention was soon drawn toward a narrow fissure in the rock beyond the cave where a small troupe of travelers entered. The first to come into view was Zeke, with the Staff of Urd held firmly in his right hand. Standing beside him, holding his left hand was Erna. Devon smiled to himself, a momentary plunge into levity as he thought of Zeke actually having a girlfriend. But he was quickly pulled from his giddiness when he saw the wagon. Its bed was filled to overflowing with gold. Pulling it was a very angry looking dwarf. His teeth were ground together while his eyes continued to shift toward Zeke. Their yellow centers seemed to pierce his back with a look of malice.

Once again a low growl emanated from somewhere deep in Nidhogg's scaled throat.

"Stop there, light bearer," Nidhogg called, his voice edgy with threat. "Stand aside so that I may see the great treasure you have brought me."

Zeke stopped abruptly and bore the staff firmly in the ground before him. He released his gentle grip on Erna's hand and then turned, looking back at Andvari.

"Move aside, dwarf. Let the dragon see the gold."

Andvari began to growl too as his sharp pike teeth exposed an ominous grin. "I'll not do it!" he bellowed. "This is my gold. I made it and I'll keep it. I won't be handin' it over to some ugly serpent."

Zeke turned completely now and faced Andvari directly, his face revealing a rare look of authority. He held the staff high and then unswervingly aimed it at the dwarf. Andvari took a giant step backward. Even the Captain found himself edging back as Zeke's sudden show of power held sway over the small group.

"You will do exactly as I have bidden you to do," Zeke said. "I hold the power of the staff. I can feel its magic start to rise in me. Do as I say or I will destroy you!"

Andvari hesitated for only a moment before he stomped his foot hard into the ground and then released the harness that kept him fixed to the wagon. He moved reluctantly to the side and sat down upon the rocky earth, crossing his arms over his chest like a defiant child.

Zeke looked back at Nidhogg while his hand waved in the direction of the treasure-filled wagon. "I have brought you the rarest of gold, Nidhogg. It is red gold forged in the land of the dark elves."

The dragon of Niflheim squinted toward the incredible cache of red and yellow gold as its uneven surface caught the light of the gray day and reflected it onto the rocks. The light seemed to dance as it sparkled, catching the dragon's eye as he stared at it greedily.

"Is this all you have brought me, holder of the stones of Odin? Surely you could have done better than this." Nidhogg shuffled toward the wagon and sniffed at the contents with an air of contempt.

"My home is filled with gold from the land of the dark elves," Nidhogg continued, though Zeke noted a tiny drop of saliva that fell from the corner of the dragon's mouth, as if the beast longed to hold the treasure, letting each and every nugget caress his scaled body. "Do you really expect me to release your friends for something as meager and unsubstantial as this?"

Zeke stood in front of Erna, protecting her, while the Staff of Urd was held firmly in front of him. "I ... I have brought you the best, Nidhogg. What more could I do?"

"That is not for me to decide, young warrior. Your task was to bring me a ransom, something of value. But this," he said, shaking his head sadly, "is nothing but a pittance. Of course I will keep it for my collection, but it is not enough to save your friends. I'm afraid I will have to eat them."

Nidhogg turned suddenly from the wagon, the gold, and from Zeke. He bared his teeth viciously at Devon, Sinmora, and Vidar.

"Wait!" Zeke hollered. He held out the staff with his right hand while his left hand pushed against the putrid air like a policeman halting traffic. "I have something else."

Nidhogg stopped and turned. A malevolent grin dripped from his jagged tooth-filled mouth. "Well, what have you brought me, slayer of Loki's daughter, destroyer of the giant Geirrod? Is it enough to save your friends?"

Zeke continued to hold the staff in front of him while he reached into his pocket. "Here." He held Andvari's ring out in front of him like a talisman of hope.

Nidhogg stared at the ring. At first his face showed nothing but indifference, but then, as he looked deeper, his eyes widened.

"Oh, Zeke Proper," the dragon whispered, the taste of pure avarice dripping off his tongue. "You have brought me the gift of a life-time. With this gift I shall be able to forge my own gold. I shall never be in want. Where ever did you find it?"

"Never mind that. Is it enough to free my friends?" Zeke said.

The dragon bent closer as an eager look of stupidity crossed his features. "It is more than enough, my little friend. More than enough."

Then, with his huge clawed hands, Nidhogg tried to reach out and grab the ring from Zeke's open palm. But Andvari, who had been sitting to the side watching the whole affair with an air of uncertainty, suddenly stood up and raced across the rocky ground toward Zeke's upturned hand.

"It's mine!" He quickly grabbed at the ring and snatched it from Zeke.

Andvari ran with the ring tucked tightly within his chubby little fist. He pushed past the Captain with a violent shove of his shoulder and then literally careened into Berling with the force of a sledgehammer. Berling landed flat on his back as a heavy "umph" escaped his mouth. His breath was pushed forcefully from his lungs.

Andvari continued to run and headed directly for the narrow fissure in the rocks that surrounded Nidhogg's cave. He tripped once and fell flat on his face, his tiny body splayed out like road kill on the rough ground. Sharp stones tore at his exposed skin, opening deep cuts on his arms and legs. He stood quickly and opened his fist slightly to see that the ring was still there, then, almost as an afterthought, glanced at his bleeding limbs. Andvari ignored them, the pain of the frightful wounds becoming a mere annoyance as he tried to slip away quickly and return to his smithy and his place beneath the waters.

Nidhogg, however, was quicker.

Before Andvari could reach the gap, Nidhogg's huge tail swept through the air with a "whoosh", its scaled end caught the dwarf fully in the chest. Andvari sailed through the rancid air while his tiny arms flailed spasmodically, almost as if he could somehow fly his way over the rocks. He landed with a painful thud on the coarse earth while the ring tumbled from his fist. It rolled in the dust and dirt until it lost momentum, spun once on its rounded edge and then toppled over on its side. But before the dwarf could rise, Nidhogg pounced heavily on his chest. He crushed the life from him as bones cracked and organs disintegrated under the dragon's weight. Zeke, who stood at the forefront, looked on in absolute horror. Behind him he could hear the moans and screams of his friends as they too witnessed the ghastly scene.

Nidhogg pressed his foot harder into Andvari's body as the tiny dwarf's form seemed to meld into the ground. Blood and entrails squished over to the sides of the dragon's foot as Andvari's life was completely obliterated. The dragon ignored the viscera that clung to the bottom of his foot and stepped toward the ring with an eagerness that bordered on obsession, his bloodied foot now coming down and hiding the ring. Nidhogg then turned toward the horrified onlookers and growled

"So this was your plan, light bearer? Pretend to offer me the Forger's Ring while another runs off with it. Is that it?"

It took a moment for Zeke to understand what Nidhogg was referring to. His mind was still caught up in the shock of Andvari's violent death. But then realization set in. Nidhogg had just accused him of being a liar.

Anger began to well up in Zeke's brain. From far across the corpse infested courtyard Devon could see the fury that began to rise. He recognized it from times past when he'd teased Zeke to the brink of madness, ire mounting as Devon taunted him and prodded him on until he screamed with frustration. But this time there was a difference. Zeke's anger wasn't the childish frustration of sibling rivalry; this was controlled rage, the substance of a warrior. Sinmora placed her hand on Devon's shoulder. Her fingers gripped his skin tightly.

"This is what we've been waiting for," she declared. "Now we begin to see the warrior within."

Devon watched with growing anticipation as Zeke lifted the Staff of Urd. He noted with a sense of awe and confusion the glowing golden light that grew from the staff's base, spinning up the sides of the polished wood and circling ever closer to its glossy tip. Then he saw Zeke advance toward Nidhogg, his limp all but forgotten, as his body appeared to strengthen under the staff's swelling magic.

Nidhogg saw the light too and his yellow eyes narrowed to slits of malice. "Be careful, friend of Shaker," the dragon hissed. "You may have defeated the Korrigan, or so the tale goes, but you are no match for me. The runes on the white stones protected you then, and perhaps you believe the Staff of Urd is yours to wield as well. But my magic is strong. It has passed the test of time and millennia. And it is dark, Zeke Proper. Oh, so dark."

There was a moment, perhaps just a brief millisecond, when Zeke thought he saw movement, like a flash just before the lights go out. He'd been looking directly at Nidhogg, his enormous, scaled body far across the courtyard still hunched over the ring. And then suddenly the beast was standing right next to him, his hot, moist serpent breath raking across his skin. Nidhogg stooped, his jagged teeth bared as he hissed into Zeke's ear.

"You see, little warrior," the dragon mocked. "Darkness always extinguishes the light."

Nidhogg rose up on his haunches and his mouth widened as he prepared to devour his victim. Zeke, paralyzed with fear, could only watch as death loomed over him. The staff, its light now smothered, fell from his hands and clattered to the ground.

Suddenly, there was another flash of movement. Zeke saw it briefly from the corner of his eye. In front of him, as a spatter of dragon saliva dripped on his forehead, Zeke also saw Nidhogg's expression change. A look of surprise had altered the wicked gaze of murder. Zeke tore his eyes away from Nidhogg and was equally shocked to see the Captain standing beside him, the Staff of Urd gripped firmly in *his* hands.

"Step aside, ya mangy reptile, or I'll drive this stick so far up yer belly you'll be usin' it ta pick yer teeth from the inside."

The Captain stood with his feet spread apart, his shoulders squared, and his jaw set. His eyes seemed to exude a kind of madness whose glare would send most men running for their lives. The staff, its tip now glowing brightly with a golden light, was held just inches from the dragon's stomach.

"Run, Zeke," the Captain said, never taking his eyes off of Nidhogg's. "I've got it from here."

Zeke began inching himself backward, but his eyes never left the dragon that appeared to be wrestling with the thought of taking on a completely new and unexpected threat. In a few moments Zeke felt the warming hand of Erna. Her grip was firm as she pulled him even farther back. Soon they stood beside the treasure-filled wagon. Berling was leaning against the cart holding his stomach where Andvari had run into him. Beside him stood Devon, Sinmora, and Vidar, who, during the massacre of Andvari and the sudden attack on Zeke, had made their way as far away from the cave's entrance as possible. Together the small group watched with growing horror as Bartholomew Gunner challenged a ferocious beast whose head towered ten to twelve feet above his own.

Tension seemed to fill the air as both combatants stood waiting for the other to make a move. Finally, Nidhogg spoke his words sharp but measured. "It seems that you and I are at a stand off, old man."

The Captain's eyes squinted, a look of disdain that cast flickers of malice at the dragon. "I'll not be havin' ya call me that, ya stinkin snake. Old I may be, but the power of the staff is all the strength I need. I know it, and you know it, too. I can see the fear in yer eyes, dragon. Do ya deny it?"

"I deny nothing," Nidhogg said. "The magic of the staff is as old as Odin. But I wonder do you really know how to make it work to your advantage? Holding a glowing stick is one thing, but wielding the magic within is something completely different."

For a brief moment the Captain felt uncertainty. He questioned the power of the staff and what it could really do. Never in his life had he taken on a task as momentous as this. And although the staff burned in his hands with power, what could he really do with it? Did he have to say some sort of spell? Did he have to swing it in a certain way? Did the holder have to be a wizard? *What,* he thought *do I do with it?*

From far above, Nidhogg saw the doubt that drew itself across the Captain's features and knew it was time to strike.

Before the Captain had time to take a breath, Nidhogg raked his claw through the air and caught Bartholomew Gunner on the side of the head. The impact sent him flying across the hardened earth. Bartholomew was dazed as tiny lights danced in front of his eyes and thick drops of blood began to pour down the side of his face. But he managed to push aside the confusion and find the staff as it lay next to him on the ground. He stood uneasily and faced the dragon as it advanced toward him, jaw agape and teeth bared. The Captain gripped the staff in both hands, its magic sending painful jolts of electricity into his hands and up his arms. Nevertheless, he held firm, once again squaring his feet and readying himself for another painful onslaught.

As the dragon neared, Bartholomew thrust the staff forward, heedless of its direction. He simply hoped for the best. The tip of the staff struck Nidhogg brutally as he tried to bat the Captain aside again with his clawed hand. This time, however, the golden light that was kept secure within the confines of the gnarled wood, burst outward, spinning the dragon on his tail, casting him aside as he lay in a heavy, curled heap on the ground.

Nidhogg shook his head violently as his eyes seemed to spin in their own sockets. He rose unsteadily and looked around him as if he'd forgotten where he was. Then he turned to the Captain and rushed toward him. The dragon's howl of anger echoed off the rock walls sending tiny shards of stone and dust to the ground. This time, however, the Captain didn't wait. He threw the staff like a spear. Its tip caught the dragon in the chest, penetrating the thick scales and entering his black heart.

Nidhogg screamed.

The tiny group of observers edged back toward the rock walls and cowered from the piercing sound that clawed at their ears. Then they looked up in horror as Nidhogg's neck stretched upward, his shrill voice calling to the heavens for help. But there was none to come as blood began to pour from the open wound in his chest and as his eyes began to pop. White puss spilled from a thousand gaping holes as the ooze stained his shimmering scales with the residue of death.

Nidhogg fell over with a resounding thump, while his head came to rest beside Andvari's ring. For a moment he stared at it, and then a revolting look of greed once again filled his features before his eyes finally closed and his breathing stopped.

Nidhogg was dead.

ᚴ

There was silence, there was gloom, and there was death, lots of death. No one spoke; there were no words that could fill the space of dreadfulness that had just taken place. Zeke embraced Erna as they watched Nidhogg release his final breath.

Devon and Vidar looked around at all the blood, and Berling sat beside the tattered wheel of the wagon and wept. Then Sinmora finally spoke, her soft words turning the heads of the shattered group in one direction.

"Bartholomew," she whispered urgently.

The six travelers scurried across the hard earth and gathered round the fallen man. Before them they saw a harrowed, bloodied figure. The Captain, completely unconscious, appeared to have aged twenty years. His skin was pale, his lips were blue, his breathing was shallow and quick, and a deep gash on the side of his head continued to spill blood. Sinmora knelt before the stricken man and reached toward Zeke, rummaging inside the pack he wore at his hip. From it she extracted several thick bandages and a yellow-topped bottle. She pressed the bandages on Bartholomew's head and sprinkled a fine powder over the dressings that were quickly filling with blood.

"Will he be alright?" Erna asked.

Sinmora looked up from her work and stared at her apprentice. "You know the answer to that as well as I do. Did you not proclaim that he would receive the gift of a warrior?"

"I ...I did," Erna stammered. "But at the time I didn't know what that meant."

"What about now, child? Do you now understand your prophecy?"

Erna bowed her head and stared at her fidgeting hands. Then she turned to Zeke as a sad smile pushed her mouth into a frown. "I do," she proclaimed. "The gift is the entrance to Valhalla. There he will feast and celebrate his life as a warrior."

Zeke stepped forward. "Wait ... what? What are you guys talking about? The Captain is going to be fine. You just put that goop all over his head. That'll make him better, right?"

Erna shook her head sadly and took Zeke by the hand. She pressed it to her breast and looked deep into his eyes. "No," she said tearfully. "Bart is going to die. But he died to protect you. This is the warrior within. What he did today will be remembered. Songs will be sung and poems will be written. This is the legacy Bartholomew Gunner leaves behind."

Zeke pulled away from the grip Erna had on his hand and knelt beside his friend. "I don't want a legacy," Zeke said, as tears began to flow. "I want the Captain back."

Chapter Thirty-One
Shape Changer

Loki's entire army was encamped in a large field just west of Vanaheim near the land of the Vanir. If they were to leave now and march quickly for thirteen days, they would reach the world of the Aesir and the Gates of Asgard. But Loki had revenge on his mind and Fenrir could sense the darkness growing in his father.

"We are at the edge of victory," Fenrir said. "Let us take rest here for a day or two and then begin our march on Asgard. We must end this war now. We must give life to the prophecies."

"Patience, my son," Loki said as he sat in his jewel encrusted chair and sipped on his horn of mead. "The moment will present itself when it is time to attack. That instant has not yet appeared. The gods are strong and the warriors of Valhalla are eager for battle. We must attack only when they least expect it."

"I understand, father. But the giants are eager for battle as well. They pressure me to push you on to war."

"Do they?" Loki said. He turned an angry eye toward his son. "And have they also decided to lead this army as well?"

"No, father," Fenrir said, cowering at Loki's sudden display of temper. "They desire only to serve you."

Loki smiled drunkenly. "That is so good to ..."

"What is it, father?" Fenrir said, suddenly aware that Loki had stopped speaking and was tilting his head as if listening to another conversation.

"Something terrible has happened," Loki said. He stood suddenly within the confines of his tent. "I feel it in the air. The Mist declares the demise of Nidhogg. How could this happen?"

"Nidhogg?" Fenrir said incredulously. "Impossible. He holds magic nearly as great as your own. He has dwelt amid the carnage and rot of Niflheim almost as long as time itself. Nidhogg cannot die."

Loki's anger bubbled over into rage. He threw his horn of mead across the room. Its contents spilled across the hide-covered enclosure. "Are you questioning me!" he bellowed. "Is it you who now wants to lead this army? Is it you who desires to rule over Asgard instead of I?"

"No ...no father," Fenrir stammered, edging himself backward as he stared at the rage in his father's eyes.

"Then listen to me when I tell you! Nidhogg is dead!"

Loki stood on a raised platform in the center of the tent, his arms raised like a preacher calling his parishioners to repentance while his face flamed with anger. He stared down at his son, his teeth bared with the fury of a dragon when he suddenly stopped. His ranting dissipated amid the hides of the tent walls like a fading echo.

Loki was immediately filled with regret.

"My son," he proclaimed sadly. He stepped off the platform and buried himself in the soft fur of the wolf. "Forgive me. I did not intend to cause you fear or pain."

Fenrir nodded slowly and relished his father's touch and appreciation. "All is forgotten, father. I am always your servant. I will do whatever I can in your time of need. You need only ask."

Loki fell back and sat heavily on the edge of the platform. He looked up dejectedly at his son.

"Fenrir," he said, his palms open before him imploringly. "Things are not going as I had planned. I have traveled so far to rid this universe of the one thing that has outdone me. Yet he continues to somehow overcome my power. First he slays my bastard daughter, the Korrigan. Then, somehow, he destroys Geirrod, the most powerful giant there is. Could he have also killed Nidhogg as well? I expected him to travel the path that leads to Nidavellir, past the land of the dwarfs, but instead he travels to the one place most men choose to avoid: Niflheim. Why? Is he a greater foe than I could have imagined? Is he in fact more than just a silly Midgard child? Has he discovered a great magic that we are unaware of? Or, is that witch casting a more powerful influence on him than we could have imagined?" Loki stood and raked his hands across his face in frustration.

"The witch is nothing to be concerned about, father," Fenrir said soothingly. "She's an idiot. A pretender. She is nothing but a maker of potions and a stupid apprentice of Var who does nothing but listen to the silly compacts of men. Pay no attention to her. As for Zeke Proper," he said with a sly grin, "we will take care of him. His earlier successes have been nothing but luck. We will destroy him. I promise you; we have the annoying girl to make sure of that." Then Fenrir hesitated, considering his next words carefully.

"But father," he said hesitantly. "Promise me, please. When the minor task of destroying the Proper boy is done, let us be on our way to the Gates of Asgard. Let us tear down its walls with our army and regain the place that is rightfully ours. I feel the call of destiny. The life of Odin is mine to take, and I will have my revenge."

With shoulders hunched in defeat, Loki fought hard to look up at his son who loomed large in front of him. Finally, after a moments pause, Loki lifted his head, a sad sort of smile creasing his lips. He nodded and gently reached out his hand to touch his favorite. "This I promise, Fenrir. Once Zeke Proper has met a painful, agonizing death, we will continue our pursuit. We will destroy the gods of Asgard, I will bring all of my children home, and we will all live and rule in peace forever."

Loki rose slowly and patted Fenrir one last time on the top of his enormous head before he regained his place at his throne. Immediately a dwarf servant entered through a heavy flap of goat hide and poured another overflowing horn of mead. He handed it to Loki with a bow and then left as quietly as he had entered. Loki sipped on the brew, swirling the contents in his mouth before he swallowed.

"Where is the annoying girl, by the way?" Loki looked up over the edge of his drink at Fenrir.

"She sleeps, father," Fenrir's furry head motioned toward a hide-enclosed alcove within the tent.

"Why does that not surprise me?" Loki said. "It seems to me there is nothing else that she does, you see. Sleeping. Always sleeping." He took another short sip from his mead horn and then motioned it toward the alcove where Taylre slept. "Wake her," he ordered. "It is time that we challenge her with more lies."

Fenrir began moving toward Taylre's private niche when Loki suddenly called to him.

"Wait," Loki said. He swirled his mead gently in front of him while his mind seemed to be working on another problem. "Before you do that, let us devise a plan. This 'Light Bearer', as the legend and mythmakers are beginning to call him, has tricked us by turning to the land of the dead. But we don't know why. Somehow we must discover what he is up to, you see."

"I agree, father," Fenrir said. He returned to his place beside Loki and the jeweled throne. "But we waste our time in speculation. Let us, therefore, send a spy."

Loki nodded toward his son with a look of pride. "Well done, Fenrir, an excellent idea. Whom shall we send?"

Fenrir looked at his father knowingly. "Why, you, of course."

"Me?" Loki answered incredulously.

"Certainly. Have you forgotten your legendary ability as a shape changer? Surely you could summon the power once again. Change into something unexpected," Fenrir urged. "You could literally be a fly on the wall if you wanted."

Loki's smile broadened. "In recent times I have practiced the art," he admitted, "but it was to no avail. Nevertheless, if I were careful and my actions were calculated I could be successful as in the days of old." Memory cascaded over his mind. Then he turned to Fenrir and looked him directly in the eyes. "I will do it," he said brightly. "I will learn all of the secrets for myself. Indeed, I may even find the opportunity to destroy Zeke Proper within the land of the dead itself. How appropriate."

ᛣ

Taylre was not asleep.

Every word that had been uttered by father and son outside her tiny sleeping quarters had been heard. She fought hard to stifle the sound of her tears amid the blankets and pillows that covered her bed.

Foremost in her thoughts was the image of her grandmother: her tear stained face and her sad eyes as she tried to convince her that Loden was not her friend. Then, more tears streamed down Taylre's face as she recalled how angry she had been at her grandmother. How she had yelled at her and told her how silly she was.

What a fool I've been, Taylre thought.

She pounded her fists against her pillow in frustration and then sat up quickly while a thin blanket covered her shoulders.

I will fix this, she thought. *If it's the last thing I do, I will fix this.*

Zeke felt numb. His emotions were shattered and no amount of uplifting words could settle his aching heart; the loss of the Captain was more than he could bear. Erna tried her best to give comfort by embracing Zeke, stroking his hand and whispering sweet words, but he would only push her away wanting nothing more than to be left alone with his thoughts.

Sinmora tried to offer comfort through potions that she claimed would help Zeke relax and sleep, but this too he pushed away. Sleep was the last thing he wanted. And Berling kept stepping forward, resting his hand on Zeke's shoulder, saying nothing, only sighing deeply and then dropping back to follow the rest.

Zeke felt responsible for the Captain's death and wanted to punish himself for the shear stupidity of his own cowardly fear, therefore he was determined to go without food and water and keep at bay the desire to sleep.

Before leaving Nidhogg's stronghold, Sinmora committed a shallow grave in honor of Bartholomew Gunner. Her words, as she spoke quietly over his place of rest, spoke of the breadth and honor of a worthy warrior. They spoke of his journey in death to his final resting place among the warriors of Valhalla where he would obtain the gifts that only a true warrior can receive: feasting among the greatest of men, the company of the Valkyrie who would serve him meat and wine, and a place of rest where he could finally push aside the burdensome cares of Midgard. All these things and more were said as the last of the earth, along with the golden Forger's Ring, were thrown upon the Captain's burial place. For as Sinmora prophesied, nothing but evil would come from the ring. Its band of magic was full of greed; its holder would eventually be destroyed by it. Thus it was best to bury it with the Captain and be done with it forever. Nevertheless, Zeke's soul still felt the weight of an enormous guilt. He remained steadfast to the belief that if he'd only held tight to the staff and wielded the power on his own, it would have been him that would have destroyed the dragon, the Captain would be alive to continue the journey. To make matters worse, Zeke began to question his companions, those who proclaimed the ability to see the future as seers.

Did not Sinmora whisper in Devon's ear, just as the dragon was about to attack, that the true heart of the warrior would be seen? Yet she lied; Zeke had faltered in his will and let fear encompass him. He dropped the staff and would have died in the jaws of Nidhogg if the Captain hadn't come to his rescue. And what about Erna? Her words of encouragement, Zeke decided, were nothing but lies as well. As far as Zeke was concerned, no one could be trusted. The entire journey had been a complete and utter waste of time. Both his father and the Captain were dead, Taylre was still missing, and his leg was aching worse than it ever had. What more could go wrong?

As Zeke continued his dark musings, he realized that the cave of Nidhogg was now several days behind them. The travelers had journeyed at an incredible pace as they scurried over tundra, scrub, and undulating land. Beyond, toward the horizon, a chain of mountains rose into view. Some were like upturned ships, some like unfinished pyramids and monstrous cones with their tops sawn off, but none of them were smiling. It was a dark and dreary place that the travelers were advancing toward.

Bringing up the rear of the tiny parade was Vidar and Devon. They were pulling Andvari's cart that was lightly loaded with some meager supplies, food, and of course Berling, whose legs were too short to keep up with the rest of the group. The gold that had once filled the wagon had been dumped next to the rotting, burning corpse of Nidhogg. All of the travelers agreed that it was now in its rightful place. Only a few nuggets had been saved by Sinmora, which she tucked safely into her tiny pouch.

As the day wore on, the six sojourners came to a fjord that joined with a deep swift channel. The air was utterly still there, and the sun had placed a dazzling hand on the water. The river before them seemed to barely move. On the far bank a figure sprawled in the midday sun; his flat-bottomed boat lounged beside him.

Sinmora gazed across the water. "The ferryman waits upon the distant shore. We must call to him to bring his boat so that we may cross. But he will require payment for the journey, hence the reason I hid Andvari's gold in my pouch."

Sinmora cupped her hands around her mouth and called, waking the sprawling figure. He stood quickly and placed his hand over his forehead to shade the glare of the sun and stared back at the travelers. Finally, after a few moments of contemplation, the man pushed his boat off the shore and into the slow moving water. He churned the water with his oars, the bulge of his muscles pulsing with every stroke. Soon he reached the opposite bank where Zeke and the others stood, their anxious minds sizing up the man who pulled the boat swiftly out of the current and stopped before them.

Sinmora was the first to approach the man. "We desire passage to the other side," she said confidently. "We have gold to pay for the journey."

For a time the man was silent as he gazed at each member of the company. Then he spoke softly, quite different from the voice Zeke expected to hear from the large man.

"Why do ye want to cross?" he asked. "This is no place for the living. It is a miserable, desolate place ye enter. Go back the way ye came."

"We seek audience with Groa," Sinmora said. "We must pass over the water to gain her advice before we continue on our journey."

"Groa, is it?" the ferryman said. "Then to be sure thy journey is worthy, but are ye worthy? Hildolf, the slaughtering wolf, entrusts this ferry to me. He is a wise man who lives on Rathsey, the Isle of Counsel. He has given me my orders: no pilferers may cross. So," said the ferryman, "if thou desires to cross ye must tell me thy name. And be quick, the waters become swifter and more difficult to maneuver as the day wanes."

"I am Sinmora the Volva. This," she said, pointing toward Erna, "is Erna, my apprentice. Beside her is Zeke Proper, he is a warrior apprentice and holder of the Staff of Urd."

At the mention of Zeke's name and the staff, the ferryman raised an eyebrow. "Zeke Proper is it. I have heard this name whispered on the wind. It speaks of battles with beasts and entities of evil. Could this be true?" he said, glancing over Zeke's exhausted, skinny frame.

Zeke stepped back a pace, amazed that this simple man who lived out his life at the edge of a lonely river would know his name. *Could there be something to this?* he thought. Zeke turned to Erna who was looking at him. Her smile was tender and full of forgiveness and love. Then he turned to Devon who was gazing at Zeke with his cheesy grin. He nodded his head stupidly. Zeke looked back at the ferryman. "We've traveled far," he said quietly, "and we're very tired."

The ferryman nodded as a brief smile crossed his face. "Come aboard then," he said with a wave of his hand. "The wagon will go in last, the rest of ye will sit yourselves near the bow."

Using the staff, Zeke sat down heavily into the weatherworn wooden seat. He took a deep breath as he felt his limbs relax and the pain in his leg lessen, when he suddenly felt the bite of a large horse fly on his neck. It bit him hard. Zeke swatted at it, but all he managed was to give himself an angry red welt at the side of his throat. The horse fly flew away quickly. It perched itself on the gunwale at the back of the boat. Zeke rubbed his neck tenderly, a slight swelling beginning to form beneath his touch. He stared toward the place where the fly landed, its multiple eyes gazing right back at him. Zeke felt a slight shudder course itself up his spine; he couldn't be sure, but it appeared as if the fly were watching him.

ᛉ

The crossing was quick and uneventful. The ferryman took a small portion of the money that Sinmora offered and then retreated quickly to his makeshift bed on the riverbank, falling asleep long before the small company set the wagon-wheels on the road into Niflheim. But darkness was beginning to settle; as it did a ghastly rotting smell came with it. Suddenly, the quiet gentleness of the growing dark turned chaotic as a cold began to burn the travelers. An unsettling wind churned the dusty ground, and tiny granules of earth scraped across the traveler's eyes.

"Take shelter!" Sinmora called, her voice barely rising above the din of confusion and swirling soil.

The group pulled tattered blankets out from the back of the wagon and began tucking them over the sides and building a makeshift tent, using the wagon as support. They huddled underneath while the blankets flapped wildly beside them.

"What in the world is going on?" Devon called.

"The gates of Niflheim are just ahead, lad. They welcome the dead with open arms, but they mistrust the living. The storm is their way of warning us," Berling said.

As the wind raged on, Erna looked at Zeke, gently reaching up and touching his swelling neck. "What has happened here?" she asked.

Zeke touched the spot and winced with pain. "A fly bit me," he said. "When we were getting on the boat."

Just as Zeke spoke, the wind outside the cramped shelter ended, almost as quickly as it began. The tiny group of travelers, huddled within the wagon-tent, breathed a sigh of relief, all except Sinmora. She had heard Zeke's proclamation over the rush of wind and hurried over to him, climbing over Devon and Vidar in her eagerness to grab hold of Zeke and tilt his head to the side. Her bright blue eyes closely examined the swollen bite.

"A fly did this to you?" Sinmora asked. She pressed her fingers lightly on the swollen sides of his neck.

"Yeah," Zeke said. "Like the ones that hang around the pastures and drive the cows crazy. But this one was a lot bigger. The bite hurts like mad, too."

Sinmora continued her close examination and reached into her pouch for a black-topped bottle. Erna leaned in close, resting her hand lightly on Sinmora's arm. "You're concern worries me," she said. "This is more than just a normal bite, isn't it?"

"Aye, lass," Sinmora answered as she spit into a cloth, emptied a portion of the black powder into the folds of the material. She then began dabbing it on Zeke's neck. "This is the work of a shape-shifter."

Erna sat upright as her eyes widened with recognition. "Loki!" she whispered sharply. Her piercing whisper, however, was not lost between Zeke and the two boys.

Zeke pulled away from Sinmora quickly as she continued to dab at the wound. "Loki," he repeated. "How is that possible?"

"All things are possible with the Sly-One," Sinmora said. "Nevertheless, our problem is not *how* he discovered our presence in the Mist, but the fact that he *has*. I fear his discovery will greatly increase the difficulty of our journey. Our hope was to find Groa, seek her advice, and depend on stealth to rescue your cousin. But now he surely knows why we travel to Niflheim. He's been listening in the guise of a fly."

"But that means he must be near. And if that's true then so is Taylre," Devon piped in.

"Not necessarily," Sinmora said. "Loki can travel far in this disguise. He's done so many times in the past. But my guess is that he's returned to his waiting place, wherever that may be. I also believe now that the storm was *not* meant for us. I think the gates felt Loki's presence and hoped to blow him away. His tricks and mischief amid the land of the dead in the past have made him an unwelcome guest."

"I knew this was a bad idea," Vidar said. "Didn't I say so from the start?"

"Hush, boy!" Sinmora said sternly. "Your fears don't help. Fear never has. So be quiet and let me think."

For a moment the travelers kept still, afraid they would disturb Sinmora and her thoughts. Finally, Erna began moving. She lifted the blankets from the side of the wagon, folded them neatly, and placed them gently in the cart. The boys rose from the ground as well, kicking aside dirt drifts that had piled up alongside the wheels and gathered the remainder of their belongings that were blown and scattered across the ground.

Eventually, Sinmora stood too, brushing off dirt and dust from her skirt. "We go to the gates," she proclaimed. "I feel that Groa waits on the other side, that in her death-sleep she anticipates our arrival. It is she that has sent Loki away. Indeed, the wind whispers that she has much to say."

She gave a quick nod to Erna who turned to the boys, beckoning them on with the wave of her hand. The group started slowly along the well-worn path leading to Niflheim, their heads bowed. They considered ominously the mystery that anticipated their arrival beyond the black gates and what dire words the seeress of the dark lands had in store for them.

ᛦ

Just as before, during the hike toward Nidhogg's cave, Sinmora whispered instructions in Zeke's ear, coaching him with words of encouragement and etiquette.

"You must recite these words," Sinmora urged. "Else Groa will not come to the gates."

"Why can't someone else do it? I'll only screw it up." Zeke whined.

"Because you are the Chosen. You hold the staff. Its power is yours to command."

Zeke shook his head. "I am not the Chosen," Zeke said forcefully. "You saw what happened with the dragon. I screwed up. Because of me the Captain is dead. I am no more a warrior than Devon is."

Sinmora swung her arm around quickly; her palm opened, and smacked Zeke crisply on the back of the head.

"Ouch!" Zeke cried. "Whadya do that for?"

"Do not question me, Chosen," Sinmora said sharply. "I've heard the whispers. The Valkyrie tells it on the wind. They speak only the truth. You may think you know better, but you do not." Sinmora pushed ahead of Zeke angrily, her confident strides once again leading the small group. But before she could get too far she turned again.

"Do not forget the words I've given you. Groa will be listening for them."

x

The ghastly rotting smell became stronger, its stench bringing tears to the traveler's eyes. Devon fought against a wave of nausea, but the puke won and he was forced to empty the contents of his stomach on the side of the narrow trail. Darkness reached up to the travelers as well, clinging on to their thoughts like oozing, thick mud.

Finally, the group stopped and looked up. Before them stood the blackened gates of Niflheim, its iron bars slick with moss and clinging entrails.

"This place," Berling began, his voice tempered to a slight whisper, "is as dreadful as the worst of fears, the worst of dreams."

"What you say is true, Berling, but sometimes," Sinmora said, turning to look directly at Zeke, "we must discover our lowest point before we can rise to our summit."

Sinmora nodded at Zeke and urged him forward with a slight tilt of her head. "Say the words," she instructed.

Zeke inched himself ahead, fighting back the same nausea

that Devon wrestled with. He pushed away the fear that trickled up his spine.

"Groa, wake! Wake, wise grandmother!" he shouted. "We stand at the doors of the dead and call on you. Bless us with your gifts and your visions of the future. Wake!"

Zeke stepped back and looked at Sinmora; a bashful smile lifted his lips. Sinmora smiled back and nodded her head gently. "Well done, Chosen. Well done."

For a moment there was nothing but silence that shuddered before a soft wind. Then the gates seemed to stir; their giant hinges pulsed like living things, easing the gates open. Zeke and the others began to slowly step forward, but Sinmora stopped them. She placed her hand in front of Zeke's chest. With her other hand she pressed her finger gently to her lips.

"She comes," Sinmora whispered, "but we must not enter. Only if we are invited to do so."

As the travelers watched, there appeared a ragged form out of the darkness that walked slowly toward them. Its hands were lifted while long, gray hair streamed from its aged head. Soon the figure of a very old woman stood before them just inside the gates. She let her eyes drift from one member of the tiny group to the other, finally coming to rest on Sinmora.

"You, apprentice of Var, I know, but the ..." she paused, her eyes leaving Sinmora's and turning to gaze at Zeke and the staff.

She looked back at Sinmora. "You give the Staff of Urd to another?" She asked. "Even though Var bequeathed it unto you?"

Sinmora nodded. "I believe him to be the Chosen One. For this reason I have given him the staff."

The old woman turned and examined Zeke much closer, her pale, pupiless eyes sending shivers up his spine.

"You have done well, Sinmora. He is indeed the Chosen. But–," she said, shaking her head slowly back and forth, "–he is weak. Oh, so weak."

"For this reason we have come to see you, Groa," Sinmora said.

Groa raised her arms, but her pale eyes remained fixed on Zeke. "Then I shall sing the ballad of the Chosen. The magic of this song will uplift you and give you strength on your journey. The road you travel is long. Your quest's path is strewn with many dangers. But love guides you," she said, glancing toward Erna. "You will achieve your aim, because the Norns favor you."

There was a brief moment of awkward silence where no one spoke. Finally Sinmora gave Zeke a slight nudge on the shoulder. "Say something," she urged. "Groa waits for your permission to sing."

Zeke fidgeted with the staff and looked around nervously at his fellow travelers. Finally he raised his head, trying to look beyond the aged, pupiless eyes of Groa. "Um...yeah," he said. "That'd be great if you sang. I think we'd really like to hear that."

Sinmora closed her eyes and shook her head, but Groa smiled and brought her arms to her sides.

"Then you shall hear the song and discover the destiny the three goddesses of the Well of Urd have in store for you. Listen, Zeke Proper. Urd, the Mother of Fate speaks. Skuld, the Mother of Being whispers. Verdandi, Grandmother and Protector of Necessity chides."

Groa began singing.

Her voice was not unpleasant, but the rhythm and variation of notes seemed to come at random intervals giving the song an ethereal tone, haunting yet deeply soothing.

"Shrug off whatever sickens you;
Discover your own strength
In the midst of one who saved your life.
A warrior's gift he received.
If not so, the fates would have declared your death.
The Staff of Urd will be your railing
To keep you on the right road,
As the rivers Horn and Ruth will part before you.
If enemies attack you on your gallows way
Your wish will be their desire,
And they'll long only for peace.
Know now that as you speak,
Your head shall be well stocked with wits,
your mouth with wise words.
Now take the road with all its hidden dangers,

And let no evil work against your love.
Carry this grandmother's spells with you
And keep them in your heart.
You'll prosper for as long as my words live in you."

᚜

Groa lowered her head, her pale eyes staring lifelessly at the barren ground. "Go now," she said. "I have nothing left to say. My soul is weary and desires the rest of the grave. Leave and be on your way."

The old woman turned to go. Her feet shuffled tiredly on the black path. The drained travelers watched her, a mixture of confusion and surprise at her sudden departure.

Zeke turned to Sinmora, his face filled with expectancy, willing her to explain the song, the ancient woman's curious words, and her abrupt exit.

Suddenly, the gates began to shut. Zeke swung back around, watching Groa slowly fade into the blackness. He exhaled sharply, anxious for some kind of closure. Something, anything that would help him on his quest.

"Wait!" he shouted, his sudden words startling those who stood patiently behind him. "I need to know something."

Sinmora approached him quickly and placed a heavy chastising hand on his shoulder. But Zeke shrugged it off, stepping closer to the closing gate. "Please! It's so important."

Groa stopped, her pale, luminescent back facing Zeke. "Speak, Chosen. But be quick; I need my sleep."

There was so much that Zeke wanted to ask at that moment. So much that he wanted to know about Loki, the Captain, but especially Taylre. Yet the words he uttered were nothing like he had expected.

"My father," he asked quietly. "Is he okay? Is he happy?"

Groa turned slowly and stared at Zeke, a bright smile prominent upon her face. "This is what I had hoped for. Your inner thoughts are not for yourself; you think only of the well being of others. This," she said, raising her finger in the air, "is the true breadth of a warrior."

Groa shuffled toward Zeke a few paces and stopped, her smile never leaving. "Do you see the jagged mountains behind me, Chosen? That is the place for the royal dead. Your father," she whispered, "lives among them, and he is at peace. He longs to see you, to embrace you, and to tell you how proud he is, but it is not the way of Niflheim. Nevertheless, know this: he watches and he waits anxiously for news of your success. So, achieve your quest, Zeke Proper! *Stop* them at the Gates!"

The gates slammed shut and Groa disappeared into the darkness, her words now just a faint echo quivering in the evening air.

Chapter Thirty-Three
Beaten and Bruised

As night descended on a field full of tents and campfires, a tattered horse fly buzzed its way like a drunken man over the grassy ground, almost as if its wings had been clipped. It fought hard to find lift, weaving to and fro in slow arches. It collided with a blade of grass here, a small branch there, until finally coming to rest on a small boulder that stood just outside the entrance to a large and regal pavilion. The fly shuddered; its multiple eyes bobbled in its oversized head, and seemed, for just a moment, to hold its breath. Suddenly, there was a flash of light, and where there had once been a fly now sat a man, a god, a fallen god, battered and bloodied. He stood slowly and arched his back as a shock of pain jolted up his spine and ended in a piercing stab between his shoulder blades. He groaned and pressed his fingers deep into his lower back, massaging the tightened muscles that cramped and moaned beneath his touch.

He stepped forward, pushing aside the silky flap of goatskin that marked the entrance to the tent and entered, making his way awkwardly toward an opulent chair, stumbling as he went. He spilled an ivory hilted dagger on the floor in one place and a torn bootstrap in another. Eventually he found his throne in the middle of the room, its jeweled backing surrounded by lush carpets and ornate pillows.

"Mead!" he ordered. He smashed his empty horn heavily on the table in front of him.

A tawny dwarf waddled in, his skin wrinkled like his faded leather tunic. He carried with him a tankard of ale and proceeded to pour the contents into Loki's horn. But before the liquid could find its way into the cup, Loki swung his arm across the tiny man's face, hitting him hard with a solid backhand.

"I said mead, you idiot!" The dwarf landed with a solid thump on the floor while the ale spilled all around him.

"My apologies, master." He stood quickly, ignoring the blood rushing from his nose and shuffled back through the door-flap from whence he came.

At the sound of Loki's bellow Fenrir entered the tent from the back where a larger door-flap allowed him a cleaner entrance.

"Father, you're back," he said, surprise and curiosity marking his furry expression. He stared at Loki as Taylre walked in behind him. "What has happened to you? Has there been a battle? Did you destroy the..." But he stopped himself, glancing back at Taylre. Taylre, however, ignored his look and kept her focus on Loki.

"Mr. Loden," she said, managing to keep her large, magnified eyes looking sad and innocent, "you look hurt. Is there anything I can do? Some bandages? A drink of mead?"

Loki managed a slight smile that looked more like a sneer beneath the rage and pain that he was feeling.

"Dear, Taylre," he said, his voice remaining silky smooth underneath the burning fire. "My needs will be met. There is no need to worry. In the meantime, if you don't mind, I would like to speak with Fenrir. Alone. We have much to discuss, you see."

Taylre bowed her head humbly and looked at her feet, and there, right next to her instep was a beautifully made dagger, its sharp edge catching the firelight from the flickering sconces on the wall. She picked it up quickly and tucked it behind her belt loop in the back of her pants. A weak smile escaped her lips. "As you say, Mr. Loden. Please call me if there's anything I can do. You have helped me so much that I feel I need to do my part to serve you as well."

"Such a sweet child, is she not, Fenrir?"

"Indeed she is, father," Fenrir said, only half listening to the conversation while he continued to study Loki's wounded face and arms.

Taylre left the room and closed the flap behind her, quickly hiding herself just outside the pavilion amid a stack of empty ale and mead barrels. Then she bent her head close to the thick hides, discovering that she could clearly hear the words of the traitors inside, thus keeping the promise to remain vigilant. The time would come; she knew it would. Loden and his furry son would make a mistake. When they did, she would be ready. She had to be. Otherwise Zeke was sure to die.

ᛦ

"Groa!" Loki spat. "She knew I was there. Somehow she knew. And with what little power she possesses, she called upon a great wind to stir." Loki eased back into his chair as a grimace of pain crossed his face. He looked at Fenrir. "Do you have any idea what a sand and dirt storm will do to a fly? Do you!"

"No, father. But I can imagine," Fenrir said.

"Look at me. Just look at me. My beautiful face will be covered in scars after this." He reached for his horn and tried to drink. When he saw it was empty he threw it across the room. "And where's that damned dwarf!"

Immediately the door-flap opened and the errant dwarf entered carrying a large jug of mead that he quickly used to fill Loki's horn. With trembling hands he walked it over to Loki. As he handed the drink to his master the dwarf looked up, seeing for the first time the bloodied cuts and scratches and the dark bruises that covered Loki's face.

"Oh, master," the dwarf uttered.

Loki grabbed the horn angrily, spilling some of its contents on the dwarf. "What is it, you sniveling little imp? Something wrong with my face, is there? Something you want to say?" Loki grabbed the dwarf by the tunic and shook him until the tiny man's teeth began to rattle. "Get out!"

The dwarf, finally released from Loki's ferocious grip, turned and ran, leaving the jug of mead behind.

Loki settled himself back in his chair, his body shaking with fury. He watched as the little man exited the tent and then turned to Fenrir. "We gather the armies tonight and begin our march to Asgard."

Fenrir, his eyebrows raised in wonder, stared at Loki. "Tonight?" he questioned.

"Yes, tonight!" Loki bellowed. "Is there a problem?

"The warriors will need to be rallied, father. That will take some time. Provisions need to be gathered and weapons must be sharpened. Besides that, the giants have had little rest since we left Midgard. They are tired. They are not ready for battle so soon."

Loki gritted his teeth but held his anger. "How long then," he whispered sharply.

"A day, father. Give us a full day to prepare. By this time tomorrow we will be ready to move."

"Fine," Loki said reluctantly. "See to the preparations. Make sure we leave by tomorrow, no later."

Fenrir slowly backed away, his gaze never leaving his father's beaten face. "What has happened, father? Why the change in plans?"

"Proper," he spat. "He travels with the witch and they've gone to the Gates of Niflheim to seek Groa's advice."

"That is not so bad, father. Groa is an old witch herself. She lingers most times in her deathbed. She has almost no powers left."

"But there is more, you see," Loki said, draining his horn of mead in one giant swallow. "My daughter's killer also carries the Staff of Urd."

Fenrir stepped back a pace, swirling in sudden bewilderment. "The staff? But how? Sinmora is the caretaker, how can that insignificant fool now be its holder?"

"You idiot," Loki chided. "Do you know nothing? The staff was cut from the roots of Yggdrasil, those that grew near the

Well of Urd. It contains the power of life and the power of death. No one can possess it. Its only true place is in the hands of the Chosen, you see. Sinmora obviously believes Proper to be the one."

Fenrir tilted his head in wonder. "Can he wield it, father? Can he control its mighty power?"

"No," Loki answered. "He appears weak and unsure of himself. But that does not mean that he won't get stronger, you see. We must, therefore, begin our march on the gods and destroy them. Let the rest burn. Surt's fiery forges will turn the tree to ashes. And when it does, it will also destroy Proper and the witch who guides him. There will be no need to chase the pest any longer. Our victory at the Gates of Asgard will be the end of him."

Chapter Thirty-Four
Wing and a Prayer

They left the wagon at the edge of the river, finding that its bowed wheels and rotting wooden sides were becoming more hindrance than asset. They were forced to carry their provisions on their backs in makeshift gunnysacks. The weight of the bags, however, slowed them down considerably, adding more aches to the pains that already existed.

Zeke found it to be a welcome relief to finally sit down at the side of a cool brook and soak his tired feet in the cold water. He watched Devon splash around in the shallows as he tried to engage Vidar in some childish horseplay, but Vidar was having none of it. He remained solemn and grave, choosing to sit farther up from the water's edge and only come down once and a while to take a drink.

Just beyond the tiny brook, Erna and Sinmora tended to a tiny campfire. Its flames were meager, but they were enough to cook the small amount of food that they still had left. Berling offered his help by exploring the thick wooded area that surrounded the brook. Among them he gathered small sticks and twigs to feed the fire.

"Come. Eat," Sinmora called, giving a slight wave toward the boys.

Devon ran with vigor to the meager offering of boiled meat and half cooked grain. Vidar slogged his way with very little enthusiasm, while Zeke limped along, the Staff of Urd his constant companion.

"I'm starved," Devon said as he shoved the food into his mouth.

"Enjoy it while ya can, lad," Sinmora said sadly. "This may be the last of it for awhile."

The tiny group gathered glumly around the crackling heat, their thoughts drifting as they chewed mechanically on the tasteless meal. Finally, in a quiet, unexpected voice, Vidar broke the silence.

"This is taking too long," he said.

Devon looked up from his now empty wooden plate. "Whadya mean? These ladies cooked a fine meal in less time than it takes to microwave a bag of popcorn."

Vidar looked at Devon, bewilderment pressing hard against his features. Finally, he shook his head. "I'm not talking about the food," he said. "I mean this traveling. It's taking us too long. We'll never get there in time if we keep going at this rate."

Sinmora bit off a tough morsel of meat and began chewing slowly. She watched Vidar from the corner of her eye. "There?" she questioned. "Where is there?"

"There," Vidar said confidently, "is exactly where Groa said: the Gates of Asgard. That's where we're going isn't it?"

"Aye, lad. Very perceptive ye are."

"Asgard?" Zeke said. "Why does that name sound so familiar?"

"The Captain told us about it," Devon said, swallowing hard on a stringy piece of meat. "It seems like a hundred years ago, but it was when he wrote a bunch of stuff down on a pad of paper explaining all about the Norse gods. I did my research, too, if you recall."

"So, what is it?" Zeke said, a little more sarcastically than he wanted to.

"It's the home of the gods, dummy," Devon responded. Sinmora sat back and smiled. She nodded her head occasionally and let Devon resume his story, finding he was a well-informed teacher.

"See," Devon continued, "there were these three brothers. One of them was Odin, the other guys I don't remember. But these guys built Asgard after they created everything: the moon, the stars, people, dwarfs, all that. But the thing about this Asgard place is that it's huge. It has a giant wall surrounding it. And the only way you can get to the gate is to cross a rainbow colored bridge called Bifrost. But it's heavily guarded. There's a guy named Heimdall who's constantly on the watch for enemies, so there's no way to get into Asgard without first going through him and some pretty hefty Viking warriors."

"And we're going there because...?" Zeke said, looking now at Sinmora. But Vidar spoke first.

"Because, that's where Loki is going. And," he added, his voice lowering slightly, "that's where you're going to need to stop him."

Zeke was about to open his mouth to object, but then he closed it quickly, recalling Groa's last words just before the entrance to Niflheim closed: *Stop them at the gates!*

He stared at the flames, their blue and yellow flickers reflected in his watery eyes. Erna rose from her place on a low stump and came and sat down beside Zeke. She put her arm around his waist and rested her head on his shoulder.

"This is a hard thing to bear," she whispered. "But know that we are here to ease your burden."

"I know," Zeke said as a sudden cascade of tears spilled over his eyelids onto his cheeks. "You've all been so patient with me. And I've been such a pain sometimes. But Groa was right. I understand that now. What she said at the beginning of her song now makes perfect sense. The Captain needed to be the warrior and kill Nidhogg. He needed to save me. Otherwise I'd be dead. I wasn't ready." He lifted the staff and looked at it, caressing its smooth wooden shaft with his eyes and admiring its keen workmanship. "But now, I think I am."

Zeke stood, but he didn't use the staff to aid him. He stood on his own, feeling heat rise in his chest as it began to fill his whole body with strength, a healing balm that penetrated him to the very core.

He looked down at his fellow travelers. In his eyes they could see a change come over him. His features exhibited strength and confidence that only a moment before held fear and doubt. And when he spoke his voice moved his listeners like a rushing river.

"I perceive that Loki has a large and menacing army at his command. I sense that he begins his march on Asgard." He looked once more into the fire, the flames suddenly becoming taller and brighter. He gripped the staff tightly, a faint golden light emanating from the tip. "And Vidar is right," he added. "We must move quickly. We must arrive at Asgard before Loki does."

Zeke turned to Sinmora. "How can we travel faster?"

Sinmora considered the fire as she pondered Zeke's wondrous change. Then, as she rubbed her hands together near the flames she began to smile and looked back up at Zeke. "We fly, of course."

Zeke tilted his head in question. "Fly? How?"

"The great eagle, Hraesvelg. Nidhogg has been slain. She is now in *your* debt."

ᛉ

The great eagle rose from its perch, high atop Yggdrasil where it sat and viewed the inhabitants of all the nine worlds. But she flew reluctantly, compelled to do so only because the Staff of Urd called. She had to obey; the staff held the power of life and death, and if the summons came by one worthy to wield it, then Hraesvelg had to abide by its holder's wishes.

As she flew, the eagle sailed over great distances, crossing the wild, wide, whispering rivers and made her way over the trembling rainbow bridge where all remained quiet and still. She soared over a ribbed and silent plain, bright with snow, and past plumes of steam that issued from whistling fissures. Soon she tilted its wings and circled, bending close to the mouth of a valley, surrounded on three sides by the purple mountains and the mighty river, Iving, the dashing torrent of rushing rapids and icy waters that divides the world of the gods from the world of the giants.

Eventually, she landed in a grassy meadow, her giant clawed feet coming to rest while her enormous wings beat the air.

At the edge of the meadow, standing amid a thicket of trees and low-lying shrubs stood Zeke. He held the staff firmly as he watched the giant bird land. Behind him stood Sinmora, a proud smile on her face as she looked at the Chosen. Beside her was her apprentice, Erna. Away off, leaning against a small tree was Vidar and Devon. They both watched with excited expectancy when Hraesvelg finally arrived. At first Devon didn't think it would really happen. He always viewed Zeke as his annoying big brother, the one he argued with, fought with, and teased, but always secretly admired. Now, as he looked at Zeke, he saw something completely different. And as he tried to put a word to it, the only thing he could think of was warrior.

Zeke strode across the meadow, confident in each and every step. There was no limp. Hraesvelg watched him approach, a glare of anger in her eyes, but also one of respect.

"I know why I have been summoned," the eagle said. "I am not happy. Never have I had to carry man or beast upon my back. But I am compelled to follow the power of the staff. When at first I saw it in your hands I felt some fear, but not enough to be concerned. Back then you were a weak little boy. But now..." the eagle looked at Zeke and then past him to where the others stood.

"Let's get this over with," the eagle hissed. "And hurry. I have seen from my perch the armies of the Sly-One begin to march. The fate of the nine worlds is in great peril."

ᛦ

The decision was difficult, but when it came right down to it there was just no way that six people could fit on the back of an eagle, no matter how big it was. In the end it was decided that Berling would remain behind, taking care that Erna, Devon, and Vidar were guided safely out of the Mist.

"Take care of them, Erna," Sinmora called. "Keep a warm fire burning and set places for us at the table. We'll be home before long."

Zeke hugged Erna tightly. He kissed her gently on her lips and caressed her cheeks lightly. He hugged Devon too, embracing him tighter than he ever had before, urging him to be safe and to tell their mom that he loved her; that he would see her soon.

Hraesvelg's wings thrummed the air, pushing her higher and higher. As she rose, Zeke looked back and waved a final goodbye, then he turned stalwartly and looked ahead, gazing at the breathtaking beauty of the land of Jotunheim and the purple mountains that towered over the land, their peaks scraping the bottom of the sky. The wind blew cold in his face, tossing his hair. But he breathed in the chill, feeling strength from its freshness, glad that the fear had finally left him and that he no longer felt the throbbing pain from his leg. The staff lay securely on his lap; he held it tightly with both hands. From behind, where Sinmora sat shivering, came a sudden shout.

"Look!" Sinmora said, pointing toward the distant ground. "Far below us is the Seam. It is faint, but look how it shimmers. It marks the border between the Land of the Giants and Midgard. Berling need only travel there to cross over."

Zeke watched the shimmering line course across the land. It reminded him of heat rising from asphalt on a hot summer day. He nodded; glad to know that Erna's journey would not be far; that his brother would be safe from the battle to come.

Hour upon hour they flew. The light of day waned as Skinfaxi, the great stallion driven by Sun, guided daylight across the sky. Soon night fell and the air grew even colder. The only light left to guide their way came from the stars and the constellations made by the sons of Bor. With the darkness Zeke's eyes grew heavy and his head nodded forward. His chin rested heavily on his chest.

He slept. The first real sleep he'd had in a long time. And he dreamed he saw his father. He was standing outside in the bright sun next to a large yellow house. There was a garden with flowers, and in it, tending to the magnificently radiant blossoms was his grandfather. Together Zeke's father and grandfather turned and looked at him. They smiled and waved. They seemed so happy. Then his father cupped his hands around his mouth and shouted.

"Hold on tight, Zeke!"

Zeke thought he might have heard his father wrong. He leaned an ear closer, calling back.

"What? What did you say?"

"Hold on, Zeke! We're about to land."

It was Sinmora shouting from behind him. Her hands shook his shoulders as she tried to wake him.

Zeke opened his eyes and raised his head, feeling dazed and confused. "Where are we?" he said as he struggled to wake and find his bearings.

"Behold!" Sinmora shouted. "The world of the Aesir and the Gates of Asgard!"

It took only a moment for Zeke to realize that what he was seeing was far beyond anything he'd ever seen before; far better than anything his mind could have imagined.

Before him, laid out like a dream come to life was the most beautiful meadow Zeke had ever laid eyes on. The green grass was dazzling, coupled with the bright colors of the wildflowers that grew in tall, vibrant stalks. The air was fresh beyond belief.

It filled his senses with images of eternal springs and endless summers. Beyond them rose gentle hills, rolling like a soothing sea that carried ships to paradise and filled their sails with hopes of red sky mornings and peaceful sunsets.

Zeke eased himself down from Hraesvelg's back and tried to take it all in. But it was impossible. There was too much to see, too much for one person to ever comprehend. Then, as he stepped forward, eager to take his first steps in the green of the meadow, Sinmora stopped him and pointed toward the rise.

"Look," she said.

Zeke followed her outstretched hand and saw another sight that completely took his breath away. It was a bridge, gilded in all of the colors of the rainbow, spanning a great chasm. At its closest edge was a watchtower. It appeared to be built of solid gold, a facade that caught the light of the new day and reflected it back on the green meadow, adding to the hue of life and eternal sunshine.

"What is it?" Zeke asked.

"Bifrost," Sinmora answered. "'Tis the rainbow bridge to the land of the gods. Few have witnessed its beauty, Zeke Proper. You are blessed, indeed."

ᚨ

Within the great tower, amidst the beauty of Asgard and the richness of the gods, sat Heimdall, the watchman, he who needs less sleep than a bird. He who can see a hundred leagues in front of him as well as by night as by day, he who can hear the grass growing as well as the wool on a sheep's back. And although he witnessed the landing of Hraesvelg on the soft meadow and the arrival of the Chosen, he was somehow unaware that Loki and his army had advanced well beyond the Well of Urd and were soon to fall upon the land of the Aesir.

Chapter Thirty-Five

The Plains of Vigrid

A vast legion of giants and dwarfs, marching in perfect cadence to the beat of a thousand drums, stirred up dust and dirt that seemed to drift a hundred feet in the air and carry a hundred miles behind them. They were relentless, stopping only occasionally to rest and drink before they set off again. They were advancing quickly toward the Gates of Asgard.

Taylre, her face and clothes covered in dirt and grime, always thought she was in good shape. She ate well, always got enough sleep, and tried to exercise as often as she could. But this, this was more than she could possibly bear. Mr. Loden's massive army was traveling fast, faster than she could have ever imagined. The muscles in her long skinny legs cried for rest, and the grumble in her stomach was a constant reminder that the meager supplies she carried on her back were running low. Soon, very soon, she would have to ask one of the giants to share some meat or a morsel of bread. Or worse, she would have to ask Teddy. But she hated to ask. They were brutes, every one of them, especially Teddy; she feared Teddy's insults and feigned attacks. She feared receiving another vicious backhand like the one she'd received once before from Surt at the forger's fire back at La Cueva del Diablo. Nevertheless, her will was strong. She would push on despite her discomfort; Zeke and Devon were the targets of Mr. Loden's wrath and she would protect them at all costs. But, she had to wait. Difficult though it was, she had to bide her time. The moment would present itself, and when it did she would act. She held the dagger in her hand and gripped the hilt till her knuckles turned white, finally returning the weapon, unseen, to her back pocket.

The army continued its march, pressing over the rising ground until the sun was directly overhead. Eventually they came to a saddleback shaped mountain. Struggling over its precipice and then climbing down, the many feet of the soldiers came to an abrupt halt at the fringe of a square-shaped valley.

Loki strode out ahead of the army as a thin-line smile parted his lips. In one hand he held a golden hilted sword and in the other was a bejeweled shield. Behind him, pushing his way through the crowd of soldiers was the enormous wolf, Fenrir. His eyes seemed to shine with blood lust as he stopped beside his father and gazed out over the immense valley.

"It has been a long time since my eyes have beheld this place," Fenrir said. "The memories I have are a mixture of joy and sorrow." He turned and looked at Loki, his expression of rage turning to sadness.

"The gods stole me from you, father. But here I was raised, and Tyr the god of war was good to me...at first. But then, like all the gods, he betrayed me. Binding me with their tricks and their magic." Fenrir's voice turned angry, his tenor becoming dangerous.

"The fire in you begins to burn, my son," Loki said. "Let it. The rage will empower you. The destruction of your enemies is at hand, for we now stand upon the plains of Vigrid. Look!" he said, sweeping his hand across the horizon. "One hundred and twenty leagues in every direction. Our great army will fill this plain. There will be blood and death as far as the eye can see. I long for it. I can taste it."

"They will be waiting for us, father. Heimdall, whose eye sees even the faintest fluttering of a hummingbird's wing, will have seen us. By now he's left his great hall and has lifted the horn, Gjall, to his mouth to warn the warriors of Valhalla. Even now they are preparing their weapons and staging their own assault. We should begin our attack before it's too late."

"Patience," Loki hissed. He pressed his hand gently against Fenrir's neck. "The black runes have been cast. Their magic is strong. The spell they weave has kept us hidden all this time."

Fenrir's look of rage suddenly left, leaving a tapestry of confusion. "But, father," he said, stepping back from Loki, "the prophecies and the legends and the myths. They have guided us since the beginning of time. They have never been wrong. The words spoken at the Well of Urd when Odin, Villi, and Ve were still young, foretold the time when Ragnarok would begin. The gods will know that we are coming. That is the prophecy."

Loki smiled, a wicked smirk that even sent a shiver up Fenrir's back. "There are many reasons the gods call me the Sly One, Fenrir. I have just beaten them at their own game, you see. They do not expect me. Therefore, their defeat will be swift and complete."

Fenrir was at a loss for words. He hated the gods as much as his father did, but something didn't sit right. Something was terribly wrong with the plan Loki had devised, a wrong that transcended the balance of Yggdrasil.

Shaking his head, he turned to look across the vast plain toward Asgard. He trembled inside. *This is not the way*, he thought. *I fear the Norns will turn their back on this day.*

ᛦ

When Zeke first laid eyes upon Shaker - the Valkyrie who saved him from certain death from the hands of Loki - he was struck by her awesome, stalwart appearance. But what he saw striding toward him now left him stunned and amazed.

Heimdall was a true god, and as he descended from his post on the great golden tower he exuded strength and power that was beyond anything Zeke could have ever imagined. His shoulders were wide and brawny, carrying on them a massive set of metal-plated shielding. His neck was thick as well, exhibiting thick bands of muscle that appeared to glide in perfect form and cadence with his own fluid strides. His hands were covered in tough leather gloves that had brass spikes protruding from the knuckles, and his legs were covered in skins, bound by leather bands that crisscrossed up his calves from the heavy sandals he wore on his feet. All of this impressed Zeke, especially the man's height that was well over nine feet tall. But it was nothing compared to Heimdall's thickly bearded face and the piercing eyes that bore down on him, a stare that seemed to grind into Zeke's very soul.

The giant eagle, Hraesvelg, lifted her head as the god approached and immediately began beating her wings rapidly as dust and dirt flew about. Sinmora and Zeke shielded their eyes from the onslaught of debris, watching with hooded expressions as the eagle took to the air coursing her way north, her duty to the staff accomplished.

As they watched Hraesvelg sail away they felt Heimdall's presence loom over them. The shadow of his huge form blocked the light of the bright sun.

"I have watched you, Light-Bearer. I am impressed with what I've seen." Heimdall stared down at both Sinmora and Zeke, his eyes wide and evaluating, while his expression remained neutral. "I've seen you destroy the Korrigan with the white stones once touched by the hand of Odin. I've witnessed your battle and defeat of the giant Geirrod. I have seen you in combat with the Sly One, and I have witnessed your bold approach against the dragon Nidhogg. I see also that you have become more adept with your use of the Staff of Urd, an impressive feat indeed. But now I ask you, Light-Bearer, why have you come to the Gates of Asgard? What is your purpose here? Have you come to take on the gods as well?" At this, Heimdall began to laugh, his head held back while his thick, muscled arms wrapped themselves around his stomach, as if he were trying to hold in the hilarity of his own joke.

Zeke and Sinmora stared at one another, their looks revealed their confusion. Finally, Sinmora turned to Heimdall. "Do you really not know, Watchman?"

Heimdall's laughter subsided to a giddy chuckle as he regarded the Volva. "Know, Seeress? Know what?"

"That now, as we speak, Loki's mighty army approaches the walls of Asgard." Sinmora said.

"Impossible," Heimdall scoffed, looking from Sinmora to Zeke and back again. "Nothing escapes my vision. I am the son of the nine waves, holder of the horn Gjall. I can see clearly a hundred leagues in every direction, in day as well as by night. I can hear the grass growing in the lowest regions of Midgard as well as the flutter of a hummingbird's wing as it bends to sip nectar near the Spring of Hvergelmir. There is nothing that I do not hear or see."

"But Groa..." Zeke began, stuttering in the presence of the immense god. "She...she said he would come. That I was to stop him here at the gates."

Heimdall chuckled again, but this time with a hint of sadness. "You must have misinterpreted Groa's words, Zeke Proper. It would be impossible for Loki to venture toward the Gates of Asgard now. The time is not yet ripe. And though it is true he has escaped his bonds, this is time only for him to gather his armies and find those that would be loyal to him. There is so much more that must come to pass before Ragnarok."

"But I saw the ship," Zeke said, his confidence building as his frustration grew. "It sailed into the Mist. I saw it."

"Indeed you did, as did the All Father. But he has sent Hafgufa, the great serpent to battle the ship and its miscreant giants. It has succeeded in destroying the ship, sending its occupants scrambling for rescue."

Zeke turned to Sinmora, a horror-stricken expression turning his face pale. "But what about Taylre?" he asked, his hands held in front of him, pleading. "Have we been misled all this time? Is she lost somewhere in the sea?"

Sinmora rested her hand gently on Zeke's shoulder, a gesture that seemed to settle Zeke enough to listen. Then she turned to Heimdall. "Something is wrong," she said. "I heard the words that Groa uttered. We have not misinterpreted them. Has the Sly One somehow fooled us? Has he somehow kept himself hidden from your omnipotent vision, Heimdall?"

Heimdall shook his head slowly. "As I have said: nothing escapes my vision or my hearing."

"But Loki has kept himself hidden from you before," Sinmora said, watching Heimdall's neutral expression turn to a frown. "Did he not conceal himself amid the streams and rivers for many years after he destroyed Balder?"

"Ah, yes," Heimdall cried. "But in the end we found him. Our nets dragged him out of the icy waters when he tried to change himself into a salmon."

"Aye," Sinmora said, "'tis true. But still, did he not escape your vision for a time?"

Heimdall opened his mouth to speak, hesitating for only a moment as he thought. "But I know his tricks, seeress. He cannot change without me knowing it now."

"Aye," Sinmora continued. "But Loki is smart. He would know you were watching."

"Then what?" Heimdall said. A sense of frustration and urgency edged his voice. "What could he have done?"

Sinmora glanced at Zeke, her mind swirling with thoughts, and then she turned to face Heimdall squarely. "He's gathered the black runes and summoned their power to conceal himself," she said.

Heimdall gasped slightly while Zeke turned to Sinmora, his right hand grasping the staff while he held his left out like an eager traffic cop. "Whoa!" he said. "The black stones? The ones that the mayor used to call the Korrigan?"

Sinmora nodded.

"There's no way," Zeke continued. "I saw them melt into the ground when that ugly beast died. I saw it! There's no way Loki could get them."

Sinmora shook her head. "You're forgetting who we're talking about here, Zeke. Loki would know where to look. And *he* was there. He went to the place his daughter died to mourn her and plot your destruction. The stones would have been the first things he would have gleaned from the earth. Their powerful magic would add considerably to his. And if he transformed them and cast them correctly, then he would have been granted the power to conceal his entire army."

Sinmora and Zeke turned to look at Heimdall. He face glistened with a pale sheen of sweat as he cast his eyes over the vast valley of Vigrid, suddenly seeing, for the first time, the gathering dust of an innumerable army in the distance.

He raised Gjall to his lips and began to blow.

Chapter Thirty-Six
Staff, Sword, and Shadow

Teddy stood right behind Taylre. She could feel his angry glare on the back of her neck. All around her were hordes of giant and dwarf soldiers, the pungent stench of their acrid body odor burned the insides of her nose. She turned a sideways glance, looked at Teddy and challenged his glare.

"Is there something you want, Teddy?" she asked, knowing full well he'd get angry at her use of his "Midgard" name, as he often referred to it.

"You know damn well that's not my name, brat. And since you've asked, yeah, there is something. Gimme all your food and water. I'm all out."

Taylre tried hard to keep her expression even, despite the fact that she was shocked by Teddy's demand. She had hoped to get some food from *him*. The supplies she had left would barely last out the day.

"I'm...I'm all out," Taylre lied. "I don't have anything left."

"You're lying!" Teddy roared. He reached out and grabbed hold of one of the shoulder straps that held the pack to Taylre's back and tore it from her, pulling her to the ground. She landed hard on her side, forcing a rush of air to escape her lungs. She fought hard to gain her breath, gasping and choking as dirt crusted the corners of her mouth. Then, just as she began to feel somewhat normal, Teddy yanked her to her feet again, using her red, curly hair as a handle. Taylre screamed in protest and reached back to try and release Teddy's tight grip. Her only defense was to grind her nails into his wrist, but Teddy's grip tightened even more as he dragged her away from the indifferent soldiers and made his way to the front of the horde. Taylre continued to kick and scream, but to no avail; Teddy was simply too strong.

He dragged her to a small rise overlooking the Plain of Vigrid, the vast valley extending beyond the horizon where somewhere, in the distance, stood the home of the gods and the gates of Asgard. Teddy finally released his grip on Taylre's hair and grabbed her around the back of the neck, pulling her to her feet. With his other hand he grabbed hold of Taylre's face and pinched her mouth and cheeks together, his face coming within inches of her own.

"I thought you said you didn't have any food, traitor." He opened the pack and pulled out a small wineskin and a meager portion of crusted bread and moldy cheese. Then he shook her head violently and threw her to the ground.

It took a moment for Taylre to find her bearings, but when she did she looked down from the small rise and saw Mr. Loden and Fenrir standing at the head of the great army. They appeared to be in hot debate with each other and with some of the giants. Taylre looked back at Teddy. "Mr. Loden will hear about this," she said angrily.

Teddy looked up from his task of rummaging through the backpack and laughed. "Oh, didn't you hear? You're no longer on Loden's 'A' list. I've been given the job as babysitter. Apparently he doesn't think you're all that special anymore. So now I get to treat you like the traitor that you really are."

Taylre felt a sudden twinge of despair. She wondered if Loden had somehow discovered her plan to stop him.

"What are you going to do with me?" she asked, her voice trembling slightly.

"Oh, that's an easy one," Teddy mocked. "We're going to teach you how to be a soldier in one easy lesson. Loden wants you to lead the army into battle."

Taylre's eyes widened and her lip began to tremble. "What...?"

Teddy laughed again as he reached down and grabbed Taylre by the arm. "That's right, brat. You're gonna be one of the first to meet the enemy head on. It'll be fun to watch you get slaughtered. It should make for an interesting afternoon."

ᛦ

Loki was frustrated. His soldiers, even his own son, doubted his ability to win the battle against the gods. But his stubborn arrogance would not yield to their pleadings. He'd come too far. He was determined that by the end of this war he would vanquish Asgard and sit on Odin's throne.

As his generals continued to argue, his attention was drawn to a small rise where Teddy stood with Taylre. He gave Teddy a slight nod and then watched as his ever-faithful minion dragged the girl down the slope toward him. He smiled with satisfaction and turned back to his men.

"Enough!" he bellowed. "There will be no more discussion on the matter. We stand at the edge of Vigrid. This is the place where the gods will meet their match. We will destroy them, you see." He turned to the giant Surt.

"Organize your men. Fill their minds with rage. Let the berserks find place in their souls and let us begin our march on Asgard!"

ᛢ

The blast of the horn made the very air shutter and bend. Its sound echoed across the plain and reverberated off the walls of Asgard itself. The colors of the Rainbow Bridge, Bifrost, twisted as if in agony and mimicked the call of the horn as it beckoned the warriors within the halls of Valhalla to arms.

Zeke tried to cover his ears against the shrill call, but it was to no avail; the noise seemed to resonate deep into his soul as it stirred up an overwhelming anger and a will to fight. He dropped his hands from his ears and retrieved the staff. He held it tightly in his fists and felt a strength course its way through his body. As the magic filled him, his mind retrieved the memory of the white stones, and how their strength made him feel light and powerful. He once again discovered that his breathing became deep and clear. He felt like he could leap over the highest tree if he wanted or race through the fields at incredible speeds. He felt clean and pure.

From behind Zeke, Sinmora watched the transformation take place. She stepped back apace, knowing all too well the overwhelming potency of the staff. "This," she whispered, "is what we've truly waited for."

Zeke began to stride down the short slope. Behind him stood Heimdall, the bellow of his horn quieted as he gazed toward the south where the footfalls of tens of thousands of enemy soldiers advanced. Behind Heimdall there came a resounding clash as the towering Gates of Asgard swung open. From its gaping maw poured a formidable force of warriors, each one screamed with the cries of battle and blood lust. But none of these things deterred Zeke from his march across the plain; his eyes were still set on the horizon and the advancing army.

He held the staff in front of him as if its carved wooden shaft were a sharpened long blade that glistened in the bright noonday sun. His expression was hardened, a determined look that seemed to glow with energy.

Behind him the multitude of warriors pouring through the gates stopped, their raised swords and shields hanging limply by their sides as they watched the boy's slow stride turn into an all out run. The burley warriors with their thick beards, their muscled backs and arms, turned to one another, looks of confusion marked their grizzled features. Then, from among them, pushing his way to the forefront came a new warrior. His smile was bright as he lifted his newly honed sword and called out to the others who stood nearby.

"'Tis the Chosen, lads. Mark my words. I knew there was somethin' special 'bout that boy the first day I set eyes on him in the café!"

The Captain cupped his hands around his mouth and called with the loudest voice he could muster. "We'll be here if ya need us, lad!" And then in a more subdued voice he whispered. "But somethin' tells me ya won't."

Zeke didn't hear the Captain. His complete focus and attention was on Loki who led the charge of the surging army. But then he saw something more, something that compelled him to stop dead in his tracks.

Taylre. She led the army as well.

ᛉ

Teddy's continual pushing and shoving began to grate on Taylre's already frazzled nerves. Besides that, her knees were now scraped raw as well as her elbows and the palms of her hands. Hot tears ran down her cheeks in little rivulets. The streaks gave her an eerie nightmarish appearance.

She tried to look to Mr. Loden and even Fenrir for help, but they ignored her; their attention was focused on the vast walled city that lay in the distance. She even tried to appeal to Teddy. She hoped by some miracle he would have pity on her and leave her by the wayside. But that was too much to hope for. Teddy seemed to actually enjoy watching Taylre suffer. Her cries for help only made it worse.

"Move faster, brat! These soldiers aren't going to stop for some stupid traitor. They'll trample right over you if you don't get a move on!" Teddy pushed Taylre again. His fist made a sharp connection in the middle of her back.

Taylre tried to keep her balance, but the shove was too hard. She fell again. This time she scraped her cheek against the rocky ground while her glasses flew off in front of her. She reached for them quickly, knowing that Teddy was right behind her ready to give her another kick in the ribs if she didn't get up. Just as she placed her glasses on her face she looked behind to see Teddy's leg swing back. Taylre closed her eyes and prepared herself for the next blow.

But the kick never came.

She opened her eyes slowly. Teddy still loomed over her, but he wasn't looking at her. In fact, none of the soldiers were moving. All of them had come to an abrupt halt, and all of them, including Teddy, stared at something on the near horizon.

Taylre, still lying face down on the dirt, slowly turned her head and gazed across the open plain. She expected to see another huge army approaching, their swords drawn and their spears at the ready. But what she saw took her completely by surprise.

It was a boy, all alone on the vast plain. A gnarled wooden staff his only weapon.

Taylre squinted as she tried to look through her dirty glasses. Finally, she sat up and removed them, wiping away the filth on her shirt. She put them back on and looked again.

It was Zeke.

It took her a moment to catch her breath. *What is he doing?* she thought. *Is he planning to take on the entire army by himself?*

Suddenly there was movement to Taylre's left as Mr. Loden and Fenrir stepped forward. Loden turned and looked at her, an expression of utter surprise etched across his face. He looked at Teddy and gave a quick, subtle nod. Teddy bent down and grabbed Taylre by the back of her shirt and forced her to stand. He shoved her again, not as hard as he'd done before, but enough to get her moving in the right direction. Soon she stood beside Fenrir and Loden, but was quickly pushed forward and forced to march out in front with Teddy walking close behind. They approached Zeke slowly, Loden's gait appeared purposeful and confident, but beneath the walk, Taylre could sense Loden's fear.

ᚱ

Zeke was sure that Taylre's mind had become so twisted by Loki's wicked influence that she now marched among his army as a loyal soldier. But then he saw her thrown to the ground and the culprit behind it was Teddy Walford. When he witnessed her abuse he almost felt a measure of gladness. Not because he would wish any harm to come to her, but because he recognized she was still Taylre, the one he knew and loved. Nevertheless, the legion of giants and dwarfs that now approached him was indeed formidable. He would have to take stock of his current situation and consider his options; he had no specific plan in mind. It was almost as if the staff led him here, drawing him out to the field of battle before his logical mind had a chance to assess the dangers.

With the staff still gripped firmly in his hand, Zeke could feel the pulse of magic, and it strengthened him. Surprisingly he felt no fear, even when Loki broke off from the horde of soldiers leading one of the largest animals Zeke had ever set eyes on. It looked like a wolf, but it was the size of an elephant.

Zeke held his ground and waited; the base of the staff bore into the gravelly earth. As the tiny, odd company approached - Taylre among them with Teddy pushing her along - they came to an abrupt halt and stopped within shouting distance. Zeke wondered why Loki didn't come closer. *Does he fear the staff?* he thought.

ᚠ

Loki stared at Zeke. The malice and hatred he felt was almost too much, but he forced himself to remain calm; mistakes were made when one acted on emotion alone. With his eyes still focused on his enemy, Loki raised his right arm and signaled Teddy to bring Taylre. Teddy, always obedient, grabbed Taylre by the arm and pulled her to his master. Loki glared across the short distance at Zeke and took hold of Taylre. He wrapped his arm around her shoulders and pulled her in tight to his chest.

"You are a wonder, Zeke Proper. You really are," Loki shouted. "You surprise me at every turn."

Zeke remained fixed, his stance wide, his shoulders squared and the staff held out firmly in front of him. "I've traveled a great distance to find you, Loki," he said boldly. "Let us not prolong this any longer than it needs to be. I have come for one thing and one thing only. Give me Taylre and I will be on my way, back to Alder Cove, back to my family. That's all I want. What you do after that is completely up to you."

"A truly worthy adversary you are, Zeke Proper. Not only are you fair, but you are direct as well. I like that. Yes, I truly do. But let me be clear on one thing. Before I give up Taylre I will need the staff, you see. In other words, no staff, no Taylre." Loki smiled bitterly; his desire to crush Zeke between his hands almost over-whelmed him.

Zeke smiled back at Loki, shaking his head as he spoke. "No deal," Zeke said. "The staff stays with me. It's not mine to give away, *you see.*"

Loki's crooked smile turned to a frown of anger as he caught the mocking tint in Zeke's voice. "How brave of you, Zeke. How very brave. Obviously the girl's life is really of no consequence to you, otherwise you would turn over the staff immediately." Loki looked at Taylre whose eyes were wide with fear as she stared out across the distance toward Zeke.

"But you see she is a burden to us too," Loki continued. "She eats too much and she whines too much. Something I just can't stand. So you go ahead and keep the staff. In the meantime I'll get rid of this burden by simply slitting her throat."

Though it was almost impossible to do, Taylre's eyes opened even wider. Then, just as quickly, those same eyes that were just a moment ago open so wide, squeezed shut as she anticipated the sharp blade of Mr. Loden's sword drawing across her throat, spilling her life blood over the dry earth.

Her brief life seemed to pass quickly in front of her closed eyes, reminding her of all the things she would miss: a thick blanket on a soft bed when the nights are cold, her grandmother's gentle voice and her soft touch, friends and picnics, warm summer nights, movies, fishing on the ocean, a knife...

A Knife?

Taylre suddenly remembered Mr. Loden's dagger, the one she still carried in her belt. With Loden's arms still wrapped tightly around her shoulders and across her neck, she reached down and felt for the concealed weapon, its sharpened steel blade with its ivory hilt hidden within the folds of a leather sheath. Slowly she wrapped her fingers around the handle and gripped it firmly until her knuckles turned white. Then she hesitated as she tried to take a deep breath, but Mr. Loden's hold on her was tight; it was difficult to expand her lungs. Nevertheless, she managed a short breath, just enough to clear her thoughts and ease her anxious mind. Then, as quickly as a thought, Taylre drew the knife, swung it upward in a wide stroke, and pierced Mr. Loden solidly in the side of his neck.

Loden shrieked with the sudden pain. He reached up to take hold of the knife still lodged in his neck while inadvertently releasing his hostage.

Taylre, who felt Loden suddenly let go, pushed away with her free hand and ran, sprinting across the open plain toward Zeke.

Teddy, the faithful minion, could hardly believe what had just happened. The painful screams of his master tore him to the core as he let out his own bellowing howl. At first he tried to go to Loden and ease him in his misery, but the sight of Taylre, the traitor, running across the barren ground toward the cowardly Zeke Proper ripped at his heart even deeper. He ran after her, his mind blurred with rage as he thought of nothing other than how he would destroy her and rip her limb from limb. He envisioned himself choking the life out of her as she screamed in pain. His leg muscles flexed as the bottom of his feet dug into the ground, propelling him closer and closer to Taylre. He reached out his hand and gripped the air in an attempt to grab on to the back of her hair when suddenly there was a flash of light, a bright, encompassing beam that filled his mind and exploded in a blinding brilliance of pain. Oh, so much pain.

Teddy fell to the ground. His body twitched only once before he died.

ช

Still holding the hilt of the knife that continued to dig deep into his neck, Loki watched as Teddy tired to recapture his hostage. But then, just as he was about to take her he saw Zeke raise the staff. Then came the light, a condensed beam of power that flew across the plain into Teddy's head and drove him back as the light filled him, burning at his insides until he exploded in white heat while his life faded from him like the dying embers of a fire.

Loki screamed again, but this time it was rage that took over his mind. It shadowed the pain from the wound. He pulled at the dagger and drew it slowly out of his neck while the muscles sucked at the edges of the blade. A fresh squirt of blood poured out when the knife was finally released. Loki then turned to Fenrir who stared in disbelief at the fallen Teddy, his head shaking as he continued to mutter. "I knew it. I knew it."

Disgusted, Loki turned to his generals. "Destroy him! Hack him to pieces if you must! But do not let him get away!"

The forward soldiers, ever obedient to the wishes of their leaders, advanced on Zeke. They raised their swords and held their shields before them, screaming their terrifying battle cry. They marched at double time, eager to be done with this minor obstacle so they could proceed with the real battle at hand.

ᛉ

Taylre literally fell into Zeke's arms. The run across the plain sapped all of the strength she had left. Her breathing was sharp and ragged. And when she looked up, Zeke hardly recognized her. Besides the fact that her face was covered with filth and tear-streaked stains, Taylre had lost weight. Her features were gaunt and harried. Dark circles surrounded her eyes and her hair hung in dirty strips, like torn pieces of discarded material. When she tried to speak, her voice was barely audible. But Zeke was able to make out at least one word: *"Safe"*.

Using his left arm, Zeke held Taylre delicately; her bones seemed so brittle that he feared squeezing her too tight would somehow break her. He tried to speak his own words of encouragement, but when he heard the shouts, the screams of the berserkers, the warrior's cries for death, he realized he had no time to deliver comfort. Instead he let the staff guide him. His right arm lifted as he extended the Staff of Urd in front of him like a shield. It began to pulse, but this time with a strength that threatened to bring him to his knees. Nevertheless, he held on, bending on his own strength to hold the staff high while a light filled the tip, as if the staff were gathering all of its magic in one powerful surge. Then, as Loki's army spilled toward him, the staff let go and Zeke could feel his own energy pour out of him, like fingers of strength that pulled at his feet and stretched up his legs, through his thighs, into his chest, and out his arms. White light filled the air and expanded in a wide arch. It struck the oncoming troops with a blinding force, sending their helmets and weapons flying, as if a mighty wind had blown.

The light continued to build. The soldiers were pushed back. Their eyes became opaque scrims of pain, and each warrior fell to his knees and placed his hands over his face to try and stop the madness that had filled his mind. But before they could ease themselves of the anguish, each and every one of them dropped their hands to their sides and fell forward. Their faces struck the ground hard as they died, their memories passing like shadows across the barren earth.

Zeke's legs began to buckle, but Taylre managed to hold him. For just a moment her meager strength prevailed. Then, Zeke looked up and saw the dead soldiers strewn across the ground. He gazed at the staff and wondered. It still had the appearance of a simple gnarled piece of wood, roughly hewn from a tree in some far off place, and yet it had destroyed a host of attacking soldiers. It literally brought them to their knees and turned their minds to dust.

Loki watched dumbfounded. Behind him stood the remaining horde of warriors and Zeke feared that another attack would come. He wondered if his strength would hold out. But his fears were soon eased when he saw the look of terror on the faces of the giants and dwarfs. He smiled as he watched each of them step back, drop their weapons, turn, and run, mindless of the consequences of their cowardly actions.

Loki, whose mind tried to comprehend the inconceivable thought that his army would abandon him, stood alone with

Fenrir. He tried to make a fist, to feel the anger that would propel him into action, but his strength receded like an ocean tide.

"Will you destroy *me* now, Zeke Proper?" he called, his voice catching the wind and drifting amid the dust and dirt.

"No," Zeke said, shaking his head slowly, his eyes squinted against the light of the sun. "That is not my privilege, this much I do know. But I sense that in the future our paths will cross again. When they do you *will* meet your demise, of that I am certain." Zeke looked at Taylre and then turned back to Loki.

"Leave now, Shape Changer. Take what remains of your dignity and remember this day. Remember it well."

Fenrir, his fur fluttering in the breeze, listened silently to Zeke Proper's taunting words and felt his own anger begin to rise. He turned and looked at his father, witnessing the defeated, mortified, pale expression that hung over his face, the look of a vanquished man. Never had he seen anything so distressing in his life.

Fenrir was heartbroken.

"I will destroy him, father," he growled. "I will tear him limb from limb and savor the sound of his screams."

Loki turned slowly to his son, almost as if the effort were too much for his defeated soul to manage, and saw him rise off his haunches, his giant paws pressing into the ground as he prepared himself to pounce.

"No. Wait," Loki said, touching Fenrir gently on the leg. "The staff he wields will destroy you. I could not bear that, you see. His magic must be challenged with another. Brute force will no longer suffice in this battle."

He reached into a small pouch that hung from his belt and retrieved a handful of black stones, each one etched with the language of magic, the runes of dark power. He held them out for Zeke to see. A wicked smile creased the corners of his mouth.

"Do these look familiar, Proper?"

Zeke, who still teetered with weakness in Taylre's arms, looked up at Loki and saw a glint of sunlight reflect off the polished surface of the stones. His heart sank. Sinmora had guessed correctly. Loki *had* recovered the black stones and their magic gave him the strength to conceal his entire army from the gods. He understood with shocking clarity that their power must be terrible. They were the antithesis of the white stones he once held, the magic that had destroyed the Korrigan. He shook his head slowly and mumbled the words of a silent prayer to any god that would listen; he needed his strength back.

Loki's voice took on a mocking tone. "Let's see, how did your silly little mantra go? Oh, yes. 'Hold the stones high, let their light shine, and live'." He raised the black stones high above his head. "I have an even better one, you see. How about, 'Hold the stones high, let the darkness fill your enemy's mind, and watch them die'!" Loki pushed past Fenrir with the stones extended in front of him and planted his feet firmly on the ground. Then he lifted the stones, almost as if he were begging the sun to take them and release their power. Instead he closed his eyes and took a deep breath.

Across the dusty plain, still clinging tentatively to Taylre, Zeke tried to stand. He used the staff as a crutch, released his grip on Taylre, and pulled himself up on wobbly legs. He gripped the staff hard, his knuckles turned white as he tried to will some measure of power from it, anything to give him the strength he so desperately needed. But the magic seemed to be used up. The staff was useless, just a gnarled piece of wood whose purpose would be better applied to strengthen the limbs of a feeble old man. Zeke looked again at Taylre, her face streaked with tears and dirt, and rested a comforting hand on her shoulder.

"You need to run," Zeke urged. "While there's still time. You must run and save yourself."

For a moment, just a breath, Taylre stared at Zeke. She took his hand from her shoulder and held it tightly in her own. "The stones that Loden holds," she said. "Will they do the same thing to us as they did to the Korrigan?"

Zeke took his eyes away from Taylre's stare and glanced at Loki who now stood within a growing, swirling mass of black smoke. It began to take on the appearance of dancing, errant spirits, their smoky, mocking fingers pointing at Zeke as they laughed.

He pulled his terrified gaze back to Taylre and began to nod his head very slowly. "I think it's going to be worse," he whispered.

The sun suddenly turned dark and Taylre turned to see that the growing mass of smoke-spirits not only spun around Loden, but also filled the sky, chasing away the light of day and turning it to night.

"I'm not going anywhere," Taylre said. "We started this thing together, and we're going to end it together. We're kindred spirits, Zeke. I knew it from the first moment I laid eyes on you. There's no way that I'm going to let you go this one alone." And then she smiled. It was weak, barely lifting the corners of her mouth, but it was enough. It was the strength Zeke needed.

Using the staff he turned his weakened body around and faced the oncoming smoke, the fiendish dance of a thousand wicked souls, brought to life by the black stones with the call of the runes etched on their surface. Zeke steadied himself and prepared for the onslaught of pain and his eventual death.

The smoke-spirits began to gather into one immense sphere, a ball of darkness that continued to spin and turn violently lashing out with the speed of a cobra. It struck at Zeke, intent on crushing him with hate and vile thoughts of murder. But before the blackness could strike, Zeke raised the staff, almost as an afterthought, a weak measure of defense that repelled the smoke for a moment, pushing it back toward the stones and the holder. Loki opened his eyes and glared angrily at the retreating darkness.

"Destroy him, you fools!" Loki hollered. "He is too weak to wield the staff. Destroy him before it's too late!"

Very slowly the scattered smoke began to draw in upon itself, churning, lifting, tilting and bending until it looked like a giant smiling skull. It rose into the air and once more blocked the light of the sun, taking the remaining shadows and combining it within itself. It stared down at Zeke and Taylre and began to laugh; horrible, piercing laughter that shook the ground and entered the minds of the two cousins like a sharpened dagger.

Taylre fell to the earth, desperately trying to protect her ears from the stabbing pain, but the sound seemed to be coming from every direction, inflicting her thoughts with utter despair as she rolled helplessly on the ground.

Zeke, dropping to his knees, released his grip on the staff and let it fall. It clattered when it hit the hard, rocky ground, and lay in front of him like a battered corpse, worthless and dead. He stared at it glumly and suddenly felt a wave of depression wash over his mind. He struggled to raise his arms, but they hung uselessly by his side. His face began to sag and his mouth hung open; he no longer had the will nor the strength to close it. And though his head hung low, he managed to raise his eyes just enough to see Taylre press her hands against her head. He knew she was screaming, but even listening was too much work. He looked past Taylre and saw Loki drawing ever closer to him, his hands still raised high above his head as the black stones released their dark power.

For a moment, just long enough to blink an eye, Zeke thought about fighting the darkness, but it quickly passed. The magic of the stones pulled him, drawing him in like the shadows. Soon he would become one of them, a swirling mass of smoke whose master is evil, a captive with no will of his own, lost in a world of sadness and despair.

A shadow, like a thick blanket, fell over his eyes and he was blind, suffocating, fighting for air. Zeke knew he would lose. It was only a matter of time.

᛭

In the east, far across the Plains of Vigrid, the Captain continued to stand amongst the warriors of Valhalla. The walls of Asgard loomed large over them all, beautiful and impenetrable. Across the great green meadow where Bifrost spanned a deep chasm, stood Heimdall's watchtower. The flags of the twelve gods snapped and flapped in the warm breeze as they sat on top of its precipice, breaking the all-encompassing silence. The Captain felt uncomfortable; it was too quiet. He watched the warriors who stood around him and noticed that they, too, shuffled nervously, as if they could sense that something was wrong. He saw that many of the warriors had their hands gripped tightly around their sword handles, while others raised their shields defensively against a silent foe.

Bor, a giant of a man, whose arms were as thick as the Captain's neck and who was the first to greet Bartholomew when he first entered Valhalla's halls, stood next to him. He fidgeted nervously, rocking from side to side like a trapped wild animal.

The Captain tapped him gently on the wrist. "What is it, Bor? What's happenin'? The tension is thicker than Atlantic fog."

"Aye, Bart," Bor responded. "There's unease to be sure. See there, far across the plains to the west, smoke is rising. Something is stirring. Something evil."

Suddenly the silence was broken by the sound of a blaring horn. Heimdall was blowing Gjall, its ring echoed throughout the nine worlds.

Bor raised his sword high above his head, his eyes widening with the desire for combat. "To arms!" he shouted. "Prepare for battle ye warriors of Valhalla!"

The Captain looked around and witnessed the contagion of the war cry spread throughout the troops, each warrior raising his sword and shouting for death to the enemy.

The Captain removed his own sword from its sheath, the stiffness of the leather marking its newness. The blade felt strange in his hand. He would have rather held a fly fishing rod than the double-edged sword he now clutched. Nevertheless, he held it firmly and gripped the hilt until his knuckles turned white. Suddenly there was a general rush, and the Captain was caught up in the movement. The warriors were moving.

Their pace started as a slow jog, but then built, increasing to an all out sprint. The Captain found himself swept up in the momentum, fearful that if he slowed he might be trampled by a wave of battle hungry soldiers.

"Where are we bound?" the Captain shouted, hoping to gain Bor's attention.

"To the west and to the smoke," Bor responded. "The gods have need of our help. We must pursue this enemy, Bart. Whatever it is, we must destroy it in the name of Odin."

The Captain ran while his fat legs screamed with pain. The exertion pulled at every nerve in his body. Still, he continued; stopping would mean a very painful transformation: a displacement through time and Mist that would eventually return him to his bunk in Valhalla. He would lose a great deal of time and the chance to face the unknown enemy. *And,* he thought, *the chance to help Zeke.*

Thousands of warriors raced across Bifrost. They passed Heimdall's tower and entered the Plains of Vigrid, their feet kicking up a huge cloud of dust and gravel. The Captain was among them, fighting to keep up the pace, but knowing that it was only a matter of time before he lost his strength and fell face first on the hard ground.

But the soldiers suddenly slowed, parting in the middle as a new sound entered their ears: hoofs galloping over the bridge at an incredible speed.

Bartholomew Gunner looked back and saw one of the most unusual sights he had ever seen: an eight legged horse with a one eyed rider prodding it along with a leather strap.

ᛦ

Odin, the god of gods, was not content to let the warriors of Valhalla march toward this unknown enemy alone. From within the walls of Asgard Odin heard the twisting call of Gjall. There was something in its tenor that pulled at his ear, something unusual that beckoned him. He recognized that the danger that stood without the walls of Asgard was more than his warriors could manage. He would have to join the fight.

Quickly, he saddled Sleipnir, the eight-legged horse, and mounted, his wide brimmed hat tilted forward and his blue cloak close about him. But before he left he searched the halls of Asgard, seeking other gods who would join him in the battle, but so many were gone, exploring among the limbs and branches of Yggdrasil. Even Thor was away fighting trolls and troll women and their wolf children in Iron Wood. He realized with some dismay that he would have to rely on his strength and that of his obedient warriors.

Racing through the gates of Asgard, Odin pulled hard on Sleipnir's reins as the powerful horse vaulted the rivers and streams that meandered across the meadows outside Asgard. Soon he came to Heimdall's watchtower and galloped past it and over Bifrost. The warriors of Valhalla, startled by the sudden appearance of the All Father, stopped their march momentarily, parting ranks to allow Odin to take the lead.

Hidden among the soldiers, the Captain stood in utter amazement when he realized who the rider was. It took Bor's heavy hand on his shoulder to bring the Captain back to the moment and the task at hand.

"Close yer mouth, lad," Bor said with a slight chuckle. "You'll have ta get used ta seein' the gods wanderin' about from time ta time."

As soon as Odin passed, the warriors raised their swords and shouted another fervent battle cry. The Captain, encouraged by the sight of Odin, joined enthusiastically and raised his voice until his throat hurt.

The warriors continued their quick march into the Plains of Vigrid toward the rising black smoke in the distance. Bartholomew Gunner found an inner strength that pushed him forward. No longer did he feel the nagging pull of weakness in his legs or the burning grip of frailty in his lungs. Now he sought only to assist Zeke and avenge him of whatever danger he faced.

ᛣ

The shadows of disembodied spirits continued to pounce on Zeke and Taylre, painfully drawing from them their souls, their substance, and their lives. Any attempt to fight the smoky wind that encircled them was immediately quashed, drilling into their minds an overwhelming sadness that erased all hope.

Zeke managed another quick glance at Taylre, her fallen body lying just a few feet to his left. Her screams had stopped; the effort to do so was too much. He tried to reach out to her one last time, but his arms refused to lift; any strength he had left had been completely sapped. Life was slipping fast, edging toward an eternity of imprisonment and despair. He tried to call out, but his voice was gone, pulled away by the shadows and lost amid the Mist.

Suddenly there was light, a small flicker, like the quick glow of a firefly, or the glimmer of a searchlight in the fog. Zeke saw it from the corner of his eye. He tried to comprehend it, but the determination to save himself and anyone else had long since left. Soon he would lose this battle and give himself up completely to the shadows.

Again the light flickered, but this time it lingered a moment longer, hovering in the distance but growing larger as each painful second passed. The light called to Zeke, its voice a whisper of hope amid the gloom and darkness. He winced with pain and pulled his hand into a tired fist. Within that fist he clasped on to the Staff of Urd, its gnarled wooden shaft pulsed beneath his grip. There was still some magic left, enough to allow Zeke to keep his eyes focused on the light.

Loki felt the change. It was subtle and it required a great deal of concentration to find, but it was there nonetheless. His hands, raised high above his head with the black stones exposed, began to shake and lower. The faint movement caused the shadow spirits to turn; they sensed the fleeting vulnerability in their master's touch, and for the briefest of moments, ceased their relentless attack on their victims.

Zeke felt the momentary delivery. It allowed him to roll to his side, his right hand still clasped weakly to the staff while his left grabbed onto Taylre's hand. Hope was building along with a small measure of strength.

Loki, suddenly aware of his falter, glared at the shadows, a reproving glance that made them turn their heads and focus on the destruction of their prey.

But it was too late.

A storm of dust and dirt filled the air. It mingled with the shadows and choked the dark spirits as they tried to resume their hammering blows on Zeke and Taylre. Then, a great wall of light, like a tidal wave pressing against a barren shore, reared up against the darkness, squeezing it like a vice until it was forced to retreat within the confines of the black stones.

Loki was thrown backward. His body flailed helplessly as he flew through the air. He landed hard on his back, a solid thump that pushed the air from his lungs with the force of a sledgehammer.

The pain was immense and he tried to call to Fenrir for help, but his voice was lost, faded to a whisper that dissipated into the stones like the errant shadow spirits. He fought to open his eyes against the churning grime, but his vision was assaulted by light, a brilliant white that stabbed at the back of his brain like a sharpened dagger.

Shading his eyes, Loki managed to see the furtive movements of a figure dismount a horse. At once he knew who was approaching. He tried to stand, but the ability to do so had left; the light was too powerful.

"Still playing your impish games, Loki?" an aged voice said. "I would have thought that a few centuries tied to a rock with dripping venom would have smartened you up. I see it hasn't. Your mind is still twisted."

Loki managed to lift his head, his eyes still shaded against the blaring light. "Enough, Odin!" he shouted. "The light from your staff sickens me. Have I not suffered enough under your hand?"

Odin chuckled, a warm gravelly hum that rolled like distant thunder. "The light you fear is not of my making, Shape Changer. Instead, fear the Chosen and the Staff of Urd. The light that assails you comes from him." Odin stepped to the side and revealed Zeke, his hand still clasped tightly around the staff as the tip blazed brightly.

"It can't be," Loki moaned. "The magic has been used up. There's nothing left. I saw it with my own eyes."

"What you saw, Sly One is a boy who has found the wisdom and the strength to become a warrior. He has passed his trial. The staff responds to his power. Thus it shines brilliantly. One day he will find his place among the gods. But today is not that day," Odin hissed. "Today is the day that *you* will return to your prison on the rocks! But this time you will remain imprisoned until the time is fully ripe and I meet you again at the battle of Ragnarok."

Across the plain, where Loki's army once stood, Fenrir, shocked and saddened by the All Father's decree, began to howl. His lament echoed Loki's own cry of dismay.

Chapter Thirty-Seven
The Binding of Loki

The warriors of Valhalla, though quick on their feet, could in no way match the rapid pace set forth by Odin and his eight-legged horse, Sleipnir. Nevertheless, the army arrived in time to see Odin grasp the wounded and weakened Loki by the back of his neck and drag him forcefully to the edge of the plain where the valley began to take a gentle rise.

Zeke watched the whole affair with a debilitated sense of indifference. Part of him was glad that the pain inflicted upon him and Taylre had finally come to an end. Another part of him was happy to see Loki receive a measure of punishment from the old man who stood before him, though he had no idea who he was. But the biggest part of him, the part that longed for home, that longed to hold Erna's hand, and that longed for a nice hot meal at his mother's table, just wanted to sleep; he was utterly exhausted. And so he continued to lie on the ground, still grasping tightly to the staff with one hand while the other held lightly and affectionately onto Taylre's.

There was movement all around him. He could hear the shuffling of feet, the bawdy shouts of some of the warriors, and the clink and clang of metal on metal. Zeke cared very little about any of it. He just wanted to go home. But then there was movement close by and a tender touch on his shoulder that reminded him of family and faraway love.

"Are ya alright, lad?"

Zeke looked up and saw a familiar silhouetted figure. He smiled, though the effort to do so was quite painful.

"Never been better," Zeke said, the aching grin never leaving his lips. "And you, Captain?" he asked. "Are you doing alright?"

The Captain chuckled and shook his head lightly from side to side. "I'm better now, lad. Much better."

As he knelt down beside Zeke he glanced toward the still unconscious form of Taylre lying beside him. Bartholomew Gunner reached a hand over to caress her cheek tenderly. The Captain frowned. "He's nearly done ya both in. Looks like we made it here none too soon."

The Captain looked up from his kneeled position and then waved a steady hand at someone beyond Zeke's view. Soon there was a giant of a man who stood next to the Captain, his long blond and braided hair kept neatly out of his way by a shining helmet. The man reached down and easily picked Zeke up. He cradled him in his arms like a small child.

"Be careful with that one, Bor," the Captain said. "He's more precious than gold."

"Have no fear of that, Bart. I'll treat him as if he were my own son."

The Captain nodded and then reached down and picked up Taylre, her limp body rested in his arms like a priceless treasure. Slowly, the two warriors started to walk. They followed the rest of the army while they carefully bore their cargo. Following Odin's lead, the men of Valhalla were guided up the steep grade toward the world of Midgard and a familiar, barren cave.

ᛉ

Zeke slept, but it was not restful; his mind was filled with nightmares, visions of demons, and the pitiful cries of his father. He woke often to find himself still held firmly in the arms of Bor while they continued to walk a darkened path through woods and valleys, over ridges and mountains, and across icy river floes. Occasionally he would raise his head to see the Captain striding determinedly next to Bor, Taylre's unconscious body clasped tightly in his arms. It felt as if they'd been walking for days, a never-ending trek amid the branches and limbs of

Yggdrasil. But then there was a general shout that woke Zeke from another fitful sleep and even stirred Taylre, but did not fully waken her.

Zeke raised his head. "Where are we?" he asked groggily.

Bor gently placed Zeke down on the uneven rocky ground. "See for yourself, Chosen. And remember this place well. It will be Loki's prison once again."

Zeke looked around and saw a high ceilinged, twilit cave, and a dismal cavern belonging to bats and the ticking drops of water that fell from stalactites. At once his thoughts drifted back to a time and place that seemed so faraway. A vision of his grandfather who urged him to look upon the form of a suffering god, a fallen god who had killed the beloved son of Odin and sent his soul to the realm of Hel. He remembered how he had trembled at the sight. It was so cruel. The god was stretched out on some jagged rocks while a huge snake dripped burning venom over his face. Zeke recalled how he'd cried out, begging his grandfather to make it stop. But then the god broke his bonds, his fury making the earth tremble and quake.

Zeke remembered that that fallen god was Loki. The evil god who had come to Alder Cove to destroy his family, who had taken the life of his father, and who had attempted to take Zeke's life many, many times.

Now they were back, back in the place where it all began.

The Captain placed Taylre gently on a bare patch of ground where the jagged rocks wouldn't cut into her skin. Zeke walked over to her and touched her cheek. It felt cold; her breath was ragged. He looked imploringly at the Captain. "Will she be alright?"

Bartholomew looked at Taylre's still form. "If you can get her home quickly, keep her warm, and get some food in her, I think she'll be fine."

Just then, there was another general shout that captured Zeke's attention. He looked toward the aged man with the pointed hat and the one eye and saw him throw Loki to the ground. Loki lay still; he looked at nobody and said nothing. Then, with the help of some powerfully muscular warriors, Odin took three slabs of rock, stood them on end and bore a hole through them. They stretched Loki over them, unwound a length of cord prepared by the dark elves of Svartalfheim, and bound him with it as no one had ever been bound before. They trussed Loki's shoulders to one slab and twisted the cord round his body under his armpits; they strapped Loki's loins to one slab and wound the cord round and round his hips; they clamped Loki's knees to one slab and tied the cord round his knees. No sooner was Loki bound than the cord became as hard as iron.

Then Sigurd, a leader among the warriors of Valhalla, stepped forward, carrying a vile snake into the cave. He fastened it to a stalactite high up in the darkness so that its venom would drip straight on to Loki's face. For all his intelligence, anger, and wit, there was nothing Loki could do.

Zeke sighed. He faltered between happiness and despair. The fact that Loki was finally bound and could no longer hurt him or his family was wonderful. But the punishment...oh, the horrible punishment. Zeke could hardly bear the thought.

Zeke looked at Loki and expected him to look back. But Loki did nothing. He lay still; he looked at nobody and said nothing. Then Odin and the warriors of Valhalla left the Sly One there. No longer did they yearn for battle. Instead they felt heavy-hearted. And as they left Loki to his fate they wept for their brother who was once a god.

ᛟ

Zeke thought that riding on the back of an eagle would be an event he would never be able to equal. But sitting astride a horse with eight legs was an encounter never to be forgotten. It moved swifter than air. Its gait was smooth and even. And the aged one-eyed rider who guided the unusual animal handled it with ease and expertise.

Zeke, still holding tightly to Taylre's comatose body, sat behind the cloaked man with the wide brimmed hat, his identity still a mystery. Behind Zeke, grasping nervously around his waist, sat the Captain. With his eyes squeezed shut, Bartholomew bent his head against the wind that rushed past at hurricane speed.

"Tell 'im ta slow down, Zeke," the Captain muttered, his teeth chattering against the chill in the air.

Zeke turned his head just enough to see that the Captain's face had turned pale while the rest of his body shivered with fright or cold - Zeke wasn't sure. He shrugged his shoulders and gave the Captain a confused look.

"I don't know who he is," he said. "I'm not sure he'll listen to me."

Instantly, the rider slowed the horse to a gentle trot and turned in his seat. "I am the Shaman," he announced. "I am the one who seeks wisdom throughout the nine worlds. When I find it I carry that wisdom to its rightful place, a location where it can be offered its greatest potential. This is why you ride with me today, Chosen. You are wisdom personified, are you not?"

Zeke's bewildered look turned to skepticism. "Me?" he scoffed. "No, I'm just Zeke Proper. There's nothing wise about me."

"Still the doubter, I see," the rider said. "And perhaps this is a good sign. It shows humility. There is no better quality.

Nevertheless, you must know that your deeds have set you on a path that leads to the realm of the gods. You, Zeke Proper, are the Chosen. You are a warrior. I have declared it and there is none that can dispute it. Now look!" The cloaked man pointed a steady hand toward a tiny cabin in the woods.

"Here is the place for wisdom," he said. "It is here that you will obtain your greatest potential."

The rider stopped his horse at the edge of a line of trees that skirted a broad meadow. Within the meadow bloomed thousands of wildflowers that stretched their heads toward the bright spring sun.

"Take the girl. She will be healed by Sinmora who waits in the cabin," the rider said. "And take care, Chosen. Spread your wisdom to protect against the wicked times to come. Continue to be brave and don't forget those who've sacrificed their lives for you."

The rider helped Zeke dismount the horse, easing him down to the soft ground while the Captain took Taylre in his arms and held her unconscious form one last time.

Then Bartholomew Gunner, the newest warrior of the Valhalla, placed Taylre gently on the ground and stepped toward Zeke, wrapping him in his arms.

Tears filled Zeke's eyes as he embraced the Captain. "I will never forget you," he said. "You have been a great teacher, a devoted friend, and a life saver, literally. You saved me from certain death, and for that I will always be thankful."

The Captain was sobbing as he held Zeke against his chest. He tried to catch his breath as he attempted to express his love for this boy who had become a man. But the only thing he managed was a tight embrace and a quick nod toward Taylre.

"Take her home; place her in the care of Sinmora." He choked back tears of sadness. "She'll be in good hands there."

Then he released his grip and helped Zeke lift Taylre over his shoulder. Zeke turned and began his slow walk across the meadow toward a sagely cabin, a white line of welcoming smoke rising from its chimney.

The Captain watched as Zeke carried Taylre away, his eyes spilling over once more with tears. Then he turned to Odin who extended a helping hand. The All Father pulled the Captain up on Sleipnir's back and then turned the horse toward the hills and the distant crest of Mt. Sif. Odin gave the horse a gentle tap with the reins and the great beast began trotting back to Asgard and the magnificent halls of Valhalla.

Chapter Thirty-Eight
Return to the Cabin in the Woods

Meteorologists called it a freak storm that originated near the island of Surtsey. It carried north toward the city of Reykjavik, and then dissipated quickly over the northeastern tip of Greenland. It was described simply as a swirling mass of black clouds that carried lighting and thunder, but produced no precipitation. Scientists were baffled.

Because of the storm, Vivian and Marjorie's flight to Halifax was delayed eight hours. When they arrived they were completely exhausted. Pulling their luggage across the airport terminal to the parking garage required extraordinary effort.

As they approached the elevator that would take them to the parking level where they'd left their car, Vivian took a moment to sit on a nearby bench. She sighed heavily.

"I say we get a hotel for the night, Marjorie. I don't think I can keep my eyes open a second longer."

Marjorie, who was watching the numbers above the elevator count down, turned to Vivian. "I'm tired too, Viv. But we've got to get back. You heard what the Draugar said."

"Heard him *and* smelled him," Vivian said tiredly. "But what he meant when he said 'it's over' still puzzles me."

"'The storm is over'," Marjorie corrected. "He said the 'storm was over'."

"I think he may have gotten that little bit of information wrong," Vivian said. "Didn't we just spend eight hours sitting in an airport because of a storm?"

"Yeah, that was weird," Marjorie said thoughtfully. "Still, I think we need to get back. I'll do the driving and you can rest. As tired as I am, I still don't think I could fall asleep."

ᛉ

"I'm not going," Vidar said, his arms crossed defiantly over his chest. "It's not that I don't like you guys; I do. In fact I've come to consider you as family, and for that I'm eternally thankful. But this is my home. This is where I belong."

Berling frowned, his brow knitted with worry. "Where will ya go, laddie? The branches of Yggdrasil are strewn with dangers, I fear ya won't last out the night on yer own."

"I can take care of myself," Vidar proclaimed. "I've done it before and I can do it again."

Erna stepped forward and wrapped her pale arms around Vidar and gave him a tight hug. "I will miss you, Vidar. I understand why you won't cross the Seam with us; the world of Midgard is a strange place, but I'll worry about you. Please be careful. Don't take any unnecessary risks."

Next Devon approached Vidar, hugged him quickly, and then patted him gently on the back. "You're a good guy, Vidar. A little on the quiet side and a bit too serious for me, but still, you're a good guy. Just be careful, okay?"

"I will," Vidar said. "You know I will."

The three remaining travelers pulled their packs up over their shoulders, cinched them tightly, and then turned and walked to the wall of shimmering air that loomed before them. Each of them turned back once more and waved a solemn goodbye to Vidar who stood steadfastly, his left hand resting on the hilt of his rusted sword while his right waved a reluctant farewell.

The group then turned back to the shimmer and stepped forward. Their images faded slowly, like winter turning to spring.

When the dizziness left them and they were able to clear their thoughts, the three sojourners looked up to see a meadow scattered with brightly colored wildflowers. Across the meadow, its roof covered in green moss, stood Sinmora's cabin. A thin line of smoke rose from its chimney.

ꝶ

When Marjorie pulled the car up in front of the wooden split-rail fence, the sun was just beginning to rise. Vivian was still sleeping soundly in the passenger seat. Marjorie tried to rub the tiredness out of her eyes.

"We're here," Marjorie said, shaking Vivian gently on the shoulder.

Vivian opened her eyes slowly, blinking once or twice before she could open them fully. "Here?" she said groggily. "Where is here?"

"The fence," Marjorie announced matter-of-factly. "Come on. It's time to do some hiking."

The deep winter snow that once marred the path leading to Sinmora's cabin had long since disappeared making the hike much more bearable, even though both women continued to feel the weight of exhaustion pressing on their shoulders. They trudged through a dense forest, thick with new spring growth and the pungent aroma of pine. Finally, the trees opened up to a brightly colored meadow, its rolling fields strewn with flowers. Across it, barely visible in the morning light, stood Sinmora's cabin. The smoke rising from its chimney seemed to beckon them with a friendly wave.

ᛟ

A warm fire crackled quietly in the hearth, emitting a soft yellow glow that brushed gently across Taylre's face. Her glasses had been removed and placed beside a down pillow where she tried to rest. But it was difficult with everyone gathered around watching her. She appreciated the attention and the kind care she'd been receiving from Erna as well as from her doting grandmother, but it was getting to be too much. She just wanted to sit up, drink deeply from a big glass of water, and eat. Eat a lot; she was starving.

"Can I get up now?" Taylre pleaded. "I feel better. I really do."

Marjorie Anders shook her head. "I think you need more rest, hon. You've been through a lot. Give yourself a chance to heal."

"But I'm sick of just lying here," Taylre whined. "I'm sore, that's true, but if I don't start doing something I'm scared I'll stiffen up and never be able to move again."

"Oh, let the wee lassie get up," Berling said, puffing on his pipe while his short legs dangled from a tall chair in a darkened corner of the cabin.

Marjorie looked toward Sinmora who had resumed her place on her favorite chair, a rocker whose wooden arms bent and twisted like gnarled driftwood. Sinmora followed Berling's lead and lit her own smelly pipe. She puffed on it vigorously before she pulled the long stem from her lips and blew out a white cloud of smoke. "Give the girl a chance to rise," she said. "My thinkin' is that she's stronger than she looks."

"Well, if you think you can," Marjorie sighed, "then I guess you can get up for awhile. But don't over do it."

Taylre's smile widened as she rose slowly and painfully to her feet. Her muscles and joints ached as if she'd just run a marathon. When she finally stood she was shaky, but Erna was there, taking Taylre's arm and steadying her until she found her footing.

"You see?" Taylre said, looking around the room at the many smiling faces that were staring back at her. "Almost like new."

Zeke stood slowly from his seat near the fire while the Staff of Urd leaned against the crooked stone façade. He put his arm lovingly around Taylre's waist and steadied her as Erna did.

"You are, without a doubt, one of the bravest girls I've ever met," Zeke said. "When we were faced with certain death on the Plains of Vigrid, you said something that I will never forget. But it's also something that I've always thought, too. From the moment I set eyes on you, Taylre Anders, I knew that you and I were kindred spirits. I felt it then. And I feel it now."

Taylre's cheeks reddened. "Do you see what you're doing, Zeke? You're making me blush."

"I'm sorry," Zeke laughed. "But it's true. Your presence there at the end, when everything seemed to be closing in...well, it sustained me. It kept me alive."

Taylre bowed her head humbly, but then she looked up, her eyes red with tears. "You don't have to say that. I know the real truth. At first I thought it was only a dream, some nightmare I thought I'd never escape, but then I woke up to see you here along with everyone else and I realized none of it was a dream. It was real. You, Zeke, are the one that saved *me*. You are the Chosen." She leaned over and gave Zeke a tight hug, ignoring the pain in her shoulders and arms. She released her grip and began pacing the floor, her memory swirling with visions of darkness, evil, and dread.

Sinmora rocked in her chair and watched as Taylre circled the room, testing her tired, swollen limbs, her face grimaced with pain and memory.

"The dreams will fade with time," Sinmora said. "As will the wounds to your body. Soon they will become nothing but a distant memory. But the wisdom you've gained will remain. For that you should be thankful."

"I am thankful," Taylre said. She winced when she raised a bruised arm to brush away an errant strand of hair. "I'm thankful to finally be back with my family. I'm thankful to be away from Loden and from that giant wolf. But I'm especially grateful to be away from Teddy; he was a brute." She sat heavily in a chair placed in front of a well-worn dining table. Its surface was loaded with celebratory food that Erna had prepared: thick stew filled with chucks of potato, turnips, and venison. Roasted chicken seasoned to a golden brown. Hard-crusted bread sliced and enfolded with cheese. And brimming mugs of buttermilk and mead, as well as a steaming pot of hot tea with a side of luscious sweet bread. Taylre stared at it and felt her mouth water. She wanted to dive into the meal and satisfy her nagging hunger, but something else tugged at her, an emptiness that couldn't be filled. She turned away from the temptation of food and stared back at the softened, worried eyes that looked back at her.

"I can't help but think that all of the tragedy that's occurred has been my fault," Taylre said.

"Oh that's just nonsense," Marjorie replied. She reached a protective, comforting hand toward her granddaughter.

Taylre raised her hand and silenced her grandmother's protests. "No. Let me say my peace. I've been doing a lot of thinking and I need to get these thoughts out. I need to ease myself of this burden."

Taylre looked up again and saw forgiving smiles that held no judgment. The eyes of the onlookers urged her to speak.

"That day, the one that compelled me to go to Loden's classroom, that's when it all started. If only I'd stayed away. If only I'd had the strength of will to walk out of that room and leave Loden behind. If I'd done that, Zeke and Devon's dad would still be alive. The Captain would be with us. And," she said, lifting her arm to expose slowly healing bruises and cuts, "I wouldn't look like a worn out punching bag."

This time it was Devon who spoke, his voice quiet and mature beyond his years. "What Zeke said a moment ago, Taylre is true. You are an amazing person. When you first walked into our house the night we moved to Alder Cove, I thought you were awesome. I still do. For that reason I can't let you go on thinking you were to blame for all of the crap that's happened. It wasn't your fault. All of the stuff that's happened started long before we were born. You couldn't help that. All those people that started bringing the Korrigan to town, they're to blame, not you. The bad stuff that happened to dad and to the Captain, they would've happened anyway. Loki was determined to get revenge. If you didn't stumble into his plan, then someone else would've. Of that I'm certain. So quit blaming yourself. If anything, feel proud; you kept it from getting any worse."

Among the watchers there was quiet agreement as heads nodded slowly. Sinmora continued to rock gently in her chair and Berling puffed on his pipe. Marjorie rose and gave Taylre a kiss on the cheek, while Zeke and Devon cuddled up next to Vivian. Erna filled a cup with tea and placed it next to Taylre, and then she resumed her seat next to Zeke and interlaced her fingers with his.

For a long time there was silent contemplation among the tiny group, thoughts that drifted from one harrowing experience to the next as each member considered the incredible stories of adventure that had been related throughout the day.

Finally, Sinmora broke the silence with a gentle sigh. She stood slowly and tenderly from her chair; the discomforts and cares of Midgard had returned.

"Enough," she said boldly. "This is a night of celebration. We've heard the tales and we've considered our wounds. But in the end we're victorious. Bartholomew is safe and happy, as is the father, Percy. All this we know. Therefore, we should rejoice. Yet we sit here like beaten warriors. So I say, enough!"

Sinmora swept her arthritic hand in a wide arch and fastened a crooked smile across her face. "See, there is food. Erna, bring out your lyre and pluck the strings with pleasant, happy music. And Berling, bring your flute; let its tune fill the air with merriment. This should be a night of laughter, not sad reflection."

Zeke stood quickly, his hand still clasped tightly with Erna's. "Sinmora," he said smiling, "you're absolutely right. What are we doing? If there was ever a time to party, it's now." He lifted Erna to her feet. She giggled with pleasure, took a piece of sweetbread, and pushed it playfully into his mouth. Zeke laughed as crumbs fell to the floor. He began chasing her around the table as the others joined in on the laughter.

Soon the tiny cabin in the woods was filled with celebration. A bright fire blazed in the hearth and cheeks were reddened by mead and dandelion wine.

The festivities drew into the darkness of night and finally into the wee hours of the morning. One by one the revelers slackened in their merriment, finding themselves weakened and exhausted, but happy to have been a part of the celebration.

Berling eventually retired to his home beneath the cabin, while Sinmora slowly climbed a narrow ladder to her cot in the cabin's loft. Devon found a comfortable place to sleep next to the fire while Zeke and Erna nestled beside each other on a wide, cozy chair falling asleep in each other's arms. Marjorie and Vivian managed to outlast them all as they continued to sit by a table that was now scattered with crumbs and left over food. Mugs that were once filled with honeyed mead and sweet dandelion wine were tipped over, adding to a mess that would require a great deal of attention, but not until the affects of the merriment had past.

Taylre, still tired and sore, slowly plodded her way toward the two women. She knelt in front of her grandmother and rested her head in her lap falling asleep quickly. Her soft snores drifted amid the heavy breathing of the other tired occupants.

"What a night," Vivian sighed.

"I'll say," Marjorie agreed. "But isn't it nice to be back together again? I mean, look at us," she said, pointing toward the sleepy room with a wave of her hand. "Could you have ever imagined after that night during the Seidh, that we'd be back here, surrounded by a happy fire, filled with food, and glad to be alive?"

Vivian sighed again as her exhausted body slumped in the softness of the chair. "I miss Percy, Marjorie. No matter how many times I've asked Zeke to repeat the story, no matter how many times I've asked him to tell me how happy he looked, I still miss him."

Marjorie leaned over and hugged Vivian tightly. "I know, hon. I miss him too. But he is happy, so is Bart. And the best part, we'll see them again. When our time comes, they'll be waiting for us with a beautiful home and a fragrant garden to wile away our time. Won't that be wonderful?"

Vivian nodded, her red eyes filled with tears. "It is," she agreed. Then she motioned toward Zeke and Erna. "But what do we do about them?" she said, shaking her head while a slight smile parted her lips.

Marjorie laughed quietly while her hand absentmindedly stroked Taylre's hair. "Those two are in love, Vivian. You're just going to have to accept that. They're young, but they've both been through more than most people have experienced in a lifetime. They've seen more, and they're far more mature. I think they're going to be just fine. Just make sure you make room for Erna in your house, and don't be too concerned when Zeke leaves for a few days to venture into the woods. Sinmora will see that they behave, and you can do the same when she comes to Alder Cove to visit." Marjorie smiled again, grasping Vivian's hand tightly in her own.

"I guess what I'm trying to say is just be open minded. What these two have is not the same as normal teenage lust. This is real love. And I think it's going to last a long time."

Vivian smiled. She thought about true love, and then she thought about Percy. More than anything in the world, she wanted her sons to know the real meaning of love, and if that's what Zeke had, then she was happy. What could be better than finding true love after all they'd been through.

She looked at Devon, his silent form sleeping soundly near the fire, and then she looked again at Zeke as her sleepy mind imagined freckle-faced grandchildren running around in a soft meadow filled with wildflowers.

Brad Cameron

is a high school English teacher who has been inspired to write Young Adult Fantasy Fiction through his countless hours of teaching and reading to students. He is an avid follower of all things mythological. When not writing, Brad spends his time in the outdoors either on his bicycle or motorcycle touring the stunning countryside near his home in the Pacific Northwest.

To learn more about the Korrigan and Loki, the trickster god who spawned her, visit www.bradcameron.net. and Brad's blog, The Young Adult Guide to Norse Myth at zekeproperchronicles.blogspot.com

29733356R00282

Made in the USA
Charleston, SC
22 May 2014